To Win a Crown

Endorsements for Rachel Hauck

TO LOVE A PRINCE

"Another compelling royal story by the master of princely tales!"
—Susan May Warren, *USA Today* bestselling,
RITA award–winning novelist

"*To Love a Prince* is breathtaking and enchanting! Rachel Hauck is the queen of inspirational royal romance."
—Teri Wilson, bestselling author of
Unleashing Mr. Darcy and *Christmas Charms*

"Hauck has taken elements we love from fairy tales and given them a fresh twist in a modern setting. A delightful read!"
—Becky Wade, bestselling and Christy Award winning author

TO SAVE A KING

"I read a LOT. And I mean, a lot. I've read several royal love stories. I read romantic suspense. I read mysteries. I have to say, this truly stands out as probably the best book I've ever read. The characters are fabulous. The secrets held for years/decades, revealed and overcome...wow! There is pain, heartache, love, forgiveness, laughs, romance, angst, every emotion one could have is dealt with in this story. I felt this story. I felt the emotions. I experienced this book! I highly recommend it!"
——Sandy, Amazon Reviewer

THE WEDDING SHOP

"I adored *The Wedding Shop*! Rachel Hauck has created a tender, nostalgic story, weaving together two pairs of star-crossed lovers from the present and the past with the magical space that connects them. So full of heart and heartache and redemption, this book is one you'll read long into the night, until the characters become your friends, and Heart's Bend, Tennessee, your second hometown."

—Beatriz Williams, *New York Times* bestselling author

THE WEDDING CHAPEL

"Hauck tells another gorgeously rendered story. The raw, hidden emotions of Taylor and Jack are incredibly realistic and will resonate with readers. The way the entire tale comes together with the image of the chapel as holding the heartbeat of God is breathtaking and complements the romance of the story."

—*RT Book Reviews*, 4.5 stars, TOP PICK!

THE WEDDING DRESS

"Hauck weaves an intricately beautiful story centering around a wedding dress passed down through the years. Taken at face value, the tale is superlative, but considering the spiritual message on the surface and between the lines, this novel is incredible. Readers will laugh, cry and treasure this book."

—*RT Book Reviews*, TOP PICK!

THE ROYAL WEDDING SERIES

"Perfect for Valentine's Day, Hauck's latest inspirational romance offers an uplifting and emotionally rewarding tale that will delight her growing fan base."

—*Library Journal*, starred review of *How To Catch A Prince*

"Hauck spins a surprisingly believable royal-meets-commoner love story. This is a modern and engaging tale with well-developed secondary characters that are entertaining and add a quirky touch. Hauck fans will find a gem of a tale."

—*Publishers Weekly* starred review of *Once Upon a Prince*

THE FIFTH AVENUE STORY SOCIETY

"Hauck intertwines the stories of five New Yorkers who each receive a mysterious invitation to join a "story society" in this exhilarating inspirational… Hauck inspires and uplifts with this mix of tales. Readers who enjoy Karen Kingsbury will love this."

—*Publishers Weekly*

"Rachel Hauck's rich characterization and deft hand with plotting and setting had me enthralled until I turned the last page of this superb novel. *Fifth Avenue Story Society* is truly a masterpiece—a one-of-a-kind novel that lingers long after the last page is turned. This is one I'll reread often, and it should garner Hauck much well-deserved acclaim. This should be on everyone's shelf

—Colleen Coble, *USA Today* bestselling author

MEET ME AT THE STARLIGHT

"Hauck pulls out all the stops!"

—*Library Journal Starred Review*

More by Rachel Hauck

Visit www.rachelhauck.com

COLLECTIONS AND SERIES

Nashville Series
Nashville Dreams
Nashville Sweetheart

Lowcountry Series
Sweet Caroline
Love Starts with Elle
Dining with Joy

Songbird Novels with Sara Evans
The Sweet By and By
Softly and Tenderly
Love Lifted Me

The Wedding Collection
The Wedding Dress
The Wedding Chapel
The Wedding Shop
The Wedding Dress Christmas

The Royal Wedding Series
Once Upon a Prince
A March Bride (novella)

Princess Ever After
How to Catch a Prince
A Royal Christmas Wedding (novella)

True Blue Royal
To Love A Prince
To Save A King
To Win A Crown

The Hearts Bend Collection
When I'm With You
Anyone But You (with Carrie Padgett)
What If I Stay (with Mandy Boema)

Stand Alone
This Time
Hurricane Allie (novella)
Georgia on Her Mind
The Writing Desk
The Love Letter
The Memory House
The Fifth Avenue Story Society
The Best Summer of Our Lives
Meet Me at the Starlight
The Sands of Sea Blue Beach

TO WIN A CROWN

RACHEL HAUCK

To Win A Crown
Copyright © 2026 by Rachel Hauck. rachel@rachelhauck.com

Published by Hauck House
ISBN-13: 978-1-7341366-4-7

This novel is a work of fiction. Names, characters, places, incidents and dialogues are either the product of the author's imagination or are used fictitiously. Any resemblance to actual events, locales, organizations or persons, living or dead, is entirely coincidental and beyond the intent of the author.

Cover Design: Kristen Ingebretson
Map Design: Penmagiccards
Interior Formatting: Author E.M.S.

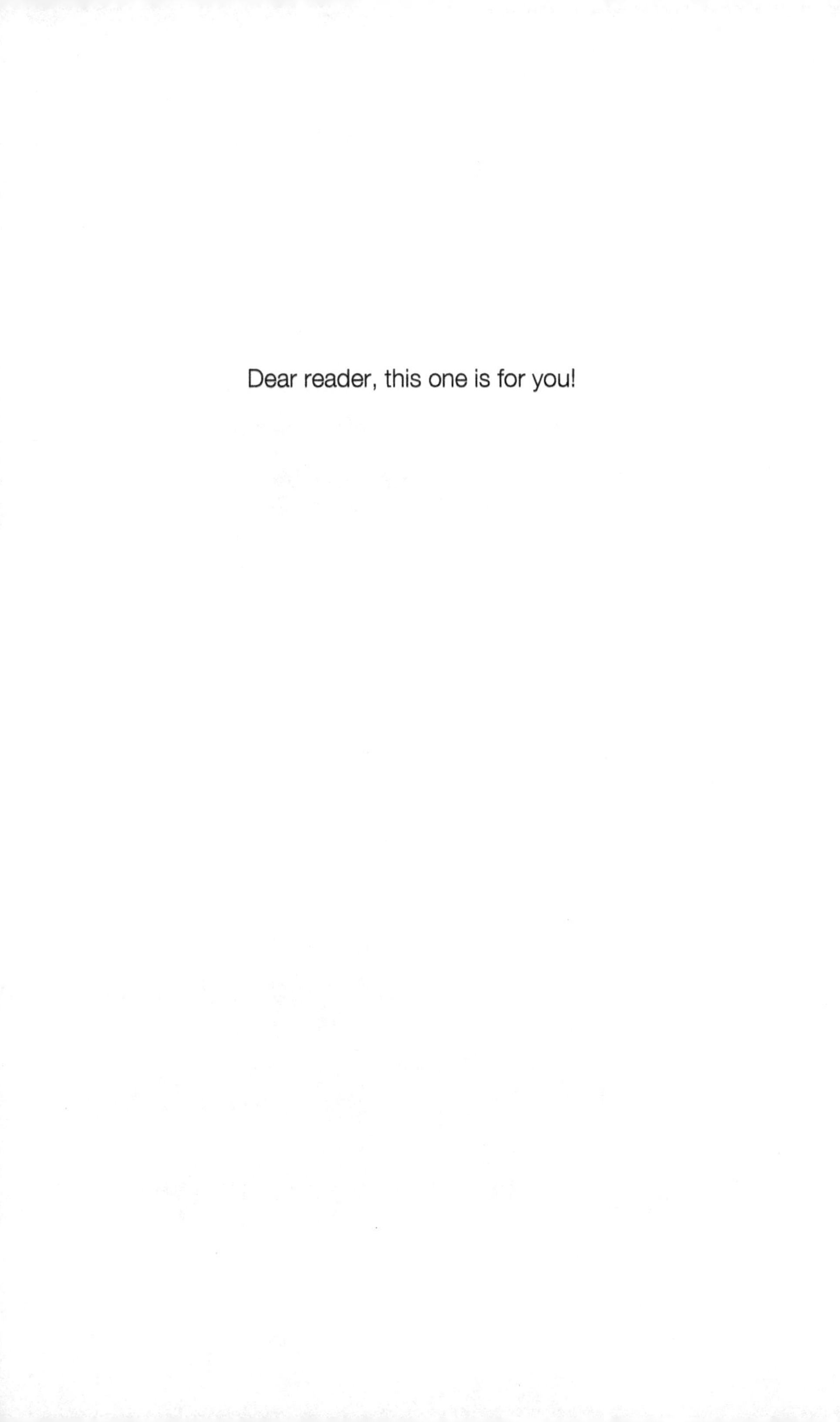

Dear reader, this one is for you!

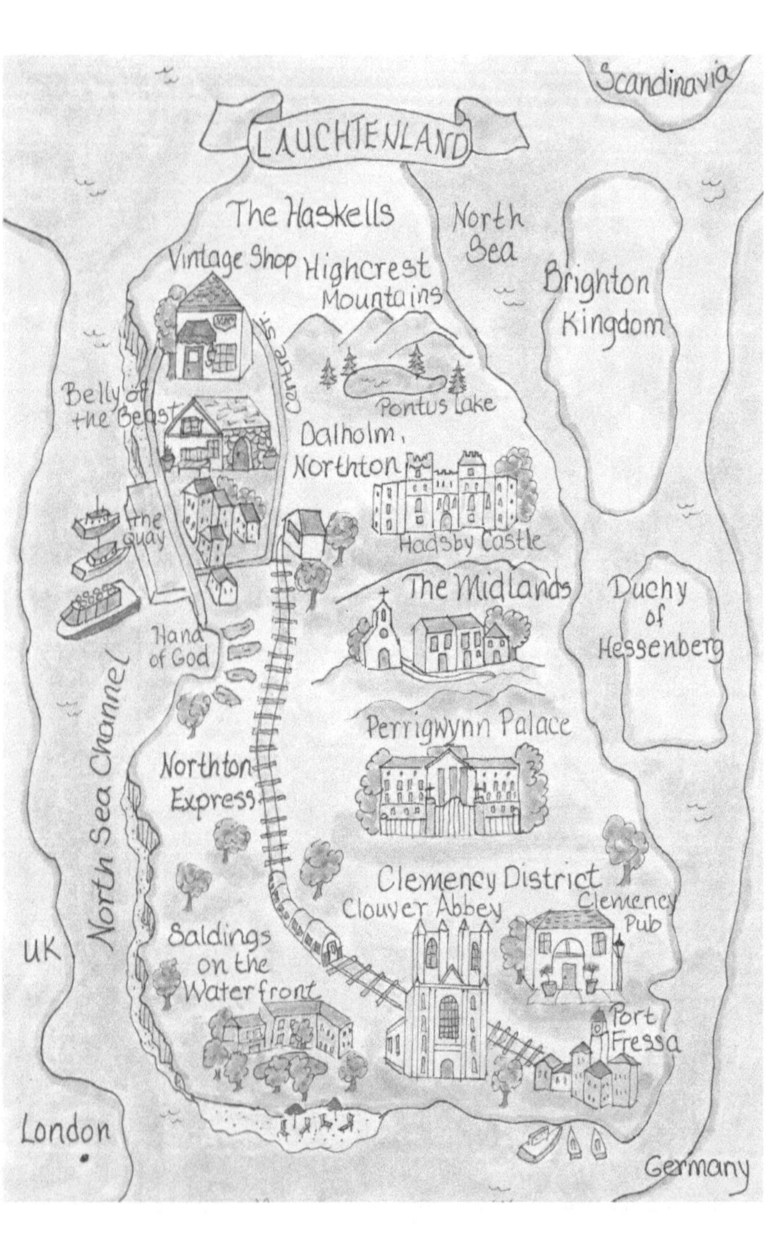
Scandinavia
LAUCHTENLAND
The Haskells
North Sea
Vintage Shop
Highcrest Mountains
Brighton Kingdom
Centre St.
Belly of the Beast
Pontus Lake
Dalholm, Northton
The Quay
Hadsby Castle
The Midlands
Duchy of Hessenberg
Hand of God
Perrigwynn Palace
North Sea Channel
Northton Express
Clemency District
Clouver Abbey
Clemency Pub
UK
Saldings on the Waterfront
Port Fressa
London
Germany

L̲ET'S BEGIN HERE...

Somewhere between the April showers and the May flowers, the flora and fauna that bloom high above the crags and cliffs, the winds of the Highcrest Mountains blew strong and stirred the crusty brown leaves of the forest floor.

They gathered and swirled, twisting on the current, skitting and flitting toward the south and Hadsby Castle, their earthen fragrance awakening our senses, reminding Lauchtenland of unfinished business.

Because once upon a time there was a girl whose mother was a queen. But she was not a princess.

December 10, 1988
To R. Vinter
c/o Henrik Dane, Lord Ostergaard
Northmark Abbey, Westfall, Port Fressa, Lauchtenland

Vinter,

Well, you asked for photographs so here you go. She's something else, Vinter. Going to change the world. Yes, that's a grandmother talking.

I've not spoken to anyone about our deal. Not even my husband, which grates my craw, but your secret is safe with me. That being said, there are honestly too many secrets resting on one little girl's head.

Yours truly,
Octavia O'Shay

July 19, 1993
To R. Vinter
c/o Henrik Dane, Lord Ostergaard
Northmark Abbey, Westfall, Port Fressa, Lauchtenland

Vinter,

I do apologize for not writing last year. We keep busy around here. Find enclosed photos of "little Shug" as I've taken to calling her. One is from a Rock Mill High football game wearing her little cheerleader outfit, bearing a sweet, toothless grin. The other was taken before a ballet recital. She and the other little girls forgot the routine and little Shug lead them in improvisation. She had the whole auditorium on their feet cheering.

She's a gift to us. Please know how much we love and care for her. I see in the news "things" have improved with your people. Congratulations on your daughter's marriage.

Yours truly,
Octavia O'Shay

September 22, 1997
To R. Vinter
c/o Henrik Dane, Lord Ostergaard
Northmark Abbey, Westfall, Port Fressa, Lauchtenland

Vinter,

Against my better wishes, Trent bought her a horse for her eleventh birthday. She's in hog heaven so I guess I can ease up on my worry. She's tall, up to my shoulders, and athletic, smart and very pretty, which puts Trent in a tizzy. He's already worried about boyfriends. Guess that's what fathers do. We're taking a family trip to Switzerland over the Christmas holiday. I'll send along photos when I can. I found an undeveloped roll in my desk drawer. Turns out they were from 1976. But it was good to go down memory lane. What wild clothes we used to wear. I see Trent in our girl, but more and more, she's the image of her mama.

As luck would have it, I found a few more photos which I'm including in this letter. One is from her middle school basketball tryout and the other from last summer when she worked in the office of the family business. After all, it will all be hers one day.

In keeping up with the news, I see you have two grandsons already! Doesn't that just bust your buttons?

Your friend,
Octavia

March 21, 1998

Dear Henrik,

Thank you for your kind note regarding the passing of R. Vinter. He telephoned last fall to thank me for our correspondence over the years. It was as if he knew his time was short. He'd become a friend to me over the years. You as well, Henrik. Thank you for your devotion, loyalty, and friendship to R. Vinter. Those are rare commodities in these modern days.

Kind regards,
Octavia O'Shay

CHAPTER ONE

SCOTTIE

For the most part, her days were the same as before. She woke early for a workout, ate a protein-laden breakfast with the occasional Danish from Haven's Bakery, captained her creative ship, O'Shay Shirts, dined at her favorite hometown hotspots like Valentino's and Ella's Diner.

She grabbed coffee with friends, played pickleball, rode horses, hung out with Dad or her grandparents on the weekend—if work didn't call—and when he wasn't consumed with the spring planting, she curled up with her boyfriend of two years, Cap Henderson.

She chatted with folks around town, most of whom she'd known her whole life, asked about their jobs or health, and wowed over the fact that Lila Smith's Great-uncle Beau was still picking and grinning around town and in Nashville. He'd once played at the Grand Ole Opry. This was Scottie O'Shay in Hearts Bend, Tennessee, the small town tucked under Nashville's shadow, defined by cozy streets, long traditions, Friday night football, guitar circles, and Sunday evening potlucks.

Yet deep down, her inner O'Shay bedrock had shifted. She'd discovered the truth. And as much as she wanted to pretend, she could carry on as usual, she found herself gazing out her office window toward the east, daydreaming about a land far, far away, and wondering *"What if..."*

"Scottie, oh my, oh my, it's here." Penny, her assistant, beamed from the other side of her desk, the latest edition of *GQ* pressed against her chest. "You are on the cover of *GQ*."

"Yes, I know. I was at the photo shoot," she said, reaching for the magazine, staring at her own image and seeing the doubt in her eyes. Could the rest of the world see it too?

"It just arrived with a bouquet of flowers from the editor." Penny disappeared for half a second to return with a very large vase containing a very large bouquet of wildflowers.

"Send him a nice thank you, will you, Penny?" Scottie flipped through the pages with marked reserve, finding her featured article, stiffening slightly at the headline.

She's a Wildflower in the World of Men's Fashion. Princess Scottie O'Shay.

She sank slowly to her chair. Why, why, why? People didn't listen. She'd been adamant with the reporter, Rance Howell, to not refer to her as a princess. Because she wasn't one.

"But your mother is a queen."

"Yes, I realize it's confusing, but her status does not change mine. Please don't use the title related to me."

He answered with a smile that said he'd write the story however he wanted.

"We're celebrating in the lunchroom with cake," Penny said, flipping through a second copy of the magazine, making notes on various pages with her black Sharpie. She liked to scout out and research O'Shay's competition. She was southern, no nonsense, skilled, and invaluable. "Scottie, these pictures of you are gorgeous and the article is—" She glanced up. "Didn't you tell him not to call you a princess?"

"I did. But it's done now." Scottie tossed the magazine to her desk. She'd read the article later. Rance Howell's faux paus aside, being featured in *GQ* was huge for O'Shay Shirts. "So, what kind of cake?"

"Two kinds. Vanilla with buttercream icing and chocolate-on-chocolate. Your fave. Haven's just delivered them. The interns are decorating, so we have a few minutes."

"This is a win for all of us, so don't put the spotlight on me."

She'd been on national morning shows repping O'Shay Shirts many times in the last ten years. She'd been in *People* and *Vogue*, for her role as a woman in a menswear world, but never *GQ*. "Besides, I've been featured in mags and other places."

She suspected *GQ*'s interests peaked when the world learned the Queen of Lauchtenland, Catherine the Second, had a secret daughter. Scottie. But so what? She'd ride a bit of notoriety for the good of the company.

"True, but you've never been on the cover before."

"Reach out to Rance Howell for me," Scottie said. "Ask him what about 'don't use the title princess' was confusing."

Penny shot her a sly grin. "Gotcha, boss." She exited the office with a final reminder. "Cake in twenty-seven minutes."

Scottie glanced out her corner office window, the one framing the western tip of Hearts Bend and a curve of the Cumberland River, and wondered what her mother, the queen, was doing about now. Sitting down to a sumptuous Perrigwynn Palace dinner?

She moved away from her daydreams toward her drawing board spread with sketches for the winter line. She was irritatingly a week behind. Her concentration kept slipping. More and more her heart yearned to explore another life.

Ah, forget it. She was just restless, and work cured restlessness. Or maybe she just needed to fall all the way in love with Cap, get married, and make a baby. Though at thirty-eight, staring down the barrel of thirty-nine, the internal drumbeats of motherhood remained a distant sound.

Stepping over a pile of fabric samples on the floor, she sat at her board and took up her pencil. She began every collection with pencil and paper. Photographs of models were strewn along the edges. Some of the men were lean, others beefier. Some bald and some with thick-styled or wild hair. She had shots of men in suits sitting in a boardroom. Others wore leisure wear on the golf course or on the beach.

Scottie caught the edge of a photo she'd taken herself and had the marketing department enlarge for her. Pulling it free, she smiled at the face of her brother Gus. Too handsome for his own good. But as modest as they came. Especially for a prince. He'd make a great model, but he'd refused her half-joking offer to work for O'Shay.

As he should. He was a working royal for the House of Blue.

The truth of it all still caught in her in a funny way. She had a brother. Two brothers. She was a big sister, and that singular reality was a big part of why her world tilted. That, and the fact her mother was not dead but very much alive, living in a Lauchtenland palace as queen and supreme monarch.

Such a reality would tilt anyone's world, no doubt. The only reason she hadn't capsized completely was because of her O'Shay roots. She was heir to the men's fashion line, O'Shay Shirts. Great-grandpa Loom had passed the company to Grandpa Fritz, who gave the reins to Dad. Scottie was next in line. A handful of O'Shay cousins worked as production managers, accountants, sales directors, quality assurance, and HR, but everyone knew the next ruler of O'Shay Shirts was Scottie.

So why, in the quiet hours, did she long for a home that was not her home? Why did she text her sisters-in-law for pictures of the kids? Why did she hate missing out on their lives? More than anything, why did she miss the mother she never knew?

Back to the drawing board. She stared at the casual suit she'd sketched, frowned, and wondered if it looked too Don Johnson, 1980s.

"Scottie?" Penny peeked in, pointing to her watch. "Cake time. And we moved the winter design meeting back an hour."

"Is this too *Miami Vice*?" Scottie held up the drawing.

"Yes, but the '80s are trending. Go for it."

"You think I can risk millions of dollars on 'go for it'?"

"If you don't want to know what I think, don't ask. Did you hear me about cake and the design meeting?"

"Yes, to both. Is Matteo ready to present his designs? I told him not to waste our time."

Matteo Rossi, whom she had stolen from Armani, was her first hire since Dad and the Board promoted her to Creative Director three years ago. He was talented, creative, and often completely unrealistic. But he excelled in designing clothes for men, so she waded through his Halloween-like ideas and the no-man-would-ever-wear-that options to find the gems. Which were plenty.

"He says he's good to go."

"Then let's eat cake." Scottie headed for the door, pointing to the UPS boxes. "Open those while I'm in the design review, please."

Boxes and packages sent directly to Scottie were, well, a bit of a sociology lesson. Some came with drawings and clothing samples from would-be designers often asking for internships, just looking for a chance to succeed.

Others contained a piece of O'Shay clothing with a wine stain and long, ragged tear. *"I caught my husband cheating wearing your shirt!"*

Most often: gifts from House of Blue fans, like a cheap crown or a home-sewn gown by a woman who thought it might be nice for Scottie's next ball.

Never mind she'd never attended a royal ball. In the three years she'd known Queen Catherine—Kate—was her mother, she'd visited with her as many times. Usually for a week around the Christmas holiday. The queen had once traveled to Hearts Bend with her son, Crown Prince John, whose wife, Princess Gemma, was a hometown girl—whom John met while on a mission from Kate to woo Scottie into the Blue family.

But the queen battled illness and rarely traveled.

In case anyone wondered, a royal presence in quaint Hearts Bend was no small thing. HB also boasted a country music star and a pro football quarterback. The weekends were flooded with tourists.

"Coming for cake?" Dad peeked in, smiling, looking youthful for his sixty-two years. Also, he was in love. Another factor that tilted her world a little. Trent O'Shay in love. Dad never dated when she was growing up. It was always the two of them, plus his parents, Shug and Fritz.

"See you in there." Scottie reached for her phone as a text from Private pinged.

Kate: Hello. It's been a while since we chatted. I
know you're busy so no reason to reply quickly. I
just wanted to say I am thinking of you.

Her mother, Kate. Texting from a double-dog top security mobile phone.

She was about to reply when a familiar masculine voice asked, "You busy?"

"Cap, hey, what are you doing in town?" Scottie met her boyfriend of two years in the middle of her office for a kiss.

Dusty and dirty, dressed in jeans, checkered shirt with a white tee peeking over the top, and well-worn work boots, Cap was the epitome of the all-American boy. Tall, good-looking, athletic and smart, devoted to his friends and family, he was a former member of the elite 75th Army Ranger Regiment turned farmer.

When he had finished saving the world, he hung up his rifle and boots for the two-hundred-year-old Henderson farm, a hundred-and-twenty acres spread along the Cumberland River.

"I came in to do some banking and stop by the post office. Here." He handed Scottie a cup from Java Jane's. "I was wondering if we could grab a burger from the Fry Hut later. Have a picnic in Gardenia Park."

"Sure. Should be fun." She sipped the hot, creamy latte. "Isn't tonight the first spring concert?" Local bands auditioned for the coveted spot on the park's stage. Being so close to Nashville, the talent was strong and the competition fierce. "They have cake for me in the lunchroom. Care to join?" She eyed him over the rim of her latte.

"Cake? What's going… Ah, the *GQ* spread?"

Scottie pointed to the magazine on her desk. "Don't worry, I won't get a big head over it."

Cap laughed. "I'm not worried, Princess Scottie."

"Stop. I'm not a—"

"Princess. So you've said." He regarded the cover for a long moment, almost sighed, then scooted over to kiss her cheek. "Beautiful cover, babe. Bring me a piece of cake to the park.

I'd love to stay, but I need to get back to the farm." He backed toward the door. "So, Gardenia Park? Seven o'clock? I'll bring the cheeseburgers with the works and fries." His eyes checked hers for confirmation.

"Seven o'clock. I'll bring you that piece of cake," she said, his stiff posture tapping her curiosity. "Cap, is everything okay?" She was still learning to read him. In the two years they'd been a couple, they'd not developed a deep relationship between his farming schedule and her workload. Still, she was hopeful.

"Yeah, everything is…yeah…" He paused in the doorway. "You, um, look beautiful."

"So you said, Cap Henderson."

Something was up. She felt it in her bones.

Chapter Two

Michael

When he sat in the Port Fressa stands watching the lads on the pitch, everything came right. No longer was he the mourning fiancé, the conflicted son, or the trained protection officer who had nearly failed his prince and the House of Blue.

No, while watching the Cross PF Youth Football Club, Michael felt whole. Yet he couldn't sit here forever, cheering on the lads with the cold spring winds blowing from the Port Fressa Bay.

He cupped his hands around his mouth. "Come on, lads, you can't all be strikers. Cross the ball."

His ten-year-old nephew Phineas ran down the middle of the pitch toward the goal. He had a clear shot. *Shoot the ball, Finn. Shoot.* Michael leaned forward, arms propped on his legs, a cup of coffee warming his hands. He loved this game. Spent his youth on this very pitch, honing his skills, rising in the ranks.

"Goal!" He jumped up, nearly dropping his coffee. A perfect soaring kick from Phineas. Just like his Uncle Michael had taught him. He gave a fist pump when Finn looked his way with a grin.

From the sidelines, Michael's brother Evan looked back with a nod. That was brother speak for thank you.

With ten minutes left in play, Michael relaxed, confident the Cross lads earned the win. Named after and sponsored by his ancient family—one as old as the House of Blue—the pitch sat in the middle of Lauchtenland's vibrant capital city of Port Fressa.

The expertly kept field stretched in peaceful defiance against the daily hustle and bustle.

The historic city surrounded the Cross facilities. Behind him, twenty-first-century high rises and luxury flats. In front of him, the six-hundred-year-old Parliament House and Ministry Hall. To his right, the peaks of Perrigwynn Palace, home of the royal Blues.

As a member of the esteemed Cross family, he was a kindred spirit to this older part of the city. His bones were honed from the same sturdy stone as those hallowed structures.

Though recent events seemed to crack his inner core a little. His boss, Gunner Ferguson, Chief of Her Majesty's Security Detail, ensured him he'd done his job the day a wild man tried to assassinate the Crown Prince of Lauchtenland, Prince John, right after his keynote address to the North Sea Island Nations' Summit in Brighton Kingdom.

The HMSD kept the attempt undercover. So much so the tabloids and mainstream media never caught wind of it. The crown prince, along with Michael and two of the hotel security guards, were the only ones there when a gunman charged Prince John, as he pulled the trigger. Michael returned fire. The shot was fatal.

Which was why he'd spent his days in the palace basement, running the Queen's Operations Room and watching CCTV while the Crown's Investigation Bureau—made up of men in dark suits with tea-stained shirts—launched a quiet investigation.

Today, after six long months, they had arrived at the palace to announce their findings. Michael had headed to the pitch to await his fate.

Speaking of which—Michael glanced in the direction of the palace just as someone plopped down next to him.

"They told me you'd be here." Gunner hunched against the chill, digging his hands into his dark wool coat bearing the queen's cypher. "Who's winning?"

"Depends on your side."

"I'm on your side."

"Then give a cheer, mate. The Cross Football Club is on top. The lad dribbling is my nephew, a top-notch striker." Michael raised his coffee for a long sip. The liquid was starting to cool. "Are you here to fire me?"

Gunner laughed. "I told you to trust the process. The CIB cleared you today with recommendation for commendation."

Michael glanced at Gunner, and the invisible yoke he'd been wearing broke off. "Thank you, sir."

"Their findings concluded you'd gone above and beyond your duty. You risked your life to save our future. The House of Blue and the nation thank you."

Lauchtenland had been through a few skirmishes in the past three years. Rogue operators had infiltrated and stirred up trouble, hoping to start a war. Prince John's adopted daughter, Princess Imani, had been in danger as well as his wife, Princess Gemma. The whole mess read like a blooming Jack Reacher novel.

"You can have your choice of assignments," Gunner said, giving a rousing shout as the Cross lads scored another goal. "The incident will remain confidential. We don't want to inspire copycats or members of the Renaissance Coalition." Gunner glanced at Michael. "So, what's your pleasure, Mick? Where do you want to serve?" As he spoke, the April clouds suddenly darkened and dusted the stands and pitch with a soft snow. Gunner shook his fist at the heavens. "It's spring, you brass monkeys."

"I rather like the dark room with all the tellies," Michael said. The atmosphere mirrored the shadows of his life. "I've been running emergency protocols and perfecting escape routes. Did you read my notes on improvements?"

"Already submitted them to the maintenance yeoman. And you're not staying in the dungeon. I only asked where you wanted to serve as a courtesy. Report to the squad Monday morning."

"Yes, sir." It was back to Her Majesty's Security Detail. Michael finished his coffee, crushed the cup, then rose up, tossing it at the bin. It hit the lip before bouncing in.

"One more thing." Gunner cleared his throat. "You good with, um, everything? The shoot. Purnell."

"By 'good,' do you mean I get out of bed every morning? Yes."

"The shoot was a clean, Mick. You acted in accordance with your training. But if you need to talk to someone, I can—"

"I'm good with the shoot, Gunner. Though I never like aiming my weapon, much less discharging it."

"And Purnell?" Gunner gave Michael a single solid pat on the shoulder.

"I'm good with her too." Almost. Getting there.

Last year had been one of those years—a year a man might have leapt over if he'd known what was coming. Yet what would he change? To strip away the ugly, painful moments meant losing the lovely, sweet, beautiful ones as well. And it was those memories, shining through the cracks, that carried him on the hardest days.

Ignoring the spring snow, the lads played on. Gunner stayed for the final minutes, which Michael found oddly comforting. The Cross PF Youth Football League bested the Clemency Park boys three to nil.

Down on the pitch, Michael congratulated the coaches—his brother Evan and his longtime mate Piers Hollings, also known as the Lord Atterbery.

Two years younger, Evan was the good son. At least to Mum. A former lawyer and advisor to the Crown on Supreme Court matters, he'd recently accepted a position at the *other* family business, Pratt Printing, which was also the *other* ancient family that formed Michael's bones. Evan headed up their legal department, overseeing the business in forty countries.

Between the Cross family, one of duty and devotion to the Crown, and the Pratt family, a heritage of entrepreneurship and business, Michael wondered if he'd ever be at peace about the direction of his life.

"Did you see me, Uncle Mick?" Phinneas knocked him back with a running hug. "I kicked it like you said. It worked, it worked, I made a goal."

"Excellent kick. I never doubted you." Michael hugged him close. He'd always wanted a family of his own but—

"Are you coming over?" Finn asked, taking his gear from his

dad, who reminded him to pack it up the next time. "Mum's making hamburgers and hot dogs, crisps, and ice cream."

"I'll be there straightaway." He'd not planned on joining the family, but the look in Finn's eyes defied anything but a yes.

While Finn dashed off with one of his mates, Michael helped Evan carry the sporting gear to his motor. "The kids love when you come round. You know that, right? Mindy and Linus love seeing you." Evan popped open the boot. "By the way, Tracy insists you come for dinner. We've seen you once since Christmas. At Easter dinner. I get it. Being a member of HMSD requires a lot of time, but we miss you when you don't darken our door. Also, fair warning, Trace thinks you're hiding because of what happened with Purnell."

"I'm not hiding." No matter how tempting.

"Then come to dinner. Here's a second fair warning. Mum will be there."

"Oh, blimey, I think I have a pressing engagement elsewhere."

"Very funny. I know Mum comes at you hard about joining Pratt Printing, but you need to figure a way to get on with her." Evan closed the boot and called for Finn. "I saw Gunner Ferguson in the stands. What did he want?"

"Nothing." Evan knew a wee bit about the events in Brighton Kingdom but only that Michael prevented an incident. "Merely gabbing about future assignments."

Piers came along and clapped Michael on the back. "Why aren't you on the sideline with us? I need you, my star footballer friend."

"Too busy. I shan't commit only to back out."

"Then come when you can. You love the sport. You love the kids. You coach from the stands whenever you're here." Piers tossed his keys to his son. "Marcus, let yourself into the motor."

"Believe me, I would if I could, but I live a life that takes me elsewhere."

"Michael, I've known you for over twenty years," Piers said. "Where's the chap I knew running round the pitch, coaching up others, life of the party, top of his class, winning the awards and top honors? And all so effortlessly. I hated you when we met our fresher year. I'm ashamed to say it, but I truly did. Then you offered to help me pen a paper, and I learned of your kindness, not to mention your wit and brilliance. Don't get me started on the lasses giving you looks everywhere we went. Seriously, just saying all this now makes me loathe you again. Are you real? The lads wanted to be you. The ladies, well, they simply wanted you. To be Mrs. Michael Cross, I say, was their dream."

"Piers, leave it out," Evan said.

"Why? Michael is an ace. Top drawer. Even in Her Majesty's Special Forces you blew off the doors."

"I said leave it out, Lord Atterbery." Evan stood between Michael and Piers. "Have you no heart? He just lost his fiancée a year ago. You speak as if he's a partying playboy without a soul."

Piers looked stricken. "Oh, Mick, mate, so sorry. I'm a bum. We all loved Purnell. Such a sweet and kind lass. Please…" He rested his hand on Michael's shoulder. "I wasn't thinking how you must miss her."

Michael glanced away, never sure how to respond to sympathy. He blamed himself. Gunner and Piers were simply being good mates.

But last year was a blur. Everything happening so fast. One day Purnell was fine, healthy, and happy. The next, falling ill, leaving him on the sidelines to watch, helpless, and unable to save her. Then came the attempt on Prince John. The moment he spotted the man's weapon, one thing and one thing only came into his mind: save the prince.

"Dad, you coming?" An irritated Marcus leaned out the passenger side window. "I'm starved."

"We were like that at his age?" Piers wondered with a laugh. "Coming, lad. Keep your knickers on. Ring Mum, tell her we're on the way." He turned to Michael. "A piece of advice? You're a splendid chap, Mick, so don't let death steal the life in you. I cannot know how it feels to lose the woman I love, but I do know letting death defeat you is not the answer. You're a champion, Michael. Remember that, please. Get on with your life. Fall in love. Raise a family."

"He's right, Mick," Evan said. "Purnell said as much to you when she was in hospital."

Michael nodded. "I'll take it under advisement."

Though he didn't mean it. At least not in this moment. Maybe next year. He might be an inch or two closer. What he wanted more than anything was to sense, feel, even hear Purnell one last time. To say what he needed to say.

For a long while, Michael sat behind the wheel of his car, motor idling. The wipers had dusted away the thin, wet snowflakes, and sunlight broke through the scattering clouds.

He wanted to be the chap Piers bragged on. But that was easier said than done.

CHAPTER
THREE

Under a spring cottonwood, Scottie sat alone on a Gardenia Park bench with a brass dedication plate.

In loving memory of Merle and Hattie Lerner. Sixty-seven years of wedded bliss.

Sixty-seven years. She happened to know Merle and Miss Hattie Lerner made it to seventy years of wedded bliss before Hattie died in her sleep. Merle lasted two more weeks. The legend around town was ole Merle couldn't breathe without Miss Hattie.

Up on the park stage, a crew worked under a bright light as they dismantled the sound equipment. Scottie watched them a moment, then returned to the memory of Merle and Miss Hattie.

More and more benches with brass plates dedicated to enduring love had popped up around the park. When Miss Jean-Ann died last year, six months after her husband, their daughter, Dolly Tuggle, wept at her funeral saying, "Mama warned us if Daddy went first, she'd not be long behind. He was her joy and light, her one true love."

There'd been so much emotional vibration in her words, Scottie actually began to believe in the fairy tale of a "one true love." Something she'd not observed often in her thirty-eight years.

She certainly didn't observe it tonight during her Fry Hut dinner-in-the-park with Cap Henderson. But his unusual demeanor in her office this afternoon finally made sense.

19

Did Scottie believe in true love? Yes, of course, the world was too big and beautiful not to believe. It was just, with the greatest of all doubts, she wondered if true love would ever aim its arrow at her.

Her grandparents, Shug and Fritz, were examples of solid, lasting love, but as the kid of a single dad with a supposedly deceased mother, true love seemed like a Disney movie. In real life, a couple like Shug and Fritz were the lucky strike.

Her whole life, Dad had lived with a broken heart beating in his chest. He loved Kate Rein, the girl he'd spied across Lauchtenland's Haxton University campus his sophomore year. He hurdled benches and bushes to chase the "vision of beauty" before him. (Dad was as confident as he was corny in his twenties.) Right then and there, he determined to marry her. Being a brash American, little did he know she was the Crown Princess of Lauchtenland.

Yet Dad being Dad, he'd won her heart. They fell in love. Conceived a child. Kate assured him the modern ways of a royal family in the 1980s would not hinder their relationship. But she was wrong. Dead wrong.

Her father, King Rein IV, dropped a bomb on their relationship that left shrapnel in Dad's heart for years. Kate had been forced to choose between the man she loved and her country and royal duty. Duty won out.

Kate delivered a daughter, left the child in her father's care, and never looked back because everyone agreed—it was for the best.

Dad's crushed heart never loved deeply again. Except for his baby girl, to whom he gave everything. He modeled a life well-lived with a solid work ethic, family loyalty, and friendship with the community. But he never modeled heart melding, you're-my-soulmate, committed and devotional love.

When Scottie met Cap Henderson two years ago, his hero's swagger, sparkling green eyes, and cocky grin made her wonder if she'd tripped into something marvelous.

Yet heart-fluttering sensations were only the start of a love story, right? The trick was making it to "sixty-seven years of wedded bliss."

Take Dad and Kate. Such a beautiful beginning with a tragic ending. Kate not only lost Dad but also her child. She'd confessed to Scottie how she wept and wept once she returned home to Lauchtenland—her arms and soul so empty.

Then on a day she was forced to fulfill her duty, she met Edric, Duke of Connought. His kind eyes and easy laugh somehow put the first piece back into her shattered heart.

If anyone understood heartache, it was the Queen of Lauchtenland. The notion *call her* whispered to Scottie. *She'd understand.*

"Scottie O'Shay, you okay?" One of Hearts Bend's finest, Officer Chris Mynheir, leaned to see her face, his gold shield glinting with the soft light of Gardenia Park. "The show's over. Everyone's gone home. The crew's packed up."

"Hey, Chris, I know… I'm not ready to leave yet." Being alone in the park was better than being alone at home.

"Suit yourself, but I'm going to sit over there, keep an eye on you. I can't allow our local princess to be exposed."

She scoffed softly. "I'm not a princess, Chris. But thank you."

Knowing he kept one eye on her restrained her tears. She had known something was off with Cap for a while now. Even more when he'd stopped by her office. Tonight, he made a shocking announcement between bites of burgers, fingers of fries, and saying hello to locals—that he was in love with his ex-wife.

"What?" Way to bury the lede, Henderson. "You talked to Freya? When? I thought you said she was 'outta here.'"

Cap had been forthcoming on their first date about his first love, Freya, who he met after college between deployments. They married in a romantic rush, but after a couple of years, she bailed, unable to deal with the stress of her husband's deployments.

"She was, or so I thought. I've not talked to her for over a year, then a couple months ago, she texted me about something and well, we started talking, apologizing, reminiscing. Two weeks ago, we met for dinner and—"

"—remembered why you fell in love," Scottie said.

"Scottie, I promise, I never anticipated this." Cap was crushing his empty soda cup in his strong, solid hand. "I wanted it to be you, but we never seemed to go beyond pals who had some amazing make out sessions. I'm sorry, I really am."

"I know. It's okay." Scottie tossed her empty cup into the trash bin. "But you should at least give me the 'it's not you, it's me' speech."

"It's definitely *not* you, Scottie O'Shay. You're amazing. I was really hoping to be your trophy husband and talk you into investing in the farm."

Scottie's final memory of her last date with Cap Henderson was when he scooped her in his arms and softly kissed her goodbye.

"Hey," she'd said as he stood to go, the final band of the evening holding out the last note of their last song. "Invite me to the wedding."

Then *ker-plunk*, the amphitheater lights shut off. The stragglers moseyed toward their cars, and except for the glow of Victorian lamps, Scottie sat in the dark.

The town clock chimed midnight.

"I'm still here," Officer Mynheir said.

"Are you on the midnight shift, officer?" She spoke toward the shadows.

"No, but I ain't leaving till you do."

Scottie smiled. "Thank you. Not much longer." She glanced down at the foil wrapped cake with two forks taped on top resting on the bench next to her. "Care for a piece of cake, Officer Mynheir?"

"Really?" He walked through the lamplight toward her. "Don't mind if I do."

When he retreated to his post, a thought ran through Scottie again. *Call her.* She stared at her phone, then with a deep inhale, dialed her mother. On the third ring, Scottie realized the six-hour time difference between Hearts Bend and Port Fressa, Lauchtenland. She was about to hang up when Kate answered.

"Hello? Darling?" Her greeting was soft yet awake. "Is everything all right? It must be midnight in Hearts Bend."

"It is and I'm sorry to wake you. I can call you later."

"No, no, I'm up, padding my way to the tea trolly. Edric rises at five for a brisk walk round the garden. I'd love to join him but, well… Goodness, you didn't call to hear about me."

"Guillain-Barré is still giving you trouble." A statement. Not a question.

"Though I hate to admit it. Two years, and I'm still fighting the usual suspects. Muscle weakness, fatigue, various pains. My physio is coming up with therapies to keep me strong, but some days the pain flat sets me aside."

"I'm sorry, Kate. What a nasty virus—and such brass nerve to inflict a queen."

Her mother's warm laugh confirmed why Scottie made the call. "My sentiments exactly. Now, how is your world? Why are you up at midnight?"

"Cap and I ended things. He's in love with his ex-wife."

"His ex-wife? Goodness—"

"He was sweet about it, Kate. He didn't know he still loved her or that she still loved him." When Scottie had visited Lauchtenland between Christmas and New Year's, she shared a little about Cap, wondering if Kate wanted to meet him. *He could be the one.*

"Are you all right, darling? What does your father say?"

"Dad? He doesn't know yet. I'm still in town, at Gardenia Park."

"Alone?"

Scottie glanced at Officer Mynheir. "No, a police officer is watching over me."

"Good. I know Hearts Bend is your city, but do take care, love. Word's out. You're part Blue now."

"No offense, but that's nothing to the country music royalty around here."

"Still, you take care, please." So far in their relationship, Kate walked the thin line between being a friend and long-lost-mother with queenly ease. "So, your young man has moved on. I'm so sorry. How can I help?"

"I don't know. What do mothers say to their disappointed daughters?"

Kate laughed. "Shall I ring your aunt Arabella? I only had sons, remember?"

"Do you think I'll find love one day, Kate? I never thought much about it until Cap. Now I'm wondering. Am I one of those girls who never marries but gives her life to her career?"

Which, in her younger days, Scottie believed was the superior option.

"I don't believe so. Love finds those who are seeking."

"How did you know Edric was really the one after Dad? I mean, you were so brokenhearted. You loved Dad so much."

"It wasn't easy, darling. I simply got on with life. What choice did I have? Once I accepted the reality you and your father were a closed steel door I could never open, I was free to move on. As much as I grieved it all, I allowed myself to believe I'd love again. Of course, I had to marry. Produce an heir. And I was determined not to live a life devoid of romance. The human heart was made for intimate love. Edric was the first man after your father to make my heart flip-flop. Here we are thirty-seven years later."

"Do you think there's hope for me?"

"Darling, of course. You are a beautiful, accomplished, talented, and kind woman. This Cap fellow just happened to give his heart to another first. Tell me, did you really, really love him with all your heart? Did you daydream about him? Was he first on your mind upon awakening? Did you surrender hours of the workday to be with him? Or rearrange an event to accommodate his schedule?"

Kate read between Scottie's emotional lines with precision. "No, never. Even after two years of dating, sometimes when we got together, the first fifteen minutes were awkward, like we were just getting to know one another."

"Then he was not your true love. Work through this sadness and open your heart again."

"You're right, Kate. Thank you. This helps a lot."

"Good. Now, while I have you on the line, darling, feeling bold from my sage motherly advice, might you fancy a long holiday?" Kate's regal and royal accent wavered a bit. "You see, everyone is leaving me this spring. Edric is off to Scotland for fishing with a mate he's known since boyhood. Afterward, he's taking my place for a technology tour in England and the States. This ridiculous GBS makes travel terribly difficult for me, but I am eager to keep Lauchtenland on the leading edge of technological developments. John is off to a trade conference in Sweden then a holiday in Corfu with Gemma, Imani, and the baby—whom I will miss terribly. He's such a jolly little chap. Gus, Daffy, and sweet little Mathilde are spending the month in Manhattan with their friends Coral and Chuck and their new baby. We all bemoaned how our bookings clashed terribly this year. John and Gus offered to cancel their holidays, but I couldn't see it. They've worked so hard, and after some terrorist shenanigans over at Titus Stadium and an incident with John in Brighton Kingdom—"

"What happened in Brighton Kingdom?" Scottie was read in on the attempted terror attack last year that put Princess Gemma and Princess Imani in danger, but nothing about her brother John.

"I'd tell you, but it's classified, and I don't want you to worry about accidentally slipping up. Rest assured, all is well. A smashing protection officer saved the crown prince. As I was saying, they're all leaving me save for Mum, who's not doing well. Arabella and Rachel will be taking on duties at Perrigwynn Palace, but I'm at Hadsby Castle beginning in May until the Rose Ball in June."

"Are you asking me to visit, Kate?" Scottie rose to her feet. From the corner of her eye, she saw Officer Mynheir stand.

"Yes, but more than visit. A stay. Roughly eight weeks. 'Tis all. Help me get through the events on my diary."

"What's on your diary? And Kate, I'm hardly a substitute for the king consort and the princes."

"We kick things off with the Garden Party. Everyone will be here for that, but wouldn't it be lovely for us to be together? As a family."

"I guess." Kate's appeal stirred a strange warmth. Scottie's family tree had always been so one-sided. Just the O'Shay's.

"Then everyone skedaddles while I go on walkabouts and make presentations. May and June at Hadsby is a long-standing House of Blue tradition. The Dalholmites have been loyal to the Crown since the Hundred Years' War."

"You want me to come for two months?" Scottie leaned forward, intrigue swirling with the yearn of being wanted, no, needed by her mother.

"If it's too much to ask, how about a month? The truth is, love, I'm not sure I can manage on my own. I've not let on how weak I am to the family. I know I cannot do it all on my own. In fact, if you're comfortable with it, you'd go to some events in my place."

Scottie laughed. "You cannot be serious. The people will not accept your illegitimate daughter as your emissary."

She hated the term *illegitimate daughter*, true as it were, and it'd become a tagline in the press. Did she want to endure two months of it along with complaints that "yet another American has infiltrated the House of Blue"?

Prince John had taken Gemma's adopted daughter, Imani, as his own when they married. Instantly there were two Americans in the House of Blue. Then the discovery of Scottie as the queen's secret daughter stirred trouble from the small but loud RECO party.

Yet what did it matter to Scottie? She had no intention of taking a title or a crown. Her kingdom was O'Shay Shirts.

"I've thought about it and want to issue a Letters Patent to bring you into the Family. I've already spoken to the prime minister about your title, and he's—"

"You want to give me a title? Like Her Royal Highness? Kate, I don't think—"

"No, no, love, that would require you to be a working royal. And to be blunt, an HRH Princess styling would need government approval." There was a guttural echo in her sigh. "Unless, of course, you married into the family like Gemma and Daffodil or were adopted like Imani."

"Kate, you don't have to make excuses. I'm not looking to have a title or win some kind of crown."

"It's just, you see, the rule of such things, over the years, has changed. And while I can call you my daughter, because you are, all day long, my great-grandfather and one of his prime ministers restricted the royal Letters Patent for fear of foreign enemies sneaking into the Family. However, I can give you a House of Blue styling, which in my mind, carries as much cachet and rank as an HRH."

Her speech was rushed with a soft passion, as if she'd been storing the words for a long time.

"What sort of title?" Scottie was curious. That's all.

"There's an ancient title—Lady Royal Blue—someone brought to my attention recently, and I thought it perfect for you. It's only been used a few times in our long history and won't require approval or ruffle the small but loud contingent demanding a reduced royal family. Nevertheless, the title gives you rank and respect. I just can't see you being my daughter without some indication your mum is the queen. The House of Blue is too distinguished, too ancient, too established to leave off."

Kate's speech was punctuated with one big exhale.

"I see." The invitation to visit for a few weeks was starting to feel complicated. "Should I expect to be eviscerated by the press?"

"No more than usual," Kate said. "Since you're not in the line of succession or earning taxpayer dollars, the people will see the title as one given to a relative in the House of Blue. You're in the fashion industry, Scottie. Surely you're used to a bit of criticism." There was a smile in Kate's voice.

"Yes, but for our clothes, not my person." Scottie paced, her mental wheels turning. "Okay… Can I think about it? I'll have to talk to Dad. We're working on the winter line and—"

"Really?" Kate's soft passion rose to a soft excitement. "You'll consider it? Marvelous. Yes, yes, of course talk to Trent. The Hadsby Garden Party is May eighth. We'll have a bit of a family reunion and then the others will be off. You and I will get to know one another over afternoon teas. Still, Scottie, love, feel free to answer honestly. A denial will not be the end of us. I'm still your mum and always will be."

"Kate, are you sure about this?" Scottie started toward her car with a wave to Officer Mynheir. "I don't want to be some sort of stir stick that creates trouble while you're dealing with Guillain-Barré and your support system is away."

"Nonsense. I'm used to stir sticks and with everyone gone, you'll be my support system. You're the tonic my tired, weak body needs. Besides, it's high time I owned up to my past and showed the world how proud I am of you."

After their goodbyes, Scottie glanced down First Avenue, so empty and peaceful sleeping under the amber streetlamps and the glow of shop signs.

She'd told Kate she'd think about it. Talk to Dad. But she already knew the answer. Now she just needed to understand why.

MICHAEL

Monday morning Gunner met him at the security entrance of Perrigwynn Palace. But instead of walking with him to the Operations Room, he said, "Come with me."

"Where are we going, mate?"

"Her Majesty would like to speak with you."

"Her Majesty?" Michael looked down at his blue security uniform and black boots. "Dressed like this?" He caught Gunner's arm as he started up the scuffed gray steps of the basement. "What's this about? Prince John? I won't be blindsided."

"She's requested you for a special project when she moves residence to Dalholm and Hadsby Castle."

Michael stepped back with a short laugh. "You're having me on. Why would the queen request me for her summer in County Northton?"

It was well known the royal family held the first garden party of the spring season at Hadsby Castle, a stone and concrete fortress and first royal residence. Michael had been to Hadsby on several occasions—starting as a boy when his father traveled north to see the queen. But at the moment, he was more than content below stairs, manning the HMSD Operations Room.

He felt close to Purnell in that place, which didn't make a lot of sense, but there you go.

"I'm not sure," Gunner said, pressing through the door at the top of the stairs, exiting the shadowed utilitarian "below stairs" into the grandeur of "above stairs." "Good morning, Nigel."

The footman nodded, waiting to escort them. "Mr. Ferguson."

It'd been a decade or so, but Michael was not unfamiliar with the palace opulence and hushed reverence. As a member of the Cross family, he'd attended receptions and garden parties with his parents in his youth. Even kicked around the football with Princes John and Gus. Then his parents divorced, and Dad accepted a different position within the government. Michael grew up, attended uni, joined Her Majesty's Special Forces, then her security detail unit. Whatever privileges he had as a child in the Cross family were long revoked.

He was out of place with his black tactical boots sinking into the blue and gold carpet of the Queen's Corridor.

Over his head, the high arched ceiling with coffered panels was painted with medallions of Lauchtenland flora—edelweiss, lavender, and the soft pink and white Linnaea—twinflower— which were part of the legend. As they bloomed, so did love.

Michael wanted to duck as he walked under the colorful, artful images and the golden glow of the crystal chandeliers. He'd become used to the darkness. As for love… He no longer believed it could be his.

"I don't have to tell you how this goes." Gunner looked back at Michael as they approached the Queen's Quarters of Perrigwynn Palace. "We're meeting her in the Audience Room."

He held his reply. What was going on? The Audience Room was for official government briefings, receiving government officials, international guests, and leaders, meetings with her privy council.

"She's waiting for you." The queen's secretary, Mason, opened the ornate and gilded door and stood aside. "You'll notice your chairs are distanced from hers. Please do not approach her. If you cough or sneeze, cover your mouth." The curt and formal secretary handed Gunner, then Michael, a fresh, disposable handkerchief.

"She's been feeling poorly, but keep that to yourself," Gunner said as they approached a second interior door, intricately carved with the queen's cypher. "But she demanded this audience with you."

Gunner and Michael entered the room, stood at attention by their chairs, clicked their heels, and bowed.

"Thank you for agreeing to this meeting, Michael. Please, have a seat." Queen Catherine motioned to the tea trolly and the waiting footman. "Would you like a cup of tea?"

"No thank you, Your Majesty. I'm too full of coffee." Which now burned inside Michael's belly.

"Princess Rachel tells me coffee is all the rage with the young." The queen, in a blue dress and matching shoes, stirred cream in her cup before sitting in her chair, a replica of the first royal throne used by her famous ancestor King Titus. "They prefer it over tea. Do you think one day we'll have completely exchanged our tea leaves for coffee beans?"

"I don't think so, ma'am." Michael sat in the tall, wide-with-thick-arms-and-molded-legs plush seat. Gunner took the chair next to him, reaching for the cup of tea and plate of fragrant cinnamon puffs from the footman. "We may be trending toward coffee, but tea is in our DNA. Our comfort on a cold, wintery afternoon."

"Quite right. You've eased my concern." Queen Catherine's famous smile couldn't hide the weariness in her eyes. She appeared thinner than Michael remembered, with a pale gauntness in her cheeks. Battling Guillain-Barré syndrome was no small feat, yet according to the last Chamber Office update, Her Majesty was overcoming.

"How are you?" she asked, her attention fixed on him. "Not about the incident with the prince and subsequent investigation, but your fiancée."

She knew about Purnell? "Faring, ma'am. Thank you."

"Your grandmother, Odessa, used to join my mother and I for tea now and then. She informed me of the unfortunate circumstances. I am so sorry. I know a bit about losing someone you love, not to death, but I'd like to believe you'll find your way again, Michael." The queen sipped her tea, glancing toward the spring light coming through the windows. "Look at Prince John. He was a grieving widower when I sent him on a mission to Tennessee to woo Scottie into our family. Who could've imagined he'd meet his next great love in Hearts Bend?"

"Yes, ma'am. Prince John was blessed to meet Princess Gemma." But Michael didn't want a *next* great love. He wanted his *first* great love.

It'd become his practice to avoid talk of Purnell Lindholm, the delicate beauty with large brown eyes, bow lips, and big laugh, who'd captured his heart. He knew he'd marry her the moment she slipped her hand into his on their first date—a move that said *I trust you.*

He'd have done anything for her, including dying. But that was one feat a Cross man, one who'd earned commendation and respect as an officer in Her Majesty's Special Forces, a man of might, and her lover, could not do.

"I suppose you're wondering why I requested your presence, Michael Cross." The queen glanced at Gunner, who had a mouth full of puffs. "My daughter has decided to spend the spring season with me at Hadsby Castle." The queen sighed and clasped her hands in her lap. "I don't mind saying I'm terribly excited, but I've yet to hear the outcome of her conversation with her father. Even so, I maintain high hopes. At the very least, I believe she'll spend the week of the Hadsby Garden Party with me. Which would be lovely, having the family all together."

"Yes, ma'am." Michael. Trying to get a sense of where this audience was leading.

"I'd like you to be her protection officer, as well as equerry." Queen Catherine leaned forward as if lasering her gaze across the room directly into Michael's. "I trust you. I trust your family. The Crosses have been devoted servants to the Crown. I'm hoping

Scottie will stay while the rest of the family is managing the Crown's business abroad, as well as taking in much needed holidays." She emphasized "much needed" with a raised chin and squared shoulders. "Are you up for the job?"

"Yes, ma'am." Michael glanced at Gunner. "I'll serve in any way you require. But are you sure? After that business in Brighton Kingdom, I—"

"Michael, do you ride horses?" she said, to which he gave a nod. "Ever fall off?"

"Several times."

"Clearly you didn't quit after the first fall. I think you need to get back on the protection detail horse and look after my daughter, whether she stays one week or eight. Your résumé from your Special Forces service is exemplary. Your final years in service were as Principal Staff Aide to our Chief Defense Officer, correct?"

"Yes, ma'am."

"I'm satisfied you're more than skilled to manage Scottie's diary and your devotion to Her Majesty's Security Detail proves you are qualified to look after her safety. Which I can imagine won't be easy. She's a small-town, wholly independent American woman who doesn't see the need for a protection detail or to inform us on when she's going out for a walk." The queen nodded at Gunner. "Remember her first Christmas here? She left the palace to see the Christmas decorations and lights on Clemency Street. We were frantic for over an hour."

"If you believe I'm right for the job, I'll serve at Your Majesty's pleasure." Michael eyed Gunner's puffs before snatching one from the plate. The sweetness combated the churning in his belly. Just nerves over the Brighton incident. That was all.

"Very good. I'll inform Gunner of her arrival and length of stay when it's confirmed. I'll be traveling to Hadsby next week, since the doctor has ordered me to rest. When Scottie arrives, you'll join her at Hadsby. I'm styling her as Lady Royal Blue, quietly, but the Chamber Office will make an announcement. If I know her, she'll want you to call her Scottie, Michael, but in public please use her title. It will help her, as well as the people, to understand she's a member of the Family. I've asked Choko Danes to be her maid and stylist. She won't want one, but our way of life is very different than what she knows. She can fit Scottie for the Garden Party and other spring engagements. My hope is she'll stay for the Rose Ball at the end of June."

In the short amount of time he'd been in the room, Michael sensed the queen's growing weariness.

"Have Mason give you access to my working diary so you can match Scottie's. Give her lots of liberty to explore Dalholm, The Haskells, and the Highcrest Mountains. I know she's curious about the Midlands, where we were once a leader in textile manufacturing. However, I do want a regular afternoon tea with her. For your ears only: Guillain-Barré sets me aside more often than not. I've assigned my sister, niece, and cousins to take on engagements out of Perrigwynn. In Dalholm, Scottie may need to take an engagement for me alone."

"It sounds as if you're sure she's coming," Michael said.

"Let's just call it faith, shall we?" The queen stood, a sign of dismissal. She wished them a good day and moved toward a far side door. "I'll keep you informed."

Michael turned to Gunner. "I was going to tell you to keep my assignment in the Operations Room."

"You've been trumped by the queen."

Out of the Audience Room, Gunner took a call on his phone. Michael continued down the Queen's Corridor to the backstairs, pulling his thoughts together in case the next few weeks did not include the dark Operations Room and hiding from the world.

He checked an iPad out from IT and secured access to the queen's diary. Those simple chores done, he decided to refresh his intel on the Renaissance Coalition, also known as the RECO party, the anti-monarchists who had elected their charismatic and vocal leader to parliament.

Michael suspected the fringe members of the party may have been behind the attack on Prince John. Though the investigation had not announced any conclusions, Michael wanted to be informed on the latest intel.

Thirty-eight-year-old Scottie O'Shay, the queen's illegitimate daughter, didn't seem to pose much of a threat to the RECOs, but they were in a lull. And a lull meant they were bored. Scottie's arrival and styling as Lady Royal would awaken the bear.

He'd just started wading through recent classified reports when Gunner returned to the Operations Room.

"What were you saying about staying in Operations?" he said. "Mate, you should be chuffed the queen asked for you by name. You do not belong in this dungeon. You're an aboveground, working-with-the-House-of-Blue sort of chap. You bear the Cross name, for crying out loud. Defender of Crown and Country."

"The world has changed since my ancestors fought the Normans with King Titus the First. We're diplomats now. Keepers of history. Lawyers and advisors."

"You served in Her Majesty's Special Forces with distinction."

"Along with every other man in my unit."

"I don't get it, mate." Gunner perched on the side of the desk. "You're a senior officer. A former aide to the head of Lauchtenland's national defense. Why would you want to remain belowground in this dark hovel?"

"If I speak it out loud, you'll think me a loon."

"I already think you are, so try me."

Michael gave a short, wry laugh. "All right, here it is. Purnell hated being alone. Hated the dark. And when I'm in this room, I feel I'm helping her bear the darkness of her death." He pointed to the small corner lamp on his desk. "I keep that thing burning for her in case she happens by to see me, if that's even possible. I wouldn't want her to be in the dark. I know, I know, she's in a reality like heaven, which is full of light, but I want her to know I'm thinking of her and that darkness is only a shadow."

There. Done. Confessed. Could he carry on with his work now? But Gunner, clearing his throat, clapped a hand of understanding on Michael's shoulder.

"That doesn't sound loony at all, mate. Not at all."

Chapter Four

SCOTTIE

She was a Tennessean. A southerner. A commoner. An O'Shay. Yet the blood of the Blue royals, the long-reigning family of the North Sea Island Nation of Lauchtenland, also flowed in her veins.

"...should've done this more," her father muttered as they crested one of the rolling hills of Dad's hobby farm. His horse, Nova, snorted against the clean evening air. "Only trouble is I don't come out as much as I want. I let stuff get in the way."

Dad rested forward with his arm on the saddle horn like an old cowboy, looking over the green rolling acres of Bar T Ranch. The scent of warm leather and honeysuckle led Scottie and her gelding, Dart, through the soft dusky light. Along the horizon, the paddocks of Bar T created a checkerboard on the ryegrass.

"You've been busy building an empire," she said, keeping her voice light.

"Still, if you don't enjoy the fruit of your labor—"

"You think ole Grandpa Loom O'Shay envisioned this when he arrived from Ireland with a bolt of cloth and pair of shears? A glass-and-steel headquarters off River Road, a production plant, and an international sales force?"

"Maybe. My grandfather always said he was a dreamer." Dad stroked Nova's neck and whispered, "Good girl." Then, "I'm feeling the pull, Scottie, for fewer meetings and more afternoons on the golf course or riding Nova. Your grandpa stopped by the office last week and asked me to go on his dream fishing trip to Alaska. Neither one of us are getting any younger. I don't want him to leave this good earth hoping his son will set aside work long enough to fish with him. When he ran O'Shay, he took time for me. Came to all my games, took me fishing, skiing, rafting."

His silhouette looked crumpled in the saddle as if he wore the weight of his words. Still, to Scottie, sixty-two-year-old Trent O'Shay was fit and broad-shouldered with thick silver hair, leading O'Shay Shirts with a young man's energy. The lines around his eyes and mouth had carved deeper in the last six months.

"Dad, is everything okay? You've been sighing a lot lately." Scottie leaned to see his expression. "Is it Remi?" Dad's new love.

"There's just a lot going on with the board," he said, tipping his head back as Nova walked on, knocking off his worries. "It happens every so often. One of them gets an idea in his head and won't let go."

"What kind of idea?" She nudged Dart forward. She attended board meetings. Never witnessed anything concerning.

"Nothing, Scottie." Dad regarded her for a long moment, sighed, then said, "I'm in love with Remi." He urged Nova into the breeze. "She's got me thinking I don't need to score another O'Shay touchdown. Maybe I should kick off and let the next player run with the ball."

"I'm the next player, Dad." Though lately, she wondered if the corner office she'd prepared for all her life really was her future. "And I can tell you're in love. I'm happy for you. Remi's great."

"You don't have to be the next player if you don't want to be, Scottie."

She laughed but not in a ha-ha kind of way. "Are you serious? You, Fritz, Shug, the extended family and half the staff at O'Shay have been preparing me to take the ball my whole life."

"I'm just saying…you have options if you want." Dad steered Nova around the large sprawling oak and headed for home. "What's happening with you and Cap? Wouldn't now be a good time to get married, start a family? Give yourself some breathing room before taking over the company?"

One would think, yes. "We broke up," Scottie spoke in rhythm with the slow clop of hooves against the hard ground and the distant rumble of an unforeseen storm.

"You what? When?" Dad exhaled and Nova stopped and then reached down to snack on the tall grass.

"A week ago. He's in love with the ex-wife. She's in love with him. He didn't know there was even a chance of getting back together. Anyway, they're getting remarried."

"If that don't beat all, Scotto. If he loved his ex, why was he dating you?"

"It's a recent thing and to be honest, I wasn't all in with him. I wanted him to be the one but work always took priority. Same with him."

Dad watched her for a moment with that fatherly look of sorrow, then started Nova moving again. "How about we grill out steaks tonight? Watch one of our favorite movies?"

"Dad, the night Cap told me about his wife, I called Kate."

"I see." He brought Nova around to face her. Scottie urged Dart to take a step back. "Is this a thing now? You talking to her instead of me?"

"No, it was spur of the moment. I felt like talking to her. I thought she'd be more objective than you or Shug. She never met Cap. Anyway, it was late here, early there, and I called. Done deal."

"Well, was her advice sound?"

"She invited me to Hadsby Castle for the spring. About eight weeks. Or however long I can spare. Everyone in the family will be gone from May through June and she wants support for the spring season out of Hadsby Castle." Scottie had texted her for more details as she mulled the invitation. "She's still struggling with GBS and asked if I'd come for the Garden Party, stay a while, attend the Rose Ball. She wants to give me a title. Lady Royal Blue."

Dad shifted in the saddle and stared into the horizon. Dart stamped and snorted as if he sensed the tension. "What'd you say?" he said after another tick-tock of silence.

"I'd think about it. Talk to you."

"It sounds like you want to go."

"I do. In fact, I'm going. I already called her."

"I see," Dad looked over at her. "Scottie, we run a business. This is not like the college semester you wanted to spend abroad. What about the winter line? Your staff? I assume you've made provisions for all of this. Don't tell me you're presenting this grand exit without a plan."

He was upset. But not as much as she expected.

"I have a plan. I've jotted down things."

Dad scoffed.

"I'll have a plan. You know I will. I'm sorry I didn't confirm with you first. But the more I thought about her invitation, nothing else seemed to matter. Dad, I have a mom. I want to know her. I've tried to put it off, tell myself it's too late, that I'm grown. She's married with two sons and grandchildren. Yet I think about her all the time. I miss her. I'm restless. I lose focus during the day. I stare out my office window toward the east wondering what the Blues are doing. What if the GBS complicates Kate's health and I can't spend time with her? What if she dies?"

"She's too stubborn to die."

"I want to know my mother, Dad."

"I know. I wanted you to have a mom when you were little." Dad spurred Nova toward the barn. "I dated a few good women who'd have made good moms, but I couldn't see any of them raising Kate's girl. A real-life princess. I decided it was my task alone, and I loved every minute of it."

"Wanting to know Kate doesn't change anything about us, Dad. We're the two musketeers for life. Maybe I didn't have a mom, but so many of my classmates didn't have dads. They were jealous of me. They thought I was lucky."

"I was telling Remi about the day I was late to your fourth-grade class party, rushing with my box of smashed Haven's cupcakes. Gracie Welch asked in the loudest possible voice, 'Where's your mom, Scottie? Everyone has a mom.'" Dad looked over at her. "You just stood there, tears in your eyes, and for the first time in your life, I knew I wasn't enough. I felt completely helpless. I couldn't fix the fact that your mother was four thousand miles away, raising her two princes, preparing to rule a small island kingdom."

"Dad, you and Shug, and Fritz…you were the best trio. I have zero regrets. Best childhood ever. But now I know… Now I have a chance to know my mother. Who I thought was dead until I was thirty-five."

"What was the reporter's name who broke the story?"

"Leslie Ann Parker." Her name was forever burned into Scottie's psyche. "I'm not asking for repentance or for explanations or to change the past. I understand why Kate left me with you. For thirty-five years it was your secret. But now it's my story. It's up to me to change my future. I want to go to Lauchtenland, which surprises me, excites me, and scares me. Eight weeks, Dad. Then I'm back and all yours. You can take those afternoons for the golf course."

Scottie was eight when Dad fed her the "truth" about her mother, his supposed high school sweetheart named Brenda Luck. They married young but shortly after Scottie was born, she died. When and where, how, he never said. They never visited her grave or her people. There were no pictures, no memories shared, or love stories told. When Scottie learned the actual truth, that she was the secret daughter of the Queen of Lauchtenland, Dad defended the simplicity of his three-decades-old story.

"Simple kept the lie straight for us."

"So you're going?" Dad said. "To become a princess?"

"No, not a princess. Just as a daughter. The title is Kate's idea. I won't be an HRH. I'll be back before you know it. O'Shay Shirts is my future kingdom. Who knows, this break might stir my creativity as well as establish new business connections in Europe."

"I don't want to lose you, Scottie. You're my girl. Your grandmother used to say when you were out of earshot, 'They best not ever come for her. She's ours.' Made me wonder if she knew something I didn't."

"You'll never lose me, Dad. You gave up everything for me. Kate will never replace you. As for Shug, my grandmother drama queen is also irreplaceable. I was the daughter she never had."

As the sun set, the air cooled, the shadows deepened, and Scottie and Dad paused at the top of a knoll.

"When you were sixteen and Kate wanted to send you a gown she'd once worn, I knew then the dam had cracked. She'd never reached out before." Dad sat back with ease as Nova headed down a hill. "So, what's your plan?" he asked over his shoulder. "Work from Lauchtenland? Do you really want to be Lady Royal Blue?"

"I've talked with Matteo and the team. I'll make it all formal next week. Jack can handle the marketing without me. There's always email and Zoom if I'm needed, but I want to be present for Kate. I want to explore Lauchtenland." Scottie tightened her grip on Dart's reins. "Matteo can steer the winter line through the final phases once I approve the designs. I'll check the tech packs when I get back. There's time."

"When do you leave?" There was a calm resolve in Dad's voice.

"End of April. She'd like me there before the May eighth Garden Party."

"Then let's cancel the movie and finalize this plan of yours over dinner. The board won't like this, but—"

"Why not? What does it matter to them? You'll still be here. You're the CEO."

"Just be back before the July board meeting."

Nearing the barn, Scottie voiced her last argument for her decision. "You know this isn't about you or the company. Not even entirely about Kate. This is about me learning who I am. Until now, I've only had half a story. If you'd married when I was little and that woman adopted me, raised me, called me her daughter, we'd not be having this conversation. Mom would've been my mom. But you didn't, and my guess is deep down you knew this day would come. You wanted me to know Catherine Blue was my mother."

His jaw flexed, just once, which meant he heard her but didn't like it. "Why don't you tend the horses while I run into town for the steaks."

"Dad," she said. "I promise I'll come home the same girl I am now."

"Let's see if that girl can finally beat her old man in a race." He pressed Nova into a run. Dart, with a reluctant trot-to-run, raced home, giving Scottie everything he had.

That's what she planned to do with her time with Kate—give it everything she had, then come home the same girl who'd left.

"By order of Her Majesty, Queen Catherine the Second, Letters Patent have been issued and sealed by the Ancient Cypher of Titus granting Scottie O'Shay the style of Lady Royal on this day, the 30th of April, thus affording the rights and privileges thereof the Houses of Blue and Lauchtenland."

—THE CHAMBER OFFICE OF HER MAJESTY, THE QUEEN

"We're blooming overrun by Americans. Do we need another snooty rich lass with a title? Didn't the Yanks fight a war to throw off the yoke of oligarchy and aristocracy? Why are we allowing them to make it fashionable again? Every North Sea Island Nation has an American under a crown. Go home, Lady Royal. MP Fickle for Prime Minister!"

—@RECOPARTYMAN2000 ON X.COM

"On the heels of the queen's Letters Patent, Hamish Fickle presented the Royal Reduction Act in parliament, intending to limit the size and power of the royal family. 'Why are the citizens of Lauchtenland still paying tribute to the House of Blue a thousand years later?' Fickle said. 'We don't need their protection. In fact, we protect them. Of course, we adore our queen. The House of Blue is our constitution representing our history and culture. But there's no need to bow and curtsy. We're not a big nation but we are influential. Let's lead the way for our North Sea Island neighbors to fully embrace the power of the people in the twenty-first century.'"

—*CLARK WILSON, THE NEWS LEADER*

Michael

Her Majesty's daughter had arrived. The dark Range Rover pulled round Hadsby's meticulously cared for circular drive and stopped by the speckled portico steps.

"Here we go, lads and lasses." Michael exited the security office through the servants' hall to rouse the staff. "Grand Foyer, please. Greet her as Lady Royal but do not curtsy or bow. She's an American."

"She is Her Majesty's daughter." Cranston, Hadsby's butler, had been in conflict with Michael about the status of the recently dubbed Lady Royal Blue, Scottie O'Shay.

Cranston wanted to treat her like a legitimate member of the House of Blue. Michael insisted she be treated in the manner of any government official or visiting dignitary.

"With respect, Cranston, I believe I have Her Majesty's mind on the matter." The queen, who'd been visited by her physician this morning, was asleep but eager to greet her daughter for afternoon tea. She'd personally rung him several times admonishing him to "Not overwhelm her with our world."

Our world? Yes, of course, the world of royals and security. As a Cross man, Michael was familiar with royal security and royal duty. Yet the attempt on Prince John's life during the North Sea Island Nations' Summit lingered with him. How had he let it happen? How had he not seen the assailant? The investigation may have cleared him, but he'd not cleared himself. He had a chance to erase that event by protecting Lady Royal. He determined not to make a pig's ear out of it.

Then there was the moment Mum cornered him at Evan and Tracy's after Finn's football match.

"It's time you come work for Pratt. I need your tactical

training and thinking in our exec room. You've done your Cross duty. You've served the Crown. You're forty years old, Mick. Time to join Pratt, settle down, and have a family. Poor Finn, Mindy, and Linus have no cousins."

Evan had defended him. *"Mum, have a care. He's still mourning Purnell."* Such a good brother and mate.

"I loved Purnell, you know that, but she's not coming back."

Over the past few weeks Mum had texted Michael a possible job description, opportunities, and a pay packet. Nearly four times what he made in HMSD. Before bonus.

Yet as he stepped into Hadsby's Grand Foyer, his only focus was the queen's daughter.

Cranston, dressed in a dark gray suit with a waistcoat, starched white shirt, and dark blue tie, stood with his shoulders back, chin up. The four footmen, dressed in red coats and dark slacks, white shirts, and gray ties, lined the Grand Staircase. Hadsby's Head of Household, Somba, wore a blue skirt and a vest with a white blouse underneath. The hem of her vest was trimmed in blue silk. Choko Danes, Scottie's lady's maid—rather stylist, as they were called these days—wore black slacks and jacket with a fitted white blouse. Chef George, representing the kitchen staff, stood at attention in his chef whites.

There were others, of course. The household maids and kitchen staff, the gardeners and technicians, plus the castle's security detail. However, the lot in the foyer would interact with Lady Royal daily.

"You all look smart," Michael said with a nod of approval, reaching for the door just as Scottie stepped onto the portico, framed beneath one of the arcade arches. The crisp wind blowing up from Whistlecrag Bluff, filled with the salt and scent of the sea, tossed her long, blonde hair with brunette undertones about her face, and for the briefest moment, time and sound stood still. She was stunning.

He'd seen pictures of her, studied her life, work, and education. She was the confident men's fashion designer with a get-out-of-my-way spark in her eyes.

Yet in this moment, those observing eyes carried a flicker of vulnerability that tugged at him. Should he step forward, put an arm around her, reassure her everything would be all right? On reflex, Michael pressed his hand against the little hitch in his chest—something he'd not experienced since delicate, porcelain Purnell.

Clad in travel clothes of jeans, trainers, and an orange University of Tennessee hoodie, she caught his eye and smiled, moving toward him with a weary elegance, her gaze drifting over Hadsby's weathered stone. She pressed her hand against one of the ancient pillars as though testing its worth. Her presence was both common and regal, an American mirror of Her Majesty.

Even with Scottie's reserved hesitations, Michael saw the iron in her core. This assignment was going to be nothing like he'd imagined.

"Lady Royal Blue." He stepped forward, hand outstretched. "Welcome back to Hadsby Castle. I'm Michael Cross, your equerry and protection officer."

"Yes, I know. Kate sent me details about you. Impressive." Kate? She addressed Her Majesty as Kate? No one employed her nickname—not friends, not family—in front of staff or her security detail.

When her hand clasped his, he forgot all about protocol or even where he was standing.

"It's good to be back." Scottie pulled her hand free. "I forgot how much I love the fragrance of Hadsby. It smells wild and watery, like the gardens and the woods, like stone and sea." She peered at Michael. "Should we go in?"

"Yes, indeed. Your staff awaits you." He gathered himself to follow her inside, pulling from the way she captured him with a glance and the poetic way she spoke of Hadsby. None of it seemed to overwhelm her, but she somehow overwhelmed him.

Cranston greeted her first, bowing. "Welcome back, Lady Royal Blue. You remember the senior staff?"

"How could I forget? We played pickleball two Christmases ago in the ball room." Down the line, Scottie shook hands, her words bowed ever so slightly with the American southern accent. "How're y'all doing?"

He'd been wrong about any vulnerability. She'd arrived with her confidence fully intact. But of course. She was an international businesswoman who'd traveled the world, been on the American morning talkies, and made *People Magazine*'s "Women of Fortune" feature.

"Am I in the Princess Charlotte suite?" Scottie glanced at Cranston then Somba. "It has such a beautiful view."

"It's all ready for you, Lady Royal," Somba announced with a curtsy. "Would you like to go up now?"

"Please and thank you." Scottie motioned to the protection officers who carried in her cases from the motor. "You can leave them by the stairs. I'll carry them up."

"Miles." Cranston snapped his fingers at the head footman. "See to Lady Royal's luggage." The young man with ruddy cheeks hopped to, and his team of red-coated footmen appeared from the back of the foyer, where he no doubt had them lined up and waiting. They carried her three pieces of luggage, backpack, and messenger bag up the Grand Staircase in military fashion.

"Lady Royal, can I prepare something for you to eat or drink?" Chef George bowed, making a sweeping gesture with his arm. "I've a light refreshing cherry drink, low on calories, you might enjoy. Along with a turkey sandwich?"

"Chef George, you are mind reader. That's perfect. Thank you." Scottie drew him into a light hug. "I do not deserve all of this attention. And please, call me Scottie. I'll be here for a while and want to feel I'm among friends." She turned to Michael. "I'm not breaking too many rules, am I?"

"You can choose what you want to be called," he said. "The queen insists."

"Good." She started up the stairs. "Kate said you'd want to go over my schedule sometime today."

"Yes, Lady Roy—Scottie. We can go over your diary after tea. You've a number in your room to call down to the security office. I'll be there until you're ready." What was he to do with the

American lass staring down at him from the middle of the stairs?

"Why don't you come to the Princess Charlotte now? We can talk."

"If you wish." Cranston gave him the eye as he stepped aside for the stairs.

What? He heard her. Lady Royal—Scottie—had invited him up. He was her equerry, after all. Truth was, he hadn't spent much time around Americans and never an American woman. Not up close anyway. He'd been on duty once when Princess Gemma traveled with Prince John, but she'd had her own security detail.

Scottie seemed different. Cut from finer threads. From something special.

Up the Grand Staircase to the Grand Gallery Scottie chatted with the first footman, Miles.

"Weren't you an expectant father the last time I was here?"

"Yes, miss. We have a three-month-old son."

"Congratulations." Scottie patted him on the back. "How proud are you?"

"Busting me buttons, miss."

To Michael, the lyrical sound of her southern words seemed to hover over him, making air curly cues. She talked as if she'd known the footman for eons. Would she be the same with him?

From his pocket, his phone buzzed. A quick glance told him it was his mother. "Leave it, Mum," he muttered. She was increasingly insistent about Michael joining the Pratt Printing dynasty.

He refused. One day he hoped she'd have the courage to ask him why.

Just before the Princess Charlotte suite, Scottie slowed by the portraits on the Wall of Princesses. Enormous, beautifully painted images of her mother when she was Crown Princess Catherine, of her aunt, Princess Arabella, and of the nineteenth- and eighteenth-century Blue princesses. Charlotte, Clemency, and Louisa. The portraits continued around the corner and down the Royal Hallway.

Scottie paused in front of the portrait of her mother. "People say I look like her." She glanced over at Michael. "What do you think?"

"Yes, miss, very much."

"Miss? Please, call me Scottie or don't call me at all." She air drummed with a *ba-da-dump*. Michael cracked a slow smile. Was he supposed to laugh? "Wow, tough crowd." And she turned for her suite.

Miles and another footman exited the large second-floor apartment as Scottie entered. One of the maids had brought round a tea trolly with a heating kettle and a covered plate of something—Michael assumed a small plate of puffs—a beloved North Sea Island Nation pastry.

Scottie collapsed onto the curved burnt-orange colored couch. "Did you ever notice the colors of this room, the muted greens and pinks, yellows and blues, match Princess Charlotte's portrait?" She glanced back at him. "It seems to whisper, 'leave all your cares here.' Do you think it was like this when Princess Charlotte was alive?"

"Hadsby Castle was renovated in the last twenty years. Princess Charlotte was born in the eighteenth century. Styles have changed. But she was well-educated, an artist, author, and horsewoman." Michael focused on the tapestried walls and carpeted floor, the coffered ceiling with the row of crystal chandeliers. Scottie was not wrong. The room invited him to leave off his cares. "This side of the castle endured several bombings from our German neighbors during the second war. I believe this room was all but destroyed by fire."

"Yet now it's so peaceful." Scottie moved to the tea trolly and raised the lid from the plate. "I can't eat all these puffs. Help yourself. Plus, I didn't realize how exhausted I was until I sat on the couch."

To where she returned, legs curled under her, eating in silence, going for a bottle of water from the ice bucket on the bottom of the trolly.

Michael did not go for puffs, though they were one of his favorite treats, but stood off to the side with a cup of tea and waited for her conversational cues. Did she want to go over her diary or rest? After all, he wasn't hanging round for a proper chinwag but business.

"Do you think I should be here?" Scottie said, glancing back at him. "Hanging out with the Queen of Lauchtenland like I'm one of *them*. Can I really pull off a title like Lady Royal Blue? What are people saying about me? That I'm a grifter? Imposter?"

Her eyes met his, and he spied again the initial vulnerability. Then, as now, it caused a movement in his chest.

"It's not for me to say, miss. As your equerry, I am to manage your schedule. As your protection officer, I'm to keep you safe."

"What about as a confidant?" Scottie munched on a puff.

"Certainly everything you say and do is privileged, miss. I'm here in whatever capacity you need."

"Okay, then *please* call me Scottie. Second, be honest with me and help me do things right. Kate acts like it's a cakewalk to come here, hang out like one of the family simply because I'm her daughter." She paced to the window, plate in hand. "The whole flight over, I kept asking myself, 'What are you doing, S.O.? Leaving the life you know, the job you love, to play daughter and aide to the woman who abandoned you?'"

"It's my understanding the queen invited you, miss—rather, Scottie. I assume she wants to know you. Undo those years of separation. Is it fair to say you feel the same?"

Touché was the look in her eye. "It's fair. I wanted to come. I spent the last two weeks preparing my team at O'Shay to take my place. But you know, sometimes you make a decision and later you"—Scottie faced the tall, mullioned window again—"wonder if you'd lost your ever-loving mind."

"You seem sane from where I stand," he said. "To answer your question, I think you *should* be here if it means spending time with people you love and who love you. Her Majesty was terribly cut up she could not come down to greet you. The doctor ordered her to rest."

"Yes, I know. She had an IVIG treatment for her GBS yesterday," Scottie said. "It knocks her out. She called me three times to apologize." Scottie pressed closer to the window, leaning to see to the left of the castle.

"Did you see something?" Michael joined her at the window.

"A man. Walking along the perimeter wearing a long duster-like jacket—I think you call it an anorak—and a wide-brim hat. He stopped, looked up at me with really piercing eyes, then seemed to disappear."

"That's odd," Michael said, joining her at the window. "Emmanuel?" By her short description, it sounded like him, a Lauchtenland legend.

He was a story children learned in school. A tale adults told round campfires. As a member of the Cross family, knowing stories of Emmanuel—God with us—visiting Lauchtenland was part of his education. His ancestors kept records of the man's appearance. If he was real, he'd be eight hundred years old, so clearly he was a cultivated Lauchten fable. Though some insisted he was real and divine, Michael had never sensed a divine being interacting with his family or his country.

"Emmanuel?" Scottie said.

"Yes, the name means God with us," Michael said. "There's a legend about the woodsman who comes down from the twin peaks of the Highcrest Mountains every blue or red moon to visit the people. We Lauchtens love our legends and lore, our fairy tales." Michael moved to another window to scan the castle grounds where a field of lavender bloomed wild on the edges of Whistlecrag Bluff. "I daresay it was one of the gardeners disappearing in the sunlight."

The sun *was* unusually high and bright on this spring day.

Scottie stared at the golden swaths falling in long drapes over the flowers and lavender, then glanced over at Michael, as if testing his story.

"You look exhausted," he said as a maid arrived with her turkey sandwich and cherry drink. Beautiful but exhausted. Perhaps more from the magnitude of her trip than the travel itself.

"Let's go over your diary later." He pointed to the end table phone then regarded her for a moment before collecting himself. "Ring down to the Operations Room when you're ready."

Once in the gallery, he gave himself a proper reprimand. "Get a hold of yourself, mate."

He'd been utterly gobsmacked by her—this lovely being from the House of Blue and the House of O'Shay. Hardly the sort of reaction listed in his job description. He wasn't ready for the flutter that came from standing too near a stranger. And it was too soon to let Purnell go. She deserved his loyalty still—and he'd give it to her in death if not in life.

"The king consort is off on a fishing trip with his mates. Prince John and his family are traveling, and I just heard Prince Gus and Princess Daffodil are in New York. Princess Arabella and her husband, Sir William, and Princess Rachel are at Perrigwynn. Which Blues will be at the Hadsby Garden Party?! I finally got an invitation!"

–@STEFWITHANF ON IG

"@StefwithanF. Us too! We got an invite to the Garden Party! We can't believe it! #whattowear"

–@LOYALROYALBLOG

"I'm quite looking forward to seeing the queen's daughter and the newly styled Lady Royal Blue at the Garden Party. I know some will disagree with me, but I think she brings such a refreshing sensibility to the House of Blue, and though she's Creative Director for a men's fashion house, her taste is impeccable. She turned heads at Christmas last year, walking to Clouver Abbey with the Family. Utterly elegant. The American women really are bringing their A-game these days, aren't they? There's something so wonderfully genuine about Scottie O'Shay. The queen inviting her to serve as companion during the spring is rather touching."

–TUPPENCE CORBYN & FRIENDS

CHAPTER FIVE

There wasn't one formal bone in her body. How could there be when she grew up running in and out of Dad's office or Shug's kitchen for a cookie before jumping back in the pool or rolling down a hill of fall leaves. Never mind four years of running up and down the basketball court of Rock Mill High with a fierce competitiveness.

Formalities weren't at play in her childhood when the neighbors left their back doors unlocked for the after-school crowd to run inside for a drink and snack.

If she was out to dinner with Dad and friends walked by, they'd just sit down at their table for a chat or even the whole meal.

Welcome to the South.

However, at Hadsby Castle, Scottie waited to be invited by a footman to Monarch One, the suite of her mother. She dined in the Grand Dining Hall. Walked the Grand Gallery under the stare of her ancestors to descend the Grand Staircase into the Grand Foyer. She wandered through the Grand Drawing Room. Everything about Hadsby Castle bore the title of "Grand."

Choko brought her breakfast and laid out her clothes—some of which did not come from her suitcases.

Since her arrival, she'd slept in. Something she'd not done since, well, she couldn't remember. She easily fell into a routine of a light breakfast, touring the castle, or reading in Queen's Library with an old first edition book until afternoon tea with Kate, who was not feeling well, and barely lasted an hour before wilting.

Yesterday the doctor again expressed his concern about infections, so in order to keep Kate healthy until the Garden Party—which she *insisted* on attending—she remained isolated except for afternoon tea with Scottie. Which the queen also insisted upon.

However, at the moment, Scottie perched on a sofa cushion and processed her conversation with Dad. She called to say hi and see how O'Shay fared without her. She'd expected some frantic *"Help!"* calls. An inbox of emails. But so far, nothing. It was like she didn't matter.

"How's Kate?" he'd said. She may be a European queen and highly respected world leader, but Queen Catherine the Second would always be Kate to Trent and Scottie O'Shay.

"Weak. I don't get to see her much. The Garden Party is coming up, then the start of her spring schedule."

"Scotto, have fun. Forget being an O'Shay and the job. Be Lady Royal Blue." He sounded like a game show host. "Little girls dream of being you."

"Forget being an O'Shay?" She stiffened at his inference. "Dad, I'm more O'Shay than the air in my lungs." This was so weird. What was he not saying? "Is, um, everything all right?"

"Scottie, stop. I'm just encouraging you to enjoy being with your mom's people. Don't worry about things here."

Okay, that made sense. "I'll be home before you know it." Said with cheer. A bit forced. Yet absolutely true.

Though she sensed something rumbling between her and Dad. Was it because she chose to spend two months with Kate? He said he understood, but did he? The tone of his voice seemed to cloak something.

At the knock on her door, she turned. When she opened up, footman Miles stood in the corridor.

"Her Majesty is anxious to see you, miss," Miles said. "She's requested dinner for tea since the hour is late."

"How is she today?" Scottie tucked her phone into her pocket and regarded Miles

"She's the queen, miss," he said with a bit of a grin. "What else can I say?"

Of course, Miles wouldn't disclose anything about Her Majesty's health. Discretion was paramount to his livelihood. Down another corridor where sconces lit the textured wall, around another corner toward the back of the castle, then Scottie arrived with Miles at the familiar door of the royal suite, Monarch One.

The footman rapped on the heavy, ornate door, then backed away. Hilda, Kate's maid, escorted Scottie to the small dining room, then exited, closing the door behind her.

"Ah, here she is." Kate smiled but remained seated, her hands tucked into her lap. She looked tired and her pale skin a bit too thin. Thank goodness her eyes were clear and bright. "I'm so sorry I've spent most of your first week napping away the hours."

"Your health is more important." Scottie sat across from her mother at a small table set for two with bone china and gold flatware, and goblets of water and wine. "Are you resting well?"

"Fairly," Kate said. "I feel like the effects of my last treatment will never end. I am in a bit of pain." She sighed, reaching for her water. "How do you like Michael? Are you getting on well?"

"I've not spent a lot of time with him, but he seems like a nice man. He gave me a tour of the Garden Party tents and explained how everything works."

"Rather handsome, don't you think?" Kate raised the lid of the blue-and-white tureen, releasing the aroma of chicken and vegetables in a thick sauce covered with a golden-brown crust. The fragrances filled Scottie with a sense of home. "He comes from the very esteemed Cross family, who have served the Crown for as long as the Blues have been on the throne."

Kate tried to serve dinner for Scottie, but she bobbled the plate and dropped the lid, clattering it against the tureen.

"Kate, hey, hey, let me." Scottie retrieved her plate and the serving spoon teetering on the edge of the table. "You don't have to be a hero. I know your treatments leave you weak."

"But it's your first week here." Kate curled her hand into her lap. "We've done nothing together except drink tea, and I'm half asleep before we finish the first cup. I want to do all the motherly things I couldn't do when you were growing up, but then I remind myself you're not a child. You're thirty-eight years old. Look, now you're spooning dinner on my plate instead of the other way round."

"Well, if you want, I'll let you pat me on the back later, see if I burp."

Kate's laugh was quick and hearty but with a swift fade, like she was out of breath. Looking down, she confessed, "I refuse to let this, *this disease* triumph."

Kate's diagnosis with Guillain-Barré was one of the main reasons Scottie first agreed to meet her long-lost, fabled mother.

Prince John came looking for Scottie in Hearts Bend two years ago and convinced her to visit Perrigwynn Palace. Along the way, he fell in love with Gemma, a Hearts Bend gal who had lost herself in Hollywood. Her love gave him hope after a year of grief. His love rescued her from shame.

Kate tried for a bite of chicken pie, but her spoon nosed downward.

"Here, let's make this a team effort." Scottie scooted her chair around, dragging her place setting along, rearranging the goblets and the ornate crystal vase, then scooped a small portion of the pie.

"I feel rather silly," Kate said, eyes locked on Scottie, not moving toward the spoon.

"Either this or get half of it in your lap. Or starve."

Kate made a face, breathing out. "Well, all right, but only Edric has done this for me in the past. Let's keep this to ourselves, shall we?"

"It will be our secret."

And so it went, a choreographed routine of a bite for Kate and a bite for Scottie. She buttered a roll for her mother, who could manage holding that on her own. And with two hands, she could sip her water.

"Arabella would have a day if she saw us." Kate exhaled back against her chair. "But God love her, she's opening the symphony tonight for me."

Arabella, Kate's younger sister, was married to Sir William, with one child, Princess Rachel. Arabella was lively and outspoken—or so Scottie had observed—and the classic younger sibling of a ruling monarch. She marched in line with the Family yet was eager to make her own mark.

Kate went on. "Edric had never missed a fishing trip with his mates until I was diagnosed, and I refuse to let him miss another one. John is tending to my duties, as well as his own, and his family. The same with Gus and Daffy. I won't be seen as the poorly queen who demands everyone stop living to hold my hand." She motioned to her plate. "Though I can barely feed myself. This was not how I envisioned our visit. I was feeling so strong when you called. As if the disease was faded." She held up one weak fist. "I was winning. Until—"

"Kate, we're together. Isn't that the point?" Scottie took a bite of the chicken pie then raised her mother's spoon to give one to her. "I'll be here for you."

Kate glanced down at her trembling fingers, folding her napkin over and over. "Well, then… So, how was your father when you left?" She'd asked the same question when Scottie first arrived. "He had to be a bit miffed by it all."

Scottie lowered the spoon. "Can we put the past behind us and go forward from here? You don't have to apologize to me or Dad or anyone. You did what you had to do, and let's face it, hardly anyone in the world has been challenged with such a decision. You didn't want to abandon me and Dad, but you weren't the ordinary girl next door. You're forgiven."

"Thank you," she said softly. "You've never said it so plainly before."

"I was being stubborn, not wanting to meet you after I knew the truth," Scottie said. "My life was set. I didn't need a mother. Especially one who'd walked away from me. Never mind learning you're a queen living four thousand miles away."

"We're living a unique experience, aren't we? You're the only woman whose mother left her to be raised by her father because she was a crown princess."

"You think they'll make a movie about us?" Scottie reached for her wine and took a small sip.

"Of course they will." Kate, with a burst of exaggerated energy. "Who do you want to play you?"

"Oh gosh, I don't know. Who do you want to play you?"

"Dame Silver Leckwin. She's a marvelous and loyal Lauchten. One of our stars."

"Maybe Chloe Daschle could play me," Scottie said. "I loved her in the Revolutionary War film *Bound by Love*."

"Edric and I enjoyed that film." Kate leaned toward her daughter. "You're good for us, Scottie. Good for me. I feel the medicine of your presence already. You'll be a smash at the Garden Party—cheered far more than booed."

Scottie set her wine aside. "Who's going to boo me? The press?"

"Perhaps, but so far, they seem favorable to you. I was thinking more of the political faction—the Renaissance Coalition—intent on dismantling the monarchy altogether. MP Hamish Fickle has been vocal lately. He and his supporters see us as relics of another age, a burden to the people. They overlook, of course, how tirelessly we serve and how deeply we care for our nation and citizens. But the RECO party doesn't speak for everyone. They're a noisy few, led by a man who enjoys the sound of his own voice. I shouldn't have mentioned it, love."

"It's okay, but—why do they want to boo me again?" Scottie *was* used to criticism, which ran rampant in the fashion world. But booing a daughter simply wanting to know her family felt petty.

"Because they're small-minded," Kate said, her tone calm but growing weary. "And envious. Mostly because you're my daughter—and American. Some feel we've enough of those in the palace already."

"I've no intention of living in the palace. I'm here for you, Kate." After the Rose Ball, she'd return home in time for the O'Shay board meeting and approval of the winter line. "I'll be gone before the RECO crowd have time to pucker up and boo."

"Quite right, my dear," Kate said, her smile faint. "You've far more important places to be. Just promise you'll always come back." She started to reach for Scottie, but her arm dropped to the table. Slowly she slipped from her chair to the floor, the color draining from her face.

"Kate—hey, Kate, what's wrong? Kate!" Scottie caught her before her head struck the floor, cradling her trembling body against her legs. "Cranston! Hilda! Miles—*help!*"

MICHAEL

Everything was too quiet, save for the North Sea wind carving at the castle's ancient stone. Lately he'd begun to hate the quiet. It left far too much room for thinking."

Technically, he was off duty. Lennox and Schueler—both former members of Her Majesty's Special Forces and now part of her security detail—manned the castle's Operations Room. He had the evening free. In four days, his schedule would be packed with the Lady Royal's diary and helping her navigate the royal world.

He took a sip of port and moved to the window. He preferred a pint from the pub down by the quay—the Belly of the Beast—to sweet, fortified wine, but Cranston had brought the port round, so he felt obliged to try it.

From the entryway clock of his flat on the third floor of the castle, a bell chimed. Michael checked his watch as if to verify: nine o'clock. By the lingering light and the short shadows of a north Lauchtenland evening, the days were lengthening. The castle grounds were starting to bloom with their famous purple flora, which meant the Garden Party should be stunning. A recent email put the expected attendance at three thousand.

He'd scheduled a review of castle security protocols with the team for tomorrow. But for now...

Michael loosened his tie and slipped off his jacket. He'd packed very little from his Port Fressa flat for his duration in Dalholm: five white shirts, four pairs of black slacks, two jackets, two ties, two pairs of jeans, and three pairs of shoes. He preferred tactical gear to suits, but escorting the queen's daughter called for more formal attire. Along with clothes and toiletries, he'd brought a couple of books, though he didn't feel like reading. He could change into workout togs and head up to the fourth-floor gym, but—

Sudden movement across the grounds and through the gathering shadows caught his eye. He darted to the next window, squinting through the fading light, barely making out heels and elbows as a runner disappeared into the north woods.

It was unlikely a staff member would race across the grounds and vanish by the woods. How would they get past the security gate? Only members of HMSD knew the code.

An intruder? Michael stiffened with the recall of the attempt on Prince John. If he allowed a second attack on a member of the House of Blue, he'd resign his post. Then his mother would win— which she did not deserve—because what other position could he take to serve the Crown?

He snatched up his phone and dialed Operations. "Did I see a runner on the north side?"

"We're checking video now, sir," came Lennox's voice. He trusted her—sharp, reliable, his backup for the Lady Royal.

"Check with Cranston and Somba about the staff. Maybe it was one of them."

Ending the call, he scanned the grounds again, then changed into jeans, trainers, a Cross PF Youth Club football jersey, and a hoodie. He might as well check the grounds himself. But first he'd pop into the Operations Room.

As he headed for the servants' stairs, his phone pinged. Mum. Dare he read it?

> Mum: I found this on my phone. Thought you might like it.

Michael stared at a picture of Purnell—the sun in her hair, laughter in her brown eyes, a secret behind her smile.

> Michael: I took that picture and sent it to you. Why would I want another one?

Mum: Didn't you delete all your photos?

Michael: So you send me this in case I changed my mind?

Not that it was her business, but he hadn't deleted *every* photo of Purnell. Most, yes. He'd saved a few. This was one of them.

Mum: I thought it might be nice to see her bright, smiling face. She loved you. She'd want you to love again.

Mum was incorrigible. First, she nagged him about his career, now his love life, which, by the by, he'd never discussed with her.

Michael: If you're hinting at setting me up, move off, Mum. I'm happy enough as I am. Good night.

Mum: I don't believe you're happy, but if you insist, what can I do? Denial is a lonely place, Mick.

Michael: Good night, Mum.

Mum: How's it going with the American? I don't see any news on her yet.

Michael: How did you know about the American?

Mum: Your father told me. Do you like her?

Dad? Since when did he talk to Mum about life?

Michael: She's fine. Liking her is not my job, is it?

Mum: Are you coming to Dad and Mum's anniversary party?

Michael: I'm on duty for the next two months.

Mum: You're allowed a personal life, surely. It's your grandparents, Mick. Talk to the queen. Surely she'll excuse you for Odessa Pratt's sixty-fifth.

Michael: Good night, Mum.

Ask the queen? Was Mum off her trolley? Surely the chief executive of an international printing company understood chain of command. Gunner Ferguson was his boss, not the Queen of Lauchtenland.

He started toward the Operations Room, but a single glance at his phone stopped him mid-stride. Purnell's face filled the screen. She was so lovely. In every way. He'd thought himself the luckiest chap alive when she'd agreed to a date.

They'd gone to Pub Clemency, talked without hesitation, laughed easily. He'd snapped this photo—the one Mum sent—the day they signed the lease on their newlywed flat. Oh, how in love he'd been. That afternoon they'd shopped for furniture and tested a hundred sofas. How had he not seen the secret she harbored? When he finally learned, it was too late.

He exhaled and pressed his fingers against his temple. Sometimes he wanted to believe Mum was right—he could love again. But it was easier to remember what he'd lost than to imagine what he might gain.

What was the Dalholm saying? Something about how the sea had a song and love bloomed like the flora and fauna—touching lives in mysterious ways. Like the stories of Emmanuel, it was all legends, fables drifting down from the Highcrest Mountains.

To be frank, Michael didn't know anyone who fell in love in Lauchtenland more than anywhere else. One thing he knew for certain—Michael Cross would not fall in love while in Dalholm. *Do your worst, song of the sea.* He'd be too focused on the American royal to think of anything else. Scottie O'Shay was nothing like the soft-spoken artist Purnell, who once wept over dying flower petals.

Shaking off the emotional sidetrack—thank you, Mum—he tucked his phone into his pocket and entered the Operations Room.

"We can't locate the Lady Royal," Lennox said, eyes fixed on the CCTV bank. "I think she was the runner across the grounds."

"Why isn't she with Her Majesty?"

"Her Majesty collapsed during dinner. The medical team is

with her. We've checked all the cameras. We can't figure how she left the palace—if she left at all."

"Did she crawl out a second-story window?" He was half joking. The windows in Hadsby Castle's high rough walls, with rows of arrow-slits, were thirty feet off the ground.

"Not unless she has Rapunzel hair. There's nothing on any of the castle cameras at the time of the runner. The staff are accounted for. I thought I'd search—"

"No, let me." He was already moving. "She's my main charge." He refused a repeat of the Brighton Kingdom incident. "Keep watch for her return. Notify me immediately."

What was she thinking, going out alone? The queen had been right. Blasted independent American.

Hadsby sat between the Old and New Hamlet where, a thousand years ago, the castle provided shelter for the locals. Farmers. Merchants. Tradesmen. The people had pledged loyalty to the House of Blue for generations, and in turn, the royal family pledged its loyalty to them. Centuries on, that mindset still lay at the heart of Lauchtenland's devotion to the royal family, especially in County Northton. Yet if Scottie were recognized among them, Michael had no idea what might happen.

In recent years, opponents had risen. MP Hamish Fickle spoke of setting aside the monarchy for a republican government. His RECO party had traction with younger voters and often used aggressive tactics.

Michael jogged across the manicured lawn set for the Garden Party toward the woods and slipped through the hidden security gate toward the Old Hamlet and the Belly of the Beast.

Crossing Centre Street, he threaded down Wells Line toward the quay lights. Music rose above the thatched cottages and dark-windowed shops, and Michael joined the stream of folks flowing toward a party.

"Please don't tell me you're in this, Scottie O'Shay, Lady Royal." Back in Hearts Bend she might slip into a pop-up street gathering, but not here. Not with a brand-new title.

A band played on the quay car park, belting out a decent

Beatles cover. Michael worked through the throng, nerves pricking, senses heightened. He stopped a passing man to ask what was happening.

"Midnight Players. Best. Sir Rodney. Tour again," the man answered in the clipped shorthand unique to the north country. Why speak twenty words when five would do? The shorthand harkened back to long, cold winters when time and breath were precious.

So, Sir Rodney Corn and the Midnight Players had come out of retirement and chosen the Old Hamlet quay as their first stop. Sir Rodney, the old rock-and-roller who'd won a parliamentary seat as the people's representative, had retired last year only to announce a return to music. He must be seventy-nine if a day.

From the stage, the Players cover of a Beatles tune segued into a '60s Lauchtenland favorite by Iron & Ash, a one-hit wonder that had proved popular for sixty years.

Michael pushed toward the bandstand, scanning for Scottie. A quick sweep and he'd head back to the Belly of the Beast. Ernst would keep her safe there, being he was a loyal, royal protector.

"Pssst, Scottie." He called softly, not wanting to draw attention. How many in this crowd kept up with palace affairs? Not many. The House of Blue's hub was Port Fressa and Perrigwynn Palace, three hours south. Hadsby was more a treasured landmark for the locals than the royal family's summer residence.

Finding a fire escape, he scampered up to see if he could spot her, and sure enough, she was trapped beside the quay.

Jumping down, he pushed toward her. "Excuse me. Pardon me."

"No, no. I'm not her," she was saying in a weak Lauchten accent. "Most definitely not the queen's daughter."

"Aye, lass, recognize. Lady Royal Blue. What doing?"

"Listen. Queen's daughter. Illegit. Go!"

Don't listen to them, Scottie. Bunch of rabble-rousers. He was almost to her, but a wall of stout Lauctens boxed him out.

"Sing now. American anthem?" someone shouted.

"Yes, American." A stout woman with a long braid stepped forward. "You. Lady Royal."

"No. Tourist." Still with the phony accent. "Love Iron & Ash."

Shouts rose. Someone yelled a RECO slogan that swelled into a chant: "No more Americans! No more Americans! No more Americans!"

A couple of drunks charged the bandstand, grabbed the microphones, and shouted anti-monarchy slogans. Sir Rodny Corn and his crew bolted from the stage and into the dark. No surprise. That's exactly how he served in parliament.

"Down with the monarchy! The Blues must go. What gives them the right to lord over us?"

"The law, igits," a voice declared. "Hush yerself. Want music."

Across the quay, the drunken lot, emboldened by music and night air, began to rumble. RECO versus devotees of Queen Catherine and the House of Blue.

"Your leader Hamish Fickle don't got half the class what the queen's got."

Another shouted, "Queen traitor! American shill!"

Let them duke it out. Michael needed to reach Scottie before the mob's momentum shoved her closer to the quay. One misstep and it was over the side with the lot of them. The drop was at least forty feet, depending on the tide, into crushing waves.

"Scottie." He sliced his voice beneath the noise and pushed through the human wall around Scottie. Perspiration beaded along his temple. He'd been here before with a Blue royal in danger. "Excuse me, coming through. Step aside."

A raw, terrified scream cut through the commotion. The crowd surged forward with a few scattering, clearing Michael's path to the quay's edge. There he found Scottie, flat on her belly, hanging over the weather-worn concrete while a woman clung to her arms, clutching her screaming child. Far below, the cold waters churned.

"Don't drop, please," the woman wailed. "Please. Don't drop."

"I won't." Scottie's reply was firm and steady, devoid of panic, as she held the woman's arm with both hands. "But be still."

Michael yanked a couple of gawking lads by their coat collars. "Anchor my legs." He dropped down next to Scottie.

"Grip slipping," the woman moaned. "Me daughter—"

"Hold on, hold on. Gents, lower me down." Michael took the woman's arm, his hands just below Scottie's. "Now. Pull us up. Pull. Us. Up."

Sirens and flashing lights announced the arrival of the Dalholm Rescue Squad.

Stretching as far as he could, Michael secured the child and handed her to a rescue worker. Then he and Scottie hauled the woman to safety. Paramedics swooped in and carried her to the ambulance as she sobbed. "Thank you, thank you, thank you."

Michael rolled onto his back for a shaky breath before coming to his senses. He had to get Scottie out of here. Grabbing her hand, he bent to her ear. "We need to be away. Now."

"Okay, but I want to check on the woman and her daughter." Scottie turned for the ambulance but didn't move. "I'm shaking... that was terrifying."

"How did you even catch her?" Michael said, his own nerves still twitching.

"I don't know... I just reached out. There was this force—" With a deep breath, Scottie pushed through the onlookers to peer into the ambulance. "Hey—are you all right?"

"Scottie," he said, low and urgent as the mob began to regroup, "if they realize who you are, I'll need the whole of Her Majesty's armed forces to hold this line. Move."

"But I just want to make sure—"

"I know. And your compassion will get you killed."

CHAPTER
SIX

Her legs were rubber as Michael steered her away from the quay. Her heartbeat still kicked against chest, and she couldn't seem to draw in enough air.

"In here, miss." Michael ducked into the Belly of the Beast, steering Scottie into a shadowed corner by the blazing stone fireplace.

She plopped into a chair, glancing around the nearly empty pub and nervously pushing her hair back from her face.

"Did that just happen?" She leaned toward Michael. "I can't stop shaking."

Michael motioned to the proprietor behind the bar—a burly man in a sailor cap and a dull white shirt with his sleeves rolled up, his long braided beard tucked into his undershirt.

"Ernst, can we have some water?"

The man raised a finger and nodded. "Stella!" He poked his head through the kitchen pass-through. "Cross man, Lady Royal, here. Fish, chips. W and P."

Scottie rested her head in her hands. "I keep seeing her dangling there, clutching her daughter. What if I'd lost my grip?"

She looked up as a pretty server with short curls and bright eyes set down two bottles of water and two frosty pints.

"Thank you." Scottie twisted off the cap and took a long drink, but the water only churned her nerves. "I might be sick."

"Take a deep breath." Michael covered her hand with his. "If you need, the loo's in the corner."

"Give me a sec." She leaned back, staring at the golden flames licking the hearth. Outside the paned window, people drifted past, heading up Wells Line toward Centre Street. "I don't even know her name. Why'd you rush me out of there?"

"Because that lot was drunk and fired up. Didn't you hear them chanting 'No more Americans'?"

"Do you think they'd really hurt me?"

"Sadly, yes. The RECO party is very anti-monarchy. Small yet vicious."

"Surely those who support the monarchy would—"

"Stand by with their phones, filming as you're thrown over the quay, then lament it later? Maybe. I am not taking any chances. What a selfish lot, letting that woman dangle there with her little girl while they gawked. We'll see how many post the footage for their socials, hoping to go viral." He withdrew his hand. "You're not in America, Scottie. You're not in small-town Hearts Bend with your white picket fences and Uncle Joe on the porch picking his guitar and grinning."

"You've been watching *Andy Griffith* reruns," she shot back. "We live in the twenty-first century in Hearts Bend, Michael. I know the world's dangerous."

"Even more so because you're now part of a unique and elite family. You can't run off on your own. What were you doing out here?"

"I needed some air."

"Air? Stand by Whistlecrag Bluff and breathe in half the North Sea but at least tell me first. Wherever you go, whatever you do, you must notify me or Operations. Your protection is my responsibility." Michael looked as stricken as she felt.

"I'm sorry… I didn't think."

"In this world, that sort of thing can get you killed."

"Is this about Prince John? Kate told me of the incident in Brighton Kingdom. The attempt on his life. You were cleared, and tonight was my fault. I'll own it."

"No, it's not about Prince John," he said. Yet to Scottie's ears, there was doubt in his reply. "But I'd like to avoid a repeat incident, Scottie. Even if you take the blame, I'm right there with you. I don't get the privilege of blaming you. So please—help me by letting me help you."

"Okay, okay." Part chastened, part grateful, she felt something deeper in his plea, almost as if he needed more from her than a daily report of her whereabouts. But what could Michael Cross possibly want from her? When their eyes met across the worn table, her trembling began to ease. The thumping in her ears faded.

"Where I go, you go," she said.

"Thank you." He exhaled and smiled faintly. "Except, not to the loo."

She laughed and toasted him with her water. "Not the loo."

"Yer royalness. Welcome." Ernst, whom Scottie had met before with Gus and Daffy, took a sweeping bow, then stepped aside for a dark-haired woman in a stained apron carrying two platters of fish and chips. "My Stella." He patted her shoulder. "Good wife. Jolly husband."

Scottie smiled as Stella bobbed a curtsy, a feminine version of Ernst, minus the beard, of course. Her figure was soft and curvy, her cheeks pink from the kitchen heat.

"Yer Blues," the woman said warmly. "Family."

When they'd gone, Michael handed Scottie a napkin roll and took up his own. "Salt of the earth, as they say. If you're ever caught in a mob again in the Old Hamlet, run here. Ernst will hide you."

Scottie stared at her plate—fish and chips, gravy, and mushy peas. It was late, and she was more tired than hungry, despite the divine aroma.

"Do you think they're okay? The woman and her daughter?"

"Yes, thanks to you." Michael raised his pint. "Why'd you need air, Scottie?"

"I don't know. I felt overwhelmed. Kate was so weak she could barely eat. I was spoon-feeding her." Scottie dipped a fry in gravy. "Please keep that between us. Also, I told her I forgive the past.

We'd agreed to move on from it when she just…collapsed. I called for help, and two nurses rushed in and dismissed me immediately. Michael, the queen has two nurses on staff. Doesn't that mean her Guillain-Barré is serious?"

"No, it means she's the queen of Lauchtenland."

"I finally have a mother, and she's gravely ill." Scottie looked away. "Sorry, I'm being dramatic."

"You're being a daughter."

"When I went for air, I heard the music, so I followed it." Scottie broke off a flaky corner of fish. "The music was good. It felt like home. Then someone recognized me. I tried to deny it."

"Scottie, how did you even sneak out of the palace? None of the cameras caught you."

She grinned. "It's a secret. A Blue family secret but Prince Gus roped me in."

"I see. I presume you also know the gate code?"

"Obviously."

He smiled despite himself. "Can you remember how you happened to lunge for the woman?"

Scottie thought for a moment, replaying the scene in fragments. "I saw a break in the crowd and was about to run when I felt a large, warm hand on my shoulder. I turned and saw the woman falling over the edge. I jumped, barely catching her arm, which yanked me to the ground. I grabbed hold with my other hand, trying to pull her up. I kept thinking someone would help but no one did. I was so grateful for the man holding my legs."

"What man? There was no one holding your legs."

"Yes. A man, with very strong, warm hands. Just like the one that touched my shoulder." She closed her eyes. "I wasn't afraid."

"I didn't see anyone holding you, Scottie. It looked to me as if you were about to go over yourself."

"Maybe he left when you got there. But why didn't he help? When I felt him let go—that's when I was afraid. My arms started to shake."

"I see," Michael murmured, glancing about the pub with a curious expression.

"What are you looking for, Michael? What are you not saying?"

"Nothing. Just interesting. Eat. You'll feel better. Stella puts peace in her food."

Scottie looked down at her overflowing plate. She'd eaten here before, and while the food was good, she didn't remember it ever tasting like peace. Yet the next bite of flaky fish, dipped in gravy, tasted like Shug's kitchen. Like home.

Across the pub, a table of locals caught her eye and gave a thumbs-up.

"Saved life. Two!" someone called, and a ripple of applause went around the room. Ernst watched from behind the bar with a guarded expression.

Michael leaned closer. "Don't respond with more than a smile."

"They think I saved her life."

"Because you did. But you also put yourself at risk."

"Excuse me?" She pushed aside her plate. "How do you make that out?"

"You're a blooming stir stick, Lady Royal. More than any royal in decades because you're a mystery. People are curious about you, the secret daughter of our queen. They gravitate to the scandalous, to what makes them gasp. Your story is the plot of every silly LTV1 film. So mind yourself. You're not free to wander about like a normal lass."

"Two lectures. One meal." She sighed, suddenly drained. "Can we go so I can tuck my silly life into bed?"

"Scottie, wait. I didn't say *your* life was silly. I said *they* were. The gawkers, the curious, the haters, even the lovers."

"Then choose your words better."

At the bar, she tried to pay, but Ernst refused. "On house," he said, patting the scarred countertop. "Back. Come. Michael." He thumped his chest. "Better. Give time."

Outside, the May night carried a sharp chill and a slice of silver moonlight. Maybe she shouldn't have come to Lauchtenland. Maybe she should've declined the title Lady Royal. Michael called her a stir stick and rightly so. How could she support her mother, the queen, if her very presence caused trouble?

Beside her, Michael's even stride carried them up Wells Line toward Centre Street, away from the quay and the echoes of the night.

"I'm sorry," she said softly. "It's just…overwhelming. More than I realized."

"My apologies as well, Lady Royal." His voice gentled. "We'll figure this out together."

"I should check on Kate," she said. "But she's probably asleep."

"We can inquire of the nurse. She'll be awake."

At the security gate tucked behind the trees, Michael punched in the code and stood aside for her to pass.

The path through the woods toward the palace, lined with lavender, heather, was narrow and uneven. Scottie ducked beneath a low branch, stubbing her toe on a root. Yet here, she felt she could breathe.

"What are these woods called?" she asked.

"Don't know that they have a name."

"Everything royal has a name."

He chuckled low. "I'll find out. Maybe something simple like Dalholm Woods or Hadsby Forest."

Scottie emerged on the north side of the castle. Lights burned from nearly every ancient window.

"It's stunning, isn't it? I try to imagine the centuries of life lived here."

"There used to be a high stone wall round the grounds until the eighteenth century," Michael said. "After Perrigwynn was built, the family neglected this place for a hundred years. When German bombs from the second war nearly destroyed the castle, they changed their ways."

"I'm glad. I love it here."

"As do I." His tone made her turn. His eyes were fixed on her. "Ah—shall we go?"

"Michael," Scottie said as they walked. "What did Ernst mean when he patted his chest and said 'better'?"

The man lengthened his stride, moving ahead.

"Was that a personal question?" She hurried to catch up. "About you?"

"Yes. And one not suited for this late hour."

"I disagree. Late hours are perfect for personal questions. The dark makes us honest."

He stopped and faced her. "I am your equerry and protection officer. Personal matters aren't part of the equation."

Yet his tone carried something deeper, and she waited. If she'd overstepped, he'd brush it off. If not—

"Why do you want to know, Lady Royal? You'll be away by June's end, back to your life in Tennessee."

"It's how we do things at O'Shay Shirts. We're a family. Since you'll be my shadow for the next month and a half, I'd like to know what's in your chest."

"Purnell Lindholm," he said quietly. "She's in my chest."

"She broke your heart?"

"In a manner of speaking."

"Any chance of reconciliation?"

"No." He started walking again. "She died."

"Goodness, Michael. I'm sorry. I'm nosy. My dad tells me all the time. I think everyone's my friend the moment we meet. Not close friends, but—"

"Lady Royal." His sharp reply hit the dark. "If I didn't want to speak of her, I'd have said so. She died eighteen months ago. Everyone knows. Even the queen. I feared my grief over her caused me to miss the foul play round Prince John at the North Sea Island Nations' Summit. Yet work...work kept me sane."

"How'd she die?" Scottie asked softly.

"She contracted an infection that turned into sepsis. She hid it from me, from her family, tried to manage on her own. By the time we caught on, it was too late."

"I'm so sorry, Michael." She was moved by his composure and resisted the urge to ask more questions. His words seemed to slice open his heart so that he could speak as he did. "At least you've known a great love. More than I've known."

He glanced at her. "You've never been in love?"

"Not really. I danced with the idea, but it turns out my one candidate was still in love with his ex-wife. Which is partly why I'm here. I called Kate the night he told me. She invited me over for the spring season."

"You were willing to leave O'Shay Shirts over a man?"

"No. Cap Henderson merely shoved me over the edge." She sighed softly. "When I first learned about Kate, I resisted. I had a life. Didn't need a mum at thirty-five. A year later she sent John after me. Then she got sick. I came to see her and…for the first time in my life, I had a mother. I thought I could carry on as usual and visit Kate at Christmas, maybe in the summer. But this past year, I've been restless. I've missed her. Missed John and Gemma, Gus and Daffy. My nieces and nephew."

"You're lucky to have a mum you want to spend time with. Not everyone's so blessed."

"That's a cloaked confession. You don't have a mum you want to spend time with?"

"As I said"—His voice cooled slightly—"not everyone's so blessed." He hunched his shoulders, perhaps from the cold, perhaps from further probing. "We should go in. It's late, and I need to report the quay incident."

"Blame it all on me, Michael. Please."

He said nothing, but the faint gleam of his smile suggested he planned to do exactly that.

At the main door, he entered the code and held it open, stopping her at the threshold. "Tell me of your secret escape."

"No can do."

"Lady Royal, the HMSD must know of any possible breach in our—"

"There's no breach. Just a hidden door. You can't get in from the outside."

"But you can leave from the inside?"

"Goodnight, Michael Cross." She stepped into the Grand Foyer. "I suppose social media will be buzzing with videos about tonight."

"Yes, so be prepared. Lady Royal, where is the passageway?"

"I don't check social media. Waste of time, thief of life. Tell me if I need to know anything." She'd once followed royal accounts after embracing her heritage, but a year of snide commentary—down to criticizing the way she held her fork—had cured her. "Michael, can we find the man who held my legs? And I'd love to meet the woman and her little girl. Invite them to dinner, maybe?"

"I'll make inquiries."

At that, they said goodnight. With his curiosity about the passageway on his august face, he turned down the corridor and disappeared around the stairs.

Scottie climbed to the Grand Gallery, the hush of the castle pressing close. Her body was worn from the chaos on the quay, her mind replaying the cries, the pressure of the woman's grip still on her arm. But beneath the exhaustion, something else lingered.

The presence of Michael Cross.

The weight of grief when he spoke of Purnell was palpable. The hesitation—no, regret—when he mentioned his mother, like a story he didn't want to tell.

Outside the Princess Charlotte suite, she met Cranston on patrol.

"Her Majesty is sleeping peacefully, miss," the butler said. "She's terribly grateful you're here. She asked after you once the nurses settled her."

"I'm glad to be here too, Cranston. My mother, however, may feel differently in the morning."

"Whatever do you mean, miss?"

"You'll know soon enough. Good night, Cranston."

The truth was, Scottie didn't know how Kate would respond to her late-night adventure or the chaos she'd stirred.

In her suite, she switched off the lights and headed to her room, beyond exhausted. She might just fall face-first into the pillows, clothes and all.

But Choko, dear Choko, had laid out her pajamas, set a tea trolley beside the bed with a warming kettle and snacks, and had even drawn a steaming bath filled with soaking salts and left a towel on the warmer.

After peeling off her clothes, Scottie brushed her teeth, twisted her hair into a knot then sank into the steaming water, burning the cold from her bones.

Again, the night replayed in her mind—music, shouts, the cold quay, the woman's cries, the strong hands on her legs. The cozy, warm pub. Ernst. Stella. Michael.

"Where I go, you go."

Scottie opened her eyes. Her promise at the pub. She hadn't meant it to sound so personal, but under the cover of night, that's exactly how it felt.

"What in blazes happened on the Dalholm quay last night? Did you see Lady Royal save that woman? If you ask me, she's earned a Crown's Distinguished Honor. It can go to anyone, right?"

—*@ROYAL WATCHER ONE*

"I saw the video. Lady Royal pushed a woman and a child over the quay. Then tried to save her. What a blooming fraud. Send her home. No more royal Americans. We're through!"

—*LAUCHTEN LOUD! ON X.COM*

"'Initial investigation on the Old Hamlet incident reveals no foul play,'" said Dalholm Chief of Police, Ian Clock. "'We've looked at all the evidence and have determined the crowd on the quay simply got too close. If anyone has more information or a different testimony, please contact the DPD hot line.'"

—*THE DAILY DALHOLM UPDATE*

"'I've watched the videos of Lady Royal leaping to save Mrs. Johansdotter and I'm telling you it's staged. Or an AI video. Look at how she seems to jerk back as she grabs on to her hand. As if someone is holding onto her. Certainly a doctored video would not be impossible for Michael Cross, a decorated Special Forces major and a member of the Cross family. He's trained, strong, crafty.'"

–LT. COLONEL ROLAND HAWKIN, FORMER CHIEF OF HER MAJESTY'S HIGH COMMAND ON TUPPENCE CORBIN & FRIENDS

CHAPTER
SEVEN

After very little sleep, he bolstered his morning with a shower, three cups of coffee, one tea, and an unknown number of sweet cinnamon puffs. But this day required protein, so he headed down to the servants' hall for eggs and sausage.

After filing his report in the Operations Room, he climbed to his quarters, exhausted and trying to settle his thoughts. But his phone kept pinging with links to the events on the quay.

Most of the videos were dark and bumpy, a muddled mess of shouts, music, and references to Scottie as the "queen's illegitimate daughter."

Yet a few of them clearly showed Lady Royal diving to catch the woman, now identified as Mrs. Agnus Johansdotter. Michael had finally switched his phone to Do Not Disturb around two a.m.

Now, at the breakfast table, he studied the videos again, looking for whoever may have pushed the woman—and who might have held Scottie's legs. Yet all he concluded was Scottie had saved Mrs. Johansdotter's life without a thought of her own.

Taking a bite of sausage and a sip of orange juice, Michael pulled up the HMSD database where their custom AI tracked national and international chatter about the royal family. As expected, Scottie O'Shay was a world headline.

Lennox arrived for breakfast. "We have more on Agnus. She's a local. Married. Her daughter is named Luca. Two more children at home. And you're going to love this, Michael." Lennox aimed the remote in her hand at the telly in the corner of the room. "She's on the *Morning Show*."

"Already?" Michael shifted toward the wall-mounted screen where host Stone Brubaker was conducting a Zoom interview with a pretty blonde woman. Her lipstick was bright red, half hiding a busted lip. A brown-black bruise spread down her cheek from the corner of her eye. Michael glanced at Lennox, who was tapping notes into her phone.

> Stone: "Mrs. Johansdotter, can you tell us what happened last night on the Dalholm quay? Remember, you're on international television, so please—no Dalholm speak."
>
> Agnus: "Well, um, thanks, Stone. My husband was…away…with sons…took our daughter to hear Knight Shift Players, we love them, you know, when suddenly…chaos. The daughter—queen—alone, mind you—a political riot."

"What?" Michael said. "A riot?"

"Did she?" Lennox said. "Really?"

"No, but she is a bit of a stir stick, don't you think?"

"Not a bit—a lot. Do you think the *Morning Show* producers coached this Johansdotter woman? Did she have that black eye last night?"

"Of course they did. As for the black eye, I don't know. I was trying to get Lady Royal out of there."

> Stone: "Mrs. Johansdotter, this is sensitive, but we're after the truth. Do you believe you were shoved over the side of the quay?"
>
> Agnus: "Yes. Hurled. Someone. Pro-monarch."

"She can't do it," Lennox muttered, snorting. "Talk straight. She's probably never put together a full sentence in her life."

"She can lie well enough," Michael said.

Agnus: "I fell—screaming. Daughter in arms." She flailed one arm and clutched her imaginary child with the other. "Arm caught. Look up. See the queen's daughter. Lady Royal."

Stone: "You must've been terrified."

Agnus: "Yes. Going to die. Daughter screaming. Clutching neck." (She mimed that too.)

Stone: "We're thrilled you and your daughter are home safe. Have you spoken to Lady Royal?"

Agnus: "No. So shook. Rescuers came." She looked down. "But, um, Stone, I've been thinking. We almost died because she was there."

"Now she speaks a complete sentence," Lennox said.

Agnus: "What was she doing there? She should've stayed home. I mean America. Wherever she's from." Another glance down. "Tennessee. We were rescued, but a whole bunch of folks might not've been."

"She's a piece of work." Michael grabbed the remote and snapped off the telly. "She'd be dead or severely injured—her daughter too—if Scottie hadn't lunged for her. Have you seen the videos?"

"I've seen them."

"I didn't witness the beginning, Lennox, but Lady Royal went for Mrs. Johansdotter without regard to her own safety. The videos don't do her justice." He paced, indignant. "Someone got to Mrs. Agnus Johansdotter."

A hall boy stepped around the table collecting dishes. Michael thanked him just as Cranston appeared in the doorway.

"Her Majesty has requested your presence."

"Of course." He'd anticipated as much. She'd want an accounting.

As Cranston escorted him up the stairs, across the Grand Gallery—its mezzanine overlooking the glass solarium—and into the royal corridor, Michael shaped a polite but firm resignation in the back of his mind, should the conversation bend that way. One the queen, wise and measured, would accept, since she'd not want her inexperienced daughter put in any more danger.

Cranston knocked—*one-two, one-two-three, one*—on the monarch's door in the old manner, indicating the butler was at the door plus one.

Hilda, the queen's lady's maid, guided Michael into a small, airy library where Her Majesty stood, waiting. She appeared rested and clear-eyed, regal, with no evidence of last night's collapse.

"Your Majesty." He bowed. "I must apologize for last night."

"Scottie explained everything." The queen sat and motioned Michael to the adjacent chair. "She's assured me she won't go off alone again. Did you see the *Morning Show*?"

"I did, ma'am."

"I don't always trust the producers, but they've shown us kindness in recent years. However, this time I'll not give them the benefit of the doubt."

"Someone got to Mrs. Johansdotter, ma'am. Perhaps one of MP Hamish Fickle's RECO shills."

"Either way," the queen said, "I've instructed the Chamber Office to invite the Johansdotters to the Garden Party. Do we know the identity of the man who held Scottie's legs?"

"No, ma'am. I've viewed everything that's been uploaded. There's no hint of anyone anchoring her."

"Quietly ask around then. You'll know what to do, no?" She smiled. "I've asked Alfred Quip, head of the Kongelig Herrer, to place the Johansdotter family in my receiving line."

"Very good, ma'am. They'll be honored."

"Let's hope," she said, a knowing glint in her eye.

The Kongelig Herrer—the Royal Gentlemen—was a time-honored corps of men of influence, and now women, who served as Garden Party hosts.

Mum was miffed she'd never been invited to serve. After all, she was a Pratt. And for twelve years, a Cross. Until she abandoned her children and the Cross name. The Pratt family was distinguished but nothing like being a Cross.

"But close enough, I'll be bound," Mum always said.

"Ah, there she is." The queen's gaze went to the doorway. "My daughter. A phrase I love to say."

Michael turned, his thoughts still on the quay and the queen, wholly unprepared for the way Scottie's presence wrapped around him.

At ease in the private library, she sat beside her mother, inquiring after her health with the natural grace of any loving daughter. She wore jeans and a fitted pale-blue blouse, her long hair loosely braided.

Seeing her again was like when she arrived at Hadsby. She whispered to the parts of him that, until now, were content to sleep.

Wake up. Wake up.

This close, he noticed a faint bruise on her chin—likely from the quay—and another on her right hand. If she'd tossed and turned through the night, her face didn't show it.

"Doesn't she look beautiful, Michael?"

"Yes, ma'am." What an odd question from Her Majesty. But what else could he say? She was beautiful. Adding that her presence set his heartbeat to a different rhythm would be wildly inappropriate—and would definitely get him sacked. Besides, the young man sensations would fade in another day or two.

"We're spending the morning trying on clothes," the queen said, rising with help from Scottie. "For the Garden Party." Passing Michael, she touched his shoulder. "Thank you for being there for her. You may have thought I called you in to sack you, but I wanted to thank you."

"My pleasure, ma'am." Michael fell into step with Scottie as she exited with the queen. "Did you sleep?"

"Well enough," she said, chin high. "I'm an easy sleeper. I can knock off anywhere, anytime."

"You'd have made a good soldier."

"That's what Cap used to say."

"Cap? Oh, yes, the almost love."

"Right. He was a former Army Ranger," she said, heading toward the Grand Staircase. "How big a headline am I this morning?"

"Mrs. Johansdotter went on the *Morning Show*, blaming you for her fall."

Scottie halted, one hand on the stair rail, eyes wide. "She *what*?"

"Blamed it on you. She claims your presence incited the mob."

"I see." Scottie peered toward the light falling through the Grand Foyer's transom. "I suppose you agree with her."

"I've concluded people are responsible for their own actions. Nevertheless, steel yourself. You've begun your time in Lauchtenland with a blooming bang. You've rocketed the people into a conversation—those for the House of Blue, those against. It's a stirring debate and has been for some time." He touched her arm gently. "Be honest with yourself, miss. If last night proved—"

"Too much?" Her blue eyes searched his. "You want me to abandon the queen when she's trying to right a thirty-eight-year old wrong? What about supporting her with the family away? And her battle with GBS? The *reason* I'm here is to stand by her when she needs me. Not run from something like last night. That's just noise. A distraction. In all my days, she could never reach out, say she needed me. Now she does, Michael. Which goes well beyond me tucking and turning tail when something goes wrong." Her certainty settled like stone. "I'm staying. What can they do to me in eight short weeks?"

She held his gaze one second, then two, as if waiting. Then Choko appeared at the foot of the stairs.

"We're ready for you in the Gold Salon, miss."

"Thank you." With a final glance at Michael, Scottie started down the stairs. "Got to pick an outfit for the Garden Party, but if you're lucky, I'll show you the secret passageway before I go home."

"Be still my heart," Michael said, hand slapped to his chest.

But as he watched her go, he resisted the urge to chase after her. *"Go home, Lady Royal, now. Please."*

What could they do to her in eight weeks? Plenty.

Lady Royal, if you only knew.

SCOTTIE

If she'd known she'd walk into the Garden Party under a cloud of scandal and scuttlebutt, she'd never have run off that night by herself.

Over the past three days, the quay incident had become its own legend. Memes and AI fakes of Scottie saving Mrs. Johansdotter flooded pro-royal feeds. The anti-monarch side pushed fabrications of Scottie inciting the mob and shoving mother and child over the edge.

Talk shows debated over it, replaying one grungy, dark clip after another, worse than sports commentators reviewing plays after a game.

Dad texted then called. "What's going on? Penny keeps forwarding posts. Did someone try to push you from the Dalholm quay? That's got to be a hundred feet."

"More like forty, Dad, depending on the tide."

"Scottie, if you want to come home—"

"Hello, who are you and what happened to my 'never quit' father? I'm fine." She ran down the details with her dad just like she would at O'Shay, keeping to the main points. Avoiding emotional rabbit trails. "I'm staying," she concluded. "Kate needs me." In the end, that was all that mattered. Her mother needed her.

The final days up to the Garden Party were a struggle. Wednesday, Kate could barely drink her tea. Even so, she insisted Scottie walk with her to the old portico by Whistlecrag Bluff. She had to turn back before they left the castle's shadow. That evening, Scottie dined alone while Kate slept.

She resolved to be diligent at Friday's Garden Party—to stay close to Kate. She'd promised John and Gus, who phoned often to check on their mother. The appeal of being a part of their inner circle—of being a sibling—was intoxicating.

Aunt Arabella and Sir William, their daughter, Rachel, and several cousins were coming to the party. The queen and her half-royal daughter could not manage three thousand guests alone.

So, with a dose of courage and a taste of trepidation, on the eighth of May Scottie dressed for her *official* debut as Lady Royal Blue, daughter of the Queen of Lauchtenland. at the Hadsby Castle Garden Party.

"Miss, which clutch do you prefer?" Choko set five designer clutches on the dressing-room island. "Might I recommend the gold?"

Scottie considered, then nodded. The gold, with matching hardware, suited her outfit. It was by a local designer in the Midlands. Eloise Bright of Eloise Ltd.

"She's very hip with the young people," Choko said. "I believe she'll be at the Garden Party."

Scottie wasn't a "clutch" girl, but she'd listened to Kate's lesson on using the small bag to avoid unwanted handshakes—or as a barrier. Even to communicate to Michael if she felt trapped.

She wore a bespoke dark-blue coatdress over a white dress, with matching hat and shoes. Luigi, the hairstylist Choko insisted do Scottie's hair for the day, swept her hair into an intricate updo.

"I feel like I'm heading to a Golden Age of Hollywood premiere," Scottie said.

"Oh, to have been on those red carpets." Choko sighed. "Glorious days for women's fashion. You'll make quite an impression, Lady Royal. Her Majesty is eager to show you to the world—especially after this week."

"Do you think she's worried about me?" Scottie asked. This was a different universe from a segment on *Good Morning America* or New York Fashion Week. "Does she think I won't impress?"

"No, miss. She wants the world to see what she sees. To love you as she does."

"Choko, I don't think even the queen can make people love me like she does." Sweet thought, though. "However, I'll do my best not to embarrass her further."

"You've not embarrassed her. Mrs. Johansdotter has embarrassed herself. You are quite charming, miss. I've styled many a lady. They don't hold a candle to you."

Scottie regarded Choko for a moment, unsure how to respond. "Thank you," she said in a whisper, squeezing the woman's hand and tucking her words into her heart.

For the Garden Party, she'd already discussed protocol with Kate and Michael. How to shake hands, how to steer the conversation, how to move on to the next guests. The Kongelig Herrer would form the guests into lines so she would know exactly where to go.

Scottie suggested responding to the quay stories, if asked, with the truth. Michael and Kate had replied in unison, *"No!"* She was to avoid it altogether.

"Don't feed the lions," Michael had said. *"Let them starve. Any comment reads as defensive. Sometimes you win by appearing to lose."*

Choko placed the gold clutch in Scottie's hand, detailing the contents of a handkerchief, sanitizer, lip balm, blotting papers, and a compact, and then turned her toward the full-length mirror.

"Stunning, miss. And I'm not saying that because you're a princess."

"I'm not a princess, Choko."

"Aren't you? Lady Royal Blue for now and one day you'll be Princess Scottie. You're here to win your crown."

"Win my crown? Is that thing? No, at the end of this, after the Rose Ball, I'm heading home. I'm here to help the queen until the princes and Edric return."

She felt like a stuck record when commenting on her status. Lady Royal was more than enough of a title. More than she'd ever need.

"As you say, Lady Royal. Cranston texted. They're waiting." Choko slipped out through the interior closet door leading to the servants' stairs.

When Scottie entered the Queen's Library, conversation stopped. Sir William, in morning coat and top hat, nodded, warmly adding, "You'll do, Lady Royal."

Then everyone talked at once, punctuated with cheek kisses as they introduced the cousins: the Duke and Duchess of Clemency, Roman and Birgitte.

"Don't we make a splendid set of royal Blues," Arabella said, eyeing Scottie. "Do I see Choko's hand?"

"Of course, Mum," Princess Rachel said. "Scottie, did you know Aunt Catherine stole Choko from Coral Winthrop?"

"She left my son at the altar in front of millions," Kate said, beautiful and bright—for now—with a humor in her voice. "That's the least I could do."

Scottie had barely followed Prince Gus's story—how an American cosmetics heiress abandoned him on their wedding day—then months later, she learned, along with the world, that the "pitiful prince" was her half-brother.

"We must go to Pub Clemency sometime, cousin." Princess Rachel looped her arm through Scottie's. The pub was a favorite haunt of the royal princes. "It's time we had more girl cousins at the pub. Gus and Daffy's little one is darling, but not exactly pub ready."

"I should say not," Arabella said. "Scottie, come to us for dinner. Bring Kate. She's not been in ages."

"Later, after the spring season. Now, we should go down." Kate led the way through the door.

When Cranston met them in the foyer, Kate squeezed Scottie's hand. "Here we go. You'll do splendidly."

Uniformed officers lined Hadsby's long, wide porch, which had been built during the reign of one King Titus or another. It stretched across the front of the castle, a grand expanse of granite and marble, the steps leading down to the lush green lawn where Garden Party guests gathered beneath fluttering royal standards and a bright North Seas sky.

Tents with an array of tea, cakes, sandwiches, and fruit were stationed at the four corners. A royal orchestra quintet played on the front walk, as well as on the back portico, with the North Sea breeze adding a faint dissonance.

Scottie scanned the row of uniformed security, finding Michael, composed and regal. Without changing his expression, he stepped out to join her, falling in a few paces behind. He was here. Near. Her welcomed shadow. Something in Lauchtenland that felt uniquely hers.

Guests gathered to sing as the orchestra played the national anthem, "One Nation for Thee." Then the Kongelig Herrer—the Royal Gentlemen—shaped the crowd into orderly lines.

"We're always the A line," Kate said, taking Scottie's arm as they crossed the lawn. Their Kongelig Herrer read from a discreet note over the queen's shoulder.

"This is Mr. and Mrs. Cornwall. He's the new director of the youth centre. She was recently Teacher of the Year."

The couple bowed and curtsied, speaking quickly in Dalholm shorthand.

"Yer Majesty, Lady Royal. Honored. Please. Thanks."

"As are we," Kate said. "Thank you for your work with Dalholm's youth. Tell me, Mrs. Cornwall, how did you get into teaching?"

They spoke briefly, then moved on—everything proper, polite. Halfway down the line, Scottie spotted Mrs. Johansdotter in a yellow dress with a fascinator perched on stiff curls. Beside her stood a portly gentleman tugging his waistcoat and fanning his face with his top hat.

"Excuse me." Scottie stepped from the queen's conversation and approached. "I'm so glad you could come, Mrs. Johansdotter." She offered her hand. "How are you and your daughter?"

Mrs. Johansdotter stepped back. "We came. See queen, miss."

"Of course—yes, she's eager to meet you." The line compressed, guests edging closer. Scottie subtly reached for Michael. "I'm so sorry about that night on the quay. I shouldn't have gone out alone."

The woman made a stern face as if holding in her *"You got that right"* reply. "Me, daughter. Fine."

"Nightmares," the husband added. "Screams."

Michael leaned in. "Ask how she likes the party."

Right. "Have you tried the cakes in the dessert tent?"

"Long line." Mr. Johansdotter cast a look of longing in that direction then straightened. "No—here for Her Maj."

The crowd parted as the queen and the Royal Gentlemen stopped before them.

"Mr. and Mrs. Johansdotter," Kate said. "Welcome to Hadsby. How are you finding things today?"

Mr. Johansdotter bowed repeatedly, awe softening his expression. Mrs. Johansdotter curtsied more than once. Kate expertly directed their short conversation before moving on. That's when Mrs. Johansdotter caught Scottie's hand.

"Didn't want…to say it," she whispered. "Made me."

"Who made you?"

"Thems. TV. Paid money. Needed."

"To say I caused the mob—and that's why you were pushed?"

She nodded, eyes wide. "Sorry, Yer Lady."

"It's okay. Thank you for telling me." Scottie glanced toward her mother, now greeting another couple. Mr. Johansdotter had already slipped toward the cake tent. "I shouldn't have been down there alone."

"Still." Agnus Johansdotter squeezed her arm. "You—*thems* don't like. Want gone." She leaned back, wary. "Careful, Yer Lady."

"Who wants me gone?" The RECO people? A handful of loud citizens?

"Thems," she repeated. "All I know."

"Thank you, Mrs. Johansdotter. Very much."

"No, Yer Lady. Thank you. Me life—you saved." Her eyes glistened. "Me daughter." She hugged Scottie quickly then backed away as one of the Royal Gentlemen approached.

Scottie glanced back at Michael. She'd have to tell him. *Thems* paid Mrs. Johansdotter to lie. That was more than a drunken music-concert mob getting out of control.

That was strategic. Calculated. And downright frightening.

"Though she's an American, Scottie O'Shay, aka, Lady Royal, looked beautiful today on the castle steps. I noticed the queen reaching for her several times. Also, did anyone see how the crowds gathered round her? She couldn't take a step without fifty people moving with her."

—@LOYALROYALBLOG

"Queen Catherine the Second stunned today in her pink suit with matching heels and hat. Her daughter, the newly-styled Lady Royal, wore a blue coatdress with matching heels and hat. Her clutch was designed by Eloise Ltd, which has already sold out. Retail power has arrived with Lady Royal, who as we know, has some notoriety as a men's fashion designer. She displayed her excellent eye for women's fashion as well. My guess is Choko played a part in her Garden Party attire. Her coatdress and hat were from Elnora. Her shoes? The one and only Christian Louboutin."

—SHARON LEE HAYES, FASHION SEGMENT ON TUPPENCE CORBYN & FRIENDS

""'Stone, Lady Royal spoke intimately with Mrs. Johansdotter, whom she saved from sailing over the Dalholm quay. When asked what they spoke on, Mrs. Johansdotter declined comment. Perhaps they've come to an understanding about that night.'"

–*MELISSA FARIS, ROYAL REPORTER,*
THE MORNING SHOW

Chapter
Eight

MICHAEL

The word stuck with him all weekend. *Thems.* Who would give Mrs. Johansdotter money to lie about Lady Royal?

He'd not put it past the *Morning Show's* higher-ups to pay for lies. Between Stone's declining ratings and the network's lust for money, integrity was an expendable.

Michael passed the information up the chain to Gunner, who reported it to Nordvagt Yard, Lauchtenland's version of America's FBI and Britain's Scotland Yard.

Even though the case was not his, he'd spent the morning digging around social media and other sources for a hint of who paid the money. The RECO sort often posted clues on socials, thinking they were being clever and cloaked.

He hadn't seen much of Scottie since the Garden Party. They had a short outing with Her Majesty Tuesday morning. Brunch with the local lord and his wife.

Wednesday afternoon, she'd Zoomed with her team at O'Shay, working through a manufacturing issue. After which, she called to say she was going for a walk. He met her in the kitchen, where she grabbed a handful of fresh strawberries and headed across the castle grounds. Michael followed several yards behind, giving her space.

Thursday evening, as he surfaced from Hadsby's Operations Room for a spot of tea, Mum rang. She talked. He listened, drinking tea and eyeing a slice of chocolate cake.

"How hard can it be, Mick?" Mum was in fighting form

tonight. "Your grandparents' sixty-fifth wedding anniversary is this weekend, and we'd like confirmation that you're attending this monumental occasion. Put aside your disgust for me and show up."

"Mum, I have to clear everything with HMSD. I'm on duty. I don't get a day off. Think of me as deployed."

"Working to protect an American? I'm sorry, Mick, I support the Crown but not you missing your grandparents' anniversary. I'll see you there."

She rang off, which didn't surprise him. It had been her thing since the day she walked out on Dad—thus, on Michael and Evan.

Michael fixed another cuppa, then sat in the servants' hall, enjoying every bite of cake, the sweetness almost erasing the bitterness from the conversation with Mum. When he finished, he set his plate in the industrial dishwasher and looked out the long, deep windows toward the cliffs and the ancient stone portico overlooking Whistlecrag Bluff.

The gold, purple, and orange hues of the evening coated the grounds still cultivated for the Garden Party. In the front and sides of the castle, squared hedges and hundreds of flowerbeds framed the green lawn. But his favorite part of the castle grounds was the field of wild lavender.

He squinted, leaning close to the glass, peeking between a thread of light and shadow. Scottie—her silhouette leaning against a pillar and gazing toward the open sea.

Retrieving a tall mug from the cupboard, he filled it with tea warming in the kettle and headed out.

"The wind coming up through the crag is cold," he said, handing her the mug as he sat beside her on the dry, cracked cement of the old world—lime, sand, and water.

"I came out to see the stars, but it's still too light." Scottie tasted the tea, glancing at him. "Thank you."

"I won't remind you to let me know if you leave the castle."

"Which you just did. Very passive-aggressive."

"Your words, not mine." With a sigh, he stretched his legs toward the edge of the stone. "Are you all right?"

"I had no idea, Michael." She cradled the warm mug to her chest. "I thought I did, but I didn't."

"About?"

"Coming here. Accepting a title. Pretending I could just slip into my mother's world without causing a stir. Blending into an established family would be a chore for anyone, but I'm trying to blend into an ancient family that symbolizes an entire nation." She turned toward him. "Are the people really tired of having a royal family? Are they really upset Americans have joined the House of Blue?"

"It's clickbait, Scottie. Something to stir emotions."

"With me as the latest stick?"

"Yes, but I saw something at the Garden Party, even amid the quay lunacy. You draw people, Scottie. They gravitate to you. It's true, you see everyone as your friend. As for the press, the media, they're conflict entrepreneurs, love. They've become millionaires by peddling your worst fears."

"I just wanted to spend time with her. I like that she needed me. No one's ever needed me before. My dad, grandparents, they loved me, raised me well, gave me a good start, but I'm not sure they ever really needed me."

"O'Shay Shirts needs you."

"Maybe... I guess." Her voice softened, a familiar southern warmth slipping in. "My friends back home keep texting memes and posts. 'Hey, Scotto, did you see this?' Like I really want to know that someone at the Garden Party called me a *minger*, whatever that is."

"The opposite of you," he said. "You were beautiful at the Garden Party. Like I said, everyone wanted to be near you."

Their eyes met, stirring early sensations he'd worked to bury. He broke his gaze as the turbulent sea below thundered against the rocks.

"The sea is angry tonight," he murmured.

"Tell me everything will be all right, Michael. The *thems* aren't coming after me."

"It will be, lass. I mean it. Nordvagt Yard will handle the *thems*.

You're strong, you're wise, you know who you are. Don't let the lunatics reroute your narrative."

"Do I know who I am? This past year I've cared less about O'Shay Shirts, which is so unlike me. I've been obsessed with that company since I could hold a pencil. Another reason I came here was to scratch the itch, you know? To discover these people who share my bloodline and heritage. All my life it's been Dad, Fritz, Shug, a few aunts and uncles. I've traveled the world for O'Shay, negotiated with factories, hired and fired. Six years of college and grad school in design and business. I'm not a natural talent. I've worked at it. Then suddenly, I'm on *The Price Is Right*. 'Come on down, Scottie O'Shay! You've won a royal family!'"

"Very good impression of a telly presenter," he said, smiling. "It's a bit much, I grant you, but don't lose sight of the big picture, love." *Love.* He must stop using that word. He hadn't called anyone *love* since Purnell. "If you do, you'll waste time and emotion better spent on knowing your mum. Consider the externals as part of your royal experience. Mrs. Agnus Johansdotter will merely become one of many anecdotes in your memoir."

Scottie sighed, taking another sip. "Hey, to change the subject, I met Eloise Bright—Eloise Ltd.—at the Garden Party. She was amazing. Thrilled I carried her clutch. She said she'd tried to buy land a few years ago but was undercut by a bigger manufacturer."

"The scandal with Princess Holland and Lord Cunningham," Michael said. "Prince John never mentioned it? His late wife schemed to sell that land to Reingard Industries after Eloise Ltd. showed good faith—even ran an environmental study."

"She said it nearly ruined her company. Now she's bought a place in the Midlands, waiting for another chance to expand, but she's getting nowhere."

"With you carrying her bag, she'll gain her global attention," Michael said. "But she told you all this in a Garden Party line?"

"We chatted at the cake tent. Do you think we could visit her shop? See if I can help?"

"Ah, royal responsibility has set in."

"Meaning?"

"Meaning those in your position often feel a duty to lend a helping hand—if they've a halfway decent heart. Which you do. You've resources, connections, respect that comes with the name Blue. I'll check with Her Majesty, but she may grant you Royal Warrant privileges. You could extend one to Eloise Ltd. Even after June, the warrant remains valid for five years."

"Explain, Michael Cross. What is a Royal Warrant?"

"A seal of approval from the Crown. Only the queen, king consort, and Prince John hold that right. But the queen might allow you one such privilege. Use it wisely. A warrant allows a business to display the House of Blue coat of arms and a legend—'By appointment of Her Majesty the Queen, Eloise Ltd. is her supplier of fine women's fashion.'"

"Really? Okay, let's ask. The wonders of royal life never cease."

"I advise you research carefully first, Scottie. You can't extend a warrant to a supplier who lacks quality or can't meet demand."

"Yeah, totally get it." Her southern lilt flared again, and Michael felt oddly proud he'd helped restore it.

"Enough about me." She patted his knee. "What. About. You."

"I'm a rather boring bloke, I'm afraid."

"You are the opposite of boring. You're a man of mystery. Tell me three things about you. Good ones."

"Let's see. I love sports. Played football for years and was decent in my day."

"Easy to believe."

"I've a brother. He coaches my nephew in football. He's very enthusiastic. The nephew, not my brother. He's married. My brother, not my nephew. Evan's also got a daughter who wraps me round her finger." He hesitated, wary of stars and surf conspiring to loosen his restraint. "I'm close with my dad but…my mum and I don't get on. I'd never risk my career to spend time with her."

"That's quite a confession, Michael Cross."

"Even to my own ears. But as a wise woman once said, 'the dark makes us honest.'"

"Is there a reason for the rift?"

"She divorced my father, thus my brother and me, when I was eight. She left without looking back."

As if on cue, his phone pinged. Evan.

> Evan: Come on, mate, you must be there Saturday. Finn says it's no fun without you. We'll wrangle Mum together. Besides, Granny and Granddad will be crushed if you don't show. You're their favorite.

Michael slipped the phone away and leaned against the pillar.

"Please reply if you need to," Scottie said.

"It's my brother begging me to attend my Pratt grandparents' sixty-fifth anniversary. There's a big bash on Saturday. The Pratts never do anything small, or quietly. The whole family will be there, and half of parliament, lords and ladies from all over the country."

"Except you?" She nudged him with her foot. "Go, you goober. Be with your family. I can be without my shadow for a day or two. There's always Lennox and…who's the other guy?"

"Schueler."

"So go."

"It's just…" He searched for a word. *Painful* sounded pathetic. *Loathsome* too harsh. "Complicated."

Scottie didn't answer, which seemed one of her gifts. She let silence do its work. He should stop talking about himself.

Then, softly, she said, "I'll go with you."

"Lady Royal, you can't be serious."

"Why not?" The moonlight traced the smooth angles of her face. "But only if you want. No pressure. And only if my presence won't make things complicated. I don't want to turn your grandparents' party into a social media heyday. And you shouldn't have to be on duty."

"There'll be plenty of security. Granddad served in parliament, has powerful friends. As for social media, it can't be helped. Can you bear being filmed and posted on socials within the first hour? Even more, what about the queen? The trip would take most of Saturday, which is time you could spend with her."

"She has another treatment Saturday morning. She'll be exhausted afterward. So, I guess I'm looking for something to do."

"Lady Royal, I'd love your company on Saturday, if you're sure. But clear it with Her Majesty, please. I'll need to do the same with my boss. A day like this will challenge our professional boundaries."

"Then we'll have to be careful, won't we?"

SCOTTIE

Afternoon tea with the queen had quickly become a routine Scottie enjoyed. It was a calming, thoughtful experience, often peppered with long moments of silence, save for the clatter of cup against saucer or Kate expressing her pleasure in the tea cakes and crustless ham salad sandwiches.

Scottie never took a breather like this in the afternoon at home. No, she began and ended her days eyeball-deep in designs, marketing strategy, and production schedules. During certain times of the year, she threw in prep for a fashion show or coordinated details for a press junket.

By four o'clock, the queen's teatime, she'd be on her third or fourth cup of coffee, picking at the remains of an interrupted lunch, nine hours into a twelve-hour day. She'd be annoyed by the long angles of gorgeous sunlight whitewashing her computer screen or blinding a staffer at the wrong end of her conference table.

Now afternoon tea with Kate made her wonder why she never took a break and walked outside. Hearts Bend was beautiful and fragrant in every season.

On this relaxed Friday afternoon with Kate, Scottie waited for the right moment to bring up Saturday with Michael. They'd chatted at the portico until the dewy chill stiffened them both, trading stories about education and culture, one American and the other Lauchten. They bonded over childhood experiences, especially being raised by single dads.

Michael's beef with his mother seemed straightforward. "She left," he'd said. "Abandoned us." The gritty details, however many or few, he'd scooched around on his proverbial plate without much elaboration, almost cautious of what he confessed aloud. Which Scottie admired.

She glanced across the table set for two, where Kate sipped her tea, staring toward the window.

"I'm weary of this illness," she said softly. "Yet I can't escape my grandfather's words: 'Chin up, lass, you're a Blue.'" She narrowed her gaze as if looking at some long-ago image. "Are you adjusting well to the way of things here? Very different from your American routine, I'd think."

"You could say that. I've asked the maids to let me get all the way out of bed before they start making it."

Kate laughed. "They are efficient. That's my mother's doing. She was a Mary Poppins, spit-spot sort of woman who demanded excellence. I can't say I envied the staff working for her. She wasn't cruel, and she gave the most extravagant gifts every year, remembering birthdays and family names. She even brought back the old-fashioned Servants' Ball. But she expected extravagance in return."

"We have the same vibe at O'Shay Shirts. People are loyal because we demand excellence, but we reward it too. Everyone gets their birthday off, along with a gift card to a local restaurant of their choice. The time isn't charged against their PTO. We close down at Thanksgiving and Christmas. Shug started throwing elaborate Christmas parties when Fritz was in command. The board complains about the cost but lose their minds if we hint at downsizing or skipping a year."

"Every worker, great or small, should take pride in their work, as well as in their employer. Employers should take pride in whom they hire. Mum never let a grumbler stay long. One warning, and after that, out on his ear should he not change. Or her."

"What was she like besides demanding excellence?" Scottie asked.

She'd studied the portrait of her maternal grandmother, Queen

Rosemunde, where it hung next to her grandfather, King Rein the Fourth in Perrigwynn Palace's Queen's Corridor. Rosemunde was composed of elegant features and a noble aura. Whether the artist saw it in her or added it for effect, there was a sparkle in her blue eyes, almost a laugh, as if someone told a joke right before the brush met canvas.

"Mum was full of life but a strict traditionalist. She was a girl during the Second World War and saw the ravages of it. The world was changing. Her father was of Danish royal blood, the Duke of Gotland, a title John now holds. Her mother, my grandmother, was Princess Elsinore from the Saxe-Coburg and Gotha line. Granddad and Grandmum witnessed the fall of Europe's royal houses after the First World War. They instilled in my mother the honor and rights of one born to such ranks. She swam in that thought like a duck in water."

"Did she try to instill that into you and Arabella?" Scottie knew the answer before she asked.

"With every fiber of her being." Kate refreshed her tea, but her hand shook, so Scottie reached over to help. "She feared the end of the Blues' thousand-year reign. She tried desperately for more children, but two daughters were her lot. So she went above and beyond to prove our worth. Taking on more charities, bolstering traditions, getting out among the people. Dad wanted to shut down the summer season at Hadsby and the three-hundred-year-old Rose Ball, but Mum refused."

"Then one day her firstborn," Scottie said, more to herself than Kate, "her pride and joy, came home pregnant by an American dude."

Kate snapped a glance at her. "I've known two great disappointments in my life—telling my mother I was pregnant and leaving you in your father's arms, never to see you again. I was an '80s girl. Thought I knew the ways of the world with my big Farrah Fawcett hair, too much makeup, long belted shirts over leggings, and high-top trainers. I had more freedom at Haxton University than I'd ever had in my life. Even more at Yale. And it cost me. I broke your father's heart, my parents', yours—though you weren't really aware of the magnitude—and my own. Only by the mercies of God do I sit here with you today."

"Shug used to tell me my mother died because God needed her in heaven. It was a simple story for a little kid wondering what happened to her mother. Then in fourth grade, our teacher invited parents and grandparents to hear us read aloud our writing assignments. I stood in front of the class and read 'Why I Hate God' by Scottie O'Shay." She grinned at the memory. "The collective gasp fueled my fire. Mrs. Watkins tried to snatch it away, but I jerked back. From the back of the room, Shug said in her commanding but calm voice, 'Let her read it. God can handle it.'"

"Goodness. And what was the moral of your piece?"

"I don't know. The moral of a nine-year-old who thought God landed a cheap blow by taking her mother. I needed her more. Lots of kids in school didn't have dads, but everyone had a mother. I felt like an outcast."

"Quite right. I suppose I'd feel the same way. Did you earn a high mark?"

"An A—but only after Mrs. Watkins called Dad in for a conference. He insisted God could handle a young girl working out her grief. He also told me a bit of truth. God didn't take Mom because He needed her, but sometimes people die, and we carry on, asking God for help."

"I'm not sure my mum ever forgave me for what I put the family through," Kate said. "It was all hush-hush, save for the Prime Minister and a small bevy of advisors. I think she feared if she spoke of it, she'd break, perhaps mention the grandchild she'd never met. Things were never the same between us. On her deathbed, we shared a moment of tenderness. She squeezed my hand with tears in her eyes. Her way of saying 'I'm sorry.' We never spoke of you. None of us. It was our way of moving on. Then the news broke, shocking the world and well, you know the rest of the story. I'm glad you meet her before she passed. She once murmured during a family dinner, not long after your first visit, that you were 'a Blue through and through. Cut from the center of the cloth.'"

"That sounds like quite a compliment."

"Of the highest order," Kate said. "You remind me of Mum, Scottie. Determined. Chin up even when you're unsure. I saw the way people gathered round you at the Garden Party. That, my love, is the Queen Rosemunde Blue in you."

They were silent for a moment as Scottie took in the conversation and Kate tried to finish her tea, gripping the cup with both hands.

"I should go," Scottie said. "Let you rest. How is your pain level today?"

"Bothersome but I'm hopeful." Kate set down her cup. "What about you, darling? I fear I brought you over only to be bored with me. Do you have any thoughts about weekend plans? You could go exploring."

"As a matter of fact," Scottie said, "Michael Cross has a family event this weekend. His Pratt grandparents' sixty-fifth anniversary. I thought I might go with him."

"Yes, I know of the anniversary. Odessa Pratt was one of my mother's ladies-in-waiting. The Family sent an anniversary gift this week. You want to go with him to the party?" Kate leaned toward her as if to see beneath the surface. "Is there something you're not telling me?"

"Like what?" But Scottie knew what she meant. "There's nothing between us. He told me he wasn't going. He doesn't get along with his mother."

"Who does?" Kate smiled faintly. "Jeanette Pratt is a law unto herself."

"I volunteered to go with, see a bit of the country, meet more people. He assures me I won't be a security risk, but he won't allow me to go without your approval."

"I can't stop you, really, and I see the merits of it. But Scottie, I must warn you to keep your relationship with Michael Cross in check. Don't risk compromising his duty. If he loves you, he'll second-guess his actions. On a personal note—"

"Love me?" Scottie laughed. "We're barely friends."

"—the man still nurses a broken heart, and you are leaving after the Rose Ball." Kate drew a breath. "Aren't you?"

"I am." Scottie nodded. "We're finalizing next spring's designs in July, then the board meeting in August. I'll have to hit the ground running." She sounded a bit defensive, but there was no need. Kate understood Scottie's extended stay in Lauchtenland was a once-in-a-lifetime break from the O'Shay kingdom. "And I know about Purnell. I don't plan on breaking his heart."

"Then go, have fun. And one more thing, remember you are my daughter. Always. Even in Hearts Bend. Even if you don't see or feel it, others do. You have the Blue aura and people love you. Even that looney Mrs. Johansdotter," Kate said. "I know it's a foreign way of thinking, but please bear it in mind. You are Lady Royal Blue. The Pratt atmosphere will be friendly but be aware. Hostiles will roam among them."

Kate drew a breath as if it took all her might. "Guard your own heart. I can't forget how you called me after your man, Cap, ended things. Though I don't think he broke your heart."

"No. Maybe cracked it a little."

"Well, we're all cracked a little, aren't we?" Kate's laugh helped bring her to her feet. "I must nap. Sorry, darling, for wearing out on you so quickly."

Scottie stood, watching her mother exit. Hilda, who seemed to have a second sense when it came to the queen, met Kate at the door.

Coming to Lauchtenland for the spring had been the right thing. Scottie would never get another chance to spend so much time with her mother.

Yet what consumed her thoughts as she made her way toward the Princess Charlotte was Michael Cross. Tomorrow night she'd be *his* shadow. His support. And it felt good to be needed.

CHAPTER NINE

It was a bonny day for the Pratt family gathering, because even the Lauchtenland skies, ruled by the tempest churning of the North Sea, wouldn't dare rain on Granny and Granddad's celebration.

When Michael finally phoned in his RSVP plus one, the event coordinator said the guest list topped out at three hundred. Good. His grandparents deserved to be honored. Sixty-five years of marriage was a stellar achievement, never mind they were two of the humblest people he'd ever known. Their daughter, however, had fallen far, far away from their tree.

"Final chance to back out," Michael said, glancing at Scottie as he parked the motor on the lower grounds of Presswick Manor, an ancient and beautiful estate perched on the cliffs of the Branford-on-the-Reserve area of Port Fressa.

"Back out? No way, dude. I'm here." Scottie grabbed the gold Eloise Ltd. clutch she'd carried at the Garden Party and adjusted her hat. "Are you sure I'm not overdressed?"

Choko had fitted her out for a high-society wedding. "Back home, a celebration like this would be in someone's open field or barn with a guitar circle and line dancing. I'd be in shorts and a T-shirt, wearing cowboy boots, ready for an evening in a hot barn."

"You'll be the loveliest woman here tonight." Michael walked around to open her door, a lift in his chest when her long, slender legs stepped out, her perfumed presence following. *Easy, chap. Walls up.*

"However," he added, "the ties and cummerbunds will come off once everyone's good and snockered—and most likely thrown over the edge of Poplar Cliff along with hats and heels."

"Another night for my memoir."

"Wait until I'm dead, please."

With that, they started up the concrete and pebbled drive, passing a car park of luxury motors and men in dark suits discreetly moving through the shadows. The security was tight tonight.

Up the final incline, Michael nearly reached for Scottie's hand but pulled back just in time. Reflex. From his days with Purnell. He was always reaching for her hand. For her.

He hadn't seen most of the extended family since Purnell's funeral. With Scottie on his arm, perhaps they'd refrain from asking how he was getting on. How he was *healing*. They'd not dare ask if Lady Royal was his new love interest. Well, except Mum. She'd bowl such a question straight down the lane.

The night on the portico when they talked, he'd refrained from saying too much about good ole mum. Scottie could make her own assessment. Why smear her with his palpable contempt?

"Kate said your grandmother was a lady-in-waiting to her mother."

"Yes, they were good friends. She may have been one of the few outside the family and Privy Council to know about you. Queen Rosemunde confided in her."

"And your grandfather?"

"A brilliant businessman. He ushered Pratt Printing into the twenty-first century. When he retired, he served in parliament for fifteen years and later joined Her Majesty's council for technology and modernization. Both my grandparents remain politically connected, which means all sorts will be here tonight, including the head of the rakish RECO party, MP Hamish Fickle."

"MP Fickle. Isn't he from the Midlands?" she said. "I read about him in the paper. Kate left it on our tea table. I'd like to talk to him about Eloise Ltd."

"Not tonight, Scottie. There's no telling how he'll spin a conversation in the press tomorrow. He lives for the talkies and his social media account. As it is, you'll be posted across the internet before the first hour of the party."

They reached Granny's signature hedge framing a carpet of green grass. The manor, to his right, was of golden red brick, trimmed in ivy and anchored with green shrubs and gold and red flowers, with royal blue woven in.

"Maybe this wasn't a good idea," he murmured.

"For me or you?" She grabbed his arm. "Come on, I'll be on my best Lady Royal behavior." She stopped. "Michael, will they wonder why you brought me? Will they think I'm your date, as in *date* date?"

"If they do, they'd be wise to keep it to themselves."

Just his luck, Mum was the first to greet them. "As I live and breathe! You came. I said I'd not believe it until I saw your face." She squeezed his arm and kissed his cheek. "Lady Royal, it's an honor to have you with us."

Mum was no fan of the House of Blue because she'd always considered them competition for her husband's (now ex-husband's) attention and for her sons. But thirty years after she left, anyone and everyone with a position was a friend to Jeanette Pratt. To be fair, the way she welcomed Scottie sounded genuine, if not a bit sweet.

"Lady Royal," Michael said, "my mother, Jeanette Pratt."

Scottie offered her hand. "Thank you for allowing me to attend."

"Of course, of course. I saw you had a bit of a rough start for the spring season, what with the business with the woman falling over the quay."

"Any one of us would've tried to save Mrs. Johansdotter and her daughter."

"Yes, but it was *you*, wasn't it?"

"Well, I did give her a push," Scottie said. "It was the least I could do."

Mum stepped back, slack-jawed, then managed a rough laugh. Michael had never felt prouder. *Touché, Scottie O'Shay.*

"Let's go meet Granny and Granddad." Michael placed a hand on Scottie's back. "Nice to see you, Mum."

Check. He'd seen his mother, and now the rest of the evening was his.

They found his grandparents in a large tent strung with lights and filled with music, guests milling to and fro. The couple sat in velvet-covered mahogany chairs atop a small platform, king and queen of their little kingdom. Granny stood when she spotted him.

"My dear lad, you came. Your granddad and I have missed you." She embraced and kissed him, then held his shoulders, beaming. "We're so looking forward to you joining Pratt Printing one day. Your mother assures us—"

"Granny, may I introduce Lady Royal Blue, Queen Catherine's daughter."

"I am well aware of Lady Royal Blue." Granny clasped her hands in her lap and peered down her nose. "I do hope you enjoy your evening and, um, your soon return to America."

Granddad received Scottie in a more congenial manner. "We're honored to have you at our celebration."

"It's an honor to be here. Congratulations on your anniversary."

"Thank you," he said, with a nod toward his wife. "Pay no attention to Michael's grandmother. She's old school when it comes to the House of Blue, even in these modern times. She was a confidant of Queen Rosemunde, your grandmother, when you were born."

"I'm sitting right here. I can hear you, darling." Granny glanced at Scottie. "Your presence is most welcome. We are honored."

"Thank you, Granny," Michael said. "And to be clear, I'm not joining Pratt anytime soon."

"I asked her not to mention Pratt tonight," Granddad said with one of his trademark smiles at Granny. "But she's on your mother's bandwagon, anxious for you to come aboard. You will. When the time is right." With that, Granddad stood and taking Granny's hand, they wandered off to join a circle of friends.

"What time might that be?" Michael muttered. "When I've lost my mind? When the world's on the verge of collapse?" He snagged two flutes of champagne from a black-tie server. He handed one of the bubblies to her. "To families."

She laughed softly and he tried to memorize the sound. "To families."

"There you are, Mick." Michael turned to find Evan and Tracy approaching, along with several friends and family members, all thrilled to meet Lady Royal. Especially Tracy.

They'd just finished introductions when Finn came flying out of the evening shadows, throwing himself against Michael. "You're here! You're here!"

With one arm, Michael lifted him up and spun him around. "Don't you look nice in your suit and tie."

"Dad made me." Finn's face, very much like his father's at that age, was alight with excitement. "Can we play football later? The lads are made up you're here. Will you show them the scissor kick, please?"

"I don't know, old chap. We're at Granddad and Granny's party."

"But all the cousins are here. Besides, we never see you."

Michael bent to Finn's ear. "Later, when the grown-ups have had too much punch."

With a wide grin, his nephew shot him two thumbs-up and darted toward the cousins—a conglomerate of grandchildren, nieces, and nephews—and friends, dressed like miniature adults. If that didn't bring back a memory or two...

"When Evan and I were young, we'd—" He was speaking to Scottie, but she was gone. "Scottie?" He tapped Evan on the shoulder. "Where'd Lady Royal get off to?"

Scanning the crowd, his affection for the little cousins and childhood memories gave way to adrenaline. Moving through the party with controlled motion, chuffed she'd disappeared, he ran through de-escalation scenarios and determined avenues of escape. Then he heard her voice.

"Do you feel your cause is just?" she was saying in her warm

Tennessee accent, surrounded by a thick crowd of men and women.

"I do, Lady Royal. Your interest surprises me." MP Hamish Fickle's rhythmic Midlands' accent cut through the air. "The RECO party now holds eleven seats in the House of Commons. We're gaining influence and—"

Michael broke into the circle of men in white-tie tuxedos and women playing coy under wide-brimmed hats, which included his mother.

"And two lords in the Senate have moved in the RECO direction," Mum added.

"Indeed," said Fickle, with a sloppy grin. In his mid-thirties, the good-looking Member of Parliament with a quick mind was becoming a thorn to the House of Blue. And his political influence was just getting started. "Lord Bexley and Lord Innis. Wise men, I'd say."

"Isn't that to their own demise? If the House of Blue goes, so will the aristocracy," Scottie said, holding the attention of those around her. "What would be your purpose for abolishing the monarchy?"

What was she doing? Rule number one of the House of Blue: *Political opinions are never discussed in the public square—* which in this case was quickly gathering a larger crowd.

"Old-fashioned. Out of style," Fickle declared. "We know now, thanks to America, what a constitutional republic looks like. We don't need a ruling class to—"

"Come now, Hamish, don't throw the baby out with the bath water," said Lord Sanzenbacher, whose family had held a Senate seat since the sixteenth century. "The American government isn't perfect, is it, Lady Royal?"

"Lord Sanzenbacher," Fickle said with a grin. "We must toss out the baby. She's all wrinkled. Been too long in the water."

"Hasn't the queen done a good job of leading Lauchtenland into the twenty-first century?" Scottie said as Michael shoved in next to her. "She's not in the way of progress. She's leading it."

The group chuckled their assent, and Fickle turned to Michael.

"Did you bring Lady Royal here to campaign for her mother's causes, Cross?"

"No, he didn't. He's probably thinking I should keep my fat yap shut." Scottie's comment earned a laugh. "I'm just curious about your animosity toward such an ancient family. Believe me, America has its problems. No government is perfect."

"Quite right," Hamish said. "But we'd rather have a balance—preventing governments from confiscating property and money without a citizen's say."

"Come now, Fickle." Sanzenbacher again, one hand on his wide girth, the other barely holding his flute of champagne. "We have laws to prevent any overreach."

"Are you talking about the Midlands?" Scottie said. "With Reingard and Eloise?"

"Perhaps." MP Fickle looked impressed. "What do you know about—"

"All right, ladies and gentlemen," Michael interjected, sweeping his left arm wide to make a path. "We're at a party. A celebration. Have you been to the savories tent? I can smell the aroma of roasting meat from here."

Gently, he moved Scottie toward the savories, giving himself ten seconds to calm down. He made it to eight before speaking. "Talking politics as a member of the House of Blue is madness. It will start a firestorm for days, if not weeks. You may have sunk your entire trip."

"Calm down," she said, pure American assuredness in her tone. "Hamish Fickle started it."

"He baited you. Hook, line, and sinker. He's craftier than the serpent in the garden who talked Eve into damning all humanity over a stinking apple. If you're going to skewer all mankind, do it for a nice steak with potatoes and warm buttered bread. Add a nice merlot and sweet pudding."

He grabbed a plate and linen napkin roll. "Beef and lamb, please," he said to the man behind the rotisserie skewer.

"I was only asking questions." Scottie took up a plate. "I'll have the same. Michael, don't let him scare you."

"I will let him, because he has power. Because he can say what he wants to the press while the Family smiles and remains quiet. Just like they said nothing to contradict Mrs. Johansdotter. Scottie, if we're going to survive the next six weeks, you must listen to me. I know our countrymen, the House of Blue, and the political landscape because I've studied our culture and laws since I was a boy. I also know MP Hamish Fickle."

"Fine, but you can't just expect me to stand there and smile when he says crazy stuff like abolishing the monarchy."

"Yes, I can, and you must. The Blues have perfected the art of silence when it comes to their detractors."

"I find it curious no one in the Family knows why he hates them. I asked John about the anti-monarchist movement last Christmas, and he said he'd never spoken to Hamish Fickle about this bee in his bonnet or why he created the Renaissance Coalition. It's one thing to want a different government. It's another to denigrate a millennium of history and the Family carrying it on their backs."

"Hamish Fickle denigrates anyone in power not under his thumb. Here—" Michael motioned her forward. "—there's a table over there."

"I just think someone should talk to him." Scottie sat across from him, her plate loaded with meat, vegetables, and buttery bread. With a sigh, she took in her surroundings—the tents, the lights, the music, the crowning gold of the western sun. "Sorry if I caused trouble." When she looked at him, regret hung in her eyes.

"No, lass, you didn't. It's just…you're in my charge. Should anything happen to you—"

"Nothing will happen. I'm not a threat. I'll be gone before anyone can formulate a plan to take me out." She grinned and sipped her champagne. "Now tell me, why is such a posh event being held outside?"

"It's a Pratt family thing. Get gussied up, then have a picnic. People love it." Michael sat back, releasing the air of tension in his chest. "I understand your curiosity about Hamish." Scottie challenged the norms, and he admired her for it. "If there's any aftermath from your conversation with him, we'll face it together. But just know, he will not come to your side. Or the royal family's. He's anti-monarch." He speared the air with his knife. "However, tonight we are to have a jolly time while we celebrate my grandparents' wedded bliss. If I married tomorrow, I'd have to be a hundred and five to enjoy sixty-five years."

"Here's to wedded bliss." Scottie tapped her glass to his. "May it not pass us by."

Michael caught her gaze and held it a moment, then tipped his flute. Indeed. May it not pass them by.

Little by little, old friends and family members came round, excited to see him, thrilled to meet Lady Royal, politely snapping selfies and moving on. He relaxed and embraced this grand family reunion.

He'd just returned to their table with two large slices of chocolate cake and a side of cream when the band under the music tent struck up a tune from his grandparents' day. The dance floor instantly filled.

"Mick, you made it." Piers slapped him on the back, then nodded at Scottie. "Lady Royal, lovely to meet you. I'm Mick's old football mate, Piers Hollings."

"Also known as Lord Atterbery," Michael said.

Scottie shook his hand. "It's good to know Mick has an old mate. He seems like a recluse to me."

Piers laughed. "He's been ignoring us ever since—" He sobered, stopping himself, then recovered. "Anyway, I'm trying to get him back on the pitch with me. He's an amazing player and coach."

"You know Mum's angling to get him working for Pratt." Evan came from among the guests and leaned in. "She'll sponsor a youth club, Mick."

"Yes, but I'll be too busy working to take part."

He let Scottie manage the conversation from there. She asked natural questions, speaking as if she belonged among this crowd—with him—filling the hollow crater he'd been carrying round the last year and a half.

A trumpeter blasted a note of celebration, and the caterer wheeled an exquisite, four-tiered anniversary cake with cream icing and chocolate flowers toward Granddad and Granny. The band singer launched into an old Lauchten love song:

> *Years may come and go*
> *but your hand will always be in mine.*
> *From the first moment I saw you,*
> *my future unfurled and I knew…*
> *You'd be my past and present too.*

Michael rose to cheer and applaud, his attention glued to Granddad as he lovingly danced with Granny.

Purnell loved this song. They were to dance to it at their wedding. An ache, a longing for her, wrapped round him, and that's when he remembered—by this time, they'd likely have been holding a child of their own.

The music faded and someone shouted, "Hip, hip, hooray!"

Granny raised the knife to cut the cake as Granddad's friends shouted corny jokes. Then, tenderly, they shared a bite with one another.

Granddad took the microphone to thank everyone for coming. "But the night is not over. We've plenty to eat, and the band will be here until carriages at midnight." More cheers. "Odessa and I want to thank our children, Jeanette, Jacqueline, and Harry Jr. You made us a family, and we love you and all the beautiful grand-children and great-grandchildren. Odessa, I'm good for another sixty-five."

"I'm all yours, Harry. All yours."

Under the applause and whistles, and the sight of his eighty-something grandparents loving each other, Michael saw the life he'd lost when Purnell died. An infection. Sepsis. How utterly unreal. Stupid and senseless.

"Excuse me," he said, heading off, pausing by the burly, dark-suited man standing at attention by the tent pole to give a command. "Please, keep an eye on Lady Royal."

Chapter Ten

As Michael disappeared beyond the edge of the lights, she almost followed. But she'd seen the pain on his face as he'd watched his grandparents dance together and decided to let him be.

The anniversary atmosphere made her homesick for Dad, Shug, Fritz, and the entire O'Shay team. She'd never been away this long—with six weeks to go.

Even more unsettling was the romantic air under the dance tent. She told herself the love of a good man didn't matter, yet she secretly longed for it.

The kind she'd witnessed with her grandparents and now between Michael's—his granny's cool reception toward her aside.

A cheer erupted on the dance floor as the band and singer belted out Kool and the Gang's "Celebration." Michael's granny started *the bump* with his granddad and sent the younger set into a frenzy.

Suddenly, Scottie was pulled from her chair by a group of beautiful young women, their hair in updos, gowns glittering under the lights, and into a dance circle, shouting that the world should "celebrate good times."

Phones came out. Videos rolled. Selfies snapped. Scottie leaned into every photo. For those moments, she wasn't Lady Royal or *the* Scottie O'Shay; she was that freshman college girl again, singing in the dorm hallway with her friends.

When Little Eva's "Loco-Motion" hit the air, someone grabbed Scottie to lead the conga line right behind Granny Pratt. As she danced, perfecting her John Travolta moves, she spotted Hamish Fickle watching, smirking. She nodded his way.

"Let there be peace between us," she murmured.

By the time she *bump, bump, bumped* to "Sweet Caroline," she was perspiring and parched, her toes pinched by her designer shoes. Kicking them off, she dangled them from her fingertips and wandered to the tea tent, where she retrieved two bottles of cold, dripping water, and scanned for Michael.

She spied him facing the arching lights rising from the streets and homes of Port Fressa, hands in his pockets, tie undone and flapping loose about his neck. Scottie pressed against the cool, sharp wind climbing over the cliffs and joined him.

"I'm going to be all over social media tomorrow," she said, handing him a bottle before drinking from her own. "Your cousins dragged me onto the dance floor. I felt like myself. Like I was back at school."

"They're a fun lot and hopefully people will be discreet regarding socials."

"Hamish Fickle kept his eye on me. Maybe he thinks I'm good for the House of Blue."

"I wouldn't count on it, Scottie." Michael took a long drink. "I'll give him this, though—he recognizes beauty when he sees it."

"If you're referring to me, that's the second or third time tonight you've called me beautiful."

"Then I'll be sure to check myself in the future."

"Good" She turned away, facing the breeze. "We shan't cross any professional lines."

Shan't? Scottie laughed. She never said *shan't*. And the lines had already blurred, but only for fun. She'd be gone soon.

Michael glanced over. "You make yourself available to people. At the Garden Party, here, at this party. People love you for it, especially my cousins. You do that, you know—invite people into your world. They gather round you before you even ask."

"I inherited something intangible from Kate and her mum, Queen Rosemunde."

"We want you to love it here, Scottie. More people than not support you."

We? Did he include himself in that plural pronoun, or was he merely employing the royal *we*?

"Possibly not Hamish Fickle," she said.

"He's a flash in the pan. Forget him," Michael said.

"I doubt it," Scottie said.

"You're probably right." Michael sighed "I forget how peaceful it is here. Nothing but crags covered in endless wild grasses and the lights of the city."

"What happened back there?" Scottie asked. "Why'd you walk off?"

"Just a memory."

"Purnell?" Again, she took advantage of the dark to ask the vulnerable question.

"We'd have been married a year by now. We wanted kids right away, so…" He gulped down half the water.

"You hoped to announce another great-grandchild at this celebration."

"Or hand one to Granddad to hold." The wind whistled past, stealing away the rest of his words. "Now you know the real reason why I didn't want to come. Plus, Mum always bears down on me with her Pratt Printing plans. Sometimes I think it's more about beating my father than actually finding me fit for the business."

"I've wondered that a time or two myself. Am I the Creative Director because I'm good or because I bear the name? It took me forever to learn to draw. My gift is for colors and fabrics. Marketing." She laughed softly. "A couple years ago, I started experimenting with smart materials. How technology could improve our clothes. Then I learned my mother, the queen, took the lead in Lauchtenland technology."

"Careful, you might just conclude you belong here."

Scottie shook her head, gulping sea air. "Nah. O'Shay, men's fashion, Hearts Bend, Tennessee—they're in my veins. They hold me together."

"How'd you meet your chap, Cap?"

"At the big Fourth of July celebration on the Scott farm, which the Castle family owns now, but everyone still calls it the Scott farm. Cap had retired from the Army Rangers and took over the family farm outside town."

"Love at first sight?"

"*Ha.* No. But we saw something worth exploring in each other. What about you and Purnell? Was it love at first sight?"

"Yes. She knocked my boots off—and believe me, I never thought I could feel that way about anyone. After my parents' divorce, I tossed true love into the rubbish bin. It was a myth curated by poets and songwriters."

"Yet Purnell made you believe and that can never be taken away, Michael Cross. Even in death. Love's an enduring gift."

Michael studied her through the haze of light in a way that made her look away. After a long moment, he said, "Finn had invited me to one of his school programs. Purnell was his teacher. When I clapped eyes on her, my heart started pounding, my palms went clammy. I've had less nerves and weakness facing terrorists."

He turned at a sound from the dance tent. A group of men had gathered, cigars lit, port in hand.

"Uncle Mick!" Finn ran toward them, kicking a football. "Will you show us the scissor kick? Please?"

"Ah, buddy, it's late and I'm in my fancy togs."

"Please," said the handsome kid with the cowlick, big blue eyes, and perfect smile, the grass stains on his white shirt, proof he'd already been playing. "You promised. We're all in our dress togs too."

Michael clapped him on the shoulder and sighed, pausing for a final excuse. "All right, but pay attention, because I'm only going to show you once. After that, you're on your own. Remember that practice is key to every man's success."

He peeled off his jacket and tie, handing them to Scottie as if it were the most natural thing. She followed him toward the makeshift pitch, folding the jacket over her arm and neatly tucking the tie into the breast pocket.

"First rule?" she heard Michael say. "Relax. It won't feel natural at first. Second? Eyes on the ball."

Yes, Scottie, eyes on the ball. Don't get caught up in the magic and wonder of Lauchtenland, of the castle, of the people…and Michael.

Tonight she saw the man behind the protection officer, and when their eyes met, or when his hand brushed hers, the feelings he stirred were the most honest she'd felt in years. Maybe ever.

On the pitch, Finn crossed the ball to Michael, and as it sailed overhead in a perfect arc, Michael hopped on his nearest leg, whipped his other across his body, and sent the ball flying through a goal made of chairs and a tablecloth. The boys erupted in cheers, clamoring for more, each desperate for his own try.

Michael grinned back at her as she settled under the savories tent, where skewers of roasted beef, lamb, and chicken continued to dwindle. There was a new energy about him as he unbuttoned his collar and rolled his sleeves.

"All right, lads, pay attention."

"Have you watched him play?" Jeanette pulled a chair forward and sat beside her. "He's brilliant."

"He's certainly mastered the scissor kick."

"The Port Fressa Capitals scouted him for years, then called him up during his uni days. But his father, and the Cross duty, won out." Jeanette slipped a cigarette from a pearl-studded clutch. "Do you mind?"

Scottie shook her head.

"The football, the fame, the real money—lost to almighty Cross and Crown."

Jeanette drew on her cigarette, then blew the smoke aside. She was captivating in her gold-sequined gown with its V-neck and gathered waist, blonde hair in an intricate updo, her complexion flawless in the party lights.

"I don't smoke as a rule," she said, stamping it out after a few puffs. "Just sometimes." She laughed softly. "Probably to irritate my mother. Isn't that a sad tale for a sixty-something woman?"

"We're always our parents' children. My dad still says, 'Don't tell Shug.'"

"Shug is your grandmother? I just love your southern endearments." She cheered as one of the boys attempted the scissor kick, landing awkwardly on his back only to pop up, grinning, ready to go again. "Michael's probably told you he and I don't get along." Scottie looked over but without reply. "I have my regrets—"

A shout from the pitch drew their attention. Scottie welcomed the diversion, half expecting Jeanette's next question to be "*How's it going with your mother?*"

"Well done, Finn," Jeanette said, rising to applaud as her grandson performed a near-flawless scissor kick. She looked down at Scottie. "Thanks for indulging me. If you'd like a ride to Perrigwynn, let me know. I've a feeling Mick isn't heading home anytime soon."

"We're heading back to Hadsby Castle tonight. But thank you."

Jeanette perched on the chair's edge. "Do you realize the similarity in your stories? You're heir to an old, established clothing line. Michael's heir to an old, established international printing company. You have royal roots. And as a Cross man, he's as close to royalty as one can come without being an official aristocrat. You never knew your mother. His mother walked out on the family."

Scottie regarded Jeanette, trying to discern the purpose of her confession. "Where are you going with this?"

"O'Shay is your future, Lady Royal. It's all well and good to play princess for a season or a holiday visit. Your mother is our queen. You've every right to your place. But you and I both know your future's back home in Tennessee. Maybe, in the course of things, you can help Michael see the world through your eyes. He's done his Cross duty and served the Crown. Now it's time to step into his future. One that will provide a good living, carry on his Pratt legacy, and lead the next generation. I've nothing against the Cross family, nor the Crown, I just want my boy with me."

"You want me to persuade him to join Pratt Printing?"

"You sound dubious, Lady Royal, but he's my heir, just as you are your father's. While the whole family's involved, the helm always passes to the eldest grandchild. Michael's Cross and military training make him the perfect leader. I just need him to see it." She motioned to the field. "Here he comes. It was nice to meet you, Lady Royal."

She kissed Michael's cheek and patted his shoulder. "I'll ring you for teatime."

"What'd she want?" Michael asked, helping Scottie to her feet.

"To tell me you're heir to Pratt Printing the same way I'm heir to O'Shay. You never said."

"Because I'm not *the* heir. It's just a tradition to pass the baton to the oldest. Evan can take it just as well as I can. Or one of my cousins."

"She also noted how alike our stories are between Pratt and O'Shay. Your Cross blood and my House of Blue genes."

Scottie paused, hearing her phone buzz from her clutch resting on the table. She reached for it—

"Scottie, I'm sorry. Mum had no right—"

"It's okay." But she wasn't listening as she stared at her phone.

"Scottie?"

She looked up. "My dad." Her voice broke as she showed Michael the photo of him with Remi. "He's engaged."

MICHAEL

By Sunday afternoon, he found himself in Brindleby and at his father's kitchen table for the first time in months.

"I don't know why I don't come home more often," he said, stirring cream into the cuppa Dad set before him.

"I've a tin of day-old biscuits from the corner bakery." Dad retrieved a white can from the cupboard. "They might crumble if you dip them, but they're sweet enough."

Michael took a round, golden biscuit and tapped it in his tea. Like always, Dad's kitchen was warm and bright, sunlight pouring through the mullioned windows. A fire crackled in the stone hearth. The slate floor smelled faintly of pine soap from an early morning mopping.

Beyond the wide doorway lay the living lounge, the same room where he and Evan had done homework, played games, watched telly, and decorated the Christmas tree. Down the narrow passage was his father's den with its dark walls, thick carpet, leather chairs, bookshelves bowing under their weight, and the old desk passed down from father to son for generations. It was cluttered with folders, notes, and tea mugs not yet washed.

Dad had done his best to make it a welcoming place. He'd carted them to practices and rehearsals, taught them to drive and manage a bank account. He sewed on buttons and placed a cool cloth on their feverish heads.

When Michael turned fifteen, Dad set him with a stack of Cross books to read and pictures to study. At eighteen, he attended his first Cross family conference where he was immersed in their family mission, in history, faith, and the Crown.

"You don't come home because you're busy," Dad said, ever practical. "You're also a grown man. I don't expect you every weekend." He dipped a biscuit, frowning when only half came out. "What brings you today? Aren't you on duty?"

"Lady Royal is with the queen."

"How is our queen faring?"

"Well enough. They don't tell us much of anything, but I see her frailty when she walks with Scottie," Michael said. "What do you hear in your circles?"

"They're keeping her health close to the chest." Dad tossed back the last of his biscuit. "I saw photos from the Pratt anniversary party. Your grandparents looked well. As did your mother."

"It was a lovely evening."

"And your charge? Did she enjoy herself? Is she as beautiful in person?"

"She did and yes, she's very much so...she looks, even acts, like her mother."

"Yet you're here, the day after the party, with a long face."

Michael laughed softly. "Can't I come home because I missed you?"

Antone Cross—semi-retired diplomat, lifelong servant of the Crown, and esteemed bachelor—still lived in Brindleby, the village where Michael grew up. Tucked on the western edge of the Midlands, north toward Dalholm, it was a place untouched by time. Stone cottages shaded by Douglas firs and oaks, a stream where Michael and Evan learned to fish threading through the green.

The eighteenth-century Cross House, a Georgian manor of pale stone and seventeen fireplaces, had been a gift from Queen Clemency to Michael's seventh great-grandfather. The grounds and gardens were still maintained by a grant from the Crown.

"You can come anytime, Mick," Dad said. "But I sense something more to your visit today."

"I don't know." Michael leaned back, one hand around his cup. "I felt something last night. Something I've not felt since..." He met his father's eyes. "Purnell."

"Which is difficult, because you've not let her go. Not all the way. Never mind Lady Royal is Her Majesty's daughter. She's not here forever. She'll return to Tennessee. And you're her protection officer. Lines are being blurred."

Saturday night at Presswick Manor felt like another man's life. As the anniversary party closed, with most of the guests gone, the band had played a final tune, "Auld Lang Syne." It gripped him, and without even thinking, he'd brought Scottie to him for a slow, close dance.

She'd rested her head on his shoulder, saying nothing of his sweat-dampened shirt, but imprinted her form into his, a sensation that had just begun to fade.

If he'd gone this far off the rails in two weeks, what would happen in the next month? He must employ every ounce of reserve to protect her, as duty warranted. Crushes and feelings had no place.

"You have always been able to read right through me, Dad."

"You're my son, of course."

A meow sounded beyond the kitchen door. Dad rose to open it, and Artemis, the world's largest and most stunning Maine coon, and quite aware of it, sashayed inside as if he were king of Lauchtenland.

"Your breakfast is in the bowl, Your Royal Highness," Dad said, scratching behind the cat's ears before sitting down again.

"What do you want me to tell you, son? Resign? How much longer will Lady Royal be with Her Majesty?"

"Until the Rose Ball. And I don't want to resign." Michael reached for another biscuit. "I just don't want to feel what I felt last night." He sighed. "I needed to tell someone. Artemis was outside, so I suppose it had to be you."

Dad's low rumble was one of Michael's favorite sounds. "What else is on your mind? Did I see a photo of Lady Royal speaking with MP Fickle?"

"You did. He engaged her first, but she didn't back away. Then she asked me why no one in the Family seemed to understand the anti-monarchists."

"Which, at their heart, is MP Fickle."

"Right. So, Dad, do you know?"

"Never had anti-monarchists in Lauchtenland, not loud ones, until Fickle. My advice? Do your job. Protect Lady Royal. Leave off politics. No need for her to stir waters for which she has no oar."

"Her dad sent a message last night with a picture of his new fiancée," Michael said. "She seemed upset by it, sorry to miss the moment in his life. My guess is Lady Royal won't make it to the Rose Ball."

"Then your heart will be safe."

"Yep. My heart will be safe."

But as he looked around the familiar kitchen, the same one where he'd once heard his mother's laughter, Michael knew it was already too late.

CHAPTER
ELEVEN

Monday started on the run. Opening the Thornwick Tennis & Racquet Club Grand Slam Tennis Tournament grass venue was second only to Wimbledon, though most Lauchtens debated that point.

When Anika Dreyer, the world's number one female player, took the first set six–love, six–love, she surprised the stadium by inviting Scottie onto the court for a little volley.

She gripped Michael's arm. "I don't play. Not well anyway."

"Then give it the college try," he said. "Isn't that what you say in America?"

As she made her way to the court, he wanted to run after her, protect her from any jeering or boos. Maybe it was his imagination, but ever since her father's text, she seemed quiet and not as present.

Yet to the crowd's delight, Scottie volleyed with Anika, diving for a cross-court lob that almost made it over the net. The stadium erupted with cheers, and Scottie wore the grass stains and dust on her white slacks like a badge of honor.

On Tuesday the queen was not feeling well, so Scottie took tea with the County Northton Bankers Association alone. And again, on Wednesday, to the tech startup AiBound.

Early Thursday morning he trained down to Port Fressa with the queen and Scottie. They had an appointment at Perrigwynn

Palace with designer Kimbra Townsen, who'd been selected to design Scottie's Rose Ball gown.

Once Scottie was safe in the palace, Michael headed down to the Perrigwynn Operations Room to check in with Gunner Ferguson. Afterward, he was off to meet Mum for tea. She caught him in a weak moment Sunday evening on his drive home from Dad's.

Then tomorrow Scottie was getting her desired visit to the Midlands for the opening of the Midlands Faire. The king or queen traditionally opened the event, as it had been for two hundred and sixty years, but the king consort was out of country, and the doctors had quietly advised the queen to rest.

And so, the American Scottie O'Shay, Lady Royal, was representing the House of Blue at the famed faire. And in RECO territory.

HMSD officers would be deployed to act as tourists, shoppers, and locals, always within reach of Lady Royal should there be a repeat of the quay incident.

MP Hamish Fickle was already active on his social media and the talkies, promoting the Midlands Faire, which was part of his Midlands Garden district. To hear him, one would think he was king of his own little Midlands universe.

In the Operations Room, Michael chatted with the lads, catching up on their news, then halted when the small light from the lamp on his old desk still burned. He snapped around to Gunner, who gave a single chin lift.

"We're keeping the lamp on for her." Purnell.

It was late when he concluded the security plans with Gunner. Mum would be waiting at Saldings on the Waterfront. Hurrying out of the palace, he flagged down a taxi on Clemency Avenue.

He arrived to see Mum had secured her favorite table in the back left corner where the view of the city and view of the port were equally spectacular. He made his way toward her between the late afternoon diners and early evening drinkers.

"Sorry for my tardiness. Business." He sat, going over the table, already set with a serving of tea and cake.

"No worries." Mum set aside her phone to fill his teacup. "Everything all right?"

"Just preparations for tomorrow." He creamed his tea and reached for a slice of cake. "What's new in your world?"

"Torben Hedgerow announced his retirement this week."

"And he is?"

"Only one of Pratt Printing's most tenured employees. He started with mop and broom and rose through the ranks to become our Chief Strategic Officer. I want you to take his place. It's your right, Mick, and you'd be brilliant in the position. We need you."

"No, you just want to win, beat Dad and the Cross family. You want me doing what you envision for me, and in your mind, it doesn't include the Cross family's service to the Crown."

"Not true. You know I'm a loyal monarchist, well, ninety percent loyal, but Her Majesty's armed services and security detail have had enough of you. Twenty years. I understood in the beginning, honestly. Now I don't. Why this unfounded resistance to the Pratt way? The money, darling, think of what you could do with the money. I know for a fact if Purnell were—"

"Mum." His stern rebuke reflected on her face, and the banger he'd been harboring in his soul for thirty plus years nearly exploded. "Purnell was on my side, not your mole. And what all did you say to Lady Royal Saturday night?"

"How alike you are in your Cross and Pratt and O'Shay and Blue stories. She's a lovely woman. I liked her."

"Well, there's an endorsement." Michael leaned her way. "Mum, I'm not playing hard to get with you. I've put in my required two years during university to be a part of the Pratt profits. I know what it's like to work there, and I can't see myself in suit and tie, locked up in an office all day. I'd rather coach kids on the pitch, earning a pittance, than be a Chief Strategic Officer. There are Pratt cousins to step up. But the Crosses, we're a dying breed. Our numbers in public service are dwindling. I feel this is my calling."

There. He'd said it.

"I see." Mum fluffed the napkin in her lap, glancing away. "Is that the sum of it? You genuinely feel it's your calling?"

She was hinting at the even deeper issue. The one they'd both avoided over the years. How Jeanette Pratt walked out on her children and seemed to forget all about them.

"Nothing more than what I just said." Because this was not the time or place to ask *What sort of mum abandons her sons?* "What else is new in your life? Are you seeing anyone?"

"That's a rather random question." Mum hesitated before she answered. "Lord Cavendish and I have dinner now and then. We went to Cannes for a long weekend in the winter. Is your father dating?"

"If you want to know, ring him."

"You think I dislike him, but I don't. I loved him very much when we married and still do in my way, but the Cross devotion to service and the Pratt innovation in business were never going to coexist. I know you're angry with me for leaving. I'm sorry, Michael, but it's the way things had to be."

Mum's words, her tone, threatened to light the fuse of the old lingering firecracker—a firecracker decades in the making. His resentment was neatly packed and fused with hurt.

Why did running Pratt mean leaving him and Evan behind?

"Were Granddad and Granny happy with the party?" he said, cutting a bite of cake. "Smashing food and music for the evening."

"We're all still talking about it on WhatsApp. Don't you ever read the messages? Mum posts dozens of pictures every day. There's a rather lovely one of you with Lady Royal."

"Take the lilt out of your voice, Mum." Michael washed down his bite of cake with a hot swallow of tea. "You know protection officers do not fraternize with their charges."

"Are you reminding me or yourself? Darling, if you ever want to fall in love again, you must get out of the protection business and join the printing business. I'm sixty-three and while I've no intention of retiring soon, I need to bring you up to speed. The business is yours to inherit."

Mum. She never listened. "Take your eyes off me, Mum. Evan is your man."

"Okay, then give me a better plan for your life than Her Majesty's Security Detail. Do you fancy following the royal Blues around the rest of your life, dodging bullets and charlatans, working their schedule, living on palace grounds in some tiny apartment? What about your own family, Mick? You're forty years old. Purnell would not want this for you."

He gulped down the last of his tea. "Thanks for the tea, Mum." He rose from the table then bent to kiss her cheek. "We'll do it again soon."

"Mick, after this tour of duty with Lady Royal… Wouldn't that be a good time to end your career with the HMSD? A perfect closure."

He regarded her for a moment and the way she almost seemed to plead with him. "Be safe on your way back to the office, Mum." He gave her a nod and smile.

The Clemency district was crowded with commuters on their way home. Michael looked toward Mum's high-rise apartment that was worth several million pounds.

She assumed he wanted to live her style of life. But he was content with his palace grounds apartment. It had character. As for money, he had a trust from his Pratt ancestors. It was enough for him.

While the Cross family was once one of the wealthiest in the country, a spiritual revival among members of the clan in the eighteenth century had them donating their time and money to the poor. The only inheritance left to present-day descendants was a half dozen lovely estates filled with rare art, furniture, and just enough in the bank for upkeep and taxes. The houses were open to the public throughout the year.

Dad dwelled in the only remaining inhabited manor.

At the corner of Clemency and Queen's Way, Michael paused. He opened WhatsApp and scrolled through the Pratt anniversary photos. Granny feeding Granddad cake. The two of them dancing to their song. Surrounded by great-grandchildren.

The last photo was from Cousin Darcy and sent privately. He tapped it.

It was of him and Scottie. Walking from the party lights toward his motor. Scottie's shoes dangling from her fingertips. His jacket over his shoulder. A warm, almost enchanting glow wrapped around them.

Michael zoomed in, his chest filling with the memories of that night. As he walked to the car with Scottie, he was holding her hand, and she was holding his.

CHAPTER TWELVE

She wanted to wear jeans, a T-shirt, a UT hoodie, and sneakers for her day at the Midlands Faire, but a militant Choko insisted she slip on a pair of wide-leg tan trousers with a sunny yellow-and-blue floral print top, and a pair of espadrille wedges.

Then she wrapped Scottie's hair in a loose braid with tendrils curling around her cheeks and neck.

"You'll be the belle of the faire, Lady Royal."

"I'd rather blend in."

"You can't. You're representing Her Majesty."

She was also cold. Did it ever warm up in Lauchtenland? The sea air sank into her bones and never let up.

"You ready for this?" Michael said when they met in the Grand Foyer. He looked regal and serious in his dark suit and white shirt. "A journey into enemy territory?" His gaze swept her up and down, but he said nothing about her appearance, beautiful or otherwise.

She'd not seen him since they arrived at Perrigwynn early yesterday, and his presence now was the warmth she craved. He'd been her rock on the solo engagements earlier in the week, and she'd become dependent on his company.

"Enemy territory? I thought we were going to the Midlands Faire."

"Six of one, my lady." Opening the door, he bowed with a

sweep of his arm, drawing her attention to his broad, thick hand. The one that had held hers so tenderly Saturday night. "Scottie," Michael added as he aided her into the car, "the faire will be crowded. Please stay close."

"Yes, boss."

Settled into the car, she retreated to her memories, where she could still feel Michael's hand holding hers. Neither one had realized what they were doing until he opened her car door. Then they broke apart as if caught making out under the football bleachers. Nearly a week later, the look he gave her in that moment, as his hand slipped from hers, still made her sigh.

As they'd driven the two hours back to Hadsby, he let her talk about Dad's engagement to Remi while the radio played a soft jazz.

He thanked her for accompanying him to the party. She replied she was grateful to tag along.

Neither one mentioned the hand holding. In some way, it seemed too surreal to speak of in the cab of a Range Rover. Whatever was happening between them fit in the annals of a summer love, of a passion fleeting on the heels of going back to school, all tied up in a thanks-for-the-memories kind of way.

Between the music and late hour, along with the hum of the road, she'd drifted to sleep, thinking she'd never felt so comfortable. Once at Hadsby, Michael parked in the motor garage and escorted her to the Grand Staircase, where he said goodnight and disappeared toward the staff stairwell.

She tried to get more engagement details from Dad on Sunday, but their calls were brief as he was in New Orleans meeting Remi's family then hustling back to Hearts Bend to tour a reception venue.

"We're thinking of an October wedding," he'd said.

"October? Five months from now October?"

"Yes." Dad had answered with a small laugh. "We're not getting younger, Scottie. We want to tie the knot, start our lives together. By the way, I want you to be my best woman. What do you say?"

"Of course. You and me, not three." But their little saying didn't apply anymore, did it?

Now she teared up, remembering, fearing she was losing him. For missing out on this part of his life where love was at the helm.

Yet wasn't her time in Lauchtenland with Kate a similar way of love? How selfish of her to explore new paths while expecting Dad to sit aside and do nothing. He put a pin in his love life while raising her. Yet seeing him pull the pin out left her a bit breathless.

Then there was the reality of Kate. She battled pain and fatigue, leaving Scottie to attend her royal tasks on her own. Kate was in bed when Scottie stopped at her apartment on her way to the faire.

This past week revealed how much Kate really needed Scottie in this season. She often reached for her hand, leaned on her for conversation or to secretly sweeten her tea or retrieve a slice of cake. At the banker's tea, she gave Kate's speech and remembered to collect every offered bouquet of flowers.

"I've learned to take the flowers home," Scottie told one woman. "Her Majesty personally arranges them in colorful vases and sets them around the castle."

"So Hadsby is perfumed with the flowers of the people."

"Why, yes," Scottie said. "I believe it is."

"We're here," Michael said as the driver of the dark-windowed Range Rover slowly maneuvered through the gathering crowd. "Lennox and Schueler are behind us." He gently touched Scottie's arm. "Wait for me, Lady Royal. I'll come round. A crowd is already gathering." Michael popped open his door before the car had completely stopped.

"Here we go," she whispered to herself as she exited the car, waving while oddly, strangely, feeling as if she'd been here a hundred times.

Down the narrow cobblestone of Ribbons Avenue, the crowd pressed close. Michael boxed her in on one side, Lennox on the other, with Schueler behind.

"Stop where you want, Scottie." Michael's voice was low and protective. "But if I say move, move."

Okay, but did she stop at one or all? If she skipped a stall or a shop, would the headlines be "Lady Royal Dissed Midlands Faire Vendor"? This was nerve-wracking.

Spying a stall with young women selling handmade knitted and crocheted throws, scarves, and sweaters, she raved over their work, encouraged them to keep going, then hovered into a large group selfie. As she departed, a pretty redhead handed her a finely knitted gold crown on blue backing.

"Your crown, Lady Royal." Her cheeks reddened as she curtsied. "I made it for you."

Scottie reached her arm around the girl's shoulders, then held the crown on top of her head. "How do I look?"

The girls, probably ranging from eighteen to twenty-five, cheered, smiling. "Beautiful, Lady Royal."

"I like them," she said to Michael as they headed on down the lane, and she tucked the crown into the clutch Choko had jammed into her hands on the way out. "Can I give them a Royal Warrant?" She looked over at Michael.

"Not sure they could meet any sort of demand, but talk to Her Majesty."

And so it went. All afternoon. Shaking hands. Sampling savory and sweet foods. Then Scottie paused at a stall manned by a fiftyish woman suffering from a disability that prevented her from engaging in real conversation. She kept curtsying and offering Scottie her cookies, saying over and over, "My dog's name is Fred. I feed him the best. We go on walks." She'd reach down to pet the ole boy that was no longer there.

"Fred is very lucky," Scottie said as she purchased a dozen cookies, paying twice the quid demanded.

"She's had a stroke," a woman said, coming from around the back of the stall. "But she loves the faire. I'm Sheba, her daughter."

"Keep doing what you're doing. Our mothers are precious and—" Scottie clipped her words. The kingdom knew Queen Catherine was ailing but not how much.

"We pray for Her Majesty, Lady Royal."

"Thank you. It means so much."

The deeper they traveled within the faire, the more they left the modern world and entered ancient Lauchtenland, where thatched roof row shops, replacing the portable wooden and canvas stalls, lined the winding and even more narrow avenue. Scottie could almost hear the old-time merchants calling to one another early in the morning.

"Oh, a bookshop." Scottie turned inside, sensing all eyes on her. She perused several book tables, then turned to the man behind the sales counter. "Any suggestions of local authors?"

"Yes, um, yes, Lady Royal." The man in neat, creased trousers, white shirt and waist coat slipped a book from a shelf. "A local chap wrote this one. I suppose he'd be akin to your American Jett Wilder."

"Then I'll take it." Scottie had only read one Jett Wilder book, a memoir-like tale about a group of strangers who unraveled their lives while meeting in what remained of a Gilded Age New York mansion, and she intended to read more of his work.

As the man rang up her purchase, he motioned to a woman with long flowing hair and a long flowing skirt who'd just entered. "Love, look, Lady Royal. Might we snag a photo with you?"

Michael stepped forward. "Lady Royal, we should be moving on."

"I think we have time for a photo, Officer Cross."

His eyes narrowed with that fiery look a parent gave to an errant child. She'd hear about this later.

Back out to the street, where the crowd had grown significantly, Michael gripped her arm. "Stay close. Where to next?"

"Eloise Ltd. I promised Eloise Bright I'd visit her shop." She stopped to face him, ignoring the raised phones surrounding them. "Are we good? Everything okay?"

Michael spoke into his com, then motioned for Lennox, whispered a few things to her before tapping Scottie's arm. "Eloise Ltd. is down the lane on the left. Stay close, please."

She stayed close as they passed relatively unnoticed toward Eloise Ltd. Inside the shop, Eloise, with her tamed red hair and fitted slacks and top, greeted Scottie with wide-smile enthusiasm.

"You came, Lady Royal. I wasn't sure you could make it this far."

"I wasn't going to miss your place." Scottie glanced about, her eye falling on one beautiful outfit after another, all displayed like art. She recognized some of the materials she'd been using for lightweight men's slacks. "I love this wool and cotton blend. We find it wears well. And you make these in the Midlands? Have you had any trouble with the sewing process?"

Talking to a designer and clothier transported Scottie emotionally to her home field.

"This is our retail location," Eloise said. "Our production is in The Haskells. You know our story of losing the manufacturing plant of our choice. But we must move on. The kind of space we need is rare and expensive in the Midlands. Yet this is the best place to be for materials, fabrics, labor."

"Do you do bespoke work?" Scottie inspected a display of women's blouses and tops. "I've been pushing for a small women's line to complement our men's fashion. I'd love an option for tailoring skirts, dresses, tops, slacks for women."

"Really, Lady Royal?" Eloise moved in close. "We do a great deal of bespoke work. I'd love to explore this idea. Wh-when would you be available?" Eloise pulled out her phone, tapping the screen, searching her calendar.

Michael stepped up. "Lady Royal's diary is set for the duration." He glanced at Scottie. "Take her card. Contact her at your leisure."

"Yes, of course, of course. I'm terribly sorry—" Eloise scurried to the counter and reached in a drawer for her card. "Thank you, Lady Royal, for thinking of us. I'll look forward to hearing from you."

"I'll be in touch." Scottie slipped the card into her clutch as Michael steered her toward the door. "I can speak for myself, Michael."

"Just doing my job as your equerry as well as protection officer. You can ring Eloise Bright whenever you like but for now, we must keep moving."

It was then the shop door burst open, giving way to a horde of photographers jockeying to catch Scottie's eye first.

"Lady Royal, over here."

"Lady Royal, Lady Royal."

Around her cameras clicked, flashed, and recorded. She heard voices but could not discern from where. With each second, more and more people crammed into the shop, shoving and pushing, calling for her.

"Let's go." Michael. His broad, thick hand that had held hers so tenderly now pressed on her back, moving her forward. Lennox and Schueler collapsed around her. "To the back door."

"Poor Eloise, they'll destroy her—" The back exit was blocked with more photographers and gawkers. The fervor was too much. They were surrounded.

"Lady Royal—Clark Wilson, *The News Leader*." A dark-haired, bespectacled reporter stood on Eloise's sales counter, holding up his phone. "Are you aware that land Eloise Ltd. was to purchase was sold out from under them to Reingard Industries? A deal largely brokered by your dead sister-in-law's father, Lord Cunningham."

"Are you serious?" She took a step back, then her gaze met with Michael's. *Steady*. The best way to deal with this was to face it. "Look, Clark Wilson from *The News Leader*, I've been in this country for all of five minutes. What else you got?"

Laughter peppered through the crowd.

"Lady Royal, here—Perry Copperfield, Cable News PF." He also stood on Eloise's counter. "How do you see your role in the House of Blue? Are you for the expansion of the monarchy or reduction? What do you think of the Family's rival, MP Hamish Fickle?"

"Boys, boys, listen to yourselves." Scottie buttered her words with her southern accent. "I'm just a girl spending time with her mother. Giving her a helping hand. I'm not here for politics."

"But you've engaged several people, including MP Fickle, on matters—"

"Indeed, she has." Hamish Fickle emerged from the crowd like he was lord of all. "I think Lady Royal's here to check out the competition. Steal industry and land from Lauchtens to expand O'Shay Shirts' global brand." He looked at her as if waiting for her to confess.

"Lady Royal has no such intentions." Eloise stepped up. "She's offered to help, even—"

"Don't be fooled, Ms. Bright," Hamish said. "Lady Royal's trip isn't about a long-lost daughter spending time with her long-lost mother. It's about a shrewd businesswoman taking advantage of her new royal connections, of our ailing queen, to expand her American business. As if we don't have enough Americans in places of influence in the House of Blue." Hamish jumped up on the counter next to Clark and Perry. "We aren't going to stand for it, are we?" He pumped his fist over his head. "Go home, Lady Royal. Go home." The chant became wildfire in the crowded shop. "Go home, Lady Royal. Go home, Scottie O'Shay. No more Americans. No more Americans."

Chapter Thirteen

MICHAEL

He had to get Scottie out of here. They were crushed on all sides. RECO activists shouting down monarchy loyalists. This scenario? His worst nightmare.

He barked commands for all officers to clear the alley behind the shop and for their driver to get into position by the back door.

"Clear the way way—" Michael shoved toward the back where Eloise stood terrified.

"Eloise, I'm so sorry about this," Scottie said as she was jostled and pulled from behind. "I'll pay for the damages."

"Lady Royal, please, be safe. I'll get that blooming mob out me shop."

Michael glanced back to see Lennox, then called to the driver. "Tru, we're coming out the back door."

"People…jamming the street." A motor horn blasted over the coms. "Almost there."

Finally at the clear, Michael pressed open the back door and stepped into the sunshine. The alley was an explosion of shouters and haters.

"Lennox, Schueler, have Lady Royal—" He glanced toward them. "Where's Lady Royal? Scottie!" Forget decorum. Forget royal titles and traditions. "Scottie O'Shay, where in blazes are you?"

Charging back into the shop, he grabbed Eloise. "Where is she? Did you stash her somewhere?"

"Me? No. She was with you."

"Except she's not with me." He searched the storeroom and the loo. Had she ducked into one of them to hide?

Back out to the emptying shop, he pleaded, begged to see Scottie pressed against some wall of clothing, frozen with fear. But she was nowhere in sight. "Scottie!"

Out the front and into the avenue, a swift river of a mob flowed toward the northern end of the faire.

"God in heaven, help me find her." And when He did, Michael Cross was resigning his post.

"Michael!" A thin call lifted above the masses.

Scrambling to a lamppost, he leapt up on the concrete base then climbed the post. There. He spotted her. As he jumped off, Lennox and Schueler came running.

"We can't find her." Lennox looked panicked as she gasped for air.

"She's in this mess. Slice through the middle. Use whatever force necessary."

"Yes, sir," and off they went. Michael cut round to the left where the mob had thinned. MP Fickle best hope Michael didn't find him first. What a git.

"Michael? Lennox?"

He followed her voice. While the crowd thinned and peeled away, those that remained compacted, becoming a crushing force. Michael's efforts to thread through from the side met a wall.

Another chant began. "Just like the quay. Just like the quay." Fists pumped over the sea of heads. "Go home, American. Go home."

"Stand aside." Michael pressed in again, sweating, finding it hard to breathe in the airless space. On his right, a uniformed member of the Metro Guard appeared, armed with a truncheon.

Scottie, where are you? She was in this crowd. He saw her from the lamppost but where? At last, he spotted her, her braided hair a tangled mess, the sleeve of her yellow shirt torn. "Lady Royal," he said, low and controlled, as he stretched for her. She screamed and jerked away. "Scottie, it's me."

With a sob, she collapsed onto him and without a thought, Michael scooped her into his arms.

"It's all right. I have you."

"So…scared." Her fingers dug into his shoulder.

"I know, love. I know."

In the distance, sirens wailed. Whistles blew. Instantly the crowd scattered, running in every direction until Scottie and Michael were all but alone in the narrow avenue, Scottie pressed against him, shivering and sobbing.

"Mick, over here… the motor." Lennox motioned to a gap between the shops. "Is she all right?"

"I think so, yes."

They said nothing as the driver sped their way toward Perrigwynn Palace. Scottie pressed against the back of the seat, every part of her taut and trembling, looking as if she might scream. Perhaps she should.

Tears leaked from the corners of her eyes and across the bruise on her cheek. Besides her torn sleeve and ratted hair, she'd lost a shoe.

As for Michael, he boiled with anger and shame. How dare his people treat Lady Royal Blue in this rubbishy manner. Banish the lot of them.

When they pulled into the palace garage, Scottie's trembling hand eased a little and she looked more irritated than scared.

"We will not tell the queen about this." She opened her door and stepped out, hobbling without her missing shoe.

"Lady Royal, I have to file a report."

"Fine. But add in small print 'Don't tell Her Majesty.'"

"Scottie, you have a bruise on your cheek. You won't be able to hide this from her." Michael slammed his door, meeting Scottie at the end of the motor. "She'll find out one way or the other. Reporters were there. It's all film-at-six-and-ten now. Phone videos captured nearly every moment. Blast, Scottie, one of the staff could say to her this very moment, 'Lady Royal almost died in a mob riot.' Wouldn't it be best if you told her before Perry Copperfield scares the wits out of her?"

"I have a bruise on my cheek?" Scottie glanced in the Range Rover's dark glass. "I felt something but—" She peered at Michael through glossy eyes. "What was it you called me? A stir stick? I make a mess of things."

"Yes, I suppose I did. You're the stick the rest of them stir. No one will blame you."

"Who will they blame? You? What about them? The crazies and MP Fickle?"

"Doesn't matter," he said. "I was responsible for your safety. I nearly let Prince John take a bullet, and now nearly I let a mob tear you apart. Look at your clothes. They'll investigate. Unlike the event in Brighton, they won't be able to keep this mob business quiet. It's the quay all over again. I've lost you to a near riot twice now."

"No, Michael, you found me in the midst of two riots."

Michael pointed to the exit for the small garden, the one in front of his palace flat. "Let's go sit. Rest before you see the queen."

Removing her one shoe, Scottie followed him to the bench swing anchored to a large, thick elm branch, the green lawn under their feet, the fragrance of spring flowers seeping into the air. With a push of his foot, Michael set the swing in motion.

She fell against his arm and the ropes of the swing. "I can still hear them chanting. I'm not wanted here. My presence puts people at risk. Most of all me and you."

"Never mind me. I've survived worse."

She was silent for a moment, breathing deep, overcoming her trembling. "You know, I hate when you dismiss me like that. Dismiss my care for you. You may be my protector when we're out there, but when we're like this, I'm your friend. You don't get the high ground all the time, which by the way, I think you're doing with your mother."

"My mum?"

"Maybe it's none of my business, but you can't stay mad at your mom forever. Life is too short. Has she ever tried to apologize? Or do you like that you can hold it over her that she walked out on her husband and sons?"

There was a passion, a truth, slicing as it was, in her words that left no room for debate.

"I thought we came out to the garden to settle your nerves and devise a plan to tell Her Majesty."

"What do you think I'm doing? Settling my nerves by telling you to make it right with your mom."

He laughed softly. "She sort of apologized yesterday when we had tea. But in a backhanded way. Sorry she left but that's the way it had to be."

"It's a start, Michael."

"Why do you care, Lady Royal?"

"Because when you're caught in a mob with people ripping at your hair and clothes and chanting for you to go home, you gain a bit of perspective."

His gaze lingered on her face a moment. "Did your father teach you to speak your mind so boldly?"

"Yes, along with my grandmother, Shug, who is no shrinking violet." Scottie turned to him, the swing still swaying to and fro.

"Thank you, Lady Royal. I mean it." Just like that, his breathing became deeper, easier. Lady Royal was safe. "Purnell was all sugar. But she spoke her mind. She was on me to make peace with Mum as well."

"I'm sorry I never met her."

He nodded, catching a swell of emotion. But if she were, he'd not be here now with Scottie O'Shay firing off truths and wrapping another layer of his affection around her little finger.

"I want to go home, Michael," she whispered into the silence. "I'll tell Kate what happened and call Dad before he freaks out. That's two mobs in two weeks and I need to be home."

"For good? Cut your trip short?"

"I don't know." She pressed her fingers to the corners of her eyes. "As much as Kate needs me, I'm not sure I'm doing much good here. And I miss being the expert on my job. I miss my friends and Dad. I barely know his fiancée. I wasn't raised in this royal world, Michael." She landed a foot on the ground, stopping the swing. "I came because she asked. Because Cap dropped a bomb on me about being in love with his ex-wife. Because I was curious and unsettled, wanting to try on the Blue name. But I'm not a Blue. I'm the American stir stick. The title Lady Royal Blue is not for me."

"I regret calling you a stir stick. You're using it as an excuse. The people cluster to you, Scottie. They want to know you. That's the good of a stir stick. Why not sleep on your decision? Speak with your mother and your father. Then decide."

"I've been thinking about it since I was swept away with the mob."

"We should go, get you inside the palace. I'll retrieve your things from the motor." Leaving Scottie on the swing, Michael walked a few feet then paused in a large drop of sunlight. "I was eight when Mum left. Evan was six. We were the rope in my parents' tug-of-war. The way of the Crosses or the way of the Pratts. When Mum left, I remember thinking, 'A family can end?' Evan cried himself to sleep for weeks. I dined on morsels of fear for breakfast, lunch, and dinner. Yet I carried on, wanting to be the strong big brother. Both parents worked long hours, so we spent a lot of time with our nanny. Eventually Dad took a lesser position in the House of Blue diplomatic core to be more present for us."

"I get it, I do. There's always been a part of me wondering who I'd be if I had my mom. Shug did her best as a substitute. But she was also the grandma who spoiled me."

"Our grandparents loved us but were drawn onto sides. I gave myself to football and running round with my mates. The Cross PF Youth Club was founded and sponsored by our family in the late 1800s, so I had easy access to the pitch."

"We are born into our families, Mick." The last of the Midlands tension vanished at her use of his nickname. "Rich, poor, common, or royal, it's what we make of ourselves, and whatever God-given talent and reason He's given us are the real tricks of life. We must choose to be the kind of people we want to be. It's ours to command."

"Then don't give up on us, Lady Royal." Michael returned to the swing. "Give us boorish Lauchtens a chance to behave properly."

"I don't know, Michael. Maybe this is not where I'm supposed to be."

"If you quit, they win. You don't seem like a quitter to me."

"I'm also not a fool. If Lady Royal was my future, I'd dig in, but right now, I need a taste of home." She stood and without hesitation slipped her hand into his. "Do you understand?"

When she looked into his eyes, he was convinced they were the only two people in the world. "I daresay, I do. I believe your mother will too."

"Thank you." She rested her head on his shoulder, and suddenly the storm of the day seemed worth it. His heart thumped a little faster, a little louder, but he'd not shift away.

Just as he closed his eyes and pressed his cheek against her hair, a loud, piercing ring blasted from his jacket pocket. Scottie bolted upright, eyes wide, and pulled her hand from his. And *poof*, the magic between them was gone.

"Friday afternoon the Midlands Faire was met with a horde of RECO activists and other protestors over the American Scottie O'Shay. 'It was like at the quay,' a man from Midlands Garden said. 'I tell you, that girl is a menace. Lady Royal, ha!' Eloise Bright of Eloise Ltd. claimed she was talking business with Lady Royal in her shop when a mob of reporters and troublemakers barged in. 'It's a disgrace how the RECO party fires people up. My shop was a mess when everyone left, chanting their madness. Lady Royal is a welcomed addition to the House of Blue and Lauchtenland.' We reached out to the Chamber Office for a response but there's been no comment from the queen or the Family."

–MELISSA FARIS, ROYAL REPORTER,
THE MORNING SHOW

"I can't believe I once posted I thought Hamish Fickle was hot. What a louse. Why is he going after Lady Royal? I just saw him on *Tuppence Corbyn & Friends* making an excuse for the RECO riot at the Midlands Faire. He claims he had nothing to do with it, but there's video evidence proving he's a liar. Midlands Garden, do not reelect him to parliament. Anyone else with me on that? Lady Royal, I'm so sorry!"

–@STEFWITHANF ON INSTAGRAM

"I had a blast at the Midlands Faire. It's a tradition in my family. Our own holiday. I missed the hullabaloo. What happened? I'm sorry I missed seeing Lady Royal. I think she's beautiful and amazing."

—GretchenGreen on Facebook

Chapter Fourteen

Scottie

It wasn't often Scottie regretted her decisions, but the moment she dropped her bag Sunday afternoon on the floor of her Hearts Bend living room, she wished she were back at Hadsby Castle.

Falling face-first onto her sofa—the glorious, custom-designed B & B Italian Bellini with its post-World War II design—jet lag, along with the weight of her decision, pushed her deep into the cushions. But she was here now. Time to resolve the regret.

Kate had been shocked by the Midlands Faire uprising, but also remarkably pragmatic.

"What did you think, love? You'd join the House of Blue without controversy? Well, I carry much of the blame. I didn't prepare you. I selfishly thought only of myself."

Yes, she had thought she could join the Family without controversy.

"Why do the people hate me?"

"They don't hate you," Kate had said in that loving-queen-yet-motherly way. "They hate anyone who's not them. They see you as a threat to their plans of toppling the monarchy. We've endured such threats for centuries. Trust me, love. More people love you than hate you."

Kate supported Scottie's wish to go home and arranged for her to fly on Royal One. But she'd made one last plea.

"Will you return for the ball? Please, Scottie."

"Of course. And thank you, Kate."

They'd shared a loving, slightly teary goodbye, and Scottie had flown home Saturday evening.

Still sprawled on the couch, she waited for the relief to wash over her. Instead, she wondered how Kate was feeling and whether Michael had stayed at Hadsby or gone back to the palace. When he helped her onto the plane, he'd bent toward her as if to kiss her cheek. She'd lifted her face to meet him, but he caught himself and stepped back.

"Hello?" Shug's voice echoed from the back door.

"In here."

Scottie sat up as her grandmother appeared through the sunlit kitchen, looking as if she'd just left Sunday lunch with the after-church crowd, and set two grocery bags on the island.

"I thought we'd make cookies." Shug joined her on the couch and gave her an affectionate tap on the leg. "I've seen the news. Are you running away?"

"You've seen the news and that's your question?" Scottie shoved to her feet, fighting a fog of jet lag. "I was caught in a crazed frenzy, Shug. It was terrifying. No, I'm not running away, but I am taking a break."

"I'm sure it was terrifying, but that's no reason to run. You only fuel their engines."

"You sound like Michael."

"Michael? The handsome man who follows you everywhere?" Shug made a funny face. "I'm on Instagram now."

"Yes, Michael Cross. My equerry and protection officer."

"My darling granddaughter, you can deal with people who don't like you. You've been managing that your whole life."

"What are you talking about?"

"Oh, this girl or that one who didn't invite you to her party. Or when you made varsity basketball as a freshman and came home crying because all the girls hated you."

"They did hate me." Scottie crossed her arms. This was not the memory lane she wanted to travel. "And teen-girl angst is not in the same league as a riotous mob."

"No, but small trials train us for big ones. When we got down to brass tacks, those girls thought you hated them. You pushed them away before they could push you."

"How do you have such a great memory? You're old. You're supposed to forget things."

Shug gave Scottie's shoulder a slight swat. "Watch it, whippersnapper, I know where you sleep. Lucky for you, I don't forget things. Do you remember how we solved *that* problem?"

"We had a party and invited everyone."

"And?"

"Okay, Shug, I get it. We became good friends and as a team, unstoppable."

"You won a state championship, but more important, you girls are friends to this day, I believe."

"Yes. And so my life is here, not over there with people I can't invite to a party. Shug, they chanted 'No more Americans. Go home, Scottie O'Shay!' I was conflicted when I first arrived, thinking I should've stayed with Kate, but now I'm glad to be home." Scottie headed for the kitchen. "Are we making cookies before jet lag knocks me out?"

Baking always grounded her after she came off the road—or when one of the clothing lines had taken all her wit and strength to launch.

"I'm never going to be a real royal anyway. Lady Royal is a courtesy title. Kate can bring me along because I'm her daughter, but there's nothing binding me to the House of Blue. My kingdom is O'Shay."

"Are you going back?" Shug joined her in the kitchen, unpacking eggs, milk, flour, sugar, vanilla, baking powder, chocolate chips, and peanut butter chips.

"I am. I promised Kate I'd be there for the Rose Ball. One of the royal jets is coming for me next Saturday. I do love spending time with her, Shug. She's fighting GBS, but there are days the virus wins."

Scottie retrieved the mixer and a couple of bowls. "Oh, I need to talk to Dad. There's a designer—a clothier, really—who'd love to partner with us to make bespoke women's outfits to match some of our menswear. It'd be a real boost to her business. But even if that doesn't work, I could invest in her."

"I see." Shug arranged the ingredients on the counter. "You've not talked to your dad about O'Shay recently?"

"No, why? He's not shutting it down on me, is he?" Scottie laughed and popped a handful of chocolate and peanut butter chips into her mouth. "I Zoomed into a meeting on Wednesday, but we agreed if I was going to do this thing with Kate, I needed to be all in, not worried about work."

"Seems wise. But before you invest in this clothier, talk to your dad." Shug retrieved her oversize bag and her big book of recipes. "By the way, we're gathering at our place tomorrow for a cookout and dip in the pool with Remi and her sons. Then on Saturday some of the family want to have a cookout before you go so don't make plans."

Scottie stilled. "Does it seem weird to see him with someone? To see him in love?"

Shug sighed sweetly. "A little. But it's his time, Scottie. And he's happy."

"Everything's changing," Scottie said quietly.

"Do you remember the first summer we sent you to camp?" Shug asked, handing her an apron. "You were ten or eleven, I believe."

"I thought you were sending me away forever." She was still in touch with a few of the girls from cabin sixteen.

"You called after two weeks begging to come home. You didn't get along with the other girls. Hmm, I'm seeing a pattern."

"Hush. But y'all didn't let me come home."

"All it took was you adjusting to a world where you had to share. As I recall, two weeks later you didn't want camp to end."

"The moral of this story is—" Scottie searched the drawers for scissors to open the flour bag.

"Think of your time in Lauchtenland as camp. What can you learn from it? How can you grow? Adversity is one of life's greatest gifts if we allow it to do its work. How could you turn the tide in your favor? Win over the people. I've seen you do it so many times, Scottie. It's your superpower."

"I'll still have people chanting for me to go home. 'No more Americans in the House of Blue.' That MP, Hamish Fickle—he's got a grudge against the royal family."

"Do they know why?"

"They don't ask questions, Shug. They try to live above it all."

"Then if you're not a legal member of the Blues, you ask. See if you can help. Resolve this issue." Shug dumped two cups of flour into a bowl, sending a white cloud into the air.

Scottie regarded her grandmother, who was not smiling but completely serious. "Shug, the world needs more people like you. But their politics are nothing like ours. This MP Hamish Fickle is not interested in hearing from me. He seems determined to end the monarchy."

"That's small thinking, Scottie. You don't know the answer until you ask. Back in the day, your grandpa had a sales rep who constantly stirred up trouble. Fritz wanted to fire him, but he was one of our best salesmen. Lots of experience. He gave us good notes on our designs."

"What'd Fritz do?" Scottie cracked two eggs into the bowl.

"He decided to be that man's friend. Took him to lunch without the rest of the fellas. Called him up when we faced an important decision. Then one day, he took his shot. 'What's troubling you, Martin?' And the man told him."

"What was it?"

"On the surface, it was something about our commission structure. However, deep down, Martin was hurting. Nothing to do with O'Shay. Fritz made changes to the way we paid commissions, and Martin started calling your grandpa just to talk. He became our champion. Landed accounts no one else dared touch. He clocked thirty years with O'Shay. Our Martin leather belts are named after him."

"He's that Martin?"

"Yes. And because of your grandpa's kindness, Martin righted what was wrong inside. When he died, four hundred people crowded into the church to say goodbye."

"So you think Hamish Fickle is my Martin?" It was a stretch. She barely knew the man. He didn't work for her. They had no personal beefs, other than her Blue blood. She didn't know Lauchtenland ways or culture well.

"I think you have a shot with this fella if you care to take it. Take a page from your grandfather's book."

"It's not that simple, Shug. For one, my Martin is a member of parliament. Two, I can't go around the Chamber Office, the House of Blue, and the Privy Council to have tea with the man. I'd be seen as involving myself in politics, which could blow up in my face and cause the Family all sorts of problems."

"Who said anything about politics? And my darling grand-daughter, what do you think every state dinner or royal ball is about?" Shug leaned close. "Politics. Now, let's bake cookies."

It was late when Shug left. They'd made four dozen cookies, eaten at least a dozen with large glasses of milk, ordered a roast chicken with all the sides from Valentino's, and watched a rom-com.

It was good to be home, with all the feels. Yet Shug had opened doors in Scottie's thinking. Could she, as an American Blue, actually have a role in helping the Family—or even Lauchtenland itself?

Still, as Scottie climbed into her bed, she was eager to return to Kate and Hadsby, to finish what she'd started. She reached for her phone, found Michael's number, hesitated, whispered a short prayer, then composed a brief text.

> Scottie: Hey Mick, I was wondering…would it be possible to get a private meeting with Hamish Fickle?

With a deep breath, she hit Send.

MICHAEL

The pitch was green. The sky, blue. The slipping breeze cooled his warm skin. And he was running toward the goal in the father-son match between the Cross PF club and the Highgrove Sports League. As the ball arched toward him, a winger raced his way—a brutish teen with thighs like tree trunks and his eye on the ball. But this play was Michael's.

"Mick, back post!" Piers, or maybe Evan, calling from the sideline.

"Go, Uncle Mick. Go!" Unmistakably Finn.

He avoided the teen as the ball dropped toward him, planted his right foot then launched, swinging his left leg round and snapping his foot, sending the ball over the goalie's head and into the net.

Michael celebrated, arms in the air, running, shouting, dropping to his knee and sliding toward midfield where his teammates, young and old, piled on top of him, patting his head, his back, his chest.

The goalie, an old uni mate, shook his head. He'd been good back in the day, but he now carried an extra stone or two. *Sorry, not sorry, Baker.*

Words bandied around and through him.

"Well played, old man." This from one of the sons on their team.

"Sport, where've you been? We need you." From a father.

The referee blew his whistle. "Time, lads, the match is over."

"Uncle Mick, smashing." Finn ran across the pitch to give him an energetic fist bump. "Uncle Mick, Uncle Mick, Uncle Mick."

Evan slapped Michael on the back, knocking out what little breath remained in his lungs from the ninety minutes of play. "You're his hero."

"Only in football."

The opposing team came round for congratulations, admiring Michael's scissor kick goal, then the old men moaned about their throbbing knees and bruised ankles.

After gathering his gear from the sideline, Evan came alongside. "Pints at the pub? Finn's going home with the Baker boys, so I have time to myself. Piers, are you buying pints at Pub Clemency?"

"No, but I'll join you for one." Piers dropped his kit bag next to Michael. "Listen, mate, I know you don't want to hear it, but you're wasting your time with the HMSD. If you go to the diplomatic core, you'll fare no better. Even worse if you sign up for the stuffy offices of Pratt Printing—no offense, Evan. You're a football man. Cross football needs you. No one's really managing the club. We don't even have a mascot. Come on, man, take up the call of the pitch. It is a Cross club after all."

"You know there's no career for me in football. That ship has sailed." Michael dug his phone from the zippered pocket of his kit bag. He was waiting for a call from MP Hamish Fickle's office. So far, nothing. He slipped his phone back into the bag.

"I'm not asking you to play for the Capitals. I'm asking you to take the helm here. Use your training and skills to expand the club. You're stellar with the boys. They'd swing from tree limbs if you said it'd make them better footballers." Piers picked up his gear, slinging the strap over his head. "I'm not fooled about your financial and social status. The Cross and Pratt coffers can easily afford you a lovely place in downtown Port Fressa overlooking the bay. I don't know why you live in that palace flat. You can't entertain there."

"You assume I'm interested in entertaining." Michael replaced his spikes for his trainers and zipped on a Cross football club hoodie with a glance toward his brother, who was fixed on organizing his kit.

Piers didn't know about the decreased Cross coffers. It was reputation not wealth that maintained the family name and status. Funds for the Cross Football Club and the three Cross grammar schools came from a strictly managed trust.

On the Pratt side, Michael had money left by his great-grandparents. Clocking two years with Pratt Printing enabled him to participate in the profit sharing. He could easily take on managing the club.

"Fine, Michael, mate of mine, but think about it." Piers hoofed toward his motor, tossing over his shoulder, "See you at Pub Clemency and I'll buy the first round."

"He's not wrong." Evan scooted toward Michael. "You look happy on the pitch, big brother. As for the kids, you're a flame and they're your moths."

"That's a little poetic for you. You seriously think I can leave Her Majesty's Security Detail to run round on a pitch with eight-to-fourteen-year-olds? I'm one of the few Cross men still in her service. Dad is practically holding down the diplomatic edge on his own."

"Mick, you have a right to live your life. But Mum's got a point as well about how the decisions made by our Cross ancestors a thousand years ago, even two hundred years ago, govern our lives. It's the twenty-first century, for goodness' sake. Do you think our twenty-first great-grandfather would hold us to his ancient ways?" Evan puffed out his chest and lowered his voice. "'Carry on for a thousand years in the same way as we do now in our stone castles and chapels, freezing to death in the winter and smelling like rotgut in the summer.'"

With a laugh, Michael started for the car park. "You think the Pratt line is any different? Mum never misses a moment to prod me to join her family line." He tossed his bag into the boot. "I'm not being stubborn, Evan. But I—" He breathed in, trying to form the words. "I feel called to do what I'm doing. Yeah, maybe for some allegiance to our Cross heritage, but it's more than our name or reputation. It's something I feel here." He patted his chest. "I'll stay true until that feeling goes away."

Why didn't Evan understand? Did he not sense what Michael sensed when he studied the Cross catechism? Every young Cross man and woman studied Lauchten and House of Blue history every summer during their teen years. They could teach college professors. The Cross family were the treasure keepers, the keepers of the gospel, holding fast to the stories the rest of Lauchtenland forgot. But in the last twenty years, the family willing to take on the life of a Cross had dwindled.

When he'd proposed to Purnell, she understood his devotion to duty. She sensed it was more than an assignment. It was a way of life. The Cross life.

"I don't know why you hang onto it all," Evan said. "How are you different than any other former Special Forces chap who joins the HMSD? Does our name really carry prestige?"

"She called me when she wanted an equerry and protection officer for Lady Royal. And yes, because of my Cross name." Without it, he'd have never met Scottie. "Besides, one day, I may be the only Cross left in service to the Crown. If you ask me, the last man standing is every bit as important as the first."

In the eighteenth century, a whole line of Cross uncles, aunts, cousins sailed to America. In the nineteenth century, typhus and smallpox ravaged Lauchtenland. The Cross dynasty was not immune. Add to that, the simple attrition of a thousand years. Families moving away. Families with no sons and their daughters marrying into other ancestries where, after generations, their Cross heritage was forgotten.

In the 1920s, one Cross recordkeeper lost his family's documentation in a fire. Then his two sons were killed in the Second World War.

No, Michael must stay the course of the Cross. It would take Emmanuel Himself coming down from the mountains, fragrant with the woods and smoke, to tell him otherwise.

"I never felt called to Cross service like you," Evan said. "Tracy and I decided together Pratt Printing was best for our future. I'm fine with you rejecting Mum's offer. I get it. But Mick, there's more than one way to be a Cross man. What if a Cross man upholds the youth football club our great-great-grandfather founded? It was one of the first football clubs in this part of Europe, other than Great Britain. Do you realize a Cross man or woman hasn't run the club since the 1950s? No Cross has ever been superintendent over our three schools. Serving the community is serving the Crown."

"We should go," Michael said, opening his car door. How could he make them understand? His calling was more than the Crown way. It was the Crown *and* the Cross. "Piers will be on his second pint and plate of chips by the time we arrive."

Evan tapped Michael's shoulder. "Think about it."

"I do, little brother. More than you know."

Michael climbed into his late-model sports car, which had been a luxury spend after a surprise inheritance from a distant cousin. He'd drive this motor to his grave.

Turning out of the car park, he considered his phone, hoping for a call from the MP's office. He'd rung up yesterday morning, requesting a meeting. The little troublemaker best not let Scottie down. Michael felt a personal responsibility to make her wish come true.

Also, he missed her. Something known only to himself. The afternoon on the pitch proved a lovely distraction. Yet now that he was alone for half a second, his feelings surfaced. He longed to see her face, peer into her deep blue eyes, then let his gaze slowly drift to her soft, supple lips. Not that he'd tasted them or ever would. But a man could dream.

He flashed on a memory of Purnell. "Sorry, love." Of course he knew she was gone to a place with no sorrow, and she'd want him to get on with life. Yet pieces of him hung onto her memory.

At Pub Clemency, he lucked into a parking spot near the door. He'd just cut the motor when his phone beckoned with a Private Number. When he answered, a stiff voice said, "Hold for MP Fickle."

Michael snapped to attention. Finally.

"Cross, Hamish Fickle here. You called seeking an audience with me."

"Actually, Lady Royal Blue requested to speak with you. She's been away but will return Sunday morning."

"My office on Wednesday, ten a.m. My aide will send details."

"Thank you, sir." Calling him *sir* felt unjust, but the man was a member of parliament, duly elected by the people of his district.

"What's this about, Cross?" Hamish filled his voice with force. "I'll not be mocked."

"To be honest, sir, I don't know. However, I doubt Lady Royal has any intention of mocking you."

MP Fickle rang off and Michael stepped out of his car, wondering what Lady Royal actually intended. There'd been a quick and thorough investigation of the Midlands Faire disruption, and several protesters were arrested. MP Fickle pulled his political strings, and the lot of them were released with a slap on the wrist two days later.

As for Michael, the HMSD performed their own investigation. Thanks to the testimony of Lennox and Schueler, along with the eyewitnesses at Eloise's shop, Michael was cleared. Again.

The press spun the story as if Lady Royal was accidentally caught up in a political march. But everyone present that day knew she had been targeted.

From now on out, the Chamber Office would not announce any of her appearances.

Her Majesty Queen Catherine offered her support, assuring Gunner Ferguson that Michael was still the man for the job.

Outside Pub Clemency's door, he texted Scottie.

Michael: Meeting with MP Fickle Wednesday morning, 10:00.

Scottie: Thank you! Did he say anything? Ask why?

Michael: He wondered if you were going to mock him.

Scottie: Mock him? I want to talk. So, am I being foolish? Risky?

Michael: Probably but sometimes things don't change if things don't change.

Scottie: Well said, Cross. What are you doing while I'm away?

Missing you.

Michael: Paperwork. Playing a bit of football.

Scottie: I felt your smile when I read you were playing soccer. Did you demonstrate ye ole scissor kick?

Michael: Scored the final goal of the match with one.

> Scottie: Show off. :)

> Michael: Finn was thrilled. What about you? How are you filling your days?

She'd left late Saturday after the Midlands Faire incident. Six days and forever since he'd seen her. Since the scent of her perfume carved a new memory for him.

> Scottie: Work. Ha! Going into the office, brainstorming the spring line while making sure the fall launch is set. Winter is almost in the can. For some reason, I'm the only one in all of O'Shay who knows how to write a tech pack. #Jobsecurity.

> Michael: But you are returning?

> Scottie: Yes. I miss Kate. I miss you Lauchten lug heads.

> Michael: She'll be delighted to have you home.

So would the lug heads.

> Scottie:…

Michael waited but the three dots never changed.

> Michael: I miss you. Do you miss me?

There. He'd said it. Of course he didn't send it. But now it was out of his system.

After the Rose Ball, she'd return to Hearts Bend permanently and he'd take on a new assignment. Because it was his calling, his lot in life.

One day down the line, he might meet a lovely woman. Fall in love. If so, they'd buy a tiny cottage by the sea, raise a baby or two, God willing, and he'd rest easy at night knowing he'd carried his cross dutifully.

The fact that it quite possibly cost him the love of Scottie O'Shay would be a distant, bygone memory.

CHAPTER FIFTEEN

SCOTTIE

Saturday as she lounged by Shug and Fritz's pool, Scottie read a book and jotted thoughts and questions on her phone nates app for her meeting with MP Fickle.

But none of it distracted hers from Dad, who was in love, snuggling his fiancée, Remi, in the shallow end. To be honest, it was a bit much, but he'd not stopped smiling.

Remi splashed Dad and he laughed, dunking her under. Were a couple of sixty-somethings allowed to act like teenagers? Remi surfaced with vigor, hopped on Dad's back, and tried to push him below the smooth, cool surface, but instead, Dad circled her around to his chest and drew her in for a lavish kiss.

Scottie ducked behind her book, the one by the Lauchtenland author. She'd never witnessed Dad as a romantic being. Never saw him as a man with sexual desires. Yes, she was thirty-eight years old and not unfamiliar with being a lover, but this whole scene tilted her world.

Worse, she was jealous at the idea of sharing Dad's attention. Since she'd arrived, he'd barely talked to her beyond a hello hug and kiss on the cheek.

Meanwhile, over by the grill, Grandpa Fritz chatted with his brother, Uncle Walt, who'd recently been widowed. His three children were out and about in the world, with no interest in O'Shay Shirts. Uncle Walt lived in north Florida after he retired as VP of Sales.

Aunt Leanne, Fritz's younger sister visiting from Boston, walked from the kitchen onto the white pool deck, a sarong wrapped around her waist, her blue one-piece bathing suit reminding Scottie of the 1950s Hollywood starlets.

"I'd tell your dad to get a room, but it's kind of fun seeing him in love." Aunt Leanne stretched out on the chaise lounge next to Scottie, a mai tai in one hand and a thick Danielle Steel read in the other. "So, how's our princess? I hear you're going back?"

"For a few more weeks. There's a ball I'm to attend. And I'm not a princess, Aunt Leanne."

"Good. Don't let them peel the O'Shay off you. We're strong, independent women. Movers and shakers."

"So are the Blues," Scottie said.

Leanne O'Shay Neuheisel had cut her marketing teeth at O'Shay Shirts, but when Grandpa Fritz promoted an O'Shay cousin to director of marketing, Leanne resigned, moved to Boston and founded one of the nation's leading headhunting firms. All five of her children now worked for Neuheisel Co.

Other than Cousin Blake, who headed O'Shay's human resources, the O'Shays had moved on. Now the future of the company fell to Scottie. She'd never seen it more clearly than this past week.

From the moment she'd walked into the office, she was bombarded with questions, drawn into meetings, brought up-to-date on the End of Fiscal Year profit projections, informed of work force adjustments, and regaled with how Jack Gillingham, Veep of Marketing, averted a disaster while on a commercial shoot.

The rest of the week, she was at her desk by seven a.m., working until nine p.m. At home, she microwaved a semi-healthy frozen dinner, sipped on a small glass of wine, watched a rerun of *Family Ties*, and fell asleep on the sofa.

She'd wake up in the wee hours and head to her room, envisioning the Princess Charlotte suite. She missed afternoon teas with Kate and walking with her along the cliffs when she felt strong. She missed the cry of the wind slicing up Whistlecrag

Bluff and the sound of Michael's voice when he met her in the Grand Foyer.

Kate had texted several times but never informed Scottie on her health or asked when she was returning. Cranston sent a message and, in his kind, devoted way, implored Scottie to return.

> Cranston: Lady Royal, you bring her such joy and joy is healing.

> Scottie: I'll be there Sunday. Thank you, Cranston.

"Refill anyone?" Shug came along with a pitcher of icy sweet tea and paused to peer toward Dad and Remi. "I've not seen Trent like this since Kate. I wasn't sure I'd ever see him in love again. A man's broken heart doesn't heal the way a woman's does."

Wait. What? Scottie leaned toward her grandmother. "You saw Dad and Kate together? In love?"

"Yes, she lived with us when she was pregnant with you." Shug set down the tea pitcher and sat on the other side of Scottie. "Well, the last four months, anyway."

"She lived with you and Fritz? I thought she was in Nashville."

"Who said? She was here. You were born in this house, Scottie. Hmm, guess that's another thing we never told you. Didn't want you asking questions. The second suite upstairs was Kate's. Her dad, the king, sent over his personal doctor and nurse for the delivery. They lived in our guesthouse until you came quietly into the world."

"Oh, that's right. Scottie, you were so quiet we thought you were dead," Aunt Leanne said. "You never made a sound. Sort of like a hiccup, wasn't it, Octavia?"

"Wait, wait, wait. Aunt Leanne also knew my mother?"

"I always thought she mewed, like a kitten," Shug said.

"I mewed?" She'd never heard any of these stories. In the first grade when LaToya Dixon told her babies were delivered by storks, Scottie believed it. She must have arrived by a bird's beak because she didn't have a mother. And no one ever told her otherwise until she learned about the birds and bees.

"I only saw her once. From a distance. I did *not* know your mother was a crown princess." Aunt Leanne shot a wry glance at Shug. "That secret was kept in a vault."

"We couldn't tell anyone." Shug sat back, sipping her tea and bringing her sunglasses from her head to her eyes. "You were the most beautiful, sweetest baby, Scottie. I thought I'd break into a million pieces when Kate realized her father was not going to let her bring you home. It was one thing to not marry Trent, a whole other thing to leave you behind."

"Looking back, perhaps it was a good thing," Aunt Leanne said. "Scottie is heir to O'Shay. Who knew the daughter of a princess would be the last O'Shay in Hearts Bend to take over?" She leaned to see Scottie. "We're all counting on you."

"Don't put pressure on her, Leanne. You never know what the future holds. O'Shay may not be around forever."

"It will as long as Scottie has breath in her lungs." Leanne huffed and puffed in her chair. "Kick butt and take names, Scottie. Marry that hunky Army Ranger, Cap. I liked him."

"Me too. But he's going to marry his ex-wife."

"His ex-wife. Well shut the front door. Did you have a clue?"

"No, but don't worry, he wasn't my true love."

"Maybe she'll meet a handsome prince at the Rose Ball." Shug tossed Scottie a wink. "You always fancied yourself a Cinderella."

"All the princes of the North Sea nations are married or too young. Besides, I don't think any of them would want to move to Hearts Bend. And I never, ever fancied myself a Cinderella."

Where did people come up with this stuff?

A splash in the pool followed by a yelping laugh closed the conversation as Dad cannonballed in front of them. "Get in the pool!" he said. "How about a game of water polo? Men against the women."

"On your own head be it," Shug said. "You have Fritz, Walt, and Fletcher. I have Remi, Scottie, and Leanne."

"Exactly," Leanne said, tossing off her sarong and adjusting her suit, tugging at her wrinkled arms. "We float. You don't."

After Dad and Leanne set up the net and argued about the rules,

Leanne called for a girls' strategy meeting. Scottie headed over, but Dad gently pulled her aside.

"Hey," he said softly. "We haven't had much of a chance to talk. You doing okay?"

"Yeah, I am." She glanced toward Remi. "It's kind of weird seeing you in love but—"

"You'll always be my favorite girl." Dad chucked her chin with his finger. "You know that, right?"

"I'm happy for you. Honest. I can see she loves you very much."

"Are you okay going back to Lauchtenland? I don't like you being caught up in these protests. What's going on? Some group trying to end the monarchy?"

"It's a small but loud contingent." She kept her meeting with MP Fickle to herself.

"You don't have to go back, Scottie. Do you feel safe?"

An image of Michael flashed across her mind. "Yeah, Dad. I'm safe. Really safe."

"Okay then…you still going to be my best girl at the wedding?"

That's when the volleyball bonked him in the head and Remi taunted him to get in the pool. Dad ran down the deck and dove into the deep end, surfacing with his in-love smile.

Scottie felt every one of his movements in her soul. The plunge into the water, headfirst, then surfacing into sunshine, into love.

All her life she'd followed in Dad's footsteps. She was his mini-me. They talked about life and sports and O'Shay Shirts, about her education and how she'd one day be in command. Yet at this very moment, Dad revealed a whole other side of himself. Scottie was undone, wanting nothing more than to follow him once again and plunge headlong into love.

But that was impossible.

Michael

The steward at Blue Hall, 03 Row Clemency, led Scottie and Michael down a wide corridor, past the portraits of former MPs looking sternly through the glow of ornate wall sconces. The carpet was plush and bound by the House of Blue cypher.

He glanced over at Scottie. She smiled, which made his heart beat faster. She seemed different to him. Lighter? As if she'd let go of an unseen burden.

"Do you think Hamish Fickle realizes everything holding Lauchtenland together comes from the House of Blue?" she said. "That the Crown defines us as a people, as a nation. The demise of the Blues would mean the demise of Lauchtenland."

"I'm not sure he's thinking about anything but his own career."

Her hand brushed his, and a small chill crept up his arm. He must put his feelings in check.

"Do you have your notes of what you want to say?"

"Yeah, but I really want to talk from here." Scottie tapped over her heart and Michael admired her all the more.

The steward stopped at a gold and mahogany door and led them into a square, paneled room with groupings of tables and chairs, a row of windows with heavy damask curtains, and a portrait of Queen Catherine on the western wall.

"Would you like some tea?"

"Yes, please." Michael aimed for a set of chairs. "Where is MP Fickle?" The man should be in the room waiting, tipping cream into his own cuppa.

"He'll be along shortly."

Scottie sat in a dark red club chair with thick arms and deep buttons punched through gold tapestry. "Now I'm nervous."

"Don't be. It'll only make you waffle when Fickle shows himself." Michael paced to the window. "He's playing games. Making us wait."

"I was so confident about this when I asked to meet him but now—"

"Scottie, hang onto that confidence. Don't let him get into your head. Have you mentioned this meeting to the queen?"

"No, I was afraid she'd demand I cancel. Besides, she looked relaxed and happy when I came back. The appointment with Kimbra this morning to fit my ball gown provided a solid cover as to why we trained down to Port Fressa."

"Two birds, one stone," Michael said, loving the plural pronoun we.

"I really want to find out what MP Fickle is about," she said.

"We shall see. This could go poorly and—"

"Don't say it." Scottie made a face, looking toward the steward entering with the tea trolly.

Michael fixed himself a cup at the trolly along with Scottie. Their synchronized movements were a kind of domestic symphony—the clatter of the tea kettle lid, the dollop of cream, and the *tink* of the stirring spoon. If he weren't in this dark, slightly stuffy government house, he might be in his own living lounge with his wife.

He glanced at her, the question "Did you miss me?" on his lips, but he dared not ask. Even in jest. Professional lines and all. But he'd missed her. Very much.

It took him six months to truly fall in love with Purnell, so this short time with Scottie presented no serious threat. His affection was nothing more than a crush. Easy to tumble in. Easy to tumble out.

"At least the tea is good," Scottie said, still standing beside the trolly, cup and saucer resting on her palm. "Michael, when I was home, I realized how much I need to be there. I have more to learn from my father. My Aunt Leanne reminded me I'm the last O'Shay to take on the company, which is something we've never really talked about. Of course there's no pretense of a life for me here. Kate's offering much more than an honorary title but—" She shrugged off the last of her answer as she looked over at him with her blue eyes. "I can visit a lot, though. I want to help Eloise Ltd."

"I came to the same conclusion. I'm not a Pratt man. I'm a Cross man, and I must cling to my Cross heritage despite Mum's pressure. There aren't many of us left serving the House of Blue. But if I choose to leave, I can serve the Cross line with the football club or one of our schools."

"Well, look at us. Arriving at our futures the same week. You're not Pratt. I'm not a Blue."

The door swung open and Hamish Fickle entered. "Sorry to keep you waiting, Lady Royal. MP business." He beelined for the tea trolly.

"I appreciate you taking time from your busy schedule to meet with me."

"You presented a great temptation. No Blue has ever taken the time to meet with me or any Fickle. My curiosity got the best of me." Tea and cake in hand, Fickle chose a chair and sat.

Michael retreated into a corner, making himself as invisible as possible, but his eyes and ears were tuned to Scottie, Fickle, and the whole bizarre setting. But Scottie waved him into the conversation, pointing to the seat next to her.

"You don't mind if Mr. Cross joins us, do you, MP Fickle?"

"Not at all. This is your meeting."

Scottie set aside her tea and took the seat opposite Fickle. "What was that crazy business at the Midlands Faire? People could've been seriously hurt, including me."

"For change, sacrifices must be made. The Lauchten people want to be heard. The Crown and the government—"

"Both of which butter your cornbread."

Michael hid a grin behind his teacup. This was fun.

"We have to take to the streets, Lady Royal. It's unfortunate things get out of hand from time to time."

"Speaking from a marketing perspective, MP Fickle, your branding stinks." Scottie stood and leaned over her chair as if ready to do serious business. "Rabble rousing, shouting down the royal family only collects the lunatic fringe. You want change? Act like you've been there before. Show you have an ounce of intelligence."

Fickle darkened for a moment but quickly fixed a smile in place. "Wise words. I'll see what I can do."

"Do you think Her Majesty is going to one day wake up and think 'Daggum, ole MP Fickle has a point. A thousand years is a long time for one family to sit on the throne. I think I'll throw my rule over to him and his undisciplined, loudmouth RECO party?'"

Fickle rose slowly, a sharp glint in his gaze. "How dare you come in here and lecture me. What business is any of this of yours? Have you asked about the shenanigans of your brother's first wife, Lady Holland? Manipulating the Reingard Industries deal behind closed doors? And you. The queen's dirty little secret. She tried to elevate you with the flimsy, archaic title of Lady Royal, but we all see through it. If you called this meeting to spout your stupid American wisdom, I think we're done."

Michael moved beside Scottie, eyes on her. Eyes on Hamish.

"No, we're not done," Scottie said. "The marketing advice was only a free preamble. My real question is simple. What's behind your beef with the Blues?"

Fickle's shoulders collapsed, but then he caught himself with a laugh. Surprisingly without his trademark mockery.

"You want to know my beef with the family Blue?" Hamish descended to his seat. "Let's begin with our government formed in the name of a monarch."

"As are most constitutional monarchies."

"I want a government formed by the people, for the people. My poor uncle died giving a speech supporting Queen Catherine and the monarchy. Assassinated. Fickle loyalty died with him."

"I'm sorry about your uncle. But are you saying the queen and the House of Blue are not for the people?"

Fickle seemed a bit taken aback by the question. As if he'd never considered it before.

"I sometimes wonder, yes."

"Listen, MP Fickle, a government for the people and by the people has plenty of its own issues. But Americans know how to work with our issues. We're formed, I suppose, in the name of our Constitution, which gives rights to the people. So we duke it out. At least Lauchtenland is formed in the name of a family. One that's been good to the people. A family built on traditions but also restricted by laws. Lauchtens don't know any other form of government. I've done my research. Post-World War One Europe tried to form republics only to fail. Do Nazi Germany and fascist Italy ring a bell?"

Fickle fell against the back of his chair. "So that means we can't succeed?"

"Do you hear that, Michael?" Scottie turned to him then back to Fickle. "Classic redneck thinking." She came around to sit in her chair, arms on her thighs, shoulders relaxed. "One Bubba watches another Bubba jump from a building without a net. When he lands splat on his face, the first Bubba goes, 'He didn't do it right. Watch this.'"

Michael choked, spewing a bit of his tea. "Begging your pardon," he muttered, reaching for a white linen napkin. Whatever Scottie's aim for the day, she was owning the pitch.

"Our cause is nothing like your American rednecks." Fickle, stiff and offended.

"So you think," Scottie said. "Can you answer my original question? Why do you hate the Blues so much?"

"For one, I still contend Princess Holland was behind the Reingard deal stealing the land out from under our own Midlands' Eloise Ltd. But put that aside. The reason that propels me is—" Fickle fired from his chair and walked off, hands in his pockets. "All right," he said, whipping around to Scottie. "I'll say it. The House of Blue *stole* everything from my family." The confession stuck in the air. "Sent us into two hundred years of poverty we're just now climbing out of, barely, by using our wits. My wits. But the damage was done. All that was ours, lost, gone, never to be regained."

"What are you talking about, Fickle?" Michael said. "Where's your proof? Or is this your fabricated backstory to justify your venom against the royal family?"

"I have none," Hamish said. "Yet."

"Because there is none." Michael glanced at Scottie. "The House of Blue is the most documented family in Europe. We'd know if land was taken unfairly. I daresay if you're a representative of your ancestors and land was taken, they probably deserved it."

"You sit there so smug with your Cross name and reputation despite the family's decreased wealth, squandered by your ancestors. Yes, I know about your financial downgrade. You still have your homes and land. But the Fickles were left destitute. Not little by little, not by choosing to give away our wealth, but with one stroke of a pen. The Midlands belonged to the Fickles. We broke our backs plowing the rockiest soil on earth and turning it into farms and fields. We built the town, laid the cobblestone." Hamish aimed his speech at Michael. "We mined the minerals and the gemstone, didn't we?"

"And the House of Blue took it away? For no reason?" Scottie said.

"Lock, stock, and barrel. Every dust of dirt, every bleating sheep and lowing cattle, the crops, the shops, the mines. All of it."

"Then there should be a record of ownership." Michael pulled out his phone to make a note. "Something in the archives. Do you have a date?"

"Why would they do such a thing?" Scottie said. "What was the reason?"

"Other than the traditional reason of greed and envy, we know of none. The Fickles were prospering outside the aristocratic circles, eclipsing the no-good dukes and earls relying on their titles for possessions and wealth. Only we weren't titled. Just hardworking commoners, proving what you Americans proved, Lady Royal. A hardworking man can go from poverty to riches in a lifetime."

"Where is this novel you quote, MP Fickle?" Michael said. "I'd love to read it."

"Every word is true. Our ancestors have passed down the story from generation to generation."

"I need names and dates, bill of sale, land deeds." Michael tapped out another note on his phone, wondering if his father knew any of this.

Hamish raised his chin as if to guard against an accusation of lying. "That's the thing...our records were lost in the Midlands fire."

"How convenient." Michael tucked his phone away. Fickle had crossed the Rubicon. A fire? Meanwhile, Scottie watched Fickle with intensity.

"Tell me what you know," she said.

"All right, since you've asked. My seventh great-grandfather could buy and sell half the Lauchten aristocracy. He was a philanthropist. A man of faith. He was becoming friends with King Rein the Second. Then in 1821, the government started levying taxes and fees against the Midlands. Exorbitant ones. My great-grandfather paid for his family and workers and most of the shopkeepers because if he didn't, they'd have gone to debtors' prison. Next, the government took land on some trumped-up charge that we didn't properly possess the Midlands. My ancestor appealed to King Rein to no avail. More land was taken. The levies increased. By the 1860s, nothing was left. That once wealthy man, Nicolas Fickle, died in poverty, as did every son and daughter after. It was only in the mid-1900s we began to see daylight."

"And this is the source of your venom?" Scottie said softly. "The House of Blue didn't stop the land grabs and the taxes?"

"For all we know, King Rein the Second was behind it. He certainly didn't stop it."

"Why have you never approached the queen on this matter?" Michael said. "Instead of the last five years of constant criticism on some chat shows and social media. You look a fool, ole chap."

"Maybe because I'm dealing with fools. I tried for an audience with Her Majesty my first term in parliament. But I was stonewalled."

From his pocket, Michael's phone buzzed. He ignored it. "If you want this matter resolved, MP Fickle, I suggest you bring proof. Act like a sane, caring citizen of Lauchtenland instead of a man bent on burning it all down." Another notification from his phone. Michael glanced at the screen, then gently reached for Scottie. "Lady Royal, we're done here."

CHAPTER
SIXTEEN

"**M**ichael I wasn't done in there." Scottie matched his long strides toward the Blue Hall exit as he ordered the motor to come round to the side door. "I was hoping to end with an action item."

"He has one. Find the proof."

"What is wrong with you? Who texted?"

"Nothing's wrong. It was time to go. You represented yourself and the family well, Lady Royal. You set MP Fickle on his heels."

"He set me on mine. He's as loyal and fierce about his family name as you and I. It's admirable. Michael, what was on your phone? I only ask because once you looked at the screen, you changed. Was it something about Purnell? Your family or Finn? Is everything all right?"

"Lady Royal, everything is fine." His shoulders relaxed as he spied one of Perrigwynn's protection officers outside the door standing by the car. "To the train station, Lou. We're headed back to Hadsby."

Once they were on the road, he glanced over at her, smiling. "Sorry to yank you away if you weren't ready. I could see he was bowing up for a fight. You've opened the door. Let's see if he walks through."

She dozed on the train ride to Dalholm. The royal car was like a five-star hotel with plush seats, an attendant and food service.

Back at the castle, Michael left her in the Grand Foyer and

headed to the Operations Room. Watching him go, Scottie noted his slightly muted demeanor. Something was off with him, but was it for her to ask, "What's wrong?" For now, she must hurry. Kate was waiting, she'd figure out what later.

"I'm sorry to keep you waiting," Scottie said, pausing to see Kate dressed so casually. "Trainers and a jogging suit. Are you going for a run?"

"A run? No. Not since I was a girl. But I am feeling better." Kate fixed a cup of tea for Scottie. "I hear you had an adventurous morning. My secretary sent a photo of you going into Blue Hall."

"News travels fast." Was that why Michael left the Grand Foyer so abruptly? "I asked Michael to set a meeting with MP Fickle. Am I in trouble?"

"Not necessarily." Kate stirred cream into her tea along with a packet of sweetener. "But I'd like to know why you involved yourself with Lauchten politics? I think you've been around enough to observe our stance on political interference. The Crown has a strict code, a way we handle things, Scottie. The Prime Minister and I are in touch at all times. MP Fickle is the government's to manage, not ours. We have enough of an uphill battle with the people to accept you without you venturing into politics. Heaven knows what MP Fickle will say now."

"I was curious," Scottie said. "Why haven't you met with him? Asked why he's so hateful toward the monarchy? You've met with other members of parliament before."

"I suspect it's because MP Fickle needs to grow up. He's tried to pull us into political situations with the North Sea Island Alliance we do not feel is best for us. He should sit down and listen, learn."

"Kate, he said nothing about an alliance. He claims King Rein the Second stole land, property, shops, mines from his ancestors. The House of Blue, according to Hamish Fickle, spiraled them into poverty. Michael asked for proof, but Hamish said they lost their records in a Midlands fire."

"I know well enough about the history of the Midlands fire," Kate said. "Evening embers from a blacksmith's shop fell on dry kindling and half the town burned while the other half slept. It took decades to rebuild. Did Hamish Fickle mention the House of Blue contributed large sums from our personal coffers to rebuild the Midlands? Because those lands have always been ours, not his."

"Why don't you meet with him? Share stories. Tell him your side of the truth."

"My side is the truth." Pronounced. No doubt. Queen Catherine not Kate, her mother, now sat at the table. "Meeting with him will accomplish nothing. I've experience with these things. Also, the House of Blue never explains. To do so will make it seem as if the crown is defensive or worse, placating Fickle. He'll go on the first chat show and declare to the world Queen Catherine tried to justify whatever he deemed to be our sins."

"He's probably already blabbing about me."

"Yes, but let's not give him any more fodder, Scottie. I want your time here to be peaceful and pleasant. So far you were nearly pushed into the quay, saved a woman who accused you of starting it all, then caught in the Midlands melee." Kate pressed her hand to her heart. "Right now, I suffer more from worry over you than the GBS treatments."

Scottie reached for her hand. "I'm sorry I didn't tell you about the meeting. I thought I was helping, doing something you couldn't, but I was out of line."

"It's all right," she said. "As a mum, I'm a bit proud. You acted with courage today. Now, tell me, how's your gown coming along for the Rose Ball?"

So the Fickle conversation was over. Scottie sighed with relief. "Kimbra is a genius," she said. "The lavender fabric and lace are stunning." Scottie took a bite of cake. "Kate, you never told me you lived with Shug and Fritz before I was born."

"To be honest, Scottie, I've pushed so much of that time out of my mind, I probably forgot."

"Shug said hearing you cry when you handed me over to Dad haunted her for years."

"Sometimes I do think I hear that wail from way down inside.

But I believe in healing, Scottie. That we can move on from our deepest pain."

"We seem to be doing that now," Scottie said. "What about you father? Did King Rein ever want to meet me?"

"I asked, even begged, but he suspected I merely wanted him to see you knowing his tender heart would break and allow you home. As I've said, Mum was silent on the subject. I'd broken all the rules. However, behind closed doors, I wonder if she fought for me. Every now and then, I'd catch something of an argument coming from their room. Mum used words like 'little girl' and 'family.'"

"Now that little girl is making trouble for you."

"As all good daughters do now and then."

"I'll try to behave, but Hamish Fickle chaps my hide." Scottie polished off her tea. "Don't you want to know why he has so much animosity?"

"If he's justified in any way, the truth will light. In other news, the Dalholm Chief Constable along with the Detective Chief Inspector interviewed half the Old Hamlet and a good many in the New Hamlet. No one claims to know anything of a man or woman holding onto you while you saved Mrs. Johansdotter and her daughter. There's nothing on the quay cameras."

"I guess there's no way to make our request public."

"You'd have a thousand claiming to be the one."

The door opened and Edric, the king consort appeared, dressed head to toe in his outdoor gear, his hair wild and long, with a bushy beard covering his cheeks.

"Am I allowed in?" he said, removing his hat. "I've been missing my wife terribly."

"Edric, you're home. I thought you had another week." Kate rose from her chair with more ease and strength than Scottie had seen since she'd arrived. Edric caught his wife in his arms for a kiss.

Scottie looked away with a thought of Michael. What? No. Not thinking of Michael. Good grief.

"We caught nothing," Edric said, approaching Scottie for an

embrace. "We endured non-stop rain the last eight days, and Jacob Mercer never met a bar of soap he could *not* resist." The king consort reached for a plate and large slice of cake. "I thought to myself, 'Why am I sitting here when my beautiful, clean, sweet-smelling wife awaits me at home.' Scottie, love, it's good to see you. Thank you for looking after my queen." He sat in the nearest chair to devour the cake. "Am I allowed to sit? I'm famished."

"Of course, darling." Kate reached for the in-house phone. "I'll ring Cranston, have a sandwich and soup brought round. Edric, I am so thrilled you're home."

"I'll leave you two to get reacquainted." Scottie recognized her cue to skedaddle. "Welcome back, Edric."

In the corridor, she texted Michael.

> Scottie: Want to go to the Belly of the Beast?
>
> Michael: Didn't you just have tea with the queen?
>
> Scottie: Didn't eat much. The king consort is back. She wanted to talk about why I was at Blue Hall. I'm wondering that myself. Craving Ernst's chips.
>
> Michael: You mean Stella's?
>
> Scottie: Funny, yes. Meet me in the Grand Gallery.

MICHAEL

He was belowdecks in the castle's dark Operations Room with its bank of CCTV screens, talking with Dad about his personal MP Fickle action items, when Scottie texted.

"Dad, I have to run." He shoved back from the desk, still pressing the old black landline receiver to his ear. "I've an appointment with Lady Royal."

"Understand." Michael used to loathe Dad's stock answer to, well, everything. Yet in recent years, he realized his father wasn't using that term frivolously. He truly understood. Even if he disagreed. "A final word on Fickle. I wouldn't trust a syllable out of that man's mouth. He's nothing short of a political hack."

"True enough, but not about this, Dad. Lady Royal hit the right button and out it came, the whole palaver about high taxes and land confiscation. He seemed sincere, even a bit humbled, by her inquiry."

"Well," Dad said with his signature exhale. "I'll look into it for you, but I seriously doubt there's any meat on those bones."

Out the door and up the stairs, Michael was glad she rang. Glad to hoof it down to the pub with her. Glad to be anywhere with her.

Making his way to the second floor Grand Gallery, Michael braced for what he'd begun to dub the Scottie flutter—the movement in his chest when he heard her voice or clapped eyes on her. Rather annoying, one might say, but easy to endure. He'd almost rid himself of the sensation while she was home in Hearts Bend, but the moment she stepped off Royal One, it returned with jet boosters.

To be fair, the flutter indicated his heart was more than the cold rock he'd been carrying behind his ribs since Purnell's final breath. For that he was a bit grateful.

Ah, there she was by the old bookcase tucked into an alcove. *Breathe deep, mate.* But Scottie's smile only made those invisible wings being to flap all the more, and with the wispy light from the window crowning her hair, she looked somewhat like a vision.

"What are we up to, Lady Royal?" he said, pushing a casual tone into his voice. "Why are we meeting here? Not to jump from a window, I hope. Or sneak down a trellis. I must insist we take the stairs."

"Very droll, Mr. Cross. We *are* taking the stairs." With a sly look, she pulled a book from the shelf. "These stairs." The bookcase became a door, revealing a lightless lower level and a spiral set of narrow iron stairs.

"The secret, secret passage?" He laughed, drawn instantly into the mystery and adventure of it. "When or how did you discover this?"

"Prince Gus showed it me during my first visit to Hadsby. But you must keep our secret. I'm only showing you because you saved my bacon twice and escorted me to see Fanatic Fickle. Otherwise, it's for royal children and a few choice friends only." She flipped the light switch, igniting a bare white bulb that did little to dispel the darkness.

"I see. Well blow me down, I'm a friend of Lady Royal Blue." The stairs creaked with every descending step.

"You might need me, come the revolution," Scottie said. "Rather, I might need you."

"You jest, but given MP Fickle's animosity toward your family—"

"—he'd gleefully lead a revolution?" Scottie glanced back at him. There was enough light to see the purpose in her eyes. "We'll see," he said. "Maybe you started a path to truth by visiting him. Blimey, it's dark. Where are we going?"

They kept going by the light of their phones until a door appeared at the bottom of the stairs. It was locked with a keypad, but Scottie punched in the numbers.

When she turned the knob and pushed, nothing happened. She tried again to no avail. "Rats. Gus said it got jammed sometimes."

"May I give it a go?" Michael reached round Scottie and with one muscled shove, the door relented. He glanced at Scottie, her face, her lips inches from his. "There. It didn't take much." He breathed in her skin, her hair, the fragrance that fanned the wings of the annoying flutter in his chest.

"I, um, loosened it for you," she said, leaning close.

"No doubt at all."

"We should—" She nodded toward the palace grounds where the late afternoon sunlight turned everything to gold.

Michael tried to speak but he had no words. Only what he *felt*. Which was passionate and dangerous.

"Go," he whispered. "I'll follow."

Scottie took a step into him. "I'll follow you," she said, her eyes on his lips.

Don't, ole chap. Don't. Yet his heart drummed too loud for his ears to hear. He slipped his arm around her waist.

"Now what?" His voice was husky, a sound he'd not heard since… Had he ever heard it?

"Come to our senses?" Scottie rested her arm on his shoulder, her long frame leaning a bit more.

"That would be prudent." Michael traced his finger across her forehead and down her temple. "But where's the fun in prudent?"

"We might say you're my protection officer. Or that I'm going home after the ball and you still love Purnell."

"You argue for prudent then?" Despite a drip of disappointment, he raised her chin so he could see her eyes. So he could read what her soul was really saying. "I argue for the here and now, this moment, with the golden light on one side, the cover of dark on the other."

"Then kiss me if you dare."

Michael wrapped her in his arms as he lowered his lips to hers, kissing her with a slight brush of his lips. As the moment lingered, Scottie locked her arms around him and raised up the few inches she needed to kiss him back. First with a breathy tenderness, then a fiery passion. He gripped her jumper and fell against the metal doorframe, lifting her up so all her weight, all her burdens, were on him.

His fingers found the ends of her hair. In the distance, the sunny wind carried the crashing sound of the sea against the rocks and the call of a seagull.

Every inhale only deepened their glorious connection and for a moment, he believed there to be no end. Find him here, dead and gone, nothing but bones, locked in her embrace.

However, the thunder in his chest stole his breath, so he lifted his head and settled his hands against her face. "Hey." Soft and low, his voice only for her.

"Hey," she replied, her warm breath brushing his chin before she rested her head against his chest. "I can hear your heartbeat."

"I can feel yours."

Then the magic of the moment began to fade a little. He was tempted to stir it again with another kiss, but could they really stand in the castle's secret doorway kissing all night? No matter how much he wanted to do so.

Scottie raised her head. "I guess we should…go. To the Belly of the Beast."

"My dear Scottie," he said. "I think we're already there."

He memorized her laugh to replay long after she'd gone back to Hearts Bend.

They started across the castle grounds toward the woods, the door to the secret passageway closing behind them. Michael glanced back to see if the door was actually there.

"It's cold," she said, shivering, hands dug deep in her jumper pockets. "Don't you ever have summer in Lauchtenland?"

"One day in July," he said, snatching her in his arms, wrapping her tight, caring not a whit if anyone saw them. "But you'll be in Tennessee."

"Let's not go over it all again. You're a Cross. I'm an O'Shay. End of story."

"The beginning and the end with one glorious kiss in the middle." One he'd experience in his dreams again and again.

Through the woods to the secret gate, they entered Centre Street toward Wells Line. Michael's hand bumped hers once. Scottie's bumped his twice. "Sorry," they'd whisper to each other, but step-by-step, the taste of her kiss and the vibration of holding her in his arms burned into him. Michael needed a tall pint to cool his blood. If he ever felt like this before, he had no memory. And mates, he'd remember such passion.

"Yer royal!" Ernst greeted them, coming out from the bar, wrapped in his signature apron. "Sit. Table." He pointed to the corner. "Stella! Fish. Chips. Pints."

Michael reached round to hold Scottie's chair, feeling more like a boyfriend than an equerry-slash-protection officer. He had to shake off this sensation.

"I love Ernst," Scottie said, scooting up to their corner table. "He's amazing."

"He knows more about Lauchtenland and the House of Blue

than anyone I know, except my dad. We should make him an honorary Cross."

Scottie leaned toward him, elbows on the table, her blue eyes so bright. "Do you think he knows anything about the Fickles?"

Michael made a face. "Maybe. But let's keep this to ourselves for now." In time, he'd let her in on his plan.

"Pints. House." Ernst patted his chest with one hand while setting down two tall glasses with the other. "Lady Royal, honor." He took her hand in his and planted a fat kiss on her knuckles.

Scottie gave him her attention, not pulling away. It was well known that Prince John and Prince Gus were friends with the Belly of the Beast proprietor. The big man with the broken speech was winning over the queen's daughter as well.

"There. Rough." He pointed in the direction of the scuffle at the quay. "Folks. Lost minds. Safe here."

"Ernst, do you know who may have held my legs that night? I reacted so fast, reaching for Mrs. Johansdotter, I didn't consider I could go over too. But two strong hands held me in place."

"Indeed. Hand. God. Emmanuel." He pointed toward the window, toward the direction of the western cliffs where a large hand had been carved into stone by time, wind, and rain. Or as legend declared, by God Himself.

"Ernst," Michael said. "Are you saying the Hand of God held onto Scottie?"

"Aye, mate. Aye."

CHAPTER SEVENTEEN

"I don't understand. We're back to this Emmanuel character." Scottie sipped from her pint, roaming her attention from Ernst to Michael, who seemed as close to her as their kiss in the secret doorway.

She could still feel his arms around her. Still taste the sweetness of his lips.

Ernst patted Michael's shoulder. "Chapel. Find. Maybe?" Off he went toward the kitchen, stopping at every table along the way, delivering one-word greetings.

"Okay, Mick, interpretation please," Scottie said. "What's he talking about? What's this Hand of God? What chapel?"

"You know Lauchtenland has three unique phenomena, right? Surely the queen has informed you. One is the eight cathedrals in Port Fressa that, when lit, form a very distinct shape of a heart."

"Yeah, the Heart of God," Scottie said. "I've seen it. Gemma showed me from the top of the palace my first Christmas. She experienced the lights firsthand when she married John. It really moved her."

"People make pilgrimages to Port Fressa to stand in the light of the Heart of God. There's also the Hand of God, which is here, in County Northton, at the Northton Cliffs. Centuries ago, shipwrecked sailors climbed to a carved-out hand in the sheer rock when their vessel shattered on the channel rocks during a storm. Miraculously, they survived the sea, scaled the rough rock face,

184

and found shelter. 'The Hand of God saved us,' they claimed. When you're out in the channel, you can see a large, distinct hand with four fingers and a thumb."

"Have you seen it? Can you climb up to it?"

"I have seen it though I've not climbed up. I believe Prince Gus and Princess Daffodil climbed the step pathway to the cleft in the rock. But does the Hand of God actually rescue people? I cannot say. Ernst believes the real Emmanuel's hands held onto you that night."

"How does he know? Did he see Him?"

"Ernst knows. He and Emmanuel are connected. He referenced the chapel, in the Highcrest Mountains. Maybe we'll find Him there."

"What chapel? Can we go?"

"The Wenthelen Chapel was built almost five hundred years ago by King Magnus the Third for his illegitimate daughter Wenthelen. It holds our third phenomenon. A filigree and glass spire called the Eye of God."

"Am I to seek Emmanuel at this chapel named for an illegitimate daughter like me?"

"You're not illegitimate, Scottie."

"Only that my parents weren't married and my mother, an unwed crown princess, could not recognize me."

"You're recognized now. Wenthelen has all but faded from our history. We know she was born in 1530 to Magnus and a woman named Crystobell," Michael said. "History tells us Magnus loved her, but for political reasons, had to marry a Danish princess. Wenthelen was excluded from Family and Crown succession. Magnus had three sons and secured the House of Blue throne."

Scottie felt a sudden warmth toward this woman from centuries past. "How has she faded from history? You don't know what happened to her?"

"Only that she married in 1549 and had a passel of children."

"How can you not know more about the child of a Blue king?"

"No records. If there were any, they might have been destroyed or burned in a fire. Fires were not uncommon in days of open fireplaces, thatched roofs, and wood shingle siding. Fickle's claim that they lost records in a fire is very plausible."

"Kate told me how the Midlands fire started."

"Lauchtenland experienced quite a few blazes over the centuries. Hadsby's had a couple of fires. Even Perrigwynn, but none that affected the fireproof Archive Room."

"So she had no title? No royal life?"

"None that we know."

"Like me?"

"Like you, well, until now."

"Why is the spire called the Eye of God?"

"Legend says that at some moment known only to Emmanuel, the spire will light up and beam down onto a simple altar where fresh bread and wine are set out daily. The beam will illuminate the Highcrest Mountains all the way down to Hadsby. After a spire lighting, the churches and cathedrals overflow on Sunday mornings for months, even years. The Eye of God has not appeared in decades. Possibly no one alive in Lauchtenland has seen the Eye of God."

Scottie sat back to absorb it all. "So, let's visit this chapel." She reached for a chip, but she was hungrier for Michael's answer.

"Not sure how. There's no road to the chapel anymore, only a climb up the mountain. The legend is real enough, but my father reminds me that Ernst is always full of crazy Emmanuel stories. He'd have everyone in Lauchtenland seeking Him if he had his way." He leaned toward her. "We can go, call it one last fun adventure before you go home. But Scottie, all this to discover who held your legs?"

"Someone held onto me, or Mrs. Johansdotter, her daughter, and I would be dead."

"Don't get your hopes up, lass, for finding this mystery chap, please." He reached for her hand. "Sometimes mysteries are just that…mysteries."

"I know, but when you started telling me about Wenthelen, I felt it here." She patted her middle. "Like she's my sister. Five hundred years older, but still… She was a love child like me. And now she has a chapel where God's eye beams down. Fable or not, I have to see this place." Scottie glanced at her platter, the fish and chips barely touched. She was too full of curiosity about this ancestor the House of Blue also rejected.

"Then we'll go. Maybe we'll discover she confronted the number one nemesis of her time as well." He laughed, but Scottie considered his point.

"MP Fickle's great-times-seven-grandfather. Or grandmother."

"Wouldn't that be a tale to tell. Now eat your fish and chips," Michael said, tossing her a playful, albeit sexy, wink. So much of her time in Lauchtenland with Kate was as expected, minus the mobs. However, meeting Michael Cross was *not* expected and, despite her promise to Dad to return home the girl who left, she changed every time she was in the presence of this Cross man.

The conversation settled over fish and chips, with Scottie asking Michael for a date to hike to the chapel. Michael promised to do research then add it to her diary first chance.

Afterward, they chatted about nothing and everything— favorite songs and movies—and not refusing two large slices of Stella's chocolate cake.

It was during her final bite of cake that Scottie realized when she went home, Michael would go back to Port Fressa for another HMSD assignment, perhaps falling in love with another Purnell. He'd kiss her like he'd kissed Scottie in the doorway.

She swallowed a taste of jealousy. She didn't want him to kiss anyone else like he kissed her. To hold anyone like he'd held her. To make *her* feel as wanted as Scottie felt.

Pushing her cake plate away, she observed him as he answered a text on his phone. He was handsome but not in a way that put a girl off. Cap was good-looking and rugged with an interesting, expressive face. Michael's features approached perfect, if one could use the term for any human, yet he was so strikingly imperfect.

"Mum," he said, tossing his phone to the table. "She can't let go that I'm more a Cross than a Pratt. Once again, she's appealing to my age and any possible vanity about my future—" He stopped, making a face. "Why am I bringing you down with my venting?"

"Did she text at Fickle's office?"

"Am I becoming so obvious?" He grinned. "Yes, again, that's not why we left. Fickle was digging in. Mum's text proved a fortuitous tool to pretend something pressing was on your diary."

"I suppose you're right," she said, sighing. "I'd hoped to get something actionable out of him." She looked in his eyes. "By the way, you look like you stepped in poo when your mom sends a text. At least when I think it's her."

"Poo? Really?" He laughed softly, exhaling, relaxing his shoulders. "I'll work on that then. Now, what were we talking about?"

"I can't remember. Isn't that nice? Shug used to say there's nothing better than frivolous chitchat among friends. It frees the soul."

"I'd like to meet this Shug one day. She sounds enchanting."

"Enchanting?" Scottie laughed, missing Shug a bit. "Hardly. She's the quintessential strong southern woman who takes no flak from anyone yet loves her family and friends with the fire of the sun."

"How lucky to have been raised by her," Michael said, his comment undergirded by the sound of a small band warming up. Michael waved the proprietor over. "Is this new? Live music?"

"Yes. You." He pointed to Scottie then Michael. "Dance. Ildlys." He clapped his hands, and patrons at the center tables began to shove them aside and stack the chairs on top.

The band's dissonant sound of the guitar and fiddle warming up turned the Belly of the Beast into a Hearts Bend barn or backyard where the melodies of Appalachia met the whine of western music. An upright bass and a bodhran joined the set, along with an accordion.

Suddenly the notes came together, and the Beast's patrons began to stomp and clap. Couples migrated to the floor, hands clasped as they danced side by side in skilled, specific steps.

"What is this?" Scottie said. "Ildys dance?"

"Ildys is an old Danish word for firelight. It's a dance for the out of doors, under the stars and around a fire, but Ernst's big fireplace will do."

Michael took her by the hand to the dance floor. The lights dimmed and thousands of bluish bulbs glowed from the heavy timber beams holding up the Belly of the Beast.

"The stars," Scottie whispered.

Michael tucked Scottie by his side, his left hand around her waist. "Take my right hand with yours. Put your left hand on mine resting on your waist. Now, step forward with your right foot, rock back on your left, then we turn to the right. Step forward and rock back."

She tripped the first two turns, learning the music and the feel of Michael. She laughed softly as he encouraged her, his warm breath in her ear.

"Turn under my arm," he said. "Now you're on my right side, step forward with your left…there, you got it, love."

The movements were melodic and romantic with couples peering up at each other. Scottie locked eyes with Michael's, only breaking her gaze when she turned under his arm for the next iteration of the dance. On and on it went, the couples moving around the floor in a large circle.

When the song and dance ended, Scottie was facing Michael, his arms firmly about her. All around them couples kissed and hugged, several gave a whoop and returned to the sidelines to see what the band played next.

But Scottie and Michael remained locked together, his gaze so intent she felt captured, unable to move. His attention drifted to her lips, and she ached for him to kiss her. But if he did, then—

"We should go." She pushed out of his arms, away from the romance of Michael, the music and the dance, and the tug of a world not her own. "Even though Edric is there, I need to check on Kate."

Cutting through the tables and chairs, she burst into the clean, cool air swirling through the street where the afternoon light gave way to the purplish light of evening. She breathed deep, clearing her head, clearing her heart.

"Scottie, wait." Michael came after her.

She whirled around to him. "We forgot to pay. We should go back and pay."

"I'll pop round later," he said, concern in his eyes. "Talk to me."

"I wanted you to kiss me in the doorway, Michael, and again after the dance, but let's remember who we are and what we're about. We're not a couple of teenagers on summer break, going back to school soon, only to fall in love with someone else."

"I wanted to kiss you every bit as much."

"Then let that be the first and the last." She swerved toward the sound of an old steamer boat horn, the large vessel drifting toward the quay. The lights, the sounds, the scent on the breeze…Kate and Hadsby…Michael…they were all becoming a part of her. "We're breaking all the rules."

"Do they matter so much? I'll request reassignment—"

"Yes, Michael, yes, they matter. I've lived my life by the rules. They held me, kept me safe when the pieces of my story didn't make sense. In Hearts Bend, I know who I am. But here?" She looked away, shaking her head. "Here, I don't. So yes, the rules that govern my heart matter very much."

They arrived in silence at the gate in the woods. Michael punched in the security code and Scottie headed off through the trees, stumbling over roots, crashing into low branches, aiming for the castle's front door, bypassing the secret of the secret passageway, leaving the taste of Michael's kiss among the flora and fauna.

"Yes, Perry, Lady Royal came to my office. Wanted to know why I'm a republican. Why I think the time of kings and queens is over. She was completely out of line and I'm wondering if the whole reason she's here, with an old title dug out from the moth balls, is to tug on the people's emotions regarding our history, to find out what I'm about and bring down the RECO party. The House of Blue is using their American relative to do their dirty work. This business of staying out of politics when the Family is the head of the country is ludicrous. Our very government is formed in Her Majesty's name. You cannot be more political."

–HAMISH FICKLE ON CNC: CABLE NEWS CHANNEL WITH PERRY COPPERFIELD

"I applaud Lady Royal for asking that bloke Hamish Fickle for the skinny. I'd like to know the answer meself."

–@LADYROYALFAN ON IG

"What do my wandering eyes see but Lady Royal and her equerry doing the romantic Ildys dance at the Belly of the Beast. It's a grainy shot but you can see it's her."

–@ALLABOUTGOSSIP ON TIKTOK

MICHAEL

He was trying to distract himself and failing. Sitting in the football stands on his day off, watching Finn on the pitch seemed the perfect elixir. But the effects were taking too long to kick in.

He relived the moment Scottie turned away from the Belly of the Beast and started up Wells Line. It stirred an old, familiar feeling, and he determined to be rid of it forthwith.

She'd been right. They were breaking all the rules. He was certainly betraying the code of a protection officer. Yet deep down, their conversation in the middle of Centre Street forced him to realize he was not enough for her. Not enough to change course. To consider him as part of her future.

"Finn's becoming an exceptional player." Michael glanced round to see Dad squinting against the afternoon sun as he made his way up the stands. "Think he'll stick with it? I couldn't get you off the pitch at his age."

"He seems keen," Michael said.

"He takes after his Uncle Mick." Dad whistled and applauded, calling for Finn to take a shot on goal. Which he did, and the ball soared into the top left corner of the net. Finn's clever approach to the net caused the goalie to go to the right.

Michael leapt to his feet, along with Dad, cheering. Football was *his* world. How he grounded himself. Forget the royal household and duty and the beautiful American daughter who'd marked him with her kiss.

Football brought him back to his center. The scent in the stands. The fragrance of the pitch. Even the aroma of sweaty lads after a rough match raised his sentiments.

In his youth, Dad and Evan, along with his Cross grandparents, cheered him at every match. For Evan, they all sat for cricket games and plays at the local theater.

These thoughts surfaced as he watched the Cross PF Youth lads take it to the boys from The Haskells. He blamed Scottie's kiss for all this ruminating. It'd done something to him.

"Dad," he said. "Have I ever thanked you?"

"For what?" Dad rose up, eyes on the pitch, ready to cheer. Piers's son just tackled the ball. "Thataway, lads," Dad shouted. "Nick the ball."

"For being there for us. For not punting us off to boarding school."

Dad looked down at Michael. "I loved you boys with everything in me. You'd been crushed enough by your mum. I wasn't going to send you away to some cold, rigorous, albeit elite boarding school where mates your own age became your family and filled your heads with foolishness. We were a family, with or without Mum."

Michael stared ahead. "Thank you, Dad. Ev and I owe you one."

"No, you don't. Well, hold on, pay me back by getting on with your life, Mick. I worry about you."

"I'm fine, Dad. What about you getting on with your life? Lady Royal's father is near your age and he's marrying for the first time."

"We're not talking about me. We're talking about you. I saw the business about you and Lady Royal. A chap from the diplomatic showed me a dark video of you—" Dad's whole body tensed as Finn dribbled the ball through a couple of defenders with skill. "Have a go, lad! Put it away!"

But Finn, in stride, crossed the ball to his teammate, who sent the ball between the goalie's legs.

"From twenty yards out," someone called.

"Brilliant," Dad shouted, hands cupped around his mouth. "Well done!"

Michael's pride swelled. Finn could've taken the shot, but he crossed to his mate. Not only was he a skilled player, but he was also a top-drawer teammate.

In celebration, the Cross PF lads carried Finn and the maker of the goal away on their shoulders.

When Finn spotted him, Michael gave his nephew a nod with a thumbs-up. The team always came first. One could not keep the ball for himself.

That was it, then. He must consider the team—the HMSD, Lady Royal, Her Majesty, and the entire House of Blue. Tonight, he'd put in a request for a transfer to another assignment. Lennox was more than capable of finishing out Lady Royal's stay.

As the family gathered in the car park, Dad called out, "Burgers on me. How about Fletcher's?"

Finn whooped—Fletcher's was his favorite—and begged to invite his best mate.

"Hurry on, then," Dad said, then turned to Evan. "Meet you there."

Michael walked with Dad to his Audi. "Can I ask you something?" he said. Of course it was rhetorical, so he went on. "Why did Mum leave? Why couldn't she have worked for Pratt while you carried on with the Cross tradition? Why weren't we enough? Evan and me? To make her stay? She never came round much once she'd gone."

"It wasn't you and Evan, Mick. It was me. I wasn't enough for her." The Audi beeped and blinked as Dad aimed his key fob. "I should've talked to you boys about it when she left, but I was hurting, angry, and afraid I'd say things you didn't need to hear. I tried a few times when you were teens, then I thought, 'The boys are settled. Don't stir the calmed waters.' As for Pratt, your mum didn't think she'd be more than a mid-level manager. She was frustrated but loyal to the family."

"The Pratts and Crosses have that in common."

"Then her grandfather retired, and her father crowned her his successor. Shocked the company and the family, he did. Jeanette jumped in, sinking in up to her neck. She loved it. She secretly feared her uncle, Hugh, would stage a coup in favor of his bungling playboy son. A woman had never headed up Pratt." Dad patted Michael's shoulder. "I don't think she intended to leave you and Evan behind. It just happened. She lost all interest in being a Cross woman or helping maintain tradition."

Michael considered his father's answer, fitting his words into the blanks of his understanding. Then he patted his old man on the shoulder. "How about this, Dad? You work on finding love again and so will I."

"Really?" Dad said, surprised. "Are you ready? Are you saying Lady Royal is—"

"No, not Lady Royal. She's going back to Hearts Bend. Her life is there and mine is here. But I think I'm ready to try again. Purnell would want me to fall in love, marry, have children."

"You may not want to hear this, son, but be glad you found out Lady Royal's intentions before you gave her all of your heart, not just a piece or two." Dad reached for his car door. "As for me? I'll give it a go but give me a head start. You've a larger selection of women to choose from and I daresay, more recent experience."

Michael laughed and offered his hand. "Deal."

"Ah, this jogs my memory regarding our phone conversation." Dad reached inside his motor for a folder and handed it to Michael. "I did some digging in the archives and couldn't find evidence to corroborate Hamish Fickle's claims. I doubt they have any merit. However, my assistant came across an old ledger listing Wenthelen Chapel as home for some obscure records. I checked with Royal Records, and they said there's nothing to it. But if you want to find your way up to the chapel, might be worth a look. If nothing else, get a nice hike in the woods, see how the old chapel is standing."

"They've still not fixed the roadway up to the chapel?"

"Not that I've heard. The Family, the Blue estate, nor the Royal Trust haven't accessed the chapel in decades, which, on the balance, seems rather odd, given its royal and historical significance. The only way to the Wenthelen Chapel, and the Eye of God, is climbing a mountain pathway."

Michale opened the folder that contained a single parchment carefully preserved and sealed in Mylar. The ornate script had faded yet clearly denoted that records had been moved from Perrigwynn Palace to Wenthelen Chapel, August 1643.

"A treasure hunt." Michael glanced at his father. "You think it's worth it?"

"That's for you to decide." Dad pointed to an old-fashioned map behind the document. "Follow the red line. See you at Fletcher's."

Michael sat in his motor, the engine idling, reversing his previous resolve. He'd not be resigning tonight. Once more, Scottie would get her wish. First, she'd requested a visit to the Midlands, then to meet Hamish Fickle, and now Wenthelen Chapel.

The "stir stick" was moving things in an interesting direction. Who knows, maybe they'd run into Ernst's friend, Emmanuel, God with us.

Chapter Eighteen

The vibrations of her kiss with Michael and the dance at the Belly of the Beast lingered with Scottie as she got on with the business of being with her mother and stepfather, enjoying afternoon walks across the grounds before afternoon tea, dining in Monarch One, followed by reading and listening to music in the Queen's Library.

She'd not seen Michael since leaving him on the edge of the woods. Apparently, he'd gone to Port Fressa to see his nephew's soccer game. She was sadly relieved yet oddly missing him. Still, she determined to regain her focus, which was not Michael Cross and his kisses but her mother's love.

Friday afternoon Scottie's calendar reminded her of the O'Shay executive team Zoom call, so she popped in to hear how the end of the fiscal year was shaping up.

Dad, Jack Gillingham, and Cousin Blake were in the office, while CFO Doug Langford and Vice President of Sales, Tricia White, were in Boston.

Everyone was surprised to see her. Odd. Why shouldn't she attend a senior staff call?

"I'm still a member of the executive team. I'll be home in a few weeks."

The meeting seemed rather benign until Jack leaned for his coffee cup and Scottie saw a reminder on the meeting board.

Fairness Option—Revised

Goldman / Morgan call Tuesday 3 p.m.

"Dad, Doug," she said. "Why are we revising the fairness option?"

Dad shot Jack a stricken glance, making a face. "Routine, Scottie. The board asked for one."

"Routine? That's a three- or four-hundred-thousand-dollar ask for nothing."

"Scottie." Doug Langford leaned toward his screen. "We noticed Boston Brothers is now our third-largest shareholder. The fairness option is the board's way of letting them know they don't have the funds to buy us out."

Scottie exhaled at that point. "They tried this before. Why aren't we buying them out?"

"We've talked about it," Dad said. "How's Lauchtenland? How's my princess?"

"Dad, please, I'm not a princess. I'm thinking how one day O'Shay Shirts will own Boston Brothers."

On Sunday, she picnicked with Kate and Edric, Arabella and William, and Rachel and her new male friend, Constantin von Thalberg, a handsome aristocratic friend from the Duchy of Hessenberg.

Any remaining cares of why Dad okayed a new fairness option blew away with the North Sea wind. As they should. Initial reports indicated O'Shay Shirts was set for record profits.

What didn't blow away was the memory of Michael's kiss and how easily she returned to that moment in the secret passageway. She felt his hand around her waist as they danced under the LED stars wrapped around the beams of the Belly of the Beast.

A few more days and she might rid herself of her feelings for him, but he messaged her Sunday night about a trek up to Wenthelen Chapel to find some forgotten documents.

> Michael: We might find evidence for or against Fickle. I'll go alone if you don't care to hike up the side of a mountain. I'm leaving at six a.m.
>
> Scottie: I'll meet you in the Grand Foyer.

No way was he making that trip without her. She ignored the twist of excitement at seeing him again.

The car ride up was comfortably quiet with Michael filling her in on his father's discoveries and what they could expect from the chapel.

"It might be a heap of stone, rotting wood, and broken glass for all we know."

He was easy to be with as always, but there was a cool distance about him. They stopped at the one and only outfitters at the base of the mountains for food and water, ruck sacks, hiking shoes and poles for Scottie, head lamps—"Do we really need these?"—a machete and shovel, matches and socks.

The climb began easily enough but as the late morning sun hit its peak, she was hot and tired, climbing through an overgrown trail with Michael in the lead, his arms taut as he swung the giant machete through brambles and branches.

"Hey, Cross," she called, reaching for a low branch, minding where she planted her foot. "Go ahead and confess. Hamish Fickle paid you large sums of money to kill me."

She paused to rest against a tree, adjusting her heavy rucksack. The climb had started at about a twenty-five-degree angle but increased around each bend.

"We're off to solve the Fickle mystery as you requested. Carry on, Lady Royal."

"Michael?" He paused to look down at her, his expression serious. She smiled, dismissing what she wanted to say. That in another world, under different circumstances, she'd fall madly in love with him. But they weren't in that world. They were in this world, under these circumstances. "Thanks for helping me do this."

"Of course." He faced forward again, the muscles in his shoulders shifting as he sliced another vine out of their path. "Take care on the rocks. They're slippery."

She leaned on her trekking poles and planted her next step. "Do you think this will give us any clues to the Fickle mystery?"

"I have minimal hopes, Lady Royal. But it's a good place to start."

They climbed higher as Michael cut a path around the hill. When they broke into a small clearing where the sunlight fell through the trees, she said, "Can we stop for a second?"

Leaning on a sizeable rock, she took a long drink from the very fancy water bottle the saleswoman sold them.

"All this gear and we've not crossed one stream or powered on our headlights," she said.

"We might need the torch on our way down. Or even in the chapel." Michael bent to move a large rock and when he did, a river of smaller rocks cascaded downhill. "Scottie, stand clear."

She tried—by leaping to the next boulder, but it was still slick with morning dew and moss. She stumbled backward, her right foot landing on the rolling stones. Arms flailing, she caught herself on a cut vine as her left foot slipped into a crevice between the rocks and thick, bulging tree roots.

"Michael, wait, I'm stuck." She tried to ease free from the trap as the last of the rolling pieces collected in the wedge.

"Scottie, are you all right?" He dropped his rucksack and machete, and his professional distance, and landed belly down by her leg.

"Oh man, it hurts." Scottie tried to work her leg from the trap.

"Be still, lass." Michael's strong hands gripped her calf, then slid down to her ankle, checking for broken bones or cuts. Then in masculine silence, he cleared the rocks holding her captive, one-by-one, tossing them into the forest. Perspiration collected on his smooth forehead and high cheeks, and the muscles in his arms strained against his shirt sleeve. "Can you move your foot, love?"

"I think…a little." Scottie breathed against the pain as Michael slid his hand down to her ankle, still unable to free her foot.

"There's a large rock in the way. It's wedged but with wiggle room." He unhooked the shovel from his rucksack "Our fulcrum." *Our.* She liked hearing the plural pronoun. It meant they were a team again. "When I tell you, move, carefully, and breathe through the pain."

With that, Michael leaned against the shovel's handle, his whole body taut.

"Move, Scottie."

She moaned as she pulled free, her ankle scraping a sharp edge.

"Gently, love. Gently."

With a final pull, she freed her foot. Michael caught her hand before she fell back, then held her against his chest.

"Are you all right?" he said.

"I think so." She breathed in, listening to the sound of his heartbeat, then remembered herself and her rules, and sat forward. Mercy a mighty, this relationship was complicated.

"Give me your hand. Let's see if you can carry on?" He peered into her eyes. "Or if I'll have to haul you round on my back."

"Michael, I'm sorry—"

"The rocks are slick. I almost took a tumble myself."

"No, about the other night. The kiss, the Belly of the Beast, my rules speech. I was—"

"Never mind, lass, you brought me back to reality." He bent to inspect her calf and ankle. "There's a mark but no blood. Your trail shoes saved you from a more serious fate."

"I promised my dad I'd come home the same girl who left." Was she informing him or reminding herself? She looked up, into his blue eyes. His granite features were set with the expression of one carved from a thousand-year-old family devoted to the service of others.

"Then you must do as you promised." He returned to his professional demeanor. "Can you walk? How's the ankle?"

Scottie hobbled forward where the ground was level. "It's sore, but as my basketball coach used to say, 'Rub some dirt on it and get out on the court.'"

He laughed softly. "I truly understand you a bit more now, Lady Royal."

"Does that mean we're friends?" She glanced up the hill, then back at Michael.

"Of course we are friends." He offered his hand as she took up her trekking poles. "Tally ho, up the hillside we go." Michael retrieved his rucksack, secured the shovel, then took up the machete. "We don't have all day."

"We literally have all day to accomplish this mission." Scottie grinned, leaned on her trekking poles, and started up the path. "But you're the boss, Officer Cross."

High and higher until it seemed like they'd never arrive at the mysterious Wenthelen Chapel when around the next bend, they broke into a clearing of thick green grass, perfectly maintained with every blade the same height. A stone path cross the lawn and along the side of weathered grey stones stacked unevenly and laced with ivy. The high-pitched roof was covered with slate tiles and supported a tall filigree spire.

"Michael—" Scottie stepped onto the stone path and into an aura she'd never encountered. A rich, thick peace perfumed with a sweet fragrance. As if the fairylands told in stories had come to life.

"It's safe to say someone has maintained the chapel," he muttered, tucking the map into his rucksack. "How does the Royal Trust not know what's going on here?"

The surrounding forest was wild but stopped on the edge of the lawn as if by an invisible barrier.

"It's magical," she said, following the path to the front, where a portico, supported by heavy beams trimmed with ivy, flickered with light from oil lanterns.

"Someone's smoothed the pebbled path to the garden." Michael motioned to a shaded area with a bench between two trees. "And the door—" He reached for the iron latch of the dark, wooden door. "Hinges are oiled. The lanterns have fuel."

"Can we go in?" she said. "Are we allowed?"

"The door is unlocked, so I daresay we're allowed." He moved aside for her to enter first. "Considering our path up the hill, I'm flummoxed over the immaculate maintenance."

In the bright narrow vestibule, Scottie slipped her rucksack to the slate floor, and her aching ankle seemed less gripping.

"Look at the beams, Michael." Overhead, wide, roughhewn beams crisscrossed the room and were supported by cream-colored plaster walls. Each end contained a tall stained glass window.

"I think we have little Highcrest elves maintaining the chapel."

They entered the nave through another set of intricately carved doors. There were no pews or chairs. Nothing but a presence. A hush. Walls of the same cream-colored plaster boasted more stained glass windows. More dark beams crisscrossed the pitched ceiling.

Their footsteps echoed in harmony as they walked toward the front, where a simple table sat under the light from the spire. On the table was a cloth-covered basket, a chalice, and a bottle of wine. The fragrance of fresh bread hung in the air.

"Someone's set a place for communion," Michael said. "But there's no pulpit or service times."

"Maybe it's come as you can," she said. "I feel like we're being watched."

"Perhaps we are." Michael pointed to the daylight draining from the spire. "The Eye of God."

Scottie gazed up and stepped forward. "It's magnificent."

"Dad emailed me some old microfiche images of testimonies where people saw a waterfall of colorful light coming through the spire. The baroque period desired a connection with the Divine. The records indicated people came from all over to wait for the Eye of God to shine. They believed it healed them, brought them nearer, gave them wisdom, answered prayers."

Scottie stretched her hand upward through the light and presence. "I don't think God only answers prayers when He shines a light."

"No, two thousand years ago a bright light shone and answered the prayers of humanity."

Scottie glanced back at him. "The Christmas story."

"Some say the greatest story of them all." Their eyes met but only for a moment. "Shall we see what we can find?" Michael glanced around then started for a door behind the altar. "There's only one door. It must be the way. Let's check it out."

Scottie followed with a slight limp, hoping to find this worth the climb. She owed it to Kate for interfering. And to Michael for his kindness in leading her up the hill. She'd bet "wild-goose chases" were not part of the HMSD job description. Though maybe it was his Cross DNA that drove him to help her.

But not the kiss in the doorway. Nope, not the kiss.

The brass knob turned under Michael's hand and the door gave way, exposing narrow wooden stairs descending into darkness. He pulled a flashlight from his pocket.

"Told you we'd need these torches." He went down first, surprised to find the steps in good condition. At the bottom, the stone floor unfurled beneath the scent of cedar and leather.

"Is there a light switch?" Scottie said, moving through the flashlight's glow toward a long wooden table. "There's an oil lamp."

"Then that's all we have." Michael produced the matches he brought and lit the lamp.

With the lamp aglow, the cellar became a warm cocoon of books. Every wall was a bookcase. Scottie dug out her headlight and scanned the shelves, looking for something to catch her eye, almost immediately discovering the private journals of past kings and queens, princes and princesses. Other shelves held leather books of government records, the marriage and death certificates of noblemen and women.

"There's a whiff of smoked meat," Michael said. "The cellar was probably used to store food at one point. Now its fragrance is archived along with these testaments of past Lauchten lives. Did you ask the queen about this room?"

"I will now that I've seen it." Scottie found another lamp and lit the wick with Michael's matches. "I didn't tell her the details of our trip."

She moved about the room, going toward the back, finding a label for textiles. She carried several heavy books to the table. Between the bindings were samples and details of working with leather, wool, cotton. There were patterns for shoes and hats, quilts, knitting and weaving.

"Michael, this is incredible. A history of textiles and patterns."

When she retrieved another book, a framed painting of a beautiful young woman on a garden swing, her yellow dress floating around her and her long reddish hair curled over her shoulder, tipped from the back of the bookshelf and tumbled to Scottie's feet.

"Who is this?" She picked up the painting, the size of a modern eight-by-ten, and moved to where Michael was bent over a stack of dated ledgers. "She's beautiful."

Michael studied the image a moment, then regarded Scottie. "If I didn't know better, I'd say you. The painting style looks like early baroque, so if I were to guess, hidden down here, I'd bet on Wenthelen. After all, the chapel is named after her."

"What do you mean, me?" Scottie aimed her headlight for a better look. "You think she looks like me? I don't have reddish hair."

"You do when the sun hits it. Your strands of brown and gold turn ruby."

She regarded Michael as he regarded her. They smiled at one another. "So," Scottie said, drawing a deep breath. "This is King Magnus the Third's illegitimate daughter." She studied the face of the woman again. "I feel you, sister."

The paint showed signs of cracking, but the conditions of the cellar seemed to have preserved it. Her bright blue eyes observed the viewer with a slight smile on her pink lips. She looked to be in her thirties, but who really knew, and she wore a gold necklace with a crown pendant.

"Hey Michael, the background of this picture is here, I think," Scottie said. "This scene is outside the chapel." The woods were smaller and the ivy less dense, but this painting showed the grounds they'd walked on from the climb.

Michael leaned over her shoulder, the scent of his skin more alluring than the warm bread in the altar basket. "The swing is where the bench is now. Isn't that the front door?"

"Let's go look."

Outside, they positioned themselves by the bench and looked toward the chapel.

"Sit there." Michael motioned Scottie to the bench. "There was a swing here once because the bench is at the same angle as the swing. The door, the portico, all the same."

"I see you found Wenthelen's portrait. It was her favorite."

Scottie whirled around to see a man coming out of the woods wearing a long, woolen anorak, a broadbrim hat over sleek, white hair that flowed into his high collar. His eyes were bright. A kaleidoscope of color.

Where had he come from? She tried to speak but the moment his gaze met hers, she was both captivated and free, seen and yet hidden.

"She'd be happy it was you, Scottie," he said, stopping a few feet from where she sat. He nodded to Michael. "Mr. Cross."

"Sir—" Michael was a deer caught in the headlights, his eyes wide, his body frozen. The color drained from his high cheeks. Slowly he deflated to his knees.

"You climbed the steep mountainous pathway to get here," the Man said.

"We, we, um, heard…um…" Scottie couldn't form a coherent sentence, and her legs shimmied like an old Ford Rambler. "You're Him," she managed. "The legend. The mysterious Emmanuel."

"Not a legend. Not a mystery. But I am He. Emmanuel." His words, His smile, everything about Him purchased her heart, her thoughts, her emotions. "I'm glad you came," He said. "The Eye of God has been watching you for a long time, but I wanted to meet you face-to-face."

An awkward *eek* escaped her lips.

"Carry on," He said. "What you're doing up here is good."

Emmanuel placed His hand on Michael's head and whispered something Scottie could not hear. Slowly Michael sank to his knees as Emmanuel headed out the way He came, pausing on the edge of the woods to look back at Scottie, His vibrant eyes invited her to follow.

She tried to move, tried to say something, but she was caught in the swirl of His presence. How long she stood there, she could not say—an eternity or a minute. They were the same to her. When the power of His presence began to release her, she gave Him her answer.

"I will," she called to the trees before kneeling knelt next to Michael. He moved as if coming from a deep sleep. "Are you all right?" she said.

"Don't…" he muttered, his hand grasping hers. "Leave me be."

CHAPTER NINETEEN

MICHAEL

He was on the ground, looking up at Scottie, needing a moment to find his bearings. Could he move? He flexed his arms, then pushed to his feet, shaking the mist from his thoughts.

"How long was I like that?"

"Not sure. I was transfixed myself, but we've been out here an hour." She collected their rucksacks.

"I must sit." He took a sloppy step before falling against Scottie. "My legs are wobbly."

"I got you." She roped his arm around her shoulder and cinched hers about his waist. Settling him on the bench, she handed over his water bottle. "He said what we're doing was good."

"Wh-who said?" Michael flipped the top of his water bottle and drank deep, feeling as if he'd emerged from a rabbit hole.

"Emmanuel. You don't remember?"

"Yes, yes, of course." He patted his chest. Something felt different.

"When He walked out of the woods, you said 'Sir' then froze. You melted to your knees when He touched you."

"Did He touch my head?"

"Yes, and whispered something to you. I couldn't hear it."

Again Michael patted his chest. Something was missing— He glanced at Scottie. "Did I say something to you?"

She lowered her expression. "No, why?"

He didn't believe her but decided not to press. "Did Emmanuel say anything to you?"

"Yes, though I'm not sure I understand any of this. He said something about climbing the mountainous pathway and how the Eye had been watching me. He wanted to meet me face-to-face. He seemed to know why we were here and said it was a good thing. He walked off into the woods but looked back at me like He was—" She stared in that direction for a long moment. "I don't understand any of this."

Michael took a breath, stirring that clean and swept feeling with the air of the chapel. "What we're doing here is searching for evidence of Fickle's claim."

"So maybe we're on the right track. We'll find what he needs to back his story, or we'll find what we need to debunk it."

"Did Emmanuel mention Wenthelen? I remember hearing her name."

"Oh yes, He was glad I found the painting. Said it was Wenthelen's favorite."

Michael sagged a bit with the weight and magnitude of what just happened. As a Cross man, he'd heard stories of his family members, and others, encountering the Man, but he never imagined he'd be on Emmanuel's call list.

"Let's go back down to the cellar, light all the oil lamps we can find, and start seriously going through the archives, beginning where you found the portrait." With another gulp of water, his strength returned with a bit of creative clarity. "Scottie, tell me, please, did I say something to you?"

She shook her head. "Besides asking how long you'd been out? Nope."

Okay. He'd believe her, though he could hear his voice in his head talking to her.

Back to the cellar, they found oil lamps everywhere. When the cellar was ablaze with the cozy, romantic light of oil lamps, Michael took it in, especially the woman in the middle of it all. He didn't care if she rejected him. He loved her. For some reason, he felt free to feel it. Maybe even say it. Even better, he didn't need her to love him back, which felt utterly and completely freeing.

"Can you believe these lamps still have oil?" Scottie heaved an armload of books onto the table.

"Scottie, love, we just encountered Emmanuel. There's nothing I won't believe going forward." She returned his smile, and the last of his heart's boarded windows opened.

What'd You do to me, Emmanuel?

"All right, let's see what we got." Scottie opened one book. Michael another.

"We should wear gloves," he said. "But—"

"Somehow I don't think our brand of preservation matters in this room."

"You might be right." He pointed to the table and the lamps. His determined rigidness toward Scottie, his determination to be nothing but profesh, didn't seem all that important in the light of the lamps, the excitement of exploration, and the realization that Emmanuel had come. "What do you think? Should there be romantic stringed instruments and a seven-course dinner on the way?"

"I don't know—" Scottie surveyed the table then the page of an open book. "Were you a romantic with Purnell?"

"Not very. Not in the beginning." He was an open book. If Scottie wanted to know something, he'd tell her. Everything. "She brought it out of me eventually. This sort of atmosphere spoke to her heart. What about you? Are you romantic? How about your bloke, Cap?"

"I'm not a romantic. As for Cap—" She thought for a moment. "He tried, but deep down he was pining for his ex-wife. I'm glad they're back together. I told him to invite me to their wedding."

"That's very big of you." Michael closed the book he'd been perusing—nothing but husbandry numbers—and selected another. Across the table, Scottie gently turned the pages of her volume of Lauchtenland annals. "You've not met the right man yet, that's all."

"Nope, guess not." She attempted to glance his way but aborted the effort. Instead, she held up the leather-bound book with its collection of uneven pages revealing a rather smooth handwriting over the miniscule clumps of threads and fibers found in the paper of the day.

"This looks like a journal," she said. "By, well, um—it's hard to read—a Lord Midlands, I think? The writing is faint and very old-fashioned. I don't recognize some of the letters." She slid the book over to Michael. "I'm not sure I believe there's a right man for me. To be honest, I'm not sure I know who I am anymore." She reached for another large leather-bound book. "But I feel different. Do you feel different?"

"From what happened? Up there?" He tilted his head toward the stairs. "Yes, I feel different." Very different. *Free* might be the appropriate word.

Michael studied the lettering on the page Scottie passed to him. "Yes, this is the journal of a Lord Midlands. For a long time, Lauchtenland spoke a blend of English and Danish, which displayed in our written word as well. We adapted more to the British English in the early 1700s." He returned the book to Scottie. "Some of these volumes will be in Latin." He tapped the page from the book he'd selected. "What I see is a record of land gifts from various kings to commanders of the Lauchten army and to various merchants who paid large taxes. The script is very faint, but I believe that's the scope of it all."

"Anything about Lord Midlands?"

"Not so far."

"It's probably nothing." Scottie sighed and closed her book. "Is there a Lord Midlands today?"

"If so, the chap's in hiding. I don't believe there's been a Lord Midlands in recent history."

Scottie reached for another book. "Wouldn't it be funny if Hamish Fickle were—"

"Not funny at all." He glanced at her, smiling. "Can you see that little man with a title?"

"If you ask me, he already has one. Self-proclaimed." She reached in her rucksack for her bottle of water and, backing away from the table, took a sip.

Michael had just perused another book of records and taxes when Scottie said, "I think I found something. It's in Latin, but I see Wenthelen's name."

"Here, let me." He came round the table, hovered over her shoulder, and began to read. "'King Magnus the Third, ruler and sovereign of Lauchtenland, declares this day, Wednesday, the Second of October in the Year of Our Lord Fifteen hundred and Forty-Nine, at Hadsby Castle, Wenthelen Blue of Dalholm and The Haskells—' Interesting, I've not heard of that styling either. '—is legally wed to Mister Caspas Matthias Fickle.' It's signed by the king and a bishop. I can't make out his name." Michael pointed to a crumbling wax seal. "It looks like the Seal of Hadsby."

"Michael," Scottie said. "You just read a historical document declaring the marriage of Wenthelen Blue to a Fickle." She rubbed against the chill running down her arm. "We just stumbled upon the irony of all ironies. Oh my stars..."

"Hold on, hold on." Michael drew a lamp a bit closer—but not too close—and read softly aloud, making sure his Latin understanding was not failing him. "'Wenthelen Blue of Dalholm and The Haskells is legally wed to Mister Caspas Matthias Fickle.' We need to find the record of her dowry." He turned the page with the tips of his fingers. "And here it is."

"The irony continues." Scottie leaned over his shoulder and into his heart. He did not resist. "This makes the Fickles related to the Blues."

"Yes, nearly five hundred years ago but—"

"So what? Are you saying they'd have no claim now?" Scottie said. "If MP Fickle saw this, he'd go on every talk show, maybe even to the courts, making his case." She turned to the bookshelves. "Do you think any of this is in the Hall of Records at Perrigwynn? Why would it be stored up here where no one goes except, well, Emmanuel and whoever supplies the bread and the wine?"

"Hold on, lass. Let me read for a moment. The dowry seems to be a declaration of a land gift and title." Michael worked out some of the faded script and used his phone to understand the Latin he'd forgotten. "Here we go. 'King Magnus the Third, King of Lauchtenland and Protector Lord Perrigwynn by the Grace of God, do on this day, Wednesday, the Second of October, in the Year of Our Lord, Fifteen-hundred-and-Forty-Nine, recognise Wenthelen Blue as his legal daughter and do elevate her husband, Caspas Matthias Fickle, to Duke of Midlands.'"

"Then the journal I found might belong to Caspas," Scottie whispered. "Lord Midlands. I can't believe all this is here. No one has ever bothered to look?"

"Sometimes we just don't want to know. Let's see, farther on King Magnus declared, 'We further grant the Duchy of the Midlands to Lord Midlands and to their heirs in perpetuity with all appurtenances, rights and privileges.'" Michael sat back with an exhale. "Scottie, the Midlands belongs to the Fickles, according to this. In perpetuity. That's a binding legal term."

"Still? Today? Then what? How was it taken away?" She motioned to the dowry page. "This seems to corroborate pieces of Hamish's story. Oh my word, he's going to flip when he finds this out. Michael, does he have a case?"

"I don't know, I don't know. The only way to break such a royal gift and grant given in perpetuity is for Lord Midlands to personally revoke the grant or—"

"Which they wouldn't, if Hamish is an example of their family constitution."

"—if there are no heirs, which we know is not the case, or for the House of Blue and or the government to revoke this charter. And by that, I mean the Crown and the Supreme Court legally proving they have a right to revoke the title and land."

"Wouldn't they'd need a reason?"

"Yes, with grounds and evidence. Like treason or heresy of some kind. It would take a lot to dethrone a duke and take his land."

"We have to take this to Her Majesty, Michael. She has to know."

"Grant you, that's my first thought as well but..." Michael stood to pace. "Let me think. There's a chance she already knows and there's a valid reason for the land seizure in eighteen-whatever, as Hamish claimed. In the ensuing decades, laws have changed." He pointed to the original document. "It may have been declared invalid by some means, though I don't know what."

"Because Wenthelen was illegitimate?" She didn't say it, but he heard her whispering thought. *"Like me."*

"No, lass, the same bishop on the wedding declaration is signed to the legal heir declaration. And there's the Seal of Hadsby." He pointed to the ancient document. "If they revoked this decree, then any decree from any monarch could be subjected to the same treatment."

"Then it must be something political. What was happening in the early eighteen hundreds?"

"I'll need to access the Cross records and Lauchtenland history for the finer details, but it was a season of political unrest over taxation."

"Then let's keep looking. See what we find." Scottie started for another book then turned back. "Does this make me a traitor to my mother? To the House of Blue?"

"No, and what did Emmanuel tell you?"

"That what we are doing is good."

"Then believe Him over your fears." Michael said it with such confidence the words didn't feel wholly his. "Scottie, about the other night, in the secret doorway and at the Belly of the Beast—"

"Forget it. Hadsby's history oozes with romance and we, um, we were caught up in it. And the Ilyds, a dangerously romantic dance."

"I believe that's the intention. However, I want to apologize for my unprofessional behavior. It won't happen again."

Her half smile was hard to read. "I'm as much to blame as you. Now, how much time do we have before we need to start back down?"

Michael reckoned they had a few more hours, which they spent shoulder to shoulder in Lauchtenland's past. Reading the records and journals of those who'd gone before humbled him. He felt connected to their lives, to what they'd built, and how he benefited from their sacrifice. And heaven help him, even more connected to Scottie.

Finally, he called time. They must trek down the path or risk life and limb in the dark. Scottie made him laugh when she attached her headtorch, declaring, "Ready, Grizzly," with a tangy, southern twang.

"How's your ankle?"

"Tender, but I'm okay. I can use the poles to help me down."

Finding a couple of decent cloths, they wrapped the two books with the evidence they needed for Her Majesty and carefully slipped them into their rucksacks. Then they walked through the checkered toward the path and down the hill. Suddenly Michael stopped and turned round to the chapel.

"What?" Scottie said. "Did you forget something?"

"No." He listened for a moment. "I thought I heard the ringing of chapel bells."

SCOTTIE

"This may change the course of Lauchtenland history." Scottie climbed over the rocks that had trapped her before, the oversize rucksack resting heavy on her shoulders. "At the very least, the Fickle family history." Michael reached back to catch her hand as she jumped from the last rock onto a level path. "Have you decided if we should we keep the matter to ourselves?"

"No, I'm of the mind the queen should know what we've found."

Scottie glanced at their clasped hands and pulled free, not wanting his touch to fan the slow, kindling fire that began the moment he woke from his Emmanuel sleep.

"What if we tell her and nothing changes?" she said. "Then we have this huge secret to carry around for the rest of our lives. So will she."

"Which would still not overshadow the secret she kept for thirty-five years. You."

"Not the same, Cross. While discovering my existence surely shocked everyone, I'm not out to overthrow the Crown." Her foot slipped on a patch of loose dirt and gravel. She landed a hand on Michael's thick shoulder to keep from tumbling forward. "My most dastardly mission as Lady Royal is being accused of starting riots and speaking to Eloise Ltd. about bespoke women's wear." Scottie paused for a drink of water and spotted the additional item in her rucksack. "I have a confession." Michael squinted up at her through the shadow and light. "I took the portrait."

He nodded once and continued down. "I know. Your rucksack has a very odd shape."

"I couldn't leave her there. In the dark. Alone. We have a lot in common." Scottie hitched her shoulders, adjusting the straps of her pack. But Michael had the heavier load. The leather record books wrapped in linen.

"You don't have to explain to me, Scottie. I left a light on in the Operations Room for Purnell. The lads still keep it on." He paused to wield his machete. "She hated the dark, and I don't know, the lamp made me feel as if I was still there for her."

"Protecting her," Scottie whispered more to herself than Michael. But he glanced back at her.

"I wasn't there for her. Not when she—" He clipped his sentence and moved on down the hillside.

Oh, Michael Cross, don't make me fall in love with you.

When they arrived at the start of the trail where a wrought iron bench was squeezed between two trees, Michael sat and patted the spot next to him, shoving his loose, dark hair from his face.

"You hungry?" he said. "I'm famished."

"Starved." Scottie perched on a rock next to him—a safe distance away. "I'm starting to get the shakes." She opened her rucksack and fished around the portrait of Wenthelen for a package of Walkers and a power bar.

The air was cool and clean and gently shaking the trees. A couple of squirrels scurried around their feet, rising up on their hind legs when Michael tossed them a handful of peanuts.

He released the last few to a bird resting on a low-slung limb.

Scottie sank into the atmosphere, using the hum of nature to take in all that happened today. Still, they couldn't rest long. The growing shadows of the dense woods pushed against the thin threads of daylight.

"Purnell was always after me to forgive Mum," Michael said, his voice so low Scottie wasn't sure he meant her to hear. "But I couldn't do it. I had no desire or reason to do so." A soft red hue spread around his eyes. "We argued about it a few times. Sitting here now, thinking how you've forgiven your mum, I'm ashamed I pushed back on the wise advice of such a kind, gentle woman. My anger had become a part of me. It felt good. Justified. What kind of mum walks out on her children?"

"What kind of dad?" Scottie whispered. "I grew up with a lot of kids living in single mom households."

"Worst argument ever with Purnell was when Mum convinced her a position at Pratt would be brilliant for our future. We were two months from our wedding, but after that row, we didn't speak for two days. Finally, I couldn't take it, went round to her place, apologized on both knees." He smiled at the memory. "Three weeks later she collapsed at work. She'd been fighting pneumonia. She'd lost weight, but she told me it was for the wedding. She coughed a lot, and by the time her mum drove her to A & E, Accident & Emergency, the bacteria had taken over. I loathe every minute I wasted fighting with her. I don't think I've forgiven myself for it."

"Michael, you didn't know. It's a tall order to live your life as if the person you love could die at any turn. You should talk to Prince John. He knows a bit about grieving a young wife."

"We've chatted. He blamed himself for not being with Princess Holland when she went riding by the cliffs and was thrown from her horse."

"She was such an excellent horsewoman he didn't even consider an accident," Scottie said. "Eventually he realized it wasn't his fault. He met Gemma and fell in love again."

He looked up, his soul resting in his blue eyes. "I wasn't there when Purnell died. I'd gone to play football with the lads. She was asleep, machines bleeping, delivering meds to fight the infection and help her rest. I only intended to be gone a couple of hours but—"

Scottie switched from her rock to his bench. "From all you've said about her, I don't think she'd begrudge you an afternoon on the pitch."

"She rallied an hour before she died. Sat up, talked to her mum and dad, her sisters and brother. Asked about me. Her mum said I'd gone out to stretch my legs. The match ran long. I raced back to her but not in time. She'd crashed. Somewhere in there, she said, 'Tell Michael I will miss the life we'd have made together.'" He wadded up his crisps and peanuts package and stuffed them in a side pocket on the rucksack. "There, you've toured my personal secret cellar." Michael hitched his rucksack to his shoulders and started down the path.

Scottie followed. "There's always treasure in cellars, Michael."

"Not always. Mostly bugs and cobwebs, maybe a snake or two. Ah, don't forget bats and rats."

"The treasure is worth facing those scary things." She let that be her last word. Any more heartfelt confessions, she'd break. Michael Cross, whether she liked it or not, was a man she could love the rest of her born days.

At the bottom of the trek, a glorious sunset enveloped the peaks of the Highcrest Mountain range and shredded the drifting clouds with gold, orange, and red.

Scottie dug out her phone to capture the scene. "This is the most beautiful place on earth."

"One of my top three," Michael said, standing next to her, his shoulder barely touching hers. "I think Emmanuel wants me to forgive my mum."

"Is that what He said over you?"

"I can't remember, but I feel different. I have an urge to ring her and say 'I give up, Mum. I'm done being angry. I forgive you.'" He headed off toward the Range Rover.

As Scottie slipped into the passenger seat, a call came in. Private. "I think it's Kate."

But it was Edric on the other end. "You must come. Kate's in hospital. John and Gemma have just now landed in Port Fressa. Gus and Daffy are somewhere over the Atlantic. She's asking for you, Scottie. She needs you."

"I'm on my way."

Chapter Twenty

"Sorry I'm late." She dragged a chair across the floor to Kate's bedside in the sterile hospital room on a wing reserved for royals, the same room where she'd met her mother for the first time two years ago. "But you're not supposed to be here. Your bedroom at Hadsby is so much nicer."

"I'm a queen, I can do whatever I want." She patted Scottie's arm. "You've been out and about. Edric said he couldn't reach you."

"Michael and I hiked to Wenthelen Chapel. It's beautiful."

"The Wenthelen?" Kate perked up a bit. "I've not been there in years. The roads have been blocked and in disrepair. I can't imagine the chapel being in good condition."

"It was beautiful, Kate. Perfectly maintained. Ancient flagstones, roughhewn beams, carved and polished doors, and an ethereal hush in the nave, the Eye of God watching."

"Still," Kate whispered, resting the hand not tethered to a machine against her chest, "I should make the climb when I'm well again. Or pay for the roads to be restored."

"So what happened?" Scottie raised her mother's hand to her cheek. "Did you faint?"

"I couldn't breathe nor manage the pain."

"It's been over two years. Shouldn't you be improving by now?"

"One would hope." It seemed to take all Kate's strength to speak. "GBS has its own rules."

Scottie scooted closer. "I saw Emmanuel, Kate."

"Ah, yes…" Kate drew a deep, weighted breath.

Edric rose from his chair in the corner. "I'll ring the doctor. Kate, my darling, can you hear me?"

She stretched her eyes open. "I can hear you. Scottie saw Him. Emmanuel."

"Well, how fine. You thought she might, no?" Edric returned to his corner while Scottie told the story of Emmanuel walking in and out of the woods. Now was not the time to speak of her and Michael's discoveries.

"You can trust Him, Scottie," Kate said softly. "Yes, Edric, I thought He'd reveal Himself to her."

Arabella arrived with her husband Sir William, and Scottie retreated to the elegant Royal Waiting Room, where she sipped tea and collected herself from the highs and lows of the day.

If Emmanuel was interested in what Scottie and Michael were doing at the Wenthelen Chapel, He had to be—must be— interested in what took place in the room next door. Michael's story about Purnell remained fresh in her memory.

Edric came into the waiting room with Sir William for a cup of tea, saying how Arabella had Kate laughing with a childhood memory. But Scottie tempered her enthusiasm. Purnell had rebounded too. Then died.

Cranston arrived with a spread from Chef George. Arabella joined Sir William while Edric returned to his wife. The aromas were so tempting, but Scottie texted Dad and Shug first, then a few friends at home. And finally, Michael.

> Scottie: She's doing better but I keep thinking of Purnell's story. She has to be okay.

> Michael: She will beat this, lass. It's who she is. She's not like Purnell, Scottie. She didn't hide her illness.

Around eight, John and Gemma arrived with their baby prince, Magnus John Edric Titus Mac—for Gemma's father—and everyone called him Mac. Princess Imani followed with Princess Rachel. Around midnight, an exhausted but happy Gus and Daffy walked in with Princess Tillie, so beautifully bright-eyed. And as concerned as they all were, the family reunion was warm and welcoming. Scottie's brothers hugged and thanked her for "holding down the fort" and probed her opinion on their mother's health.

One by one, the family took a turn with Kate, returning to the waiting room to dine on Chef George's cuisine and exchange stories from their time apart. Scottie sank into the center of it all, surprised this company of royals she called family embraced her.

She'd grown up with the love of the O'Shays, but she'd also grown up alone, save for the family gatherings at holidays or a week in the summer. She believed she didn't need siblings or cousins, aunts and uncles, because she had her real extended family—O'Shay Shirts. Wasn't that enough?

Yet now, in this royal waiting room, she was part of a blood family with siblings and in-laws, nieces, and a nephew. She had an aunt and uncle, a cousin. A stepfather. It was suddenly enough to make her want what she constantly denied. To be a wholehearted Blue.

"So far, Tuppence, we've seen nothing of the royal ball gowns from the House of Blue. Sometimes Princess Daffodil gives us a sneak peek, but we're two weeks out, so we're speculating the gowns will be from Melinda House or Elnora, standard designers for our royal women. But Lady Royal? She's a mystery."

–SHARON LEE, FASHION EXPERT, TUPPENCE CORBYN & FRIENDS

"The investigation continues into the riot at the Midlands Faire. MP Hamish Fickle has offered assistance in the investigation. The head of the RECO party has also apologized to the citizens of the Midlands but not to Lady Royal or the royal family."

–CABLE NEWS PF @ 6:00

"Does it feel like the Rose Ball is going to be exciting this year? Who's coming besides the usual royal set? Is Lady Royal planning to attend? Will she have a date? I'd go with her equerry Michael Cross to the edge of the earth. He's dreamy."

–@ROYALLOYALBLOG

"The Chamber Office announced today that the
Queen has been hospitalized due to ongoing GBS
complications. She is reported to be in good spirits,
and her medical team expects a full recovery. The
King Consort, along with the princes, princesses,
and Lady Royal, are currently with Her Majesty at
Hadsby Castle."

–CNC, CABLE NEWS CHANNEL

MICHAEL

Saldings, one of the finest restaurants in all of Lauchtenland, maybe among the North Sea Island Nations, was not ten minutes from Pratt Printing. Mum often wined and dined prospective clients and employees here.

When Michael called to book the reservation, the reservationist knew exactly who he was and suggested Mum's favorite table.

A server brought a basket of bread. Michael reached under the cloth for a piece. He'd skipped breakfast for an early meeting with Dad. They'd spent the last three days digging through archives, another trip up to Wenthelen Chapel while Lady Royal spent time with her family, then piecing together the two-hundred-year-old event that caused the House of Blue to revoke the rights and privileges of the Fickles.

"You're here." Mum floated up the steps into the exclusive dining corner.

"Where else would I be?" Michael rose to kiss her cheek and hold her chair. She was, like it or not, a force to be reckoned with. Beautiful, stylish, brilliant. But Michael knew things too, didn't he? Like how it felt to be abandoned by one so elegant and fierce as if he and Evan were not good enough.

"I was on my way out when Liv Collier caught me in the hall," Mum said, reaching for the folded linen napkin. "If that girl, woman I should say, used her wits on the job as much as she used them to film her makeup tutorials for social media, she'd probably solve world hunger. How are you? Oh, a bottle of Lauchtenland grapes. From The Haskells. Nineteen sixty-one. Very nice."

"I'm not a total oaf. Are you hungry?" Michael held up his menu, nodding for the sommelier to pour the wine.

"I'm famished, but more with curiosity as to why you set this luncheon. I nearly shouted for joy, but Evan warned me not to get my hopes up."

"This isn't about me joining Pratt, Mum."

"Not yet but give me the length of our luncheon." She swirled the wine in her glass, breathed the aroma, then took a taste. "Excellent." She opened her menu, read a few columns, then closed it, giving her attention to Michael. "So what is your purpose today? I can't imagine."

Her posture, expression, and lack of imagination almost made him abandon his mission. Yet this wasn't about his mother. It was about him and the moment on the mountain that had changed him.

"Scottie and I trekked to Wenthelen Chapel."

Granddad Cross used to say, *"If you don't know where to begin, anywhere will do."*

"Really? And where is your royal charge today?"

"Hadsby Castle. With the Family."

"I've never been to Wenthelen Chapel," Mum said. "I'm not sure I believed it was real. Did Lady Royal take you exploring or were you on some royal mission? Was the chapel falling down round your ears?"

"The chapel is very beautiful and carefully preserved."

The waiter arrived to take their order. Mum chose a watercress salad with grilled sea bass. Michael selected the Caesar salmon with a side of parmesan potatoes.

"How is Lady Royal?" Mum said. "She's kept herself out of trouble for the week."

"She's well, thank you, and she's never sought trouble. It finds her."

"Is there a difference, Mick? Trouble finds you. You find trouble. Same coin, different sides."

"Are you attending the Rose Ball?" Michael raised his wine glass to his lips, backing away from the end of the story to small talk. "The king consort, Prince John, and Prince Gus have arrived home from their holidays. Lady Royal is rather caught up in the hustle and bustle." Emmanuel help him—he'd reverted to small talk.

"I am attending, yes. Bought a frightfully expensive dress. How's the queen? Has she recovered? GBS is a tricky virus."

"Mum, you know I cannot talk about intimate details of the Family."

"Then talk to me about intimate details of our family. What are we doing here, Mick?"

Here we go. Chin up, lad. Michael shifted about, took another taste of wine, and debated where to start since beginning at the end didn't get him very far.

"Mum, after you left," he said, setting down his glass, fiddling with the perfect alignment of silverware, "you took all the love and warmth of our home. Dad tried, but he was lost and hurting. Evan and I were scared, coming home every afternoon to a nanny who looked at us as if all the puppies in the world had died. For six months, Dad served takeaway as dinner. We were two little boys and a broken man trying to make sense of their lives." He braved a glance in her direction. "Dad might have been hoping you'd return soon."

Mom stared toward the window and the view of the Port Fressa port. "He knew I wasn't."

"Why did you walk out on us? We needed you. Ev cried himself to sleep for a month."

"What? He never said."

"None of us have said. You didn't give us a chance. You didn't want to know."

"So you reserved this lovely terrace table with a view of the southern waters to tell me what? I'm a terrible mother? Is this advice from your therapist?"

"I don't have a therapist." Unless he considered the past month with Scottie O'Shay therapy. "I invited you here to tell you I've missed you, Mum. Very much. You may have walked away from us without a backward glance, but we vigilantly looked forward to your return."

She sighed, glancing down at her lap, a tense line along her lean jaw. "Did you? Really? I thought I could go. Leave you in your father's, and Cross family's, safe care."

"Yes, and we were well loved, but he's not you. The family is not you. We only have one mother," Michael said. "Remember when I rode my bicycle to Pratt Printing? I was twelve, I think."

"How could I forget? You frightened the wits out of me. Fifteen miles through neighborhoods and one very dangerous stretch of busy motorway? I shudder now to think what might have happened to you."

"Yet you picked a row with Dad over it. To me you were angry that I frightened you. That I bothered you at work. We hardly saw you, Mum. That's why I came round."

"I was angry, but you never, ever bothered me."

"How was I to know? You never attended football matches even when Dad insisted I leave you messages of dates and time. The irony being that your flat looked down on the Cross PF Youth League pitch. Even now. Evan and Finn are there every week."

"I never put myself up for Mum of the Year. My career…the family business…fell on me. I was a woman in a man's world. I had to work twice as hard." She scowled at Michael's expression. "Why the look? You know it's true."

"Mum, you were the boss's daughter. And I'm sorry, but the 1990s were not the dark ages for women's advancement. Plenty of fathers left work to watch their sons on the pitch. Dad included."

Mom chucked her napkin down on the table and scooted away, then rose and walked toward the window, arms folded tight around her torso. "All right, I could've come, but it was too painful. I knew what I'd done and decided to stick to it. Believe me, I had no advantage of being the boss's daughter. I had to prove myself all the more."

"Painful? Mum, did you ever consider the pain two little boys, without mature emotions, might have felt?"

"Of course I did. But Antone, your father, gave me no choice to…" She spoke to the glass, to the city scene beyond the window. "Knowing you could never come home with me… That we'd never celebrate a victory… It was just easier to stay away."

"What do you mean he gave you no choice? Dad invited you to dinners and outings, to school functions, to parties. You never came.

We saw you on holidays and birthdays. Maybe."

The waiter came round, and Mum returned to her seat. But Michael only stared at his plate, his belly full of the confession clinging to him since that day at the chapel. Since Emmanuel's touch. He had to say it. Get it out.

"Any other complaints?" Mum said, stabbing her salad, her fork tinging against the white china bowl. "Care to list more of my shortcomings? How am I doing? Am I taking it like a woman?"

"All right, here it is," Michael said. "I hated you because nothing mattered but Pratt Printing. You stopped being our mother. Purnell pushed me to forgive you, but in my mind, you didn't deserve it."

The waiter paused on the edge of the terrace with a fresh basket of bread. When he caught Michael's eye, he turned away.

"I should get back to the office." Mum shoved her bowl forward but didn't move. "I've lost my appetite."

"Mum." Michael scooted his chair closer to hers. "I'm sorry for hating you." There. He said it and instantly felt a release. "Please forgive me. Hating you is why I never considered working for Pratt. Plus, honestly, Mum, it's too corporate office and quarterly reports for me."

"I've always known you were a Cross man through and through. I've always known you hated me but—"

"You were the only topic Purnell and I ever had a row over."

Mum deftly caught the solo tear that dripped from her chin. "I'm the one who's sorry." She raised her gaze to Michael, her blue eyes resting in brimming pools. "I was so mad at your father because he was right. I couldn't be your mum *and* take over Pratt. It wasn't in me to be divided. Some women can have a career and be a great a mum, but I was not one of them. In my early days, I was never a candidate to take over. I was sure Cousin It would rise from his drunken drool and charm Grandfather, Dad, and the board to give him the helm." The fire in her voice dried her tears. "I couldn't bear to see it. Then, one day, Dad came to my office and said, 'How'd you like to be Chief Executive?' I thought he was having me on, but the board voted me in, and I was so humbled and thrilled—" She reached for her wine goblet. "Does that make me a horrible human being?"

Michael's low laugh shook off his final crustations. "No, Mum, you're just human. Does Cousin Shrieve know you call him Cousin It?"

"Yes, and he hates it." She tasted the wine and smiled. "Can you forgive me? I know it's too late, but I never meant to abandon you and Evan. Never. You were always, always in my heart."

"It's not too late, Mum. I forgive you. It hurt, not having you round, and still hurts sometimes. But I had no right to hate you. Every breathing human needs forgiveness. Please forgive me."

"Oh, my dear boy, yes, of course." Mum slipped from her chair, took Michael's face in her hands, and kissed his forehead. "Do you know how awfully proud I am of you?"

"Are you? No more Pratt pressure then?"

"It pains me to say it, but no more Pratt pressure. But you'd be splendid as our logistics executive. And Evan will need you to help steer things when I'm gone. He's not the leader you are, Mick."

"Finn will be there for him. I'll make sure."

"Finn?" Mum laughed softly and returned to her seat, taking up her fork and knife. "You'll do well to get him off the pitch for his own wedding."

He couldn't be sure, but he felt like Purnell was smiling on him. Even Emmanuel Himself. And in the light bearing against the windows, as Michael listened to the murmur of diners, the spike of laughter, the hum of waiters clearing cutlery and glasses, the haunting sense of not being enough began to fade.

This was a good beginning with Mum. But there was a path still to trek. The irony of it all? Without Scottie, he'd be locked in his unforgiveness. Michael had been changed by her presence, and the question that rested on him now was simple—how could he truly let her go?

CHAPTER
TWENTY-ONE

SCOTTIE

S he was alone with Kate at Hadsby again. After three days in the royal wing of The Queen's Hospital, her physician cleared her to return home.

Yet she had strict orders to rest. A steady train of nurses and physios rotated in and out of Monarch One throughout the day.

This morning Edric trained down to Port Fressa for patronage duties and to retrieve his tux for the Rose Ball. John and Gus, with their families, also returned to the capital city to settle into their apartments, handle the queen's business, and prepare for the ball.

At the moment, Scottie had a more serious issue on her mind than the ball. The books. The ones she and Michael had carried down the mountain. She was set to tell Kate this morning, but now it was teatime, and as the queen sat across from her at the windowed corner table, Scottie glanced toward the door, waiting for someone to announce Michael.

Would the queen think she was intruding? Or trying to change things that were none of her business? Was the queen strong enough to hear the news?

"You look pensive," Kate said, setting down her cup of tea. She'd lost more weight, and her skin had a thin, angelic appearance. "Are you nervous about the ball? Did you finish your dance instructions?"

"Yes, last night." Michael had joined her in the ballroom with

Lady Carla Everstone for instruction on the waltz, two quadrilles, and the finer points of the Ildys dance.

Once again, she'd rested her hip against Michael's, her right arm across his body with her hand firmly settled in his while his left hand secured her waist.

The moment the music started, she was back at the Belly of the Beast, moving through the dance, ending face-to-face with Michael.

Speaking of… Where was he? He was supposed to be here.

"Scottie, can you push the window open?" Kate said. "Breathing in the North Sea air will cure me."

"Maybe we can walk out to the old portico before dinner," Scottie said, glancing at her watch. "I can push you in the wheelchair if you're too tired."

"And have the spying eyes see me old and broken, being pushed by my nursemaid daughter? Never. I'll get some rest after tea, and we will walk together." Kate lifted her chin with determination. "I'll have you to lean on."

Scottie started at the knock on the apartment door, listening, waiting, as a maid answered, then entered the living room.

"Mr. Michael Cross to see you, Your Majesty."

"Bring him in," Scottie said.

"What's this about?" Kate glanced over her shoulder as Michael bowed, then approached with the leather books from the chapel under his arm.

"About after I went to see Hamish Fickle," Scottie said.

"Interesting," Kate said in a drawn out, inquiring tone.

"He said some things about the Blues and stealing land, so Michael talked to his dad, wondered if there was a way to prove any of it."

"And?" Kate turned her attention to Michael. "Did he?"

"Yes, ma'am. He found a carefully preserved parchment listing records that had been moved from Perrigwynn Palace to Wenthelen Chapel, August 1643." Michael covered the edge of the parchment with a white cloth and passed it to the queen. "Dad was surprised to see older, more obscure records and documents had been moved out of the Hall of Records."

"To a damp, cold cellar?" Kate said, reaching for her reading glasses. "Who would approve such a thing?"

"King Louis the Fourth."

Scottie took up the story. "Michael has spent three days with his dad digging into historical records, documenting a claim made by MP Fickle. Did the House of Blue steal from the Fickles?"

Kate peered at Scottie, then Michael, over the rim of her eyeglasses. "Out with it, Cross. What did you discover?"

"The House of Blue revoked the Midlands from the Fickles. But they were given the duchy with all rights and corresponding titles."

"Impossible." Kate sat back, hands folded on her lap, her queenly nature emerging. "How has MP Fickle convinced you of this web of lies?"

"It's true, Kate." From her rucksack, Scottie produced the portrait of Wenthelen. "Let's start here."

"Wenthelen. Stars above, where did you find this?" Kate carefully held the frame in her hands.

"In the chapel cellar. Tucked behind some large leather-bound books."

"She's so beautiful. I've only seen a pencil sketching of her in history books. She was beloved for her charity and kindness." Kate dusted lint from the corner of the frame. "We must put this in the Royal Art Museum. Who is the artist?"

"We don't know," Michael said. "But we think it was painted in the early sixteen hundreds. The style is a mix of rococo and early Baroque."

"What does Wenthelen have to do with the claim of the Fickles? And don't look at each other like you're afraid to tell me."

"We don't have to recap the history of Magnus the Third's political marriage to Margarite, Princess of Denmark."

"We do not." Kate regarded Michael then Scottie. "My father reminded me of this story when he refused to let me marry your father. Magnus the Third was a great and beloved king, he said, and if he could find happiness, then so could I." She motioned for

Michael to pass over another book. "Magnus built the chapel for her before he died. She was an example to us all of Christian piety and love for others. I know she married, but there's where the story ends."

Michael directed Kate to the marriage decree. "Look at the names, ma'am, and the endowed gift from Magnus."

"The rocky land of the Midlands," Kate said, leaning closer to the documents. "She married a Fickle? Why is none of this known in the royal records?"

"It was," Michael said. "Before the lands were taken. Then the records were moved."

"Well." Kate sighed and slowly pushed to her feet. "I'm not sure what to think or believe but I feel as if I've known this my whole life. If not my whole life, since Hamish Fickle arrived on the scene. So a Blue ancestor married a Fickle? What was his name?"

"Caspas, styled as the Duke of Midlands." Michael pointed to the spot on the decree where Magnus conferred the title, but Kate was not looking.

"Go on," she said.

"Between the marriage and gift of land to the family, they prospered. The land had minerals and gemstones. They became farmers and experts in textiles from access to natural resources and the port. In the late seventeen hundreds, King Titus the Tenth imposed heavy taxes on the Midlands near the end of his reign, sort of an in-country tariff." He handed Kate a delicately preserved newspaper. "The Fickles became vocal about taxes and the monarchy for fifty years, all the way to King Louis the Fourth. He tried to broker a trade deal with Germany, but the Lord Midlands, a Bane Fickle, undercut him by negotiating a private and better deal for his own ducal territory, the Midlands. King Louis declared the act to be treason and took the land by royal decree in 1821."

Michael produced several more documents. "My father and I tracked down these documents."

"These were all in the chapel cellar?" In Scottie's eyes, Kate seemed to wither a bit.

"Most, yes, ma'am. From what we can tell," Michael said. "The Midlands were prospering, and the duke took a bold step." He produced his phone with a snapshot of another preserved newspaper page. "This was too fragile to bring, but you can see the Lord Midlands, in 1820, pronounced himself part of the Crown through his great-great-grandmother, Wenthelen."

"An illegitimate child would've never been in line to the throne. Even now." Kate glanced at Scottie, then quickly away.

If she'd been born from a legal marriage, she'd be the crown princess, the heir to the Lauchtenland throne instead of O'Shay Shirts. But they never talked about it.

"That's true, ma'am, but the law for succession from a legal marriage was not enacted until 1588. Wenthelen was born in 1530."

"Then if Magnus wanted her to be his heir—"

"It seems my ancestor"—Michael swiped to another photo—"Wilhelm Cross was the presiding priest over the argument for the rights and sacrament of marriage, and that all legal heirs to the throne must come from a wedded union."

"Goodness. I feel as if I'm following a spy movie. Does MP Fickle know all of this?" Kate sat, clearly weary, handing back Michael's phone, then taking up the white cloth to turn the pages of the record book.

"Only that the Crown confiscated the Midlands by claiming treason and sedition, utilizing the courts in their favor, and within fifty years, the Fickles were impoverished outcasts. Hamish has no idea he's a descendent from the House of Blue, nor that the Midlands were a ducal given to his ancestor, nor that he is Lord Midlands. Their records were lost in a fire."

"I need to speak with the king consort and the prime minister." The furrows on Kate's brow deepened as she raised her teacup. "I'll be candid. I do not want Hamish Fickle in the House of Blue. He's a menace. Not that we've been devoid of our own menaces in the past, but one cannot kick out a son or daughter. But inviting into the Family a man like the MP and his Renaissance Coalition—" She brushed her finger under her eye. "Who stirred up a mob that nearly killed my daughter? It would be the end of the House of Blue. Which I will not tolerate on my rein."

"Maybe, but Kate, what if learning he's a Blue will bring him to our side?" Scottie said.

"Or what if he uses it as fuel to further his cause? No, I cannot see it. World wars have been fought between royal relatives. I'll not have war in my own land, in my own house." Kate reached for her sweater and started for her room. "I'm exhausted and with this news. We'll have to return to Port Fressa tomorrow or the day after. I'll have to meet with the prime minister and the privy council. Please, pardon me."

Scottie stood as the Queen of Lauchtenland left the room. "Michael, we wore her out."

"She'll be fine, Scottie. Let her rest and process."

"What do you do when you find out your political enemy has the same blood in their veins as you? I didn't think she'd have to return to Perrigwynn."

"She can return the way she came—by Helo One. The flight is forty minutes. As for when your political enemy is your cousin? Well, I don't recommend starting a war," he said.

She smiled. "Speaking of…how was lunch with your mom?"

"Things went…well," he said with single nod. "I took a page from your book."

"What page would that be?"

"Forgiveness. We chose love over war. Anger, hate, resentment, all of that is so exhausting."

Scottie zipped up her rucksack, leaving the painting of Wenthelen with Kate. "Do you think we did the right thing in telling her?"

"Why second-guess? We've told her. What's done is done."

PERRIGWYNN PALACE, PORT FRESSA

MICHAEL

Four days later, he gathered in the Audience Room of Her Majesty's private apartment with an esteemed company of leaders. There was Prime Minister Elias Goodwill, Lord Andrew True, senior lord for the House of Lords, MP Julian Dalgaard, leader for the Commons, Antone Cross, senior member in the Cross family—known as Dad to Michael—Edric, king consort, Prince John, crown prince, various members of the privy council, the Solicitor General, the chiefs of the Lauchtenland Investigative Services and the Crown Investigation Bureau, Lady Royal and Her Majesty, and least of all, Michael Cross.

Yet he was in the thick of things. Not tucked in the corner, disappearing among the tapestries in his dark suit and tie, hearing but not listening.

After his initial delivery of the news to Her Majesty with Scottie, he returned to Wenthelen Chapel to blow the dust from the books on the highest shelves. It'd been a long two days, trekking up and down the mountain, renting a cottage by the outfitters— nothing like the day he'd been there with Scottie.

Without her, the chapel cellar was moody and dusty, and the flickering lamps were hot and devoid of any romance. The research was shoulder-aching work.

More than anything, there was no Emmanuel. No sense of wonder or purpose. Even the bread those days had been stale and the wine goblet nearly empty.

Now, the leaders of Lauchtenland had heard the story of the Fickles and were inspecting the proof.

"So these pamphlets were from the last Lord Midlands?" The queen, wearing a white glove, lifted the pages of the collected pamphlets, leaflets, and circulars produced by the duke asserting the rights of Lauchtens as citizens, not as subjects. She shifted her attention to Michael.

"Correct, ma'am. Beginning from 1770 until 1821. But we see in these letters"—he pointed to a collection of twine-bound woven paper with fragile and aged edges—"between Bane Fickle, King Louis the Fourth, and the Cross advisor about the royal rights of the Fickles. However, in these letters between the king and Isaiah Cross, His Majesty merely believed Bane was inspired by the American and French Revolutions. Or somehow inspired by the antics of Guy Fawkes and the Gunpowder Plot of 1605. In the end, the king determined to wait him out. Giving in would be, in his words, 'a chink in the royal Blue armor.'"

"You've read all the letters?"

"I have, ma'am." More than once, mulling over every word, thinking through all possible conclusions. He'd been up late going over the details, unwilling to let anyone catch him out for missing something.

"So did the Lord Midlands from 17"—she glanced at an open pamphlet—"1770 want to dethrone the Blues or join them?" Her Majesty released a spiked sigh, her skin pale, her eyes tired.

Michael exchanged a knowing glance with Scottie. She'd warned him the queen had a rough go of it lately. Only this time, GBS was not the source of her trouble. Their visual glance lingered for an extra moment. Then she broke away, being interested in what his dad, Antone, was saying.

But Michael took her in—standing with confidence in this room of leaders, dressed in black slacks and jacket with a pink top, her hair in a loose weave. Her presence seemed to fill his senses. Since that day at the chapel where Emmanuel touched him, he knew he was changed. But how much?

Dad spoke his name, so Michael tuned in to the conversation. "—scoured the chapel archives, then together we combed through those in the Royal Records Muniment Room. In our best summation, Lord Midlands wanted to be acknowledged by the House of Blue as a descendant of King Magnus through his daughter, Wenthelen, who was never officially recognized by the Church or government, as she was born out of wedlock. Though in the documents found in the Wenthelen Chapel, she was recognized by the king as his daughter and sealed by the standing bishop of the day."

"But never by the Crown." PM Goodwill was studying the archives set out on the long, square-legged table. "Let me recount. In 1549, a Caspas Fickle married the illegitimate daughter of King Magnus the Third and became a nobleman. He prospered. His wife, Wenthelen, daughter of the king, had many children. The Midlands flourished. Over time, the Crown fretted over their success, and thus imposed a tax. Then descendent Bane Fickle picked a fight with the Crown, citing his own bloodline was of the Blues." Hands locked behind his back, he returned to the rest of the circled council. "Why was the land taken in 1821?"

"He didn't merely pick a fight. He fought back. The Midlands were being taxed an exorbitant amount," Michael said. "You'll see in the government tax records. The duchy drew all sorts of tradesmen and artisans, weavers, tailors and haberdashers, milliners." Michael retrieved the first map of Ribbons Avenue from the table. "The shops were along here. Manufacturing grew north into the farmlands."

"The records Michael uncovered," Dad said, "showed that eighteenth century Midlands' wealth far outweighed the rest of Lauchtenland's GNP. High taxes were the government's way of getting what they considered their share. They couldn't annex any of the land because King Magnus the Third's charter had strict and irrevocable provisions."

"Magnus had to know how this gift and title would be perceived by the peers of his court," the queen said. "Bestowing land and title to poor, no name, albeit industrious, Caspas Fickle, invariably put a target on his back. The charter had to be irrevocable. Such lavish gifts were typically rewarded to victors in battle or those devout to the Crown. So why grant such a thing to Caspas? Because the man married his no-name, commoner daughter."

"Magnus gave Caspas a kingdom within the kingdom." Indeed. The prime minister got the sum of it.

"No, Elias," Edric said. "He gave his *daughter* a kingdom within a kingdom because she couldn't be recognized for who she was, for who Magnus wanted her to be."

Michael was impressed. The king consort so deftly summed up the first chapter of their story. As Finn loved to say, *Mike drop.*

"Yet by the late seventeenth century," Scottie said, "Wenthelen had been blotted from the House of Blue history."

"Save for the chapel named after her." The queen retreated to her chair with the aid of her husband. "Get to the bottom line. Why were the Midlands confiscated?" She glanced to Michael's father. "Antone, please ensure these letters and journals and records are added to the Muniment Room."

Dad nodded for Michael to answer Her Majesty's question. "The Lord Midlands' efforts to provoke the Crown into a conversation about their Blue blood, his pamphlets, and stump speeches got him labeled as a rebel. In 1821." Michael presented the tender document revoking the Fickles' right to the Midlands. "King Louis the Fourth claimed Lord Midlands was treasonous and inciting sedition. The parliament and courts sided with him, thus allowing him to revoke the irrevocable charter."

"In modern terms," Dad added, "the Crown staged a hostile takeover."

"So we created our own enemy, which now exhibits in MP Hamish Fickle. How much does he know?"

"Nothing, really," Michael said. "Only that land and titles were taken, causing severe hardship, making the Fickles outcasts, and sending them into poverty. As previously stated, any documents they'd collected burned in a fire."

The queen accepted a cup of tea from her husband. "Do we win points for the irony of making his case for him?"

"The question now is what shall we do?" This contemplative inquiry came from the prime minister.

"We fix it, of course," the queen said, in all of her majesty. "We restore his title and hope that little popinjay can bear it with dignity. We restore the fortune stolen. Calculate the taxes levied at the higher percentage and—"

"In modern money?" Edric demanded. "It could be hundreds of millions of dollars, Catherine."

"I'm not sure Hamish Fickle could handle that sort of windfall." Prince John entered the conversation. "He'd go mad."

"I'm inclined to agree with His Royal Highness." MP Julian Dalgaard weighed in with his south Port Fressa accent. "His whole identity is wrapped up in the common man, the chap fighting for a better life, pulling himself from poverty to achievement. No, no, MP Fickle identifies as one who has worked hard and beaten the ruling class. An influx of riches will… Well, we've no idea what it will do to him."

"There's a bigger concern. He's not earned it," Dad said. "Her Majesty said it best when she reminded us land and titles were always given to warriors and leaders. To men of valor who served the Crown faithfully. Loyally. We cannot say those things about MP Fickle."

"Besides marrying Magnus's daughter, what did Caspas Fickle ever do that was noble?" The prime minister raised his teacup in expectation of an answer.

"Nothing." The Solicitor General chimed in with his summary of the case.

"He loved Wenthelen." Scottie's voice was a silk thread slipping between the coarse twine of the men. "For King Magnus the Third, the man who loved his daughter was a hero. He didn't care about her illegitimate status or that the Church and the Crown didn't acknowledge her existence. Can you imagine not being recognized by your own people as living and breathing? Caspas brought her out of the shadows, doing what the Crown, the government, and the Church could not or would not do. He married her. He gave her *his* name. Which her own father could not. He made her legitimate. Based on all I've learned, I believe Wenthelen lived a grand life with a man who loved her, with her many children and grandchildren. For crying out loud, they named a chapel after her."

"There's the document with the signature of Bishop Cross. Don't cast stones at the Church on this one." Lord Andrew True, senior lord for the House of Lords, injected his piece. But Scottie interrupted.

"They didn't recognize her officially. That piece of paper is a sidebar perhaps meant for us to find all these centuries later. Look around. We're standing in the palace with the head of every government body, talking about *her*. I can only hope someone will remember me five years, ten years after I'm gone. Let alone five hundred. Wenthelen achieved something greater than what she was owed as the daughter of a king. She had her father's love. Her husband's love. She earned respect and a good name. If you ask me, those are the things MP Fickle is searching for—he just doesn't know it."

Michael grinned as Scottie's humble passion silenced the room. As she silenced his own angst regarding his mother.

"Gentlemen, my daughter has spoken." Queen Catherine handed Edric her cup and saucer, then rose to her feet. "We shall deal with MP Fickle in a manner worthy of Wenthelen and of this royal family. With gratitude and love." The queen reached for the telephone on next to her chair. "Mason, please arrange a meeting for MP Fickle at his earliest convenience. Tomorrow if possible."

Michael caught the six o'clock train with Scottie back to Hadsby. The queen remained at Perrigwynn to rest.

In the royal car, Scottie drifted to sleep on the luxury seat wrapped in plush royal blue velvet at the first whine and rumble of leaving the station.

He ensured the car's safety, then took the seat behind her, vigilant of his duty, all the while longing to take her into his arms and hold her to his chest. Instead, he mentally reviewed the events of the day while sorting texts and emails on his phone.

Once they'd left the Audience Room, Scottie had joined Princesses Gemma and Daffodil in the White Salon to preview the haute couture and prêt-à-porter fall fashions. Eloise Ltd. was one of the designers on hand.

Michael had taken lunch with Dad, then met Piers at the Cross PF Youth Football League facility. In fact, he was reading a message from the man now.

"What did Piers want?" Scottie said, stretching awake, looking back at him.

Why did it feel so right to be with her? As if she belonged next to him and he to her.

"The usual. Join the league. Be the leader. It's not being run well. Piers is doing what he can, but he has other responsibilities. Besides, he's not a Cross man, so why should he be heading it up? He argues that if I take the helm, the Cross league will dominate, thus making all the other leagues up their ante."

"Is that what you want to do?"

"I don't know. Maybe. In theory. I love the game and fancy myself a coach and teacher but—" Her face was inches from his. All he had to do was lean forward to taste her lips. "You were amazing in that room today. You brought Wenthelen from the shadows."

"When everyone was talking about her, I felt so defensive of her. In some way, it was like they were talking about me. Is that crazy?"

He moved a loose curl away from her eye. "Not at all. You defended her and thus yourself."

"I was lucky. My father gave me his name. That means something, Michael. A father's name. Royal rejection didn't keep me from my father's name and legacy, but it did for Wenthelen."

"I'm going to miss you," he whispered, setting his forehead against hers. "I'm not trying to start up anything, but I wanted—"

"I think I love you, Michael. Today made me realize—"

"W-what?" He bent to see her face, touching her chin with his fingertips, making her look at him.

"I love you." She twisted around to face forward. Michael jumped over the back of the seat, dropping down next to her.

"I just wanted you to know. But Michael, it changes nothing. I have a job, no, a duty to my family at home, to the company, our history and employees, the shareholders and the board."

"Yes, of course, but what if I came with you? Maybe my indecision about my future is for this very reason."

"You'd give up everything for me? You'd leave your home, your name, your legacy, all you've known, to go to some small, strange town in the American south? Wh-what would you do with yourself?"

"Love you with all my being. Be your protector. Heart, mind, soul, and body." He traced his finger along the curve of her neck. "I love you, Scottie. Perhaps from the moment I saw you."

Scottie stood, hands gripped together. "This feels so…strange. Wild yet…" She rubbed her hand down her arm. "I have goosebumps." She turned to Michael. "When I said all that stuff about Wenthelen, I knew I wanted the love of a man like Caspas. But I don't know, maybe her life is in our imaginations. King Magnus could've paid Caspas to marry her with the promise of land and a title. Yet right here"—she patted her middle—"my gut tells me they were a great love story." She returned to the seat. "For the first time in my life, I want to be one part of a great love story. I want children. Maybe not as many as the Fickles, but—"

He snatched her up for a kiss, sealing every word and confession in his heart. Scottie lengthened the kiss as the train zipped around a corner into the long dark tunnel.

"It's a sign," she whispered, her lips against his. "The tunnel of love."

He laughed softly. "You're not afraid of the dark?"

"Of course not. It's easy to be vulnerable in the dark."

Michael settled her against him, his arms linked around her waist, and kissed her until the train emerged into the light.

CHAPTER TWENTY-TWO

If this was his day of reckoning, he needed a Lauchtenland storm brewing over Perrigwynn Palace. The kind producing lightning that knifed through the Darth Vader clouds gathering over the tempestuous North Sea.

He'd been summoned by the queen, and it didn't take rocket science to know why. Lady Royal informed her of their conversation. Well now, he'd inform Her Majesty on how her family destroyed his.

Be honest, Fickle. His boldness only lived in his head. His so-called courage in the political arena melted into a form of bravado as he made his way from Blue Hall to Perrigwynn. Whatever personal feelings he held about the Lauchtenland royal family, he was proud to be in a country with the longest-reigning, most-respected royal houses in recorded history.

Outside, the June day defied clouds and lightning. It seemed the good Lord decided to send MP Fickle to an audience with Her Majesty under a great yellow ball of sun in a sky of blue like a holiday in Saint Tropez.

The North Sea waters rolled peacefully against the cliffs, as if they'd never wailed and thrashed, bursting against their boundaries. Even the garden flowers lining Row Clemency greeted him cheerfully as he walked by.

The summons to the Audience Room came late last night. He'd been out with friends, imbibing to his heart's content, which didn't leave him in the best of forms this morning, regaling them with the story of how Lady Royal came to his office demanding—as if she had any right—to know why he hated the House of Blue.

And he ruddy well told her, didn't he? Because her family had stolen everything from his. Land and fields, homes, reputation and pride, all ripped away under the pretense of treason. If it was treason they wanted, he'd show them treason. He'd be a menace, an agitator, refusing to bend. The Blues had written his family's ruin. Now he would write theirs.

Blast, but his head was pounding, and the three cups of morning coffee had yet to kick in. However, his anger and bitterness went way deeper than the effect of too many pints. Every step toward the Audience Room was a step toward truth or treason.

At the palace gates, he crossed through the welcoming gardens, down the white concrete path to the main door, and lifted the knocker. The door opened immediately.

"Welcome, MP Fickle. Do come in." A palace butler, in a short red jacket and sleek black trousers, led him up the Imperial Staircase, down what he called the Queen's Corridor, under the large portraits of royals past, and to the queen's apartment.

Her secretary, Mason, ushered him into the esteemed Audience Room. "Please remain standing until Her Majesty arrives," he said. "When she does, bow, shake her hand, sit only after she's taken to her chair. When you first greet her, refer to her as Your Majesty, then after as ma'am. At the end of your meeting, bow and back out of her presence toward the door."

"Yes, I know," Hamish said as Mason exited. "I'm not a complete clot." Only a partial one.

Glancing about the room, Hamish inspected the décor, slightly approving. It was a bit garish for his tastes, but it was a royal palace, after all.

The heavy blue carpet was woven with green, gold, and silver. The damask curtains were a cream color, while the ornate tray ceiling was painted with intricate, detailed history of the House of Blue. He took a photo with his phone. He did. No one said otherwise. He might suggest this sort of thing to the designer redoing his home décor.

What surprised him, however, was the sense he was not alone—that the ghosts of men and women from Lauchtenland's past lingered in the corners and round the furniture.

"You're my witnesses," he whispered to them.

A far door opened at the end of the long room. He came to attention. A footman wheeled in a tea trolly laden with white china rimmed in gold and two shelves of cakes and sandwiches. Hamish's stomach rumbled. But he knew he could not eat in Her Majesty's presence.

"MP Fickle, forgive me for my tardiness." Queen Catherine's unannounced entrance set him off guard. He was struck by her poise, her beauty, and the sheer awe of her name and station. She was no ordinary woman. The history of the Crown and the country sat on her shoulders.

"Your Majesty," he said with a curt bow, taking her offered hand. "It's an honor to be here."

"Is it? I'm sure my note came as a surprise. Thank you for such a quick response." She paused by the tea trolly. "Tell me, how do you prefer your tea?"

"Oh, ma'am, none for me."

"Of course you'll have some tea. Cream and sugar?"

"Yes, ma'am. Thank you." He stood helpless as the Queen of Lauchtenland served him a cup of tea and a plate with selected sandwiches and desserts.

She was gracious and kind, more than he cared to admit. She looked smart in her pale green dress and heels. If she struggled with her health, there was little evidence.

When she'd fixed her tea and plate, she sat in a wide chair with a mohair upholstery over a frame of dark, ornately carved wood.

They started with small talk, which she made an art form. Hamish took a few mental notes. More than anything, she made him feel comfortable.

"H-how is your health, ma'am?" he said, resting his teacup and saucer on his knee. "You're looking well."

"Thank you. It's been a battle, I must say, but the doctors are optimistic. I wouldn't wish Guillain-Barré on my worst enemy."

"Then I'm safe," Hamish said with a slight laugh, thinking maybe he should just shut his yap. But the queen caught his eye and smiled.

"I should get down to business," she said. "After Lady Royal visited you, she, along with her equerry, Officer Michael Cross, found archives we did not know existed."

"How is that possible, ma'am? With the Royal Trust and Royal Records? What sort of findings?" And why was she telling him?

"It seems my family, in years past, chose to store archives in an unofficial manner in an unofficial cellar." She walked to her desk for a packet of papers. "For your reading pleasure, but it appears, MP Fickle, you and I are very distant cousins."

"Excuse me?" He shot to his feet, toppling his tea all over the gold emblem on the royal carpet. "We're what?"

"We're cousins, MP Fickle. Here's what I propose."

"Stone, I'm in the village of Dalholm as they prepare for the Rose Ball and I've never seen such excitement. Nor have the shopkeepers. The mayor tells me this level of tourism and excitement is unprecedented. The weather is fabulous, and shops are open round the clock with free wine, food, and music. String lights crisscross Centre Street from one end to another joining the Old and New Hamlet. The hotels are booked. When I inquired about a room, I was asked if I wanted to join a two-week queue. Something is going on in Dalholm. I just don't know what, but it feels… Fabulous."

–MELISSA FARIS, ROYAL REPORTER, THE MORNING SHOW

"Anyone? Belly of the Beast? There's a queue! Wells Line to Centre Street. Tables on quay. Ernst, fish, chips!"

–@DALHOLM DAILY TWITTER

"The Cross PF Youth Football League made tourney play for the first time in twenty years. They bested Club Football at Port Fressa with winger Finn Cross scoring the winning goal."

– THE NEWS LEADER SPORTS ROUNDUP

"On the eve of the Rose Ball, the Chamber Office announced Lady Royal will be wearing an original gown designed by Kimbra with a cape from our own Eloise Ltd. What a win from the designer and shop owner in the Midlands who lost in a land deal three years ago. Can't wait to see the gown but more excited to see the cape."

—@ROYAL WATCHER ONE

"I've been thinking, my fellow patriots. Her Royal Highness Princess Scottie has a nice ring to it."

—MP HAMISH FICKLE ON X.COM

"As a final note tonight on News @6:00, servers went down all over Lauchtenland when MP Fickle posted on X.com he thought Lady Royal, the queen's secret daughter, might make an excellent HRH Princess. We reached out to his office for comment but they've yet to respond."

—PERRY COPPERFIELD, CABLE NEWS PF

CHAPTER TWENTY-THREE

SCOTTIE

I t was true. There were places on earth reflecting heaven. Or at least a slice of it. Tonight, that place was Hadsby Castle's Glorious Ballroom—so dubbed by Princess Clemency after the room had been restored from a fire in the 1860s—and now Scottie O'Shay from Hearts Bend, Tennessee, walked in the midst of it all.

Tonight, in this magical place, she allowed herself to feel like a princess in her purple layered gown with the fitted bodice and handsewn embroidery, complemented by Eloise's velvet cape with the Snow White collar. Choko set a delicate House of Blue diamond tiara in Scottie's updo, pairing it with a sapphire pendant and earrings from her mother's personal collection.

"They were my grandmother's," Kate said, her voice soft when she settled the necklace on Scottie. "One day, they will be yours."

Kate's declaration awakened something in Scottie. The truth of who she was and perhaps, who she'd always been.

Last night, the family had dined with a changed Hamish Fickle, his parents, and sister. He arrived at the dinner clothed in gratitude.

Queen Catherine of Lauchtenland changed the fate and history of the Fickle family with her wisdom, embracing the truth and correcting wrongs.

While they lingered for hours over an eight-course meal, Dad called twice. By the time Scottie noticed, she was falling into bed, exhausted.

She awoke late this morning, hurrying off to brunch with the family, melting like butter in the hot Tennessee sun when Gus's daughter, little Princess Mathilde, spotted her and ran into her arms singing, "Auntie."

Brunch led to a walk along the cliffs with John and Gemma, Gus and Daffy, Kate and Edric, while the kids napped. They arrived back at the castle in time to change for tea with arriving guests, dignitaries, and extended family. Cell reception was horrible by the sea at times, and Scottie missed another call from Hearts Bend.

She was stepping into her gown with Choko's help when her phone had chimed from her bedroom. The maid stocking clean towels and refilling bath salts appeared in the doorway.

"The caller ID says Dad. Shall I answer?"

No. But while Choko styled her hair, Scottie had shot off a quick text.

> Scottie: Hey, sorry to miss your calls. It's been a crazy few days. I'm off to the Rose Ball. Call you tomorrow? Even better, I'll come on the day after and talk to you face-to-face. I have lots to tell you. Love you.
>
> Dad: Have fun at the ball but call when you can, please.

Now she walked into the ballroom with her heart and soul full. Where to begin her story of time in Lauchtenland? Perhaps with this moment right here, right now.

A sentry of ten thousand candles and lamps created the ambiance through which stringed music flowed, the genius notes of Strauss, Tchaikovsky, Mozart, and Beethoven.

Men dressed in white-tie and polished shoes, their hair coiffed into place, their jaws shaven or beards trimmed, some with medals on their chests, others with sashes, watched as the women paraded in from the north side of the ballroom. Their eyes were sincerely delighted at the sight of such beautiful women in their flowing gowns, hair swept away from their glowing faces.

The Kongelig Herrer stood on the mezzanine, surrounding the royal Family as they gathered. Below the doors to Whistlecrag Bluff and the old portico stood open letting in the fragrance of the sea and the perfume of summer flora.

Scottie leaned against the mezzanine railing and scanned the faces of the security team dressed in dark tuxedos and milling about, casually inspecting the guests. She looked for Michael and the face she was beginning to see in her sleep.

"It's pretty spectacular, isn't it?"

Scottie turned to see Gemma approaching. "Otherworldly," she said.

Gemma wore a pale blue dress with a silver underlay, fitted bodice, and wide skirt, her long hair swept away from her face, a diamond pendant around her neck and teardrops dangling from her ears.

A warm affinity filled Scottie. She and Gemma were more than sisters-in-law, they were hometown sisters.

"Can you imagine ole Hooley in white-tie trying to dance a waltz?" Gemma said. "I'm sure he'd insist on bringing his bullhorn to organize everyone."

Scottie laughed. Hooley ran the three-legged race every year at the Scott farm's Fourth of July bash, and he was as fun as he was militant. "Or Jeb Kornowsky who always has a critter or two in his pockets."

In his early seventies, Jeb grew up running through the woods and canoeing up and down the Cumberland. Never met a creature he didn't like.

Gemma laughed softly. "Remember the time he came to the barn dance with a snake?"

"Which got away. You never heard so much screaming," Scottie said. "Most of it from me."

I'm glad you're here." Gemma slipped her arm through Scottie's. "You bring home to me. Even more, you brought peace to us—John and me, Imani and our little prince, Max. Knowing you were with the queen allowed John to unplug and relax, even heal from the attempt on his life. He'd randomly declare, 'I'm so glad Scottie's with Mum. I don't have to worry.' Same with Gus and Edric." She gave Scottie a squeeze. "And me. I needed the holiday for our family."

"Believe it or not, Gemma, I needed to be here. I just didn't know it. I resisted being a Blue for the first year after the news got out. I didn't even want to think about it. Then John showed up with an invitation from the queen, which I could've resisted until you fell in love with him and begged me to go with you to meet Kate."

"I like to think everything worked out for our good. I know it's a lot to take in, Scottie," Gemma said. "It's one thing to learn your dead mother was alive but even more to discover she was a living queen." She nodded toward a tall, stunning and regal-looking woman who passed by, heading toward Kate and Edric. "Have you met Princess Corina from Brighton Kingdom? She's another piece of home in these North Sea Island Nations. She grew up in Georgia. Oh Scottie, is there any possibility of you, well, staying? Or at least visiting more often?"

"Stay?" Yes, a thousand times yes. She loved Michael, but was it enough to break her promise to Dad? "Gemma, you know what's on my shoulders with O'Shay Shirts. But I'll do all I can to fly over more. If I contract with Eloise Ltd., I'll have to come back."

"Then that will do," Gemma said. "Tell me, how was your time with Mum the queen?"

"Amazing. When Cap broke up with me, all I wanted was to talk to Kate. It was the first time I truly felt like she was my mother."

"She loves you very much. The boys tease her, saying you're her favorite. But they don't mind. You were the revelation that added a piece to the puzzle they never knew was missing."

"Same for me, and now I'm in this room that's like something from two hundred years ago. Eighteen twenty-five or eighteen forty. Before the hoop skirt."

Gemma agreed with a sighing laugh. "Maybe that's what this

ball is about. For us to step into another time and remember the splendor of days gone by.”

“As well as the ills,” Scottie said. “Every century, every decade, every year—shoot, every day—comes with some sort of injustice or backward thinking along with the good, the progress, the advancements.”

“John told me about what you and Michael did for MP Fickle, Scottie. He was convicted by your actions. He could’ve done the same thing—gone to see Fickle—but never bothered.”

“Except I stepped out of line, Gemma. I’m darn lucky it worked out. But after being caught up in that RECO mob, I sort of felt like I had nothing to lose.”

“You showed MP Fickle the Family cares about understanding the ideologies that differ from theirs. They want to hear the voice of the people. John’s talking with his team about a citizen council to open critical dialogue between the palace and political opponents.”

“What’s going on here?” John approached, champagne flutes in hand. “Call the Kongelig Herrer. I smell a conspiracy.” He leaned to kiss his wife.

“A conspiracy to keep the Rose Ball going forever and ever,” Scottie said with a glance at Gemma.

“It is rather magical, isn’t it?” John handed Gemma and Scottie the flutes of bubbly. “Speaking of magic.” He nodded toward a dark-headed gentleman in uniform, medals decorating his chest, and moving head and shoulders through the dancers. “I think he’s looking for you. Gemma, darling, is that love in his eyes?”

“Why, John, you’re so clever. I believe it is.”

“Hush, you two. Mr. Cross is my equerry and protection officer. He’s on duty tonight.”

“Notice, Gemma darling, she did not deny the magic?” John took his wife’s hand. “Come on, we’ve a night together without our little crown prince. I want to hold you in my arms and dance all night.”

Below the mezzanine, couples swayed together, hands clasped over their heads in the folk dance Sølvkring, the Silver Circle. It was slow and romantic, like Ildys, but with a sense of purpose.

The men turned the women away from them, hands still clasped, and stomped. The women moved back to their sides then out again and stomped. Then they box stepped to the next position, where the movements began again.

Kate and Edric joined the floor. The queen was strong tonight, the lost hope gone from her eyes. Day by day, her pain lessened. At the moment, she was openly kissing her husband as he roped her to him, encompassing her with both arms.

Scottie shifted her gaze away, feeling as if she were spying on a private moment. But there was Gus and Daffy, also kissing, and Princess Corina and her husband, Prince Stephen.

"Lady Royal," Michael said with a nod and sly grin.

"Officer Cross. On duty, I see?"

"Yes, I have a very special charge." He lifted one of the tendrils of hair around her neck with the crook of his finger. "I can't take my eyes off of her."

His touched grazed her skin, causing her to shiver. "I'm sure she considers you handsome and sexy with your dark hair and deep-set eyes and row of medals on your chest."

He stepped closer, his gaze dropping to her lips, then to her eyes. Leaning against the rail, he motioned to the floor. "Doesn't it feel like some sort of romantic mating dance?"

Scottie rested in the husky tone of Michael's voice. "Everywhere I look, couples are kissing."

"Each stomp of the dance is as if the man, then the woman, are demanding their individual rights, yet their hands never let go." He propped one arm on the rail and lightly laced his fingers with hers. "They come back together, moving in rhythm to the next station. Just like life." He peered at her. "I want to be down there with you, holding you in my arms."

She accepted everything she saw in his eyes, heard in his tone, felt in his feathery touch. If this was love… "Maybe toward the end of the night?"

"Maybe," he said. "I am on duty."

"For me. And I say we will dance." She cupped his clean-shaven jaw. "I'm falling fast, Michael. What are we going to do?"

He covered her hand with his, then kissed her palm. "I'm sinking deeper and deeper as well, love," he whispered. "We'll figure it out. We will."

He hooked his arm around her waist, glanced about, then tugged her backward into a dark, cozy alcove. Propped against a hidden door, he held her flush against him and brushed a kiss against her cheek, then found her lips.

Scottie relaxed into his chest and let the kiss drift from one river of love to another as the orchestra began a waltz, the violins drawing rich bass notes from the strings.

She didn't want to let go when he exhaled and raised his head. Propping his forehead against hers, he laughed gently, lifting her up to spin her around.

"You're changing my world, Lady Royal." He set her down and peered into her face.

"Michael," she said, rising to kiss him, sensing he was hers in a way Cap never was. "Before we lose ourselves in blood-boiling passion, can we do this? Are we being realistic? Remember I promised Dad I'd return the girl who left."

"Is that realistic? We can't stay stuck in one place, Scottie. In a plan we made before we knew all the world had for us. I don't know how we shall maneuver our situation, but we're here now, love. We've made it this far. Tonight, let's simply be swept away in the magic and mystery of a royal ball. Who knows, perhaps the Eye of God is watching."

His arm tightened about her, inviting her to curl into him. Closing her eyes, Scottie rested her head against his arm as they emerged from the cover of the alcove.

"Lady Royal?" Scottie jerked up, away from Michael, who disappeared into the space between the crystal lighting. Hamish Fickle approached, surprisingly splendid in his tuxedo and parliament member sash. He stopped in front of her, gave a curt bow, and smiled. When not fighting the world, he was handsome and somehow, a little bit taller. "We didn't speak much at dinner last night, but I must convey the gratitude my family and I feel for what you've done for us."

"I hope you will be more kind to the Family now."

His laugh was robust. "It does seem rather ironic, doesn't it? I was engaging in a one-sided family feud." A slight blush ran over his high, slightly freckled cheeks. "You heard about my conversation with Her Majesty."

"Yes, and congratulations, Duke of Midlands. I hear she's announcing your title and the restoration of some lands at midnight."

"Yes, we agreed it was the perfect hour to symbolize the start of a new day, a new era, between the Blues and the Fickles," he said. "I woke up this morning with so many questions settled. Questions I didn't know to ask. Our whole family has changed. We're gathering next weekend, and family members who have not spoken in decades are traveling from across Europe to be there." The duke looked away as he cleared his voice. "The truth brought us salvation. I need to thank the Cross contingent as well. I've been humbled greatly by all of this."

"I wish you the best, Lord Midlands." He smiled when she used his title. "Good luck to you, and I mean it."

"One more thing, Lady Royal. I want to apologize. I'm sorry for all the trouble I caused, even putting you in danger. I've been boorish and unkind since you arrived on our shores, and all you wanted was to know your mum. None of us ask for our birth rank and right, and while I was going about trying to destroy yours, you were restoring mine." Slowly but with ease, Hamish Fickle bent to one knee, then two. "I am your humble servant, Lady Royal." An honest smile lit his face. "I've never understood true mercy until you. Can you forgive me?"

"Of course." Scottie drew Hamish into a southern gal embrace. "Grudges cost more than any of us can pay. Now use your powers for good."

He laughed. "Understood, miss."

"Also, buy me a pint tomorrow night at the Belly of the Beast. It's my last night here. I fly home the day after."

"It will be my honor. Eight o'clock?"

"Eight o'clock."

As Hamish disappeared toward the stairs and into a swirl of dancers, Scottie searched for Michael, but Lennox guarded her back. Michael was off, swallowed up by duty somewhere in the glittering crowd.

She inhaled and pressed her hand to the bodice of her gown, the reality of the last eight weeks settling on her. Being here for Kate. Uncovering a long-buried House of Blue secret. And surprise of surprises, falling in love.

"Hey, sister of mine." Her prince of a brother Gus strode her way, wearing his white and winning smile, a replica of Kate's. "Come dance." He grabbed her hand and led her toward the stairs. "I just got home and you're leaving. Should I take it personal?"

"Should I take it personal you left before I arrived?"

Laughing, he spun her onto the dance floor where one dance turned into another and another. She'd never danced nor laughed so much—even during the Scott farm's Fourth of July square dance—in one evening.

She waltzed with her brothers, reeled with her stepfather, the kings of Brighton Kingdom and Luxembourg, and the Grand Duke from the Grand Duchy of Hessenberg—Tanner, who was married to the Grand Duchess, Regina.

At the punch table, she accepted a crystal cup of lemonade, then spying the opened doors to the portico, she rushed out, craving a gulp of fresh air. Sneaking around the ballroom and ducking behind a gathering of men and women with port and cigars, she then kicked off her heels and skipped down the ballroom steps and raced across the soft grass and purple heather toward the original ancient pillars that once fortified a fort watching over the cliffs.

The lights and music from the ballroom chased her into the moon's glow and the symphony of the North Sea. She leapt onto the stone base and leaned into a thick, scarred column.

With a sigh, head back, eyes closed, she tried to memorize every detail of the evening and how she truly felt like a princess. Was any of this real? Was she truly in love?

Please, don't let me wake up six months from now, or maybe a year, straightening up from my drawing table, back aching, and wondering if all of this had only been a dream.

"Beg pardon, miss, would you care to dance?" Michael stepped onto the portico, his arms open, the moonlight in his eyes.

"What have you been doing since our alcove kiss?" Scottie moved past his hands and into his arms, locking against him and brushing her lips against his.

"Watching over you. What a jolly time you were having on the dance floor." Michael clasped his arms about her, deepening their kiss with a breath, gently swaying to their own music. "I fell for you all over again."

"I love you, Michael Cross."

"Yes, well saying such a thing won't do when I want to scold you for wandering off alone. Again."

"It's our thing, you know?" She roped her arms about his neck. "I run off. You come find me."

"Do you know Lauchtenland's legend of love?" he asked, still swaying to their private lullaby.

"I do. Why do you ask?"

"I overheard someone say that tonight, the legend of love is alive in all of Lauchtenland. The atmosphere has changed. Call me crazy, but I think it's because the queen settled a debt with MP Fickle."

"Tell me the legend," she said, resting her head on his chest, never wanting to leave.

"It's said in the north country of Lauchtenland"—he began the story with his lips against her ear—"that the sea has a song and love blooms from the earth the same as flora and fauna. It perfumes the air and touches lives in ways no one quite understands. So beware then, if you travel north to County Northton, where the wind sings through the Highcrest Mountains. Expect a bit of fairy dust on your heart. Expect to fall in love. Yes, even you, Lady Royal, Scottie O'Shay."

"Even you, Michael Cross."

CHAPTER
TWENTY-FOUR

With Scottie's head against his chest, his heart beating in time with hers, Michael Cross felt whole. He could stay here forever with the winds and song of the sea.

With Lady Royal, time stood still. Until crackling, rude voices shouted through his earpiece. "Eyes on LR?"

"Anyone have eyes on LR? HM making announcement."

Michael moaned as the real world broke the magic of the moment. "On the old portico. I've got eyes on her."

He looked down at her with a wink, to which she made a funny face. He roped his arm about her again and kissed her. What was it Kevin Costner said in the American film *Open Range*? *"I'm going to need a thousand of these."*

"We need to go in," he said. "Her Majesty is about to make the announcement."

"It's midnight, then." Scottie brushed her fingers over his medals. "I don't want to go in, because then tomorrow will become today and the spell of the ball will be broken and I go back to Scottie O'Shay, menswear designer."

"You can stay, Scottie."

"If this were a fairy tale, yes. But this is real life, Michael." As she turned for the edge of the portico, stooping to pick up her shoes, she tripped, and arms flailing, tumbled forward.

"Scottie—" Michael bounded off the concrete and scooped her

into his arms. "You're dead set on giving me a heart attack, lass, aren't you?"

"My foot caught." She stretched to get down, but he held onto her. "You can put me down, Mick."

"Not a chance." He cradled her close and started for the lights of the ballroom. "I can't have you or your pretty dress mussed, not while you're in my charge."

She seemed to weigh nothing in his arms. A sweet burden he'd gladly carry to the end of his days. But just before the ballroom doors, he set her down. Did he offer again to go with her to Tennessee?

"How do I look?" she said, lifting her face to his.

"Like a woman kissed." He tried to tuck a lock of hair freed from her hairdo into place, but it swung loose around her neck. She was so pretty with her disheveled updo, her lipstick faded, her shoes dangling from her fingers. "I'll be watching the announcement from the corner of the mezzanine. Lennox will be on your three o'clock. Schueler on your six."

"Whatever you say, Officer Cross." She clung to his arm as she put on her shoes, then worked her way to the ballroom's side stairs up to the balcony. Michael cut through the crowded floor for another set of stairs, scanning the guests, the edges of the room, and the hidden corners. Gunner communicated in his ear that every corner of the ballroom was secure.

He was about to jog up to the balcony when Mum appeared. "I've been looking for you all night." She kissed his cheek. "You look splendid in a tux with your chest medals."

"Good to see you, Mum, but I must dash. I'm due at my post."

"I only wanted to say hello." She pointed across the floor. "Your father sends his love as well." Dad gave a curt chin bob.

"What? Are you here with Dad?"

"He's my plus one now and then as I am his. It's easier than dredging up a proper date." She brushed something from his shoulder. Probably the scent of Scottie, which, if it was all right with Mum, he'd like it to remain. "Can we have lunch again soon? I really—"

"Yes, but I must be off." From the corner of his eye, he saw the queen moving into position at the mezzanine balcony.

"Esteemed and most welcome guests." Queen Catherine's refined House of Blue cadence carried gracefully across the room. "Once again you grace us with your presence, and Lauchtenland is the grander for it. You are our friends and allies, our neighbors and kin. The North Sea may churn with its famous storms, yet we remain bound by centuries of commerce, devotion, and goodwill.

"We have fought wars *with* one another—and *against*—yet through the long decades and the longer centuries, we have remained friends, and indeed, family." She let her gaze sweep the ballroom, pausing to acknowledge several guests by name with a nod of genuine regard.

"Tonight, I wish to right a wrong of the House of Blue. More than two hundred years ago, our family—supported by both court and government—conspired to deprive a nobleman of his title, his lands, and his fortune for political gain. After careful research and counsel—due in great part to the efforts of my daughter, Lady Royal, and members of the Cross family, most especially Officer Michael Cross—I have issued a Letters Patent to restore the Duchy of the Midlands to the Fickle family, together with all rights and privileges pertaining thereto.

"MP Hamish Fickle will henceforth be styled Lord Midlands, Duke of the Midlands. I thought no finer time than the Rose Ball to make this announcement."

The response was a deafening silence, then rapid and quick spurts of shouts.

"You must be joking."

"He's brainwashed Her Majesty and the Crown."

"Long live Queen Catherine and Lord Midlands. Hip, hip hurray!"

The ballroom exploded with conversation embroiled in laughter, chatter, and some anger. Michael leaned over the railing, eyes sharp, then toward Lady Royal, who stood smiling beside her brothers.

Queen Catherine settled the room and continued her elegant speech, describing in detail the Blues' crime and then apologized—again—to the Fickle family.

"I ask your forgiveness on behalf of my ancestors. May you and your family be blessed, Lord Midlands, and restored to the good fortune once given you by my great ancestor, King Magnus the Third."

Hamish stepped forward, bowed to the queen, shook her hand, and uttered three very loud words. "All is forgiven."

No sooner had the words left his lips than a blinding kaleidoscope of light filled the ballroom through every window, every open door, and if possible, the stone walls.

The guests stirred with awe and wonder and exited en masse through the doors onto the castle grounds, hands shielding their eyes, phones raised as if man's invention could capture God's eye.

Michael thundered down the stairs with eyes anxious for Lady Royal. Gunner and the team were frenetic over the coms, calling for locations on Her Majesty and the king consort, the princes and their wives, and the royal guests... Who had eyes on their royal guests?

Yet out on the lawn, the air was calm and the waters below at rest. Michael came to a halt, along with everyone else, and gazed toward the Highcrest Mountains as a river of light streamed down through the summer trees, down the mountain pathways, into the Dalholm streets, spilling onto the woods and gardens of Hadsby Castle.

His coms went silent as shouts rose from the Old Hamlet along with a cacophony of car horns. The Eye of God bloomed wider and brighter, holding a glowing pulse, and then even the street noise fell silent, and a hush seemed to blanket the whole world.

All is calm. All is bright.

Michael barely felt the pressure of a hand on his shoulder but turned at the first hint of Scottie's perfume.

"The Eye of God," she whispered, resting her chin on him. "Why now?"

"Forgiveness. It inspires miracles." Michael brought her round to settle her back against his chest, wrapping his arm about her. Someone, somewhere, began a song. Then another. The Eye continued to flicker and glow, changing colors, eliciting *awes* of wonder.

Time became endless. For all Michael knew, days had passed while he stood there holding Scottie.

Then, as soon as it came, the Eye left, drawing up from the hamlet, through the forest trees, subtly fading until all that remained was a waving peace and the magic of wonder.

No one moved. To where would they all go? They'd just caught a glimpse of true Royal Majesty.

Michael suddenly realized everyone could see Lady Royal's equerry caressing her in a romantic hold, but he didn't care. He loved her. She was his. They'd witnessed the Eye of God together. She glanced up at him but remained against his chest, speaking with others as they began to stir, talking in low whispers, each one, down to a man, stammering to put words to what they'd seen.

"Beauty."

"Incredible."

"Eye."

"God. Undone."

Ah, perhaps the Eye of God was the origination of Dalholm's shorthand speech. Not the harsh winter cold.

Everywhere Michael's gaze landed, he felt a warm affection. He didn't know two-thirds of these lads and lasses, but he loved every one of them. He caught sight of Mum and Dad and swelled with pride and good feelings. When Hamish Fickle came into view, he had a strange urge to offer him a hug. To what kingdom had they been transported?

He released Scottie when Her Majesty appeared in front of them. He offered his queen a curt bow.

"Michael Cross," she said. "We've seen the Eye of God. Whatever do we do now? Your father said you'd know."

"Ma'am, I have no idea." Then he remembered the day at the chapel with Scottie. "Wait, perhaps we should be grateful. The day Lady Royal and I trekked to the chapel and Emmanuel happened by to speak with us, He noted our mission was good. Perhaps restoration was on His mind."

"I believe you're right." The queen glanced at Scottie, then squeezed Michael's hand. "Now we've seen heaven breaking into earth. We shall never be the same."

"Kate?" Scottie reached for her mum as she turned for the ballroom, her security detail and the king consort waiting. "Thank you for everything. I love you."

"My darling daughter, I have always loved you." Kate embraced her and kissed her cheek. "Now, let's dance the night away."

"Mum, please, don't wear yourself out."

"Scottie love," she said, a hitch in her voice, "I've never felt more alive."

"We thought the legend of flora and fauna was about romantic love," Michael said, more to himself than Scottie. "But the legend is about Emmanuel's love for us and our love for Him."

"After tonight," Scottie said, "I don't think anyone will ever call Him a legend."

He peered at her through the moonlight, and the affection he felt for every beating heart tripled for Scottie.

"Don't go, love. Stay. Please. At least until the end of the summer. We can sort out if we're for real or just caught up in a rare story. Go to Hearts Bend if you must for work—but come back." He pressed her hand over his heart. "I'm all in, Scottie." He pulled her to him. "Tumbling over the side of the quay, twenty, thirty feet, shouting *wahoo* the entire way down."

"This satellite shot of the Eye of God—I'm speechless. It's the most incredible thing I've ever witnessed."

–STONE BRUBAKER, THE MORNING SHOW

"Stone, I can't begin to describe the spectacular events from last night's Rose Ball. As Her Majesty Queen Catherine announced the restoration of Hamish Fickle's family title and duchy, the Eye of God ignited the north country from the Highcrest Mountains down to the Midlands. Stories are coming in of true, bona fide miracles. A little girl in the hospital suffering from an undiagnosed illness recovered. A man on the street claims his sight was restored. I'll be collecting these stories and more from Dalholm, but Stone, we've witnessed an event not seen in more than two hundred years."

–MELISSA FARIS, ROYAL REPORTER,
THE MORNING SHOW

"I owe a great debt of gratitude to Lady Royal, Officer Michael Cross of the HMSD, and Her Majesty Queen Catherine for recent events. I fully accept Her Majesty's apology and offer one of my own for my uneducated venom toward the House of Blue. As a member of the House of Lords, I will continue to fight for the freedom of all, including the RECO party. However, I will no longer be their voice. I've been humbled by the queen's kindness. To wit I say, let there be peace among all who live in Lauchtenland. There is always a story behind the story, and if we seek truth, if we dare ask questions with an ear to listen, we make life better for us all."

–MP HAMISH FICKLE, LORD MIDLANDS, X.COM

"AP Morning Business News—Boston Brothers of Boston, Massachusetts, announced today the acquisition of O'Shay Shirts, a men's apparel company founded in Hearts Bend, Tennessee, in 1902. The deal comes after almost a year of negotiations. 'There is a great deal of synergy between Boston Brothers and O'Shay Shirts,' said Boston Brothers CEO Briggs Carson. Trent O'Shay, CEO of O'Shay Shirts, was unavailable for comment. As of this writing, no RIFs are planned in the Boston or Hearts Bend location."

–THE LAUCHTENLAND BUSINESS JOURNAL

SCOTTIE

She woke slowly, clinging to sleep and her dreams from last night. A real royal ball. A handsome sort-of-prince. Music and dancing, a supernatural moment, shared kisses, confessions of love, and not one single, solitary care in the world. Truly. Scottie rolled over on her belly and sank into her pillows, snuggled and warm under the blankets.

"Miss?" The maid knocked softly on her door. "Breakfast."

"Hmm." Scottie sat up. Breakfast sounded nice. "Come in," she said, reaching for her robe, a necessity when one lived in a castle where staff entered and exited her suite. "What time is it?"

"Almost noon." The maid, Soto, set a tray on the table by the window.

Not going to lie, she could get used to this. "Did you see the Eye of God?"

"Everyone did, miss. How spectacular." She poured a cup of tea and passed it to Scottie. "What would you like to wear today?"

"Jeans, sneakers, T-shirt. I need to pack for tomorrow, walk along the cliffs one last time, then join Lord Midlands at the Belly of the Beast tonight for a pint."

"Very good, miss. I'll tend to your laundry and packing as well. We'll miss you round here."

"Thank you, Soto. You spoil me," Scottie said, raising the cover from a plate of eggs and bacon.

From the bedside table, her charging phone pinged. Please be Michael wanting to meet on the old Grand Portico. Or for a walk through the woods and up the hill. She'd dreamt about his confession of love, his request for her to stay in Lauchtenland for the summer.

When he'd delivered her at the Princess Charlotte suite's door a little after three a.m., he kissed her goodnight, and a yes to his request nearly tumbled from her lips.

But she needed to talk to Dad first and—

Dad. She owed him a call. He'd just be waking up about now. A perfect time to chat. Crawling over the mountain of pillows for her phone, she swiped open to see Cap Henderson's name on the screen. Opening his message, she saw two links. One an online Save the Date wedding invitation. The other to an AP article. She clicked on the Save the Date invitation.

"Is Lady Royal awake?" Scottie looked up when Michael's voice came from the living room, her sleepy heart coming alive.

"Michael, I'll be right out," she called, smiling all the way to her toes. Collecting her tray, she headed for the living room. "Have you eaten? I'll call down to Chef George for a plate."

He looked good in his suit and tie, and his hair still wet from his shower. "Have you heard?" he said. "Has anyone rung from America?"

Michael came around the couch with an old book in one hand and his phone in the other, his countenance serious, his posture professional. He was nothing like the romantic hero wooing her heart last night.

"Heard what?" She set her breakfast tray on the round table by the window where the noon light, muted by gray clouds, filled the frame. "What do you mean has anyone rung from America. Michael, what's going on? Has something happened?"

"Nothing from your father?"

"I missed a couple of calls from him this week, but with the Fickle hullabaloo and events around the ball, we never connected. Michael, what's going on?" She placed her hand on his. "Tell me."

With a sigh, he tapped on his phone then handed it to Scottie. "I'm so sorry."

She read the story from the *Lauchtenland Business Journal* as if standing on the moon. "O'Shay Shirts sold? To Boston Brothers? No. No, no, no, no." She tossed Michael his phone and reached for hers. The AP article Cap sent. Was it related to this?

> Cap: Did you know about this? Are you coming home? Just checking on you.

Scottie opened the link. Sure enough. The *Hearts Bend Tribune* headline for Friday, June 26, was the sale of O'Shay Shirts. The font size was like one used to announce a war.

"No. Impossible." Hands shaking, Scottie dialed Dad, but the call went to voicemail. "Hey, call me. You sold O'Shay?" She tried Shug and Fritz, but neither one answered. "So the revised fairness option wasn't a just in case. They knew this was coming. They had to have known." She stared at Michael. "He lied to me. *They* lied to me. What is with my father and secrets? My mother, which I now understand, I do. But Remi? Now this, this sale."

Move. She had to move. But the cold quake in her legs against the burning angst in her middle kept her anchored in place.

"What, love, can I do?" Michael said.

"This makes no sense. None." She tried Jack Gillingham and then Doug Langford. Neither one answered. Even cousin Blake was unavailable. "How could he? This is betrayal. Isn't it, Michael?" She sank into the nearest chair. "The worst kind."

"I don't know the details, love. But yes—" He shifted the book he held from one hand to the other as if he didn't know what to do with it.

"It is definitely betrayal. Did you know about this? Was it kept a secret so I'd stay? Or a scheme to keep me here?"

"Scottie, you know your mum would never conspire this sort of thing to keep you here." He glanced at the book as if he wanted to say something, then changed his mind. "I'm certainly not privy to the dealings of O'Shay Shirts."

"You're a Cross man. You could've been given the inside scoop. Does Kate know?"

"Scottie, as these things go, no one knew but the reigning principals. Everyone is probably shocked. Her Majesty heard this morning on the news."

She paced, dialing her father again. No answer. She returned to the article, reading more than the headline. "It's been in the works for a year? How is that possible?"

"Why don't you hold your conclusions until you talk to him?"

"I'm so stupid." She slapped her palm to her forehead. "The

quintessential southern fool. To let myself get caught up in all this Lady Royal business. Don't you see? I dropped the ball, Michael, and everything I was raised to believe was mine has been sold out from under me. But, oh, wasn't I high and mighty when I confronted Hamish Fickle, when I trekked up to Wenthelen Chapel to dig around in a musty cellar. Just stick me on the back shelf with the portrait of another illegitimate royal baby. I should've never come back when I went home four weeks ago. I could've stopped this thing." Back in the bedroom, she dragged her suitcase from the dressing room. "Getting caught in a RECO riot was a cakewalk compared to this." Michael watched from the doorway, arms folded, his jaw set. "I need a flight home today, Michael. Please."

"Wheels up on Royal One in an hour," he said, turning to go. "Her Majesty will want to say goodbye."

"Michael, wait. I'm sorry but I have to go or I'll explode. My mind is a train wreck. My heart is thumping so loud in my ears—" She took his hand into hers. "You understand, don't you? You'd do the same, Michael, I know you would. I must fight this."

She turned back to her packing, dumping clothes from the dresser into her suitcase.

"I know this is terrible for you, Scottie, and I'm here to listen, but fight for what?" He crossed over to her. "The legal work is done. Your Trade Commission approved the deal. The only thing you must decide is where to bank your share of the money."

"I'd like to tell them what to do with their money." She shook a pair of jeans at him. "Did you arrange last night? Have some tech company fake the Eye of God?"

"Are you mad?" He stood rigid. "How? Do you not know me? Even if I could strike such a deal, I would not. I'm not Emmanuel, Scottie. Emmanuel is Emmanuel."

"You're right. See, I'm looney. I know the light came from the Wenthelen Chapel spire. I have to go home, see Dad, talk this out." Scottie dumped another drawer into the suitcase and smashed down the clothes, braced for Michael to lash back. To tell her to act her age. Instead, he squeezed her hand, drew her into his arms.

"Whatever the circumstances may be at home, Lady Royal, last night was very, very real. This sale doesn't change any of the love and beauty from last night."

She fell against him, weeping. "Then why did I wake up from an amazing dream into this nightmare?"

He held her until the last shivering tear, then dried her eyes with his handkerchief. "The dream will be here, waiting. For now, the motor will be at the front entrance. Ring for Cranston when you're ready to carry down your luggage." His voice was calm as he headed out still carrying the leather book. "Please say goodbye to Her Majesty. You have twenty minutes."

"Michael, wait, what's in your hand—"

"Something for Her Majesty." He glanced down at the book, flipping the pages. "I want you to stay, but I understand. I'd offer to go with you if I thought I'd be of service—" He backed toward the door. "I'll be in the Grand Foyer."

Choko arrived with the gown and cape from last night neatly bagged and folded over her arm. "Are you leaving?"

"Yes, there's an emergency at home."

"Then let me help." She removed Scottie's wadded up clothes from her luggage and began refolding them. Soto entered to help

"Don't pack the gown," Scottie said. "Leave it here. Princess Rachel can wear it. Or you, Choko. You're my size. Take the cape too."

"Your gown and cape? Where would I wear them? To the Belly of the Beast?" She laughed. "No, I'll store them in your dressing room for when you return."

The cacophony of her emotions began to settle as she sensed some of the warm embers from last night… But she'd taken her eye off *her* ball. And lost her future.

"Wear the gown to the Beast, Choko. Give Ernst and Stella a good laugh."

"Ernst. Laugh. Out. Door." She tapped her chest in rhythm with a broken Dalholm dialect.

After a quick shower, Scottie dressed and wrapped her wet hair into a sloppy topknot and rang for Cranston and Miles.

When they carried out her luggage, she stood alone in the Princess Charlotte suite. Alone with her memories, her churning emotions, and what felt like an empty life. Exhaling, she dropped to the couch to take in the walls, the carpets, the simple elegance of the suite, thinking back to the first time she walked into Hadsby Castle and how much it'd overwhelmed her. Now the place felt like home.

There was no time to linger. She must say goodbye to Kate. Out of the Princess Charlotte with the click of the closed door vibrating through her, Scottie made her way to Monarch One.

"Love, I'm so sorry." Kate, *Mom*, embraced her. "Surely you'll sort this out with Trent and find yourself on right footing again."

Scottie stepped back feeling the resolve of the situation. Michael was right. The sale was signed and sealed.

"I don't think so. It's done." The waning fury and angst made her weary and weak. "Thank you for everything."

"Come back soon," Kate said, her eyes glistening. "We shall miss you."

"I'll miss you." With a final hug, she slung her bag over her shoulder and headed out, meeting Michael in the Grand Foyer.

Out of Monarch One and down the corridor, Scottie found Michael waiting for her on the Grand Gallery

"What about us?" he said, walking toward to her. "I can't just let you fly away without one more try."

"I don't know," she said, heading for the Grand Staircase. "Nothing makes sense anymore."

"Maybe that's because you think everyone is out to fool you because your father and grandparents lied to you for thirty-five years about your mother." Michael walked around in front of her, grabbing her attention, stirring her pulse. "You say you understand why they never told you, but deep down, Scottie O'Shay, you don't understand. You resent it."

"Why are you lecturing me? I thought we had to leave in *twenty minutes*."

"Twenty-two minutes won't alter the flight."

"Then what's your point, Michael? Did any of them consider

how being motherless impacted my life? If she'd really died, then okay. I'd have my grandparents, aunts and uncles, cousins to tell me about her. But there were no stories. My mother was a world of nothingness. Now that I know, I admit it, sometimes I resent losing my childhood and teen years with Kate." All her stories, her thoughts, were raw and exposed. "They didn't even give me a chance to be trusted. Why couldn't I have met her, been told she was a distant relative or someone who loved me for only God knows why and then one day, tell me the truth?"

"They were never going to tell you the truth, Scottie."

"Exactly." She all but shouted as she arrived at the stairs. "That's what burns me the most."

She'd tiptoed around this depth of honesty ever since she learned the truth. Today's news shook her enough to spill her secret.

"You were born between a rock and a hard place," Michael said, leaning on the banister, looking up to where she stopped on the first tread. "Which story would you prefer? Your mother died but you were the apple of her eye, or she chose another life and left you behind? I know what being left behind feels like Scottie, and I'd prefer a dead mother a thousand times over one who walks away. Then her absence was not her choice.

"You think learning the truth at thirty-five makes you an expert on how a father or mother should convey an impossible choice? You've no idea how the truth, at any age, would've wounded your soul. To compound it with a lie such as Her Majesty being your long lost relative or a random woman who fancied you would not have made the truth any easier. They fed you a simple story to protect you. Trust me, watching my mother walk out destroyed me and Evan. It continued to tear at my soul until Emmanuel showed up that day at Wenthelen Chapel. I forgave Mum because He gave me grace to end my own self-inflicted darkness. Maybe you should consider asking Him for the same."

"Why are we talking about this again? I have forgiven them. I'm going home because of O'Shay Shirts being sold."

"The stories are connected, Scottie. Once again, your world has been turned upside down so you're going back to the motherless little girl clinging to the small world that made her feel safe— Hearts Bend and O'Shay Shirts."

"My world was not small."

"Yes, it was, love. All your life it was you, your father, and grandparents. Period. If you leave to never return, you'll be returning to the nothingness of not having a mother. You can't go back. You know the truth. You know what is possible here with your Blue family, with your mother and yes, your title. You leave, nothing on either side of the Atlantic will ever be the same, Scottie. Your mum loves you. Your brothers love you, and I daresay, you love them. I saw how you laughed and danced with them last night. It was genuine. Moreover, I love you. More than you know and more than I ever thought possible." With a glance at his watch, he started down the stairs. "Just remember those things on your long flight home."

"I'm broadcasting *live* in The Haskells this week, where residents in the villages and hamlets of the Highcrest Mountains recount their sighting of the Eye of God. So stay tuned for *Tuppence Corbyn & Friends*!"

–Tuppence Corbyn & Friends

"Eloise Ltd. announced a partnership with Reingard Industries this morning. 'Eloise Ltd. will begin production with our everyday women's wear right here in the Midlands,' said designer and Eloise Ltd. founder, Eloise Bright. 'This will up our productivity and provide hiring opportunities. As of this deal, we've come full circle for textile and clothing production in the Midlands. Lady Royal played a vital role, and we're thankful.'"

–Clark Wilson, The News Leader

"The sale of O'Shay Shirts to Boston Brothers leaves a gaping hole in Lady Royal's life. I say she come home to Lauchtenland. She's won her crown. In my book, she's already acted more like a princess than most."

–Hamish Fickle, Lord Midlands
speaking to the House of Lords

"The electrical surge from the Eye of God knocked out power grids across the northern and middle part of Lauchtenland. However, residents are reporting no loss of light or energy to their homes or businesses. Figure that one out, Stone."

—WILLIS FAREGATE, NEWS REPORTER ON THE MORNING SHOW

CHAPTER TWENTY-FIVE

SCOTTIE

She exited the stairs of Royal One, loaded for bear. The hot Tennessee sun met her without mercy.

During the long flight, between tea service, a lovely dinner, and a movie followed by a fitful night of sleep, and a long hot shower in the early morning, Scottie constructed not one, not two, but three robust speeches for Dad.

They'd talked long enough at the Lauchtenland airport for him to say he'd discuss everything with her when he picked her up. He'd sounded defeated. Hit by a Mack truck.

"Scottie, it was not what we wanted. The takeover was hostile."

Hostile? She mused over that word the entire trip. Boston Brothers didn't have the power, the money, to buy out O'Shay Shirts, let alone be hostile about it.

Scanning the chain-link perimeter, carry-on slung over one shoulder, she spotted Dad leaning against his restored dark red 1956 Chevy truck with the O'Shay Shirts brand on the door. He drove the truck. The precious relic from Great-grandpa's post-war years. It was his pride and joy, purchased with cash after the company reached a million dollars in sales, somewhere around 1955. Every O'Shay CEO inherited the truck. Dad taught Scottie to drive stick in the O'Shay "Shinner," grinding gears all over town.

The moment hit her with a teary-eyed sentiment, trembling fear, and hurt. Anger. Dad, in his jeans, T-shirt, and boots, his silver hair loose, looking more like a rancher than a deposed CEO, stared off to his left at something unseen, his lips drawn, and his countenance pale.

Oh Dad. Now she knew. He carried the weight of recent events, knowing he'd lost the hundred-twenty-four-year history of O'Shay Shirts. He glanced around and seeing her, he waved and stepped around the fence.

"Welcome home," he said. "Was it a good flight?"

"Y-yes." He stood three feet from her, but it felt like a thousand miles. "Oh Dad, what happened?" A tear burned in the corner of her eye as she picked up the soothing scent of his cologne. "How could Boston Brothers manage a hostile takeover?"

"Scottie." He lowered his head. "I never wanted this to happen." He released a sound she'd never heard from him, something like a gravelly moan, but he rose up, breathing in, capturing whatever wanted to escape.

"Dad, oh Dad." She grabbed him in a hug and squeezed. "It's okay. Really. It's okay."

Forget O'Shay Shirts. Forget her fears and anger. Anything for her father to not stand before her broken and ashamed, choking back his sobs.

He held her in his big arms, rocking her side to side. "I wanted O'Shay for you, kiddo. Wanted to hand you the reins."

They remained in mutual grief until Homeland cleared Scottie through security. Her bags were loaded in the back of the truck, and as she walked around to the passenger-side door, Dad tossed her the keys.

"Want to drive?"

She caught the keys along with a rush of tears. "It's been a while. I might grind a few gears."

"It'll be music to my ears."

When she got behind the big round wheel, it all came back to her. She pressed the gas to prime the carburetor, mashed the clutch, and turned the key.

"Attagirl," Dad whispered, reaching across the bench seat to squeeze her hand. When she shifted into gear, he added, "Shug's made all your favorites. Let's head to the old homestead and we'll tell you everything."

Windows down, the warm Tennessee air flowing through the cab, the old truck bouncing down River Road, Scottie eased her grip on the wheel and exhaled. Really exhaled.

Kate, Lauchtenland, Lady Royal, Michael faded into the leafy trees, the mowed fields, and the scattering of brick ranch-style homes set back off the road.

Today was the first day of all her tomorrows.

Shug met her with a motherly, protective hug, and Fritz, dear Grandpa Fritz, who never said much but was always there, held her close, kissing her temple.

"Let's eat," Shug said, turning toward the kitchen. "I made—"

"No, please, I can't until I know what happened." Scottie pressed her hand to her middle. "I'm full of questions and anxiety, anger and sorrow."

Fritz suggested sitting out back on the pool deck where the white concrete and blue water remained under the morning shade. Where the morning breeze stirred the leaves.

"I tried to warn you, Scottie." Dad kicked off the conversation. "I left you voicemails to call me but—"

"I know, I know. The last few days were the busiest of my time in Lauchtenland between the ball and the whole Fickle business—"

"We read about that this morning," Shug said. "I can't help but think your purpose in Lauchtenland went well beyond a daughter spending time with her mother."

"I kept telling you all, Scottie was a reckoning force." Fritz, with his chest puffed out, sat back like he owned the world. The only thing missing from his demeanor was his signature "I told you" huff.

Dad gripped his hands together as he leaned forward, arms propped on his knees. "It started late last year with Boston Brothers buying shares. When I brought it to the board, they blew it off as if BB's interest showed our strength. All those great financial minds and that's the conclusion they came up with. Anyway, by the spring, they'd gained another five percent, then eight. Doug was very concerned. But we still had controlling interests. One of the family would have to sell out for them to take over. I was sure that would never happen."

"But someone sold out, right?"

"Your Aunt Leanne gave her shares to her kids." Dad crunched his fist into his palm. "She had fifteen percent of shares given to her by my grandfather when she left as an appeasement for not promoting her up the O'Shay ranks. But in the '80s, we weren't on the open market. Flash forward, cousin Ethan wanted to expand Neuheisel and sold eight percent of the shares. Boston Brothers snapped them up. We're not sure how they got anyone to give them the capital, but they gained controlling interests."

"Ethan." Scottie was on her feet. "Why didn't he talk to us?"

"He never was the brightest bulb in the box," Fritz said.

"He claims he didn't think eight percent of the fifteen percent would make a difference. By the time we learned, it was too late."

"BB has wanted O'Shay for a long time, and they found a way." A bird perched on a low-swinging branch began to sing his song. For a moment, Scottie stood among the lavender fields of Whistlecrag Bluff. She leaned back into Michael's arms but—

"Ethan had little to say for himself when confronted," Fritz said.

"He sold out the family business. He sold me out." Scottie huffed away from the imaginary scent of the bluff and phantom feel of Michael's arms. "What does he have to say for himself?"

"Nothing. But when Leanne called to profusely apologize, she went on and on about you being a princess and no one thought you'd want to be bothered with running a shirt company."

Scottie sighed. This whole thing was on the edge of comical. "She can say that all she wants, but she knew I wanted to run O'Shay."

"To be fair, Ethan didn't know Boston Brothers had gained such a foothold."

"He would if he'd have asked," she said.

"He thought selling would help our stock portfolio diversify and he'd get a windfall to improve Neuheisel. As for me not telling you, the tender offer came right after you were here in May. It went straight to the shareholders."

"And that's what the fairness option was all about."

"We fought a poison pill proxy fight. But with so much of Ethan's block gone, the shareholders' best interest trumped our heritage. Three days ago, we knew about the merger. That's when I called you." Dad glanced at Fritz. "I should've flown over. I wanted to fly over."

Scottie returned to her seat, a resolve settling over her. "So what now?"

"We're wealthier than ever, as if that matters when losing a family legacy." Dad laced his voice with irony. "O'Shay Shirts will remain open in Hearts Bend with the plant and the team. Jack is staying on as Vice President of Marketing. Matteo is the new Creative Director—"

"Matteo? He's still designing clothes to be shown in art museums. And he can't write a tech pack to save his life."

"He'll have to learn," Fritz said.

"One more thing, Scottie. There's a three-year noncompete."

"Three years? What am I supposed to do in the meantime?"

"Get married. Have babies." Shug finally spoke. And with authority. "Trust me, darling girl, family is the greatest thing in all the world. It trumps career achievement all day, every day, and twice on Sunday. Our ancestor Loom O'Shay would be busting his buttons over who you three have become. Not over how O'Shay Shirts became a brand menswear line."

"Spare me the platitudes, Shug." Scottie's initial resolve solidified into a rock stuck between her ribs. "Who am I supposed to marry and have these babies with?"

Michael Cross. She squeezed the name from her mind.

"While I regret losing the company on my watch—" Dad glanced around the small family circle. "—I can't help but think it's a good thing. Freeing. I love Remi and want to give everything I've got to our marriage for whatever time I have left on this earth. Scottie, I want love and a family for you." He sighed. "Maybe I took my eye of the ball, let my relationship with Remi—"

"Oh gosh, I am *so* your daughter," Scottie whispered. "I said the same thing to Michael when I found out about the sale. That I'd taken my eye off the ball. Got caught up in all the royal business and—" *Michael.* She was completely caught up in Michael in her final days at Hadsby.

"Dad." Scottie knelt in front of him. The man who'd stitched her prom dress at the zero hour as the limousine pulled up to the house. The one who'd watched chick flicks and rom-coms, who listened to her babble on and on about school while she did her homework and he cooked dinner. The one who did everything in his power to keep her from life's pain.

He'd dedicated his whole life to her. Her heritage wasn't O'Shay Shirts, it was him. Dad. Fritz and Shug. She flung her arms around him.

"I love you, Dad. I don't care about O'Shay Shirts. I care about you. About us. The family, you and Remi, and your happily ever after."

He batted away the tears resting in the corner of his eye. "I didn't want to hide another story from you like I had to with your mother. I wanted you to know before the news and—"

"Dad, stop. There's no blame in any of this. Businesses are raised up and brought low. Bought and sold. Started and ended. Few things go on forever. But we're forever. Our family." She squeezed his hand, the one that had held hers through fevers and first heartbreaks. "I can't wait to see what the future has for you and Remi and our newly blended family. I'll find something to do." Scottie shot a look toward Shug. "Don't say marriage and family."

"I'll say it if I have a mind and don't tell me what to do, young'un."

Dad's laugh was solid and genuine. "I'm famished. How about that lunch, Mom?"

"Just the ticket." Shug stood, popping her hands together. "Y'all sit tight. I'll bring it out to the patio. It's not too hot yet. How about a swim later? Water polo? Boys against girls."

"Sounds good, but I want to partner with my girl," Dad said, his eyes boring into hers with gratitude and love. "Just the two of us. One last time before everything changes."

Scottie kissed his cheek. "One last time, but Dad, in case you haven't noticed, everything has already changed."

OCTOBER

MICHAEL

In the new wing of the Cross PF Youth Football League hub, Michael toured Her Majesty, Queen Catherine the Second, showing her round the construction to the architectural renderings framed and hanging on a wall.

Not long after Scottie returned to Hearts Bend, he decided life was too short to wait for right moments. He'd taken a chance with Scottie and his heart, why not with his career? He resigned from Her Majesty's Security Detail, moved into one of the quaint Cross cottages along the old Port Fressa quay, and over the summer became the leader of the Cross youth football league.

This was what he was meant to do.

"All of this will be new. We've finalized the plans and obtained the permits. Construction should start next week."

Queen Catherine had rung him up out of the blue, inquiring about a tour of the new Cross PF Youth Football League's facilities.

She seemed strong and healthy, wearing a bright yellow dress coat, her dark handbag swinging from a gloved hand as she leaned toward the glass case containing old photos of the league. "The article I read said you've plans for a hub in Dalholm as well."

The queen looked at him for confirmation, but he knew the football facility was not on her mind, didn't he? She wanted to ask about Scottie.

"We do, ma'am. We'd like one in The Haskells, and Branford-on-the-Reserve."

"Marvelous. Sport is good for our young people." The queen walked on, inspecting the drawings attached to the wall. Her team of two protection officers circulated through the enclosed space and stayed on her six. "It suits you, Michael, leading the charge for the entire Cross Youth Athletic Association. It's run aground of late."

"Thank you, ma'am. With everything that happened… I felt it was time for a change."

Queen Catherine's expression was one of a mother speaking to the man who loved her daughter.

"I miss her," she said softly.

"As do I."

"I'd planned a grand final day for us."

"Yes, ma'am." Michael had been made privy to her plans the night of the ball. She'd wanted Scottie's last days to be fun and adventurous.

"Lunch at a vineyard in The Haskells, then a ride on the gondolas over the mountains." The queen walked toward the doors opened to the pitch. "I wanted her to see some of the shops in the old foothill villages. My father used to take us there every year when Arabella and I were girls. We were allowed to run free across the wide board floors, the proprietors smiling on us, letting us choose whatever we wanted from the candy jars. My favorite doll was handmade by a Grandma Moses sort of woman. I can still see the lines fanning out from her bright eyes."

"If I may, ma'am, Lady Royal never saw our world, our way of life, as hers. I think we all forgot how American she is, forthright, determined, stubborn."

"And broken, as we all are. I wanted to help her heal. She certainly helped me heal."

"She only recently admitted she was wounded."

"Michael, don't you think she could've learned our ways? Princess Gemma has adapted into royal life. As has Imani. I forget sometimes they're American. What of the Brighton Princesses,

Susanna, Corina, and Avery? Even the Grand Duchess of Hessenberg, Princess Regina, is an American. They have southern American roots, yet have taken to their duty and positions quite well. Even splendidly."

"They all fell in love," he said. "And the truth about their mother was never a secret turned national headline."

"She resented it, resented me, I think. I could see it on her when she came to say goodbye. How perhaps I'd gotten between her and of her calling." The queen made her way to the green pitch, her protection team close behind. "I loved football as a girl. I was quite good."

"You should come play sometime. We'll have a charity match. As your health allows."

"I'm improving every day. Since the night of the ball, the restoration of the Fickle family, the awakening of the Eye of God, the pain lessens, and my strength is returning." She nodded at Michael, smiling. "May I be candid? I was quite certain Lady Royal fell in love with you."

"She said she loved me. And I love her. But when the news hit, she claimed it was all a fantasy, ma'am. Even suggested we staged the Eye of God with tech chaps from New Hamlet."

"Really? I should send her an article on how impossible that light is for man to make. But I won't. I know Trent losing O'Shay knocked her sideways. I wish he'd have telephoned, let me know it was coming."

"He tried to speak with Scottie, but she kept missing or putting off his calls until after the ball."

"I suppose things happen as they do for a reason." Spying a soccer ball on the sidelines, the queen quick-stepped over and gave it a kick. "Do keep me posted on your progress. Do you need investors? The king consort and I like to give from our private coffers to worthy ventures."

"Pratt Printing has been generous, ma'am. But if you care to give, we won't say no."

"I'll speak with my husband. And let's work on that charity match."

Outside the hub, as a fall breeze nipped at golden and burnished red leaves, the queen took a moment to take it all in. For a moment, she wasn't his sovereign or one of the most esteemed royals in the world—she was the mother of the woman he loved.

"Did you know her father is getting married this weekend?" Queen Catherine started for the tinted-window Range Rover where a protection officer waited by an open door. "I sent her a text of encouragement, but she only responded with a smiley face."

"She does the same with me."

Queen Catherine paused by the motor with a final glance at Michael. "One last thing. You know that *very* special and surprising leather book you discovered in the chapel cellar? I was wondering if you might do me a favor?"

Chapter Twenty-Six

SCOTTIE

For the most part, her days were nothing like before. Except for the month of handing over O'Shay to Boston Brothers, going through the days like a robot, she slept in and then made a late breakfast-slash-early lunch, eating it on her back deck, watching fall swallow up summer.

She avoided coffee with friends, thus the cloaked inquiries about Lady Royal and life in a castle. She canceled her pickleball membership, and when she saddled Dart for a ride, she aimed him west, wishing she could ride all the way to California.

She gave herself to Dad and Remi's wedding, finding purpose in helping where needed, even designing bespoke bridesmaids' dresses that O'Shay's head seamstress created in three days.

On this crisp fall evening with edges of gold on the fading horizon, Scottie watched the newlyweds from the wedding party's table. Handsome in a cream-colored fine wool suit, and Remi in a pink-champagne fitted gown, Dad danced with his bride to Bob Seger's "Shame On the Moon."

He was completely enveloped by her, lost in her eyes, sinking deeper with each swaying step.

Suddenly, within the span of a single note, Scottie was in the Belly of the Beast, dancing the Ildys, falling into Michael's gaze like Dad fell into Remi's.

"Hey you, why the distant look?" Cap Henderson dropped his athletic, graceful form into the vacated chair next to her.

"Tell me you're not thrilled for your dad."

"Of course I am."

"Hey, Scotto." A tipsy Uncle Festus pounded her on the shoulders. "I never thought I'd see this day. Trent O'Shay in love and married."

Cap steadied Festus, helping him move on. "Remi's good for your dad," he said, reaching for the dish of peanuts and popping a few in his mouth, his posture every inch that of an Army Ranger. "Isn't Lauchtenland in your future?"

"Remi is amazing and Dad deserves this," she said. "And no, Lauchtenland is not in my future."

This notion of "never Lauchtenland" had crept into her mental processes. The entire wedding week, friends and family had speculated about her royal connections, wondering when she'd return to her "mother's country."

"Don't you have a royal title?" they asked.

"By the way, what exactly was a 'Lady Royal?'"

Scottie retreated. Head in the sand.

"Come on, Scottie," Cap said in his jovial way. "I saw the pictures of you as Lady Royal and, girl, it fit. You looked more like yourself than ever, even with the scandal at the quay. What was that about?"

"Craziness. Mostly, people not wanting another American royal."

"But you're half Lauchten, aren't you? A Blue blood, a member of the royal *we*."

"None of that matters to the citizens of Lauchtenland. For them, it's about culture and national pride. Under their microscope, I'm not House of Blue material." Never mind the one-eighty turn of Hamish Fickle, Lord Midlands, campaigning for her to win her princess coronet. "Never mind me." She gave Cap's knee a pat. "How. Are. You?"

"I'm good. The farm's good. We're going to turn a nice profit this year. Have you saved the date for my wedding? Yesterday Freya and I finalized the deets for our Wedding Chapel wedding the first Sunday in December. She wanted a Christmas wedding when we married the first time, but we had to rush everything for my deployment."

"I'm happy for you. And yes, your wedding is on my calendar."

"So…when Taylor Gillingham was walking us around the chapel one last time she might have mentioned you've been a bit adrift."

"Did she, now? Wait until I see her." Taylor was a friend from high school, owner of the Wedding Chapel and married to Jack, VP of Marketing for O'Shay—no, no, make that Boston Brothers.

"She's worried about you, Scottie. We all are."

"Please. I'm fine. I promise."

Dad's high school best friend, Andy, danced past the table with his wife. "Finally, a bride for Trent, Scottie. We're so happy for him. Aren't you happy for him?"

"Good to see you, Andy. Delaney, I love your dress."

Then it was back to Cap, who seemed stuck on Scottie's well-being. "What are you going to do now the business has been sold?"

"I don't know…maybe buy an island in the Caribbean and surround myself with cabana boys."

"Very funny. So not you."

"What do you want me to say, Cap? That I'm crushed? Lost? Struggling through sleepless nights or how nothing makes sense even when I try to concentrate on what's next? My grasp was so firm on the golden ring and now—"

"Scottie." He leaned toward her. "For the first time in your whole thirty-eight years, you're free. You're not heir to O'Shay. You have no family or corporate obligations. You can go anywhere you want. Do whatever you want. Go, be a princess." He shot her one of his I-dare-you looks. "I'd like to see it. While you're there, Princess, find a prince. Fall in love. Use all of your amazing skill and training to help people like that chick, the local designer. You carried one of her bags, right?"

"Now how do you know that, Cap Henderson? Fashion was never your thing, as I recall."

"Hey now, I've dressed for a few military balls. You went with me once. But Freya told me about the bag and how the designer was scrambling to fulfill orders."

"Yeah, I'm happy for Eloise. But Cap, you make it sound like I can just choose a life in Lauchtenland. It's not so simple. I can't hop on a plane to Port Fressa, knock on Perrigwynn Palace's front door and say, 'I'm back, make me a princess.'"

"Why not?"

"Besides, I can't go back." The confession she'd been pushing aside welled up. "I think the entire trip over was a mistake. I allowed myself to get wowed by the glitz and glamour, the handsome equerry and protection officer, and the Lauchtenland lore of love. I thought I could be a permanent member of the Family. While all that was going on, O'Shay was being stolen."

Cap slipped his hand into hers. "Maybe that's the point, Scottie. While you were discovering this whole other side of your heritage, O'Shay ended, clearing a new path for you." Pushing back from the table, Cap said his final words. "One more thing before I go. If the acquisition fell through right now and Trent came rushing over to tell you O'Shay Shirts was yours once again, how would you really feel? Would you suddenly be at peace? Settled? Seeing the future like you used to?" Cap leaned forward to kiss her temple. "I don't think so."

Soft electric guitar notes rose from the bandstand. Cap shifted his attention across the room, instantly finding Freya as the mellow voice of the male vocalist harmonized with the guitar, singing about a dream where he'd lost his one true love.

"This is our song. 'Die with a Smile.' Lady Gaga and Bruno Mars." He started to go but took a step back. "You okay?"

"Yes, you goober. Go dance with her." Scottie waved him off. "And thanks for the pep talk. I mean it." She waved to lovely Freya, who swooned into Cap's arms. Scottie never swooned in Cap's arms. But there were a pair of arms she could feel around her if she closed her eyes. Firm. Strong. Muscled. Protective. *"Hey love,"* Michael's phantom voice whispered past her ear. *"I won't let you go."*

But he did let her go, didn't he? Because she was so determined to do it her way.

"Can I have this next dance?" Fritz stood on the other side of the table, hand extended as the singers sang out the last melodies of "Die with a Smile."

"Did Shug give up on you?" Scottie said.

"She's talking with Remi, and I was remembering how I taught you to dance all those Friday nights you stayed over." Fritz led her gracefully through his box step as a new song came from the band. A modern rendition of "Moonlight Serenade," yet still so Glenn Miller. "You were such a joy to us." A mist dusted his old blue eyes. "You are the absolute best thing that ever happened to your dad, Scottie. Well, to me and Shug too, can't lie. We tried to tell him as you got older to step out a little, find a nice girl, but you were his girl."

"I know, Fritz. I'm grateful. It's just everything is changing all at once."

"Darling, everything's been changing since you learned the truth. You just weren't paying attention." He bent to see her face. "You're free, Scottie. You can—"

"You sound like Cap. Free to do what, Fritz? I never wanted to be free. I never felt trapped." She rested her head against him. "Are you really okay with all of this? Losing O'Shay?"

"I admit it was a bit of a shock, but Great Grandpa Loom's legacy isn't shirts and trousers, it's us—his sons and daughters all the way down to you, me, and your father. Even Ethan who unknowingly put the nail in the coffin. The sale gives you something you never had before Scottie. A choice. Your dad and I often talked about how we'd locked you in as heir to O'Shay before you even knew how to read." The trumpets played their muted *mwah, mwah* melody from the stage. "O'Shay turned out to be a fine company. But it's not my greatest achievement, nor your dad's, nor my father's. Our greatest achievement is our family, friends, and what we do with our time, money, and words."

"Maybe so, Fritz, but you did create a new fabric for men's

outdoor wear that greatly impacted hunters and campers, hikers and mountain climbers."

"We were desperate for something to keep us afloat in the '70s. Desperation will make you find a new way of doing things." Fritz waltzed Scottie around the floor. "Hint, hint."

"I hear you, I hear you." Scottie smiled. How she loved her grandfather.

"Did I ever tell you the first time I saw Octavia Broadripple?"

"Many times. But tell me again."

"I spotted her at a dance and nudged my buddy. 'I'm going to marry her,' I said. Which was no easy feat, I tell you. She was beautiful and a bit stuck up. No, not a bit. All the way stuck up. Every fella in town wanted to drive Octavia to the movies."

"But you won her over." Scottie never tired of hearing her grandparents' love story. Fritz, in his wisdom, was grounding her to everything that mattered.

"A few months later, we were at another dance, and Shug's date abandoned her on the dance floor for a nip of hooch out back with a couple of hoodlums. She was fuming. I'd just come home from basic training, looking all spiffy in my uniform, so I slipped between the dancing couples, took her in my arms as the band leader sang "Unchained Melody" by Les Baxter. Never heard the song before, but it would become our song. She was spitting mad, ready to knock the other fella's block off, but I hung on to her, never let her go. Even stole a kiss as the song ended, and seventy years later, Scottie, winning her is my greatest achievement. Our love is my greatest legacy. I want that for you, my girl, more than anything. Your dad finally found his love story. It's time you found yours too."

Image after image crossed her mind. Michael at the quay. Michael by her side at the Garden Party. Michael reaching for her in the Midlands mob. His scissor-kicking lesson with his nephew at the anniversary celebration. His eyes looking so intently at her as they danced the Ilyds. Pints at the Belly of the Beast. Climbing up to Wenthelen Chapel and making so many discoveries about the Blues and Fickles. Emmanuel emerging from the woods with fire in His eyes. The Rose Ball. The Eye of God. Their quiet ride from Hadsby to the Port Fressa airport.

"I'm not sure he'll have me," she said without explanation, though Fritz probably already knew. "We've texted a few times, but we've whittled down to communication by emoji. I was so upset, eager to get home, I ignored everything between us."

"Here's my final piece of advice," Fritz said, scooching her away from the dance floor as dozens and dozens hurried out for a line dance. "Don't sit and wait for some new path to magically open for you. Take the one you're already standing on, Scottie. Consider all the good you did in your short time in Lauchtenland. You have privileges ninety-nine percent of the population can only dream about while watching a movie. I think there's more for you to do, Lady Royal."

"Any other words of wisdom, dear grandfather?" She'd always loved the calm timbre of his voice. "What about him? What do I say to him?"

"Don't let the sun go down one more day without reaching out, Scottie. Don't wait."

Chapter
Twenty-Seven

As Dad and Remi dashed toward the waiting limo through a shower of glowing, colorful confetti, Remi glanced back at Scottie then shot the bouquet at her with the might of a major league pitcher.

While everyone cheered, Cap caught her eye and winked. Fritz did the same.

"You're next."

Okay, okay, simmer down. Maybe. No, probably not. She'd given Michael every reason not to trust her. Once the bride and groom whisked off in a carriage drawn by Dad's beautiful shire draft horse Sampson, Fritz's advice resounded.

"Don't wait."

There, under the twinkle of the tent lights, a wedding bouquet in her hand, Scottie knew beyond all doubt, she loved, really loved Michael.

Everything about the O'Shay takeover, the long-held secret of her mother's identity, the notion her future was crushed, gave way to an overwhelming freedom.

She was free. Her feet were no longer cemented in Hearts Bend's bedrock.

Spinning around to go, she ran into Jack Gillingham and his wife, Taylor. "Hey," he said with a laugh. "Where're you going in a hurry? Some of us are heading to Buck and JoJo Mathews's place for—"

"Jack, Taylor, hey, I'm sorry, I can't. But thank you." She hurried around them toward her car.

"How about dinner next week?" Jack called. "I want to debrief with you, ask how you're doing? What are your plans?"

"Can't, Jack. But thanks." She took a long stride back to him. "By the way, congrats on Boston Brothers taking you on as Marketing Vice President. You're going to blow it out of the water." She hugged him, then Taylor, before spinning away.

At home, she hammered up the stairs, her thoughts well ahead of her heartbeat. Yanking a large suitcase from the hall closet, she tossed it on the bed.

"Choko, where are you when I need you?"

Full of energy, full of wonder, Scottie folded clothes from one drawer after another into the case. She packed her toiletries and loaded up her carry-on bag. Online, she booked a first-class ticket to Port Fressa. It cost the moon, but who cared? Michael was worth it.

It was only after she'd crawled into bed, exhilarated and exhausted, that doubt crept in. Was she really doing this? Hopping a plane without telling anyone? Was she actually going to walk up to the palace door and reach for the polished brass knocker?

"Hi, Mom, I'm home."

Communication with Kate had been sweet but sporadic. With Michael? Minimal at best. Lately, a series of emojis.

Her heart thumped as she considered her options. Stay home and cling to her safe and former life, such as it was, or take a chance to explore a brand-new life?

Breathing deep, she nestled down on her pillows and slowly drifted away, the events of the evening—Dad dancing with Remi, Cap with Freya, Fritz's loving advice—melding into a sweet lullaby. She pictured the night of the ball, laughing and dancing with her brothers and the crown heads of the North Sea nations, then with Michael, looking into his eyes, feeling his breath against her cheek, his strength holding onto her.

Suddenly a light filled her room. Startled, she sat up into a glow so like that of the Eye of God. She heard His voice. Emmanuel's.

"What you're doing is good."

A million questions marched through her, but none formed into words. There was no need. He already knew what she wanted to ask, and the answers were within Him.

Trembling, Scottie snatched up her phone to text Kate.

Scottie: Can I come home?

She waited, plopped down against the pillows, a peace blanketing her. When Kate's ping finally replied, Scottie smiled.

Kate: Yes, darling. Absolutely.

The next moment it was morning. Or so it seemed. She'd slept so deep and so soundly. Out of bed, she rushed about showering, dressing for travel, texting Dad, Shug, and Fritz, letting them know her plans.

Dad: I'm proud of you. Remi says we'll fly over for Christmas.

Christmas? Would she be there that long?

Fritz: Shug and I are doing a happy dance. Well, as good as an old man and old woman can do. We'll miss you but we always knew this day would come.

In the kitchen, bright with steams of sunlight, Scottie made a cup of coffee, called for a car to the airport, texted her house-keeper and lawn maintenance with instructions. The pool still needed to be covered, so she called Ned and asked him to tend to it this week.

At the sliding doors, she took her first sip of coffee and breathed in, awakening a few more rattling nerves. But she was locked in. Committed. In her line of sight, the fall colors had just begun to touch the trees. In a week, Hearts Bend would be ablaze with gold, orange, red, and brown leaves. The season was changing. She was changing.

Finishing her coffee, she washed the cup, put it away, then rolled her luggage to the front door. Taking out her phone, she tapped the screen then hesitated. Should she text Michael? Or let her arrival be a surprise? This trip was about more than Michael. It was about Scottie and the House of Blue.

No. No, this wild hair trip was all about Michael Cross. She loved him more now than she did last night.

Scottie looked up when a distant car door slammed. Was her driver here already? The rideshare app indicated he was still ten minutes away. Scottie checked the driveway through the surveillance cameras to see a black sedan down by the gate and a man walking up the driveway. Didn't she text the driver the gate code?

Opening the door, she moved to the porch and squinted through the light. The man moved toward her with strong, controlled strides and the confidence of one trained in Her Majesty's Special Forces. Dark hair flowed loose about his forehead, his deep and piercing blue eyes locked on her.

"Michael?" Scottie jumped off the porch, running toward him, not stopping until she flew into his arms and was locked against him. "You're here. You're here! How are you here?"

He caught her and held her tight, carrying her toward the house, filling her with his presence and the clean scent of his skin.

Dropping to the porch steps, he held her on his lap and kissed her slow and sweet, as if discovering something about her he never knew before. She felt weak with love as she savored his kisses, each one declaring over and over *I love you.*

When it seemed neither of them could breathe, he rose up. "I've missed you so, Scottie."

"I was on my way to see you." She brushed his hair away from his face. "I texted Kate last night. Why are you here?"

"Her Majesty sent me on a special errand yesterday. I'm booked at the Hearts Bend Inn." He kissed her again. "She has a special gift for you. But Scottie, can we begin again? Can we be husband and wife, lovers, partners? I'll go where you want to go, be where you want to be."

"I want to be with you, Michael Cross." She kissed him tenderly. "And did you just propose to me?"

"Yes, love, I believe I did."

Four hours later, aboard Royal One, Scottie once again opened the leather journal her mother had sent by a very special messenger. Her mission crossed in the night with Scottie's revelation of love.

She's flipped through her Grandfather Rein's journal of letters from Shug while on the porch steps, but she was too excited, to bursting with love, to give it her proper attention. So she waited until now.

Michael stretched around her to switch on the brass and crystal sconce anchored beside her seat. Scottie met his gaze, then rested her head on his shoulder.

"I can't believe Shug and King Rein wrote to one another." She'd confirmed with Shug before leaving, tears in her eyes as she hugged Scottie goodbye.

"Our letters were how I knew this day would come. He wanted to know you, Scottie. And so he did, in his way."

Between the journal's linen pages, the king had secured Shug's letters and photographs of Scottie. Shug's even script flowed across her personal stationery embossed with the initials OBO. Octavia Broadripple O'Shay.

"I like this one," Michael said, tapping a Polaroid of Scottie in her high chair, covered with mashed sweet potatoes. "What a mess, love." He laughed and kissed her cheek.

"Yeah, well wait, buddy, until I see your mom and ask for baby pictures of you."

"Which she'll gladly show. I was a beautiful child." Scottie threw her arms about him, drawing him in for a kiss. "Your mum says to read the unfinished letter first." He gently turned the pages to the end. "Here, this one. The king died before he could send it. When I found the book in the cellar, his letter was tucked in the front. R. Vinter was his code name. R for regent. Vinter is Danish for winter."

Scottie smoothed her hand over the crisp paper lined with her grandfather's handwriting.

December 19, 1997
To: Octavia O'Shay
P.O. Box 9702
Hearts Bend, TN

Dearest Shug,

I cannot tell you how much your letters and photographs of our Scottie have meant to me over the years. It was lovely to speak to you in October as well. I wish to heaven I could share all of this with Catherine, but I fear it would undo everything she's worked so diligently to put behind her.

She's a fine mother of her sons and it is often best to let the past lie in its own dust. As for me, I continue to battle heart disease. I've often thought to fly to Tennessee to see Miss Scottie, kiss her before I depart this life, but I could not return home with such a secret. Take care of her, my friend. Love her extra for me.

Wishing you and yours joy and peace this Christmas season and a Happy New Year.

Yours,
R. Vinter

FROM THE CHAMBER OFFICE

CATHERINE THE SECOND, Regent by the Grace of God, Queen of Lauchtenland, Head of the Commonwealth, Defender of the Faith, declares this day, her daughter, Lady Royal Scottie O'Shay, daughter of Trent O'Shay of Nashville, Tennessee, SHALL by these Letters Patent under the Great Seal of Lauchtenland, be CROWNED and STYLED as Her Royal Highness Princess Scottie O'Shay Blue, a princess in the realm with all rights, honours, precedence, and privileges.

IN WITNESS we have caused these Our Letters to be signed and sealed at Clouver Abbey on this day, the First of December in the Year of Our Lord.

"Stone, news is rolling from Perrigwynn Palace this week. The Chamber Office announced today Letters Patent by the queen. Lady Royal will be granted HRH status as Her Royal Highness Princess Scottie O'Shay Blue. Michael Cross will be knighted as Sir Michael Cross of the Realm of Lauchtenland."

–MELISSA FARIS, ROYAL REPORTER, THE MORNING SHOW WITH STONE BRUBAKER

"Swoon times a million. The new Princess Scottie gets to spend her life with that gorgeous Michael Cross. Did I miss when the queen knighted him? Does anyone have a link?"

–@STEFWITHANF ON IG

"Rumors are flying that designer Eloise Bright, owner of Eloise Ltd., will design Princess Scottie's wedding gown. Eloise Ltd. lost a property battle with Reingard Industries two years ago, crushing plans to build a ready-to-wear design house. 'The princess has been generous to us. We're grateful she's become a friend,' said Bright. Stay with @RoyalWatcherOne for updates on our next royal wedding."

–@ROYALWATCHERONE

"Great question, Tuppence. I've not become a fan of Princess Scottie merely because she discovered the truth of my family's misfortune and thus fortune. Nor because Her Majesty restored the land and title taken from us. But she ostensively ended a family feud. The princess has a lot in common with our mutual ancestor Wenthelen, also the unrecognized love child of a sovereign. She's helped me understand the power of truth and forgiveness. She won her crown, in my book. After all, a true princess wears the crown of healing and that's what Lady Royal has done for us."

–HAMISH FICKLE, LORD MIDLANDS, ON TUPPENCE CORBYN & FRIENDS

"The Secretary of Infrastructure announced road repairs and beautification initiatives to begin in the Highcrest Mountains today. It's rumored HRH Princess Scottie and Sir Michael Cross's wedding will be held in the ancient Wenthelen Chapel."

–THE NEWS LEADER

"The RECO party announced their disbandment today, citing lack of interest and funding."

—CNC, *CABLE NEWS CHANNEL*

"Is Princess Scottie getting married in The Haskells? What's up there besides ski lodges and woods?"

—*@EYEONPRINCESSSCOTTIE ON IG*

CIIR

The Lord Chamberlain of the Chamber Office

Is commanded by The Queen to invite you

To the marriage of

Her Royal Highness Princess Scottie O'Shay Blue

of Tennessee and Lauchtenland

To

Sir Michael Cross of Port Fressa, Lauchtenland

Son of Antone and Jeanette Cross

Friday the 7th of May 4:00 p.m.

The Wenthelen Chapel

Let's end here...

LET'S END
HERE...

WEDDING DAY

SCOTTIE

In the open landau carriage, Scottie O'Shay rolled through the gossamer dusk that hovered above the flora and fauna of the Highcrest Mountains. The wind gently stirred the green, leafy trees as if in celebration. As if they all knew.

The daughter of the queen had finally become a princess. Business was finished in Lauchtenland.

A throng of well-wishers lined the roadside, waving Princess Scottie banners bearing her new cypher: a scripted *S* beneath a ducal coronet. Their cheers rose like a jubilant tide.

As the carriage rounded the bend, the chapel appeared—Wenthelen Chapel—its glass and filigree spire catching and reflecting the late afternoon light. Ever since she'd returned to Lauchtenland, ever since she'd accepted she was becoming—Michael's wife, a future mother, a philanthropist, and yes, a princess—Scottie found her thoughts turned more and more toward Emmanuel, whose Eye had always been on her. As she embarked on the biggest moment of her life, she believed it.

Kate, whom she now called Mom, had told her stories of Emmanuel's appearing. Scottie had wondered if He'd shown Himself to her because Kate was queen. But Mom only laughed.

"Ernst at the Belly of the Beast has seen Him more than anyone, and he never speaks in full sentences."

Scottie glanced over at Dad sitting straight-backed, dashing in his black-and-white vested tuxedo, top hat perched with pride, his whitish-gray beard neatly trimmed. A sparkle moved through his eyes—one he hadn't lost since she walked out of the dressing room at old Haskells Manor wearing her wedding gown.

"I never saw this coming"—Dad he murmured, leaning toward her—"when Kate left you in my arms."

"It's wonderful, and strange," she said. "And I'm right where I belong, Dad. I know it through and through."

"I believe you are," Dad replied softly.

Even so, the grandeur of a royal wedding was nothing compared to her love for Michael. She had never been that swoony girl who dreamed of her wedding. Yet she'd surrendered to it all—the invitation and privilege of loving one man, and her God, all the days of her life. At thirty-nine, she was a bit late to the party. She had a lot of kisses and prayers awaiting her in the days ahead.

As the carriage slowed, rounding the curve toward the chapel, the cheering swelled into a single, harmonious note. Scottie caught sight of Mrs. Johansdotter with her children and husband on the side lawn. The woman smiled and dipped her head in greeting. Scottie mirrored the action. She'd recently introduced Eloise Bright to Mrs. Johansdotter, who just so happened to be an expert seamstress.

What had once been meant for harm had turned into good.

As they arrived at the chapel, the Grandsire Triples Quarter Peals rang from the chapel bells. Dad stepped out of the carriage surrounded by Kongelig Herrer and offered his hand to Scottie.

Lining the polished slate path stood her family—Mom and Edric, her brothers and their wives—John and Gemma with Imani, Gus and Daffy—and woven among the Lauchtenland royals were the royals of Hearts Bend—Shug, Fritz, and Remi.

Inside, seventy-five guests waited—friends, family, a few dignitaries. They'd chosen a small gathering for the ceremony. Dad and Her Majesty would host a grand royal reception in Port Fressa in June.

Today was for Scottie and Michael, one dedicated to love, to healing, to hope, and to Wenthelen, the forgotten daughter of a king.

"Daddy…" Scottie touched his arm. "Thank you. For everything. For raising me. Protecting me. Letting me go, even when I didn't see it was time. I thought you were preparing me to run O'Shay Shirts. But you were raising me for life. For this moment right now."

"Come on now, you'll make me blubber."

When Dad kissed her forehead, she felt a presence behind her. Turning, she saw Emmanuel by the bench where she and Michael met Him last June. He wore His mountain coat and wide brim hat. Releasing Dad's hand, Scottie stepped toward Him.

"You're always with me, aren't you?"

His eyes brightened with an ancient and perfect story of love. *"Always."*

"Scottie?" Dad touched her shoulder.

"I'm coming." She glanced back at Dad. "I just…needed to say hello to someone."

When she looked again, Emmanuel was gone, but His presence remained.

Trumpets played as the chapel doors opened, and the waiting family became the procession ahead of her. The queen and Remi wiped their eyes while Dad and the king consort continually cleared their throats.

Guests were gathered in a buoyant atmosphere beneath the soaring spire. The room remained as it always had been, airy and open without benches, except for the simple table with bread and wine at the front, waiting.

Potted trees from The Haskells lined the walls. Flowers crowned the sides of the altar. A quintet began to play "I Will Extol You," the wedding piece first heard at Princess Clemency's vows.

For a moment, she rattled with nerves—a blend of excitement and anticipation. Then she began the stroll down the aisle, her hand locked with Dad's, through the familiar faces and foreign royalty toward the only one that mattered. Michael. The nearer she got, the more love pumped through her veins. He was breathtaking in his military dress uniform, his gaze pulling her forward like gravity itself.

"Then we shall proceed," the archbishop declared. "Who gives this woman to be married to this man?"

"Her mother and I," Dad said, settling her hands into Michaels. Dad looked at Mom. They shared one full, radiant smile.

"Her mother and I do."

Michael squeezed her hands, blinking away tears. "Hey, I was hoping you'd show up."

She smiled. "At least this time I didn't have to climb the back of the mountain to be here."

With a muted giddiness, they spoke their forever vows. They both said, *"I do"* and slipped a ring on each other's finger.

"Let us consider," the archbishop said, "that the best love stories begin with a wedding. Michael and Scottie are embarking on that journey today." He turned to Michael. "You may kiss your bride."

Taking her in his arms, he held her in a way that made her feel her own strength wasn't needed. He kissed her slowly and tenderly. Not because of the archbishop's command or as a show for the guests. But for her. A true kiss of love that sealed their vows.

She clung to his broad shoulders as he smiled against her lips, filling her with joy.

"I guess you're my wife," he said.

"I guess you're my husband." What a fabulous reality!

Around them, the chapel exploded with shouts and applause.

"Ladies and gentlemen." The archbishop lifted his voice above the noise. "Lords and ladies, and Royal Highnesses, may I present to you Sir Michael and Mrs. Cross."

As the chapel once again erupted with cheers, a radiant, joyful light shot through the spire and spilled over the table with the bread and the wine, and over the newlywed couple.

FOUR MONTHS LATER

"The Chamber Office announced the Wenthelen Foundation, a joint effort between HRH Princess Scottie and Lord Midlands. The foundation, named in honor of King Magnus the Third's daughter, will support businesses in the Midlands and vendors of the Midlands Faire. For more information visit www.wenthelenfoundation.ll.gov."

– MELISSA FARIS, ROYAL REPORTER, THE MORNING SHOW WITH STONE BRUBAKER

"Perrigwynn Palace—Her Royal Highness Princess Scottie, along with her husband Sir Michael, are very pleased to announce the Princess is expecting their first child in early spring. The families of the Blues, Crosses, and O'Shays celebrate the news."

– THE CHAMBER OFFICE

"The medical team of Her Majesty, Queen Catherine the Second, have declared she is in full remission from GBS. Happy Holidays."

– The News Leader

The End

Acknowledgments

Thank you for journeying with me through the world of the True Blue Royals. *To Win A Crown* was years in the making—interrupted by other stories along the way—but I believe Scottie's story arrived at exactly the right time.

It's bittersweet to say goodbye, at least for now, to the Blues, Lauchtenland, and all our friends in the North Sea. They will forever live in our hearts. Writing royal stories has been one of the great joys of my career, and I'm deeply honored to have shared this world with you.

Until we meet again in Lauchtenland, wear your crown well. We're all princesses on the inside.

If you enjoyed *To Win A Crown*, I'd love for you to leave an honest review. This will help your fellow readers. (And okay, me too.)

Special thanks to...

All the shout-outs in the world to Susan May Warren and Beth Vogt, who have walked beside me on this writing journey. One patiently sharpens my technical skills at her kitchen island; the other always answering when I call to talk through a scene. Your generosity, wisdom, and friendship have been a true gift, and I thank God for you both.

Thank you to Erin Healy for reading the first draft—it wasn't so bad this time, was it? As always, your insights helped make the story shine.

I'm deeply grateful to Barbara Curtis for thoughtful line edits and careful proofreading, and to Terry Doherty and Beth Vogt for careful proofing.

Thank you to Amy Atwell for her kind and knowledgeable production support.

Thank you to Kristen Ingebretson for the beautiful cover that captures the heart of this story.

Much appreciation to Louise Lee for bringing Scottie and Michael to life in audio. I'm so glad our paths crossed.

To Debb Hackett, thank you for your patience and kindness as I navigated British phrasing and customs. Lauchtenland may be fictional, but your guidance helped make it feel grounded and true.

To my husband—thank you for saying yes to this crazy mission of novel writing again and again. You are a gift.

And to you, dear reader—thank you for showing up, for reading, and for asking for more royals. Your encouragement continues to inspire me. I hope Scottie and Michael's story reminds you that love, calling, and grace often arrive in unexpected ways.

RACHEL HAUCK is an award winning, *New York Times*, *USA Today,* and *Wall Street Journal* bestselling author.

She is a double RITA finalist, and a Christy and Carol Award Winner. Her book, *Once Upon A Prince*, first in the *Royal Wedding Series*, was filmed for an Original Hallmark movie.

Rachel was given the prestigious Career Achievement Award for her body of original work by *Romantic Times Book Reviews*.

She is a writing workshop presenter and mentor.

A graduate of Ohio State University (Go Bucks!) with a degree in Journalism, she's a former sorority girl and a devoted Ohio State football fan. Her bucket list is to stand on the sidelines with Ryan Day.

She and her husband live in sunny east coast Florida.

Sign up for Rachel's newsletter
www.rachelhauck.com.